CONTRACT TO KILL

Also by Andrew Peterson

First to Kill
Forced to Kill
Option to Kill
Ready to Kill

CONTRACT TO KILL

A Nathan McBride Novel

ANDREW PETERSON

THOMAS & MERCER

This is a work of fiction. Names, characters, organizations, places, events, and incidents are either products of the author's imagination or are used fictitiously.

Published by Thomas & Mercer, Seattle

www.apub.com

ISBN-13: 9781477827666
ISBN-10: 1477827668

Cover design by Chris McGrath

Printed in the United States of America

To the memory of Patricia Taylor (1925–2015).
Aunt Pat was a matriarch in our family—her
kindness and compassion will be missed.

PROLOGUE

Shindand District of western Afghanistan
Summer 2009

Tanner Mason tuned out the engine's drone and fought off a nagging fatigue. Outside the comfort of his vehicle, if he could call it that, a drab desert loomed under a twilight sky. Anything not beige was either brown or gray.

Looking around the cramped interior, he wondered if the MRAP truly was mine resistant and ambush protected. So far it hadn't been tested, which was just fine with him. He'd seen the hulks of other MRAPs in the scrapyard, and some of them looked pretty bad. Fortunately, his employer spared no expense when it came to protecting his people. Mason didn't know what one of these twenty-five-ton babies cost, but the Marine Corps variant, the 6x6 Cougar, went out the door at $750,000.

Mason's convoy held four vehicles, three of them belonging to Beaumont Specialists, Inc., plus one German unit for support. This was a private-military-contractor mission, with Mason in command.

Each MRAP held ten men, consisting of two operators and eight combat personnel. Mason didn't like the term "mercenary" and never referred to himself or his men that way. They were private military contractors. PMCs. Technically, they were guns for hire, but didn't that describe all combat troops?

Sitting across from him, Chip Hahn looked straight ahead with his usual neutral expression. A Korean American, Chip was the same age as Mason at forty-one. He'd rarely met a tougher individual than Chip, and he valued him as his second-in-command. Chip had once said that Mason looked like the blond villain from *Die Hard*. Mason conceded a slight resemblance—at least from the neck up. The rest of Mason mirrored a professional cage fighter, because he'd once been one.

Today's objective sat in the middle of a remote village sandwiched between two seasonal river basins. A local bigwig known as Mullah Sanjari had been positively identified as the man responsible for coordinating and conducting more than two dozen IED and RPG attacks against coalition forces. BSI's mission was twofold. First, kill or capture the mullah. And second, recover or destroy any weapons or ordnance found inside his walled compound.

Over the past eight days at varying times, Mason's convoy had driven in and out of the village without incident. Their MRAPs would roll in, drive around, and then leave. The strategy created a sense of normalcy, a ploy that had worked well in other locations.

Today would be different.

Mason made eye contact with Chip and mouthed, *You okay?*

Butterflies, Chip mouthed back.

Mason nodded. *Me too.* He pressed the transmit button and spoke calmly through his boom mic. "Two minutes. Final weapons and radio check. Everyone check in with squad leaders."

After the sequence of radio calls ended, Mason told his troops, "No one hesitates. We shoot first and sort things out later. Sixty seconds."

Just inside the village, the convoy detoured east to avoid using the same route they'd taken the day before. The ride got rougher as the convoy increased its speed.

Mason received his twenty-second call from the driver.

"Everyone brace yourselves. We'll be braking hard. Turret gunners on my mark. Ten seconds."

The M2 gunners were already in their slings, so all they had to do was straighten up.

The roar of the engine stopped and the rear doors flew open.

"All squads, move out!"

Warm air assaulted Mason's face as he started a mental stopwatch.

As rehearsed, the Germans fanned out to position themselves at each cross street.

Three seconds.

Mason yelled, "Eighty-fours!"

Half a dozen stun grenades flew over the compound's wall toward the buildings in the northeast corner.

Everyone crouched.

Concussive blasts shook the wall, creating waterfalls of dust.

One of Mason's men stepped forward and used a shotgun to make a ballistic breach of the compound's only door.

Six seconds.

In a crouch, Mason led the assault team through the opening.

He pivoted toward the buildings and saw three ethereal forms materialize through the dust and smoke.

Mason dropped to one knee, leveled his M4, and waited an extra second to verify they were enemy combatants. They were. AK-47s had a distinctive shape.

Before the Taliban could recover from the stun grenades, Mason fired three quick bursts.

Two went down, but even with multiple chest wounds, the third gunman tried to bring his AK up.

Hahn finished him while Mason changed magazines.

Ten seconds.

The rest of Alpha squad followed them over to the closest building and ducked next to its wall.

He'd keep Bravo and Charlie outside until needed. If this turned into a Taliban trap, there was no sense in risking more than one squad.

Although Mason spoke Arabic, he nodded to his translator, who yelled for anyone inside to surrender. When no one responded, Mason issued a hand signal. His men stayed low, broke the windows, and tossed stun grenades into the buildings.

More concussive thumps compressed the air.

At the fifteen-second mark, a single muffled shot rang out.

"Bravo, advance, advance!"

His second squad sprinted into the compound.

Mason used a forefinger to point at the door next to him, then drove a fist into his palm, like a hockey referee signaling a boarding penalty.

Bravo breached the door and entered the building, leapfrog style. Calls of "clear" sounded as each room was searched and secured.

Mason and Chip followed them inside through air smelling like rotten eggs and burned electrical wiring. In the back room, his men stood around the source of the gunshot. Rather than be captured, Mullah Sanjari had taken his own life.

Chip put a forefinger to his lips and pointed to a rug under the table.

Mason issued a hand signal for everyone to clear the room, putting a wall between them and the mullah's chamber.

"Go get Hutch," Mason whispered to Hahn. "It could be rigged with an IED."

As Hahn left, Mason signaled for his men to hold positions. Special Agent Hutch worked for the ATF as an explosives and arson expert, and his experimental embedment with BSI's special ops unit was being evaluated by the ATF brass. As far as Mason was concerned, Hutch was an invaluable asset, and Mason hoped he'd be able to keep him permanently. Mason really liked the ATF guys because they treated him and his contractor colleagues like equals.

Hutch appeared twenty seconds later.

"Sergeant Hahn thinks we've got something under the rug. Give it a look. I'll cover you."

Mason took a knee, pulled his Glock, and nodded to Hutch. He pointed his weapon at the center of the rug as Hutch flattened himself on the dirt floor. Before pulling the rug aside, the ATF agent checked its entire undersurface for trip wires. Beneath the rug, a three-foot piece of plywood served as a trapdoor entrance to a typical spider hole.

Hutch rechecked it for trip wires, then produced a pen magnet and slowly passed it over the entire surface of the plywood. He looked at Mason and issued a thumbs-up. Hutch made a three-finger gesture with his right hand, then grabbed the plywood with his left hand.

Mason nodded, and Hutch counted to three with his fingers. On three, Hutch flung the trapdoor aside and rolled away from it. Mason squinted and kept his handgun pointed at the dark hole.

In Arabic, he ordered anyone who might be hiding to speak up and identify himself. When nothing happened, he looked at Hahn and made a gesture like breaking a twig. Hahn reached into his belly pack and removed a couple of light sticks. He snapped them, shook their contents, and tossed them into the hole.

Hutch rolled back to the hole and peered inside. "Jackpot."

"What have we got?"

"A shitload of RPG and mortar rounds," Hutch said. "They're stacked in wooden crates. It also looks like there's close to fifty thousand rounds of AK ammo . . . Chinese made."

Mason looked at Hahn and Hutch. "You two get down there and check it out. Don't touch anything until SA Hutch clears and photographs it." He pushed his transmit button. "We're checking out an underground chamber. All squads maintain positions."

Hutch followed Hahn down a primitive log ladder.

"We've also got a cardboard box full of ball bearings," Hutch said. "There's some electronic shit, batteries, cell phones, wires, and thumb switches. I'd say we're looking at a bona fide IED factory. It looks like someone's been prying AK rounds apart for the powder. Gotta be several thousand empty casings down here . . . Wait, there's another box under the table. *Holy shit!*"

"What?" Mason asked.

"Greenbacks," Hutch said.

From the hole, Hahn issued a low whistle.

"I'm coming down."

Mason told the rest of his squad to stay alert and then descended the ladder. Hahn pointed his flashlight into the box, and Mason stared in stunned disbelief. He'd heard of this, but he'd never seen it. After all the violence he'd seen in Afghanistan, he thought it strange that a box of cash would affect him so strongly. He felt its undeniable attraction even as he despised the ugliness it represented. Temptation came in many forms, but this had to be one of its most powerful lures. A childhood memory surfaced of finding a twenty-dollar bill on the street outside a video arcade. Mason had been exhilarated. It was like discovering a pirate's treasure. He'd known about money—the tooth fairy had left him a few quarters—but he'd never held a twenty-dollar bill before. Later that night, he'd studied it with a magnifying glass, every little detail. Someday, he'd vowed, he'd have lots of bills like that.

He sensed Hahn's stare and averted his eyes from the money. As inviting as it might be to pocket several bundles, Mason resisted the urge. *Blood money*, he thought. *This stuff paid for dead soldiers.*

"How much is it?" Hahn asked.

Mason picked up a bundle of twenties and thumbed it. "Each wad is probably two grand. Some of them are fifties and hundreds. I'd say we're looking at a minimum of two hundred grand."

"What's this guy doing with so much cash?"

"We'll let command figure that out. After Hutch checks the box, we'll take it with us. You're on the money, Sergeant. None of it disappears on the way to HQ."

"No sir, it won't."

Mason climbed out of the hole and told his interpreter to make a video recording of the entire compound to document the kills, the secret bomb-making stash, and all its contents. Maybe the CIA had a way to trace the cash. For all Mason knew, the money might be marked. Again, not his concern.

Once the video was complete, he had his men move the dead Taliban over to the compound's door. He saw no reason to deny his enemy proper burials. Mason then ordered photos taken of all the KIAs for the CIA's facial-recognition software. He sent Hahn into the hole to collect the cash and bomb-making materials, but told him to leave the AK ammo, RPGs, and mortar rounds there.

Next, Mason's engineer put several C4 blocks in the spider hole with the remaining ordnance. Everyone hustled back to the MRAPs and crouched on their far sides.

After his squad leaders confirmed a head count, Mason nodded to his engineer, who detonated the charges.

Like the beginning of an earthquake, the ground shuddered.

Half a second later, a yellow-white fireball shot skyward, followed by a towering mushroom cloud. Secondary explosions rocked the compound as ordnance cooked off. Baseball-sized chunks of mud brick and splintered timbers bombarded the entire area, pinging off the MRAPs and surrounding buildings.

Chip stood and yelled, "Get some!"

Mason smiled and waved him back down.

He ordered his radio operator to relay the news: six Taliban dead, including Mullah Sanjari; a weapons cache and bomb-making center destroyed; and a large amount of US cash recovered. But most importantly, no friendly casualties had been taken. The raid on Mullah Sanjari's compound was another gold star on BSI's record.

A little over six minutes after arriving, the vehicles sped away.

Two clicks from the village, the terrain got steeper and more rugged. Before NATO's ISAF troops arrived, the only access in and out of the village had been a footpath. Several years ago, bulldozers had carved it into a one-lane track. Although wider, it remained the village's only access. For a click or so, the road weaved its way through a series of small canyons and seasonal creeks. The terrain sloped steeply away on one side and climbed sharply on the other. Coalition engineers had this road targeted for additional realignment, but it didn't rank high on the priority list of projects. Mason had argued otherwise but to no avail.

A sudden radio call broke Mason's thoughts.

Now what?

The lead MRAP had eyes on a motorcyclist on the far side of the arroyos.

"Is he turning around?"

"Negative, sir."

Solo motorcycles and scooters weren't an uncommon sight, but all Afghans knew to avoid close contact with coalition convoys.

"Bravo, increase speed and intercept." He slowed the remaining MRAPs to a crawl and increased their separation. "Fire a warning burst."

He couldn't see Bravo's MRAP, but the clatter of its .50 caliber M2 echoed across the rocky slopes like cracking thunder. Mason knew the salvo of white tracers sent an unmistakable message. If the motorcyclist kept coming, he would be fired upon.

Mason switched positions with his turret gunner to get an unobstructed look. When his vehicle cleared the next curve in the road, he brought his field glasses up. Four hundred meters distant, the motorcyclist had stopped where a dry creek crossed the road, but he wasn't turning around.

Mason ordered a second warning burst.

More M2 fire roared from the lead MRAP, and this time Mason saw the tracers extend across the valley. They skipped off the road and raised a dust cloud. That did the trick. The man turned the motorcycle around and sped away in the opposite direction. He hadn't gone ten meters when he lost control and went down.

Dumb shit, Mason thought. Through the magnified image, Mason watched the guy right the bike and repeatedly stomp on the starter pedal.

"Bravo, one more burst. Make it close."

White tracers reached across the valley again. The motorcyclist ducked and covered his head. When the salvo ended, the man threw his arms up and kicked dirt toward the convoy. He was clearly frustrated at being forced to leave his ride behind. *Well, too fucking bad.* The idiot had picked a bad time to use this road—paid for with US taxpayer money *and* BSI's blood.

The man began walking along the side of the road, constantly looking over his shoulder.

That's right. Just give me an excuse.

Mason ordered the convoy to stop well short of the sidelined motorcycle. In an act of pure defiance, the man stopped walking and turned toward the convoy. He didn't seem the slightest bit intimidated by the firepower facing him. Studying the guy more closely, Mason saw it was a younger man, but he had a hard look. Desert-schooled for sure. Mason grabbed the bullhorn's mic with the intent of ordering the kid to keep going or die.

Without warning, the canyon's wall erupted in three fierce blasts.

Chunks of rock plinked off the turret's faceted surface, forcing Mason to duck. The concussive explosions rocked his MRAP and choked the entire area with dust and smoke.

"Did anyone see RPG trails?" Mason called to his squads.

None had.

Mortars.

"All units, reverse course! Reverse, reverse! Launch smoke!"

He had to get his vehicles moving before the Taliban adjusted their aim for a second salvo. Mason believed the next round of mortars would be targeted farther along the road, not behind.

He guessed right.

More explosions cratered the road where they would've been had they continued forward. After his radio operator reported the attack to command and relayed their GPS position, Mason was told air support was being dispatched from Shindand Air Base.

Believing the Taliban had a spotter somewhere on high ground, Mason opened up with the M2 and walked his tracers along the rim of the canyon. Chunks of pulverized rock blasted free from the cliff's face. He saw no dust cloud from the launch of the mortars, which probably meant they lay beyond the canyon's rim, well out of his line of sight.

He told the other turret gunners to open fire on the rim.

Radio chatter from the lead vehicle informed him the downed biker had jumped into the dry creek and ducked out of sight. Mason swung his turret in that direction as his driver continued to back up. More chatter came through his headset.

The motorcyclist was back up—shouldering an RPG!

Mason lined up on the kid and thumbed the trigger.

The Browning answered the call.

Clenching his teeth, Mason walked a burst of tracers onto the human form. The kid's body shuddered as though being pulled in every direction at once.

He pivoted his turret back to the north, where hundreds of slugs peppered the canyon's rim. Mason added his fire to the barrage. The air shimmered in ghostlike pulses as the supersonic bullets tore through the atmosphere. Expended brass and links began piling up next to his weapon. Mason reached down and tossed some of it over the turret's armor.

"Ammo!"

One of his men handed up another can. He fired the remaining rounds, tossed the empty can into the canyon, and replaced it.

After feeding the belt into the Browning, he cranked it three times until a link came out. His M2 was good to go.

Decision time.

Mason had no way to know if an IED had been planted up ahead or if the motorcycle was rigged to explode, but there hadn't been any bombs along the stretch of road they'd just traversed. With no room to turn the MRAPs around, they had two choices. Go forward or go backward.

Or take the fight to the Taliban.

Mason was sick to death of this damned stretch of road. It was time to neutralize those Taliban assholes once and for all. The question was how.

Bravo's MRAP held the platoon's sniper. If Mason could get him deployed, he might be able to take out the Taliban's spotter. At a minimum, his shooter could put some suppression fire on the spotter, forcing him to scramble. But even if successful, that wouldn't end the threat.

Despite the risk, Mason decided to attack the mortar teams on foot. He ordered the German MRAP to increase its speed and continue reversing course until it cleared the arroyos. Once it reached flatter ground shy of the canyon, he ordered it to leave the road and swing around to the north, cutting off any Taliban escape in that direction.

Mason yelled into the compartment below. "Get ready. We're deploying in thirty seconds. We're taking out those mortar teams." He repeated the command to the other BSI vehicles and ordered a man in each MRAP to stay behind and lay down M2 suppression fire as needed.

Chip volunteered to lead Alpha's ascent up the canyon—a gutsy offer. Without knowing the number of combatants they faced out there, it could be a suicide mission. If a platoon-sized force of Taliban lurked on the high ground, his men could be pinned down and made vulnerable to another mortar attack.

Three more explosions thumped the rocky slope. Once again, pulverized stone and shrapnel pinged off the MRAPs' armored surfaces. One of the blasts hadn't missed by more than a few meters. The Taliban mortar teams were now firing at will, no longer concerned about being simultaneous.

Mason believed he was facing 81 mm shells. If they were HEAT rounds, the high-explosive anti-tank projectiles would penetrate the plate steel atop their MRAPs, creating a very unhappy result. As long as he kept his MRAPs moving along the winding road, they'd be difficult targets to hit. Reversing the convoy had temporarily confused the enemy, but it wouldn't last. Mason fully expected to see explosions any second in the direction they were traveling.

He ordered his remaining MRAPs to launch more smoke grenades and slow to a crawl. The smoke wouldn't be super effective under the current wind conditions, but he didn't need much of a margin to execute his plan. When the white smoke reached its peak, he gave the order to stop. Including himself, twenty-one BSI personnel jumped out the rear doors of their MRAPs. The entire off-loading took less than four seconds; he and his men hunkered on the low side of the road as the MRAPs resumed backing up.

Deafening explosions continued to erupt all around them. Geysers of dirt and rock were flung in every direction. Goggles protected their eyes, but the white smoke assaulted their lungs.

Fifteen seconds after they exited the vehicles, the engine noise from the last MRAP faded and they lost sight of it around a bend in the road.

An eerie calmness ensued as the mortars went silent and the cover smoke thinned.

Were the Taliban teams already on the move? If so, Mason had no intention of letting them escape.

Sounding like crackling thunder, short bursts of turret fire continued to echo down the canyon. Mason ordered a battlefield cease-fire. If the mortars started up again, he wanted to hear the launches.

Mason was an old southerner at heart and believed in dividing his forces to gain a tactical advantage. They'd make a three-pronged advance up the slope. Alpha squad would take the left, Bravo the center, and Charlie the right. He told Bravo's sniper team to remain behind and find a good shooting position. At his order, all three squads sprinted across the road and began their ascent. Not only was the terrain steep, but it also made it hard to find footholds that didn't give. If the Taliban were going to attack, now would be a good time.

Mason took a moment to call his command MRAP for a gunship update—still no ETA on the chopper.

Low, rumbling whomps resonated through the canyon. The Taliban mortar teams had resumed. Either their spotter didn't see Mason and his men down here, or he deemed the MRAPs to be more valuable targets.

As near as he could tell, the launchers were at his two o'clock, just beyond a V-shaped protrusion of the rim. It was a tactically sound location, protected by a steep wall of rock that couldn't be easily or quickly climbed. The best route to the rim was a snake-shaped ravine just south of the protrusion. If they could follow that up, they could get behind the Taliban mortar position.

A single rifle shot echoed down the canyon.

"Everyone get down!"

Too late.

The man behind Mason grunted as a bullet smashed into his ballistic vest.

"Sniper!" Mason yelled. "Did anyone see the flash?"

Mason's radio crackled to life. He knew from the calm voice it was Bravo's sniper.

"I've got him."

A second shot boomed, this time from behind their position. Near the tip of the protrusion, a single Taliban tumbled down the rock face. The lifeless body slid the last ten meters and stopped.

"Good shooting, Finn. Any sign of the mortar's spotter?"

"Negative, but that could've been him."

"Double-time to a new SP and keep eyes on the rim."

"Copy."

His man who'd taken the bullet in the chest grimaced. He looked like he was about to vomit.

"Breathe, Tucker," Mason told him. "Hang back for a spell. You've probably got a few cracked ribs."

"I'm okay. I'll be . . . right behind you."

"Sit tight, Corporal. That's an order."

"Yes, sir."

Mason patted his wounded man's shoulder and resumed his ascent.

If Bravo's sniper had neutralized the Taliban's spotter, the mortar attack might be over. Hit-and-run was a common tactic, but Mason wanted to find more than footprints up there.

He looked across the canyon and didn't like the way Alpha and Charlie were no longer synchronized. He ordered Charlie to slow down so Alpha could make a parallel ascent. He wanted his two squads to arrive at either side of the V-shaped protrusion simultaneously.

The mortars fell silent again. Had the Taliban spotted his men? Mason diverted his squad to the south so they could take advantage of the ravine for additional cover.

Thirty meters from the rim, all hell broke loose.

Half a dozen Taliban appeared at the top and opened fire; the white twinkling of their AKs stood out against the deepening twilight like a fireworks display.

Mason and his men leapt into the deepest part of the ravine and slid down its rocky bank. Each man protected his face as hundreds of 7.62 mm bullets thumped through like a maelstrom of exploding firecrackers. Once again, they found themselves mired in choking dust. One of Mason's men took a round in the thigh and cursed. A dark stain began saturating the man's pants.

"Tie that off and fall back to Tucker's position," Mason yelled.

Bravo and Alpha opened fire on the rim.

Bullets peppered the cliff face, creating tiny craters in the rock face.

Mason ordered Charlie squad to keep going.

The boom from Bravo's sniper echoed through the canyon again. Another Taliban slid down the slope like a rag doll.

Then, as abruptly as it began, the AK fire stopped. Mason had seen this before. The Taliban weren't stupid. Fearless, but definitely not stupid. They would typically open fire, relocate, then fire again.

"Sergeant Hahn, you're with me. The rest of you stay here and cover our ascent. Conserve ammo. Don't fire unless you have positive targets in sight."

If the Taliban's intent was to slow them down to allow the mortar teams time to disassemble their tubes and beat feet out of there, they were going to be sorely disappointed. Mason intended to raid their party. He estimated they could be at the rim in just under forty seconds.

More mortar-launch whomps reverberated off the canyon walls.

With no way to know where the projectiles would land, Mason ordered all his squads to take cover.

Time seemed to stretch as they waited for the high-arcing munitions to detonate.

Mason watched in horror as one of the rounds landed in the middle of Charlie squad.

Shit. He didn't know how bad it was, but he knew there'd be serious wounds or even fatalities. Charlie's squad leader radioed that his unit had taken three casualties, one serious. Mason told them to stop their advance and take cover.

Where was that chopper?

"Let's go, Chip. Balls to wind. We're putting those assholes out of business."

"I'm right behind you."

More explosions rocked Charlie.

Mason now knew the launch tubes were at his two o'clock position, in roughly the place where the AK fire had come from. So far, the AK-wielding Taliban hadn't returned, likely cautious of the sniper who'd taken down two of their comrades.

After half a dozen explosions, the mortars fell silent again.

Worried about ricochets, he told the MRAPs to cease firing at the ridge. He and Chip were twenty seconds from the top and really huffing. Mason concentrated on breathing and dug harder to get footholds.

He could no longer see Bravo or Charlie; the V-shaped protrusion blocked his line of sight. A quick radio call confirmed Charlie's arrival to the summit was ninety seconds. Mason reminded them about the cross-fire risk.

For the last ten meters, he and Chip would be dangerously exposed. The shallow ravine they followed got gradually shallower until it flattened out with the rest of the slope. If any Taliban appeared directly above them, they'd have little chance of surviving.

Another solo report echoed down the canyon.

Not knowing its source, they dived for the deck.

Like something out of a western movie, a Taliban soldier tumbled down the rock-strewn slope right in front of them.

Bravo's sniper. He'd been covering their ascent.

Half a second later their world turned into dust, shattered rock, and zinging bullets. They lay flat and hoped a lucky shot wouldn't find them. Mason felt a hornet-like sting on his calf and knew he'd just taken a bullet fragment, likely a tiny piece of deformed copper. He stole a look at the rim and saw the muzzle flashes. Fortunately, they were at the tip of the protrusion and too far away to be accurate. Most of the bullet impacts were separated by several meters.

Mason keyed his radio. "Bravo. Hold position. Suppression fire only, short bursts, conserve ammo."

Below and to their right, his second squad peppered the rim at the source of the twinkling AK fire. Over the crackling M4s, Mason heard the low woofs of Bravo's grenade launchers. A fiery blast near the tip of the protrusion collapsed the rim, and two Taliban found themselves without any ground under their feet. They cartwheeled down the slope like spastic gymnasts.

Multiple M4 bursts nailed the tumbling men.

The Taliban rifles fell silent again.

Shaking their heads to dislodge the worst of the dirt, Mason and Hahn used the break to advance the remaining distance. If they were going to get shot, it might as well happen while attacking. The distant rumble of M4 fire continued to crackle through the canyon. He ordered another battlefield cease-fire, but excluded his sniper from the order.

The terrain was so steep near the top of the ravine, they had to sling their rifles and use both hands to steady themselves. For the last three meters, they couldn't use their weapons. Just below the rim, Mason stopped and pulled a grenade. Chip did the same. They nodded and tossed the frags over the top. The air seemed to shimmer as the concussive blasts shook the entire area.

Agonizing screams followed, then went silent.

With Chip following, Mason clawed his way up the last of the slope and lay flat. Dust and smoke hung everywhere. He could scarcely see his hand in front of his face.

Being blind created the worst kind of stress. He didn't want to fire into the dust because there was no way to know what was right in front of them. They might fire into a boulder and take themselves out with ricochets.

Patience, he told himself. Sometimes no action was the best action.

Slowly, the dust from the grenade detonations cleared enough to see five meters.

Then ten.

He told Hahn to be ready; both had their M4s shouldered.

What materialized looked like an ant farm.

No more than a tennis court away, several dozen Taliban were scrambling to take down their mortar tubes and pack the remaining ammo.

"I'll take left to center," Mason said. "You take the right."

With surgical precision, they walked the bursts from either end of the scrambling men into the middle.

The result was devastating.

Six men went down, with four others clutching their stomachs and chests.

Their M4s empty, Mason yelled, "Grenades."

They rolled onto their sides and hurled the frags. Some of the Taliban recognized the gesture and dropped, but others weren't so fast.

"Eyes," Mason said, reminding Hahn to avoid being flash blinded.

Two more blasts slammed the desert. Mason felt something thump off his helmet.

They used the newly produced chaos to reload their carbines.

"Charlie, you're clear. Advance! Advance! Alpha, follow our route. Advance!"

Both squads copied his orders.

He was about to send another M4 salvo when a chain of eruptions headed straight toward them. One of the Taliban had taken a knee and lined up on them.

And Hahn was on the business end of the chain.

Without thinking, Mason shoved Hahn out of the way.

Mason felt his arm tear open as if struck by an invisible hatchet. His brain told him to curl up and wait for the volley to stop, but adrenaline ruled the moment. He rolled back to his right and discovered his left sleeve was shredded from elbow to wrist.

Oh man, he thought. *That looks bad.*

The next thing his mind registered was blood.

Lots of it.

He ignored the overwhelming desire to cover the wound and yelled for Hahn to return fire.

Hahn's M4 answered the call.

The desert fighter shuddered as bullets tore through his body. Remarkably, the man tried to get up, but his legs wouldn't work. Hahn finished him with a second burst.

The rest of the Taliban abandoned their tasks and took off in a dead run, their loose clothing flowing in the wind. It was clear they didn't know how many men they faced.

With one hand, Mason shouldered his weapon and emptied the magazine. Two more Taliban went down.

"Alpha, ETA?"

"Thirty seconds."

"Hold your fire until you reach the rim. I'm hit. Hahn's returning fire. Charlie will be at your three o'clock across the plateau. You copy that?"

"Affirm, Charlie at our three. Hang on, sir, we're on our way!"

"Charlie, Alpha will be at your nine."

"Copy, Alpha at our nine."

Damn. His arm felt like a swarm of hornets had attacked. From the look of the fabric, the bullet was probably tumbling when it cut into his flesh. The wound needed a pressure bandage, but until the rest of Alpha arrived, he'd have to let it hemorrhage.

Instinctively, Mason tried to reload his weapon, but couldn't get the necessary leverage.

At that moment, Alpha scrambled over the summit to their left.

"I've got you," Hutch said. "Lemme see that arm."

The retreating Taliban were several hundred meters distant when everyone heard the sound. The distinctive, low whooping of a main rotor.

"Sergeant Hahn, press my transmit button."

"You got it, LT."

"All units freeze positions and pop smoke." He radioed to air support that none of his forces stood above the rim of the canyon. Everything else was fair game.

The Apache roared over their heads and executed a steep 360-degree turn, the pilot identifying the locations of all friendlies before beginning his strafing run.

As grisly as he knew it would be, Mason had to watch.

Across the plateau, the Taliban were retreating as quickly as they could. Some of them fired at the chopper in desperation. Mason could only imagine the fear they felt. Being defenseless against a gunship had to be terrifying. They were completely caught in the open with no place to hide.

He didn't disrespect the Taliban—quite the contrary. They were tough as nails and formidable enemies. They believed they were defending their homeland from foreign invaders, fighting for their freedom.

But this was war, and Mason believed in his own cause.

Growling like a leopard, the aircraft let loose with its 30 mm chain gun. The large-caliber slugs quite literally dismembered the Taliban soldiers. Cartwheeling limbs and strips of flesh flew in every direction. Mason didn't understand the hydrodynamic forces at work, but the outcome was absolute.

Wholesale slaughter.

Like a cattle brand, the visual image indelibly seared his mind.

He tore his gaze away and glanced at Hahn, whose expression matched his own. Mason wanted to feel bad but couldn't. All he had to do was conjure up an image of being captured, tied to a post, and slowly flogged to death. Yes, seeing butchery like this was terrible . . .

But it was justice.

CHAPTER 1

Russell Senate Office Building—three years later

Re: The November Directive
December 14, 2012

Dear Stone:

I'm deeply outraged at the escalating violence in California and Arizona along our Mexican border. As you well know, November's death toll stands at 119:

6 US federal agents
12 Mexican law enforcement officers
14 US citizens
87 Mexican citizens

I won't stand idly by while criminal gangs and organized cartels terrorize and murder America's sons and daughters. Such heinous and depraved criminal behavior cannot stand.

I'm tasking both you and your Committee on Domestic Terrorism to come up with a two-phased plan to counter this growing threat to both American and Mexican citizens at home and abroad. I'm calling this operation the November Directive, honoring those who've paid the ultimate price this month.

The purpose of phase one will be, simply put, to stop the bleeding. Short of declaring martial law along the border regions of San Diego, Tecate, Calexico, Yuma, Naco, and Douglas, the violence must end. DNI Benson has been briefed, and he's firmly aboard, so you'll have every available asset at your disposal for planning purposes.

The second phase will address prevention. I want you to create and implement a long-term campaign to interdict the flow of weapons being smuggled across our border into Mexico.

I'd like your proposal on my desk within three days. Assemble your committee and come up with a concrete strategy to begin implementation of both phases.

It should be noted that while on American soil, Mexican nationals engaged in the wanton murder of US citizens do not fall under the umbrella of our Constitution and therefore do not enjoy the protections thereof.

Even though we stand on opposite sides of the aisle, this isn't an issue driven by political pressure. The violence along our border is a cancer, and it must be surgically removed. Make it happen, Stone.

Sincerely,
Barack

Senator Matthew "Stone" McBride read the handwritten letter for the third time and squinted in thought. Closing in on his eighty-sixth year on earth, he'd been a senator for thirty of them and he'd never seen anything like this. Handwritten presidential letters weren't unheard of, but this one had "destroy after reading" written all over it. One thing was certain: the language was carefully crafted. He didn't think Obama was condoning an "anything goes" operation, but his letter clearly gave the green light for something more than traditional law enforcement. Stone knew the use of military force on domestic soil was not being sanctioned, hence the *short of declaring martial law* wording, so where did that leave things? How far was he authorized to take the November Directive? Before he could proceed, he needed a face-to-face.

He pressed a preset on his phone. "Is he in town? I need a meeting."

"You know that's not easy to arrange."

"I'm holding a handwritten letter."

"Hold, please."

Stone listened to the silence stretch. When the voice came back on, it held more urgency. "Tomorrow at seventeen hundred. Ten minutes."

"I'll only need five."

CHAPTER 2

Present day

Nathan McBride ended the cell call and glanced at his watch: just after 9:00 PM. He didn't believe the situation was truly an emergency, but he didn't mind jumping through a few hoops now and then. Jin wanted his help, and he'd deliver. Simple as that. Whatever issue she had with her daughter, she believed it required his personal touch. Besides, he hadn't seen either of them in a couple of weeks. *Too long*, he thought. He wanted to play a bigger role in their lives.

Nathan was a big man. At six foot five, 240 pounds, his height and build belonged to less than one-tenth of 1 percent of the earth's population. His dark blue eyes were complemented by reddish-brown hair with invading areas of gray. Three long scars marred his face, grisly souvenirs from a decades-old mission in Nicaragua that had ended his career as a CIA operations officer. Although the scars had been dulled by a plastic surgeon, they couldn't be missed. Holly had once told him he appeared intimidating, then quickly assured him that he had a kind heart despite the horrors he'd endured. He'd known she was right, but the truth still stung. Seeing his reaction, Holly had backpedaled, telling him that the scars gave him a rugged, tough-guy look.

Again, probably true. But Nathan no longer wanted to wear that persona. He'd moved on.

Leaving the garage of his Clairemont home, he turned on the wipers. Nathan didn't mind the dreary weather. San Diego saw such little precipitation it was actually a welcome change.

On the phone, he'd told Jin he wasn't alone—that Holly would be with him. Jin said she didn't mind if Holly came along but made it clear that Lauren would speak to no one but Nathan. Apparently, Lauren was on her fourth night of giving her mom the silent treatment. For her part, Jin refused to cave in their dispute, insisting that her daughter behave like a normal human being. But Lauren had clearly inherited the McBride stubbornness, a trait not limited to grandchildren. Nathan could've written a thesis on the subject.

He understood Lauren's frustration. Raised as an only child, he'd often felt as though he were being suffocated. There were times when he simply wanted to be left alone to sulk. He didn't have any experience with the mother-daughter dynamic but imagined it paralleled the father-son thing.

Nathan parked in the driveway, and he and Holly approached Jin's front door. His half sister must have been watching, because she opened the front door before Nathan could knock.

Jin was dressed in blue jeans, a T-shirt, and socks. Fifteen years older than Nathan, she had classic Eurasian features that defied her age. Jin possessed an extremely rare genetic marker. She had one blue eye and one brown eye. *Heterochromia* was the official medical term. The blue side came from Stone and the brown side from her mother, now deceased—an unfortunate victim of the Korean War. Jin often wore colored contacts to hide the trait, but not out of embarrassment. In a former life, she'd been an assassin and spy for North Korea, and the French still maintained a hefty bounty on her head for her theft of Exocet missile specs in the early '80s. Years later, she'd struck a deal with the United States and traded everything she knew for asylum.

He gave his sister a hug and introduced Holly. They shook hands, and Jin turned back to Nathan, her expression showing the kind of stress a mother often faces when she can't communicate with her daughter. "I'm sorry to drag you down here, but she won't talk to me."

"What's going on?"

"She thinks she's an adult, that's what."

Nathan nodded. "Thirteen can be tough."

"Tough? She's impossible. She won't listen."

"We were all that age once."

"I just want her to enjoy being a kid awhile longer."

"Is she in her room?"

"She won't come out, won't eat, won't do anything. I don't know what to do."

Nathan smiled. "Maybe Uncle Nate can help."

"Good luck," Jin said.

Holly sat down with Jin while he walked down the hall. No sound came from Lauren's room, but a small strip of yellow light spilled under her closed door.

"Lauren? It's Nathan."

No response.

He rapped softly. "Lauren, you in there? It's Uncle Nate."

Thinking Lauren might have a headset on, he tried the knob. It turned, so he pushed the door open a crack and peered in. Dressed like her mom, Lauren was lying on her back on her bed. She made eye contact but didn't move.

"Is that all I get? I interrupted cleaning my guns to come over here."

He saw a half smile.

"That's more like it. How about a hug?"

She slowly got up and hugged him. They settled on the edge of her bed, facing the same direction, the mirrored closet doors giving them a view of each other. Matching his own, her eyes were the color of deep arctic ice. Somehow, the McBride genetic stamp had survived her Korean ancestry. Her natural black hair, combined with those blue eyes and fair complexion, made her look like a heroine from a science fiction movie. He truly believed she was the most beautiful child he'd ever seen, but knew his opinion was biased. In contrast to his own, her skin was flawless, despite the pouty expression.

Nathan didn't say anything, knowing Lauren would fill the silence.

"She hates me."

"Your mom doesn't hate you, but it's not her role to be your friend right now. She said you haven't talked to her in days."

"What's the point? She doesn't listen. She only cares about herself."

"You don't really believe that, do you?"

She didn't say anything.

"Sometimes it's harder to listen than to talk."

"Not for me."

"Come on, you know what I mean."

"I guess."

Nathan waited again. Like him, Lauren needed intervals of silence.

"She thinks I dress too *provocatively*. But all my friends get to wear cool clothes."

Nathan smiled. "Cool or provocative?"

"Both."

It was Nathan's turn to say nothing.

"Okay, okay . . . Point taken."

He used the phrase all the time, and Lauren had adopted it.

"You're at a tough age. You want to be treated like an adult, but you still want kid benefits."

"I don't feel like a kid."

"You're turning fourteen in a couple of months. Ever heard the expression: youth is wasted on the young?"

She shook her head.

"It means we adults wish we were young again, kinda the opposite of the way kids wish they were older. Don't fall into the trap of wanting to be someone you're not."

She didn't say anything.

"Brunettes want to be blondes. Short people want to be taller. White people want tans." Nathan pointed to the mirror. "You and I have something those popular girls at school will never have. A life-and-death combat bond. We've been through hell and back, you and me."

Lauren shuddered. "I still can't believe what I did to you in that abandoned house."

Nathan put a hand on her shoulder, still looking at her in the mirror. "Hey, we wouldn't be talking if you hadn't."

"That was crazy."

"You aren't kidding. I've been on some rough ops, but that was right up there with the worst of them. Look, my point is, you don't need to prove anything to anyone."

"I don't?"

"Absolutely not." Nathan put a fist to his chest. "If you're comfortable in here, you don't need to show off or hang with the popular girls. The girls who need to wear tight clothes to get attention from boys are insecure. They use their bodies to hide who they truly are, scared little girls."

"Put that way, they sound kinda pathetic."

"Don't condemn them. It's just part of growing up. Much of what they think is important really isn't. Ask yourself this: What's more important? The way you look, or the way you feel about yourself?"

Lauren looked straight ahead, but Nathan knew she'd gotten his point.

"Why don't you compromise with your mom? I have a feeling you're both coming from extreme perspectives. If you give a little, she will too."

"I guess."

"You're in transition from childhood to womanhood, and it's going to be tough sometimes. Every girl goes through it. It will take patience and understanding on both sides. Your mom didn't have a happy childhood. I'm not going to give you all the gory details, but let's just say she was forced to grow up much faster than you."

"In North Korea, was she, you know . . ."

"Yes. Many times, and when she was younger than you."

"That's horrible. She never talks about it."

"Maybe someday. You're still kinda young for the specifics. Do you remember how you felt when you saw my chest, all those scars? We were on top of that wrecked car, and we needed to use my shirt on the barbed wire?"

"Yeah, I'll never forget it. I was like totally freaked. I felt really bad for you."

"Your mom has scars like mine, only you can't see them."

Lauren thought for a moment. He didn't need to explain what he meant.

"She yells a lot. It's hard not to yell back."

"You need to understand her anger isn't directed at you. I get angry too."

"As bad as my mom?"

"Worse."

"No way."

"It's true. But I've learned to control it. Your mom has a harder time. What happened to me occurred over a three-week period, but your mom endured years of abuse."

"I told her she was a bitch, and then I felt really bad because she cried for hours."

"Look, Lauren, people say things like that, but they forgive each other. Your mom loves you. She left North Korea so you wouldn't have to grow up like she did. There were other reasons too, but she wanted a better life for you."

She leaned in close and put an arm around him. "I wish you lived with us."

"Hey, I'm only ten minutes away."

"I'm glad you came over. I was mad she called you, but not anymore."

"I know it's tough not having a dad like the other kids, but you can call me anytime. I'll always be here for you, twenty-four-seven. You've earned it."

Nathan got up and took a knee in front of her.

"This won't be easy, but you should tell your mom you're sorry you haven't talked to her. Your mom has a lot of faults, but she's not a narcissist. She'll accept your apology and not use it against you."

"What's a narcissist?"

"Narcissists are people who think they never make mistakes and are never wrong. They never say they're sorry and, to make matters worse, they expect everyone to apologize to *them*."

"Are there a lot of people like that?"

"More than you'll ever know. They also don't have any friends. To have a friend, you have to be a friend."

"They sound like assholes."

"Language, young lady."

"Sorry."

Nathan laughed. "See? It's easy to say sorry. Now, if you say you're sorry to your mom, she'll also say she's sorry. It's a way to open dialogue. When you apologize to a regular person, they see it as a sign of strength, not weakness."

"Is that a Christian thing?"

"Yes, absolutely, but not exclusively. We make lots of mistakes, but we own up to them and say we're sorry when we do something wrong. We also forgive those who've wronged us."

Lauren looked confused.

"Let me tell you something about forgiveness. It's from a sermon I heard while I was on vacation."

"You went to church on vacation?"

"Sure, lots of people do. Anyway, it was a small Presbyterian church somewhere along the 101. Templeton, I think. The pastor's name was Charlie Little, and he said that when you forgive someone, it doesn't diminish or erase what was done to you. You don't have to understand why they did it, and you certainly don't have to be on friendly terms with someone who's hurt you. When you forgive someone, you're doing it to release their debt to you."

"Debt?"

"Yes, you're moving on with your life and you don't require anything from the person who hurt you."

"Have you forgiven the man who, like, you know . . . tortured you?"

"Yes, but I'm never going to be friends with him and I don't have to understand why he did it."

Lauren thought for a few seconds, then asked, "Can I go with you on Sunday? You know, to church? Just the two of us?"

"I'll pick you up at a quarter to nine, but you'll need to dress . . . appropriately."

She rolled her eyes in that cute kid way.

They fell silent again, looking at each other in the mirror. Nathan saw her face brighten a little. She looked so innocent and fragile, but underneath was one tough kid. Tested and proven.

"I still want to be a Special Forces soldier."

"Have you told your mom that?"

"No way. She'd totally freak."

"Then it's better not to mention it for now." He paused. "Hey, do you think they're talking about us out there?"

"Duh."

"Try again."

"Yes, they're talking about us."

"Come on, we'd better get out there before they decide they don't need us anymore."

CHAPTER 3

Toby Haynes never looked for trouble. Not anymore. A few years ago, he'd pursued confrontations on a regular basis. For most of his adult life, he'd mistakenly believed that bullying people made him feel better about himself. Epiphanies can be sparked from an infinite number of circumstances, but Toby's had come from a force of nature in the form of Nathan McBride.

At six foot eight and 270 pounds, Toby looked like an NFL defensive end—minus the ink—and there had been a time when he'd used his bulk to intimidate people. Even though McBride was three inches shorter and thirty pounds lighter, Nathan had been all *but* intimidated. After an ill-advised fistfight in which he hadn't landed a single punch, Toby had been bloodied, broken, and completely defenseless. He remembered looking up at McBride and thinking, *This guy's going to beat the living hell out of me*, but something quite different had happened—something he'd never forgotten.

He couldn't remember all of McBride's advice that night, but one thing had stuck with Toby: *Life is full of details. Start noticing them.* And notice them he had, starting with a thorough self-examination. Toby had been so impressed with McBride and his friend Harvey Fontana that he'd followed in their footsteps and enlisted in the Marines, where he'd spent two years as an MP until a car crash ended his career.

Six months later, after his physical therapy ended, he'd applied for a security guard position at McBride's company but hadn't passed the background check. Although he didn't have a criminal record, he had a really lousy credit score, and if you wanted to work for First Security, Incorporated, you needed near-flawless credit.

But to Toby's surprise, failing the credit check hadn't been the end of it.

The following day, he'd received a call from Nathan McBride. Not only was Toby going to have the chance to be a security guard—he'd be attending a security guard academy. Toby hadn't known such things existed, but this school was the best in the country—the prestigious Beaumont Academy in Gallup, New Mexico. McBride was offering Toby a personal loan on nothing more than a verbal promise to repay it after he graduated and landed a job.

Now there was no guarantee of employment after graduating, much less with the esteemed Beaumont Specialists, Inc., one of the country's biggest private military contractors. Determined despite the odds, Toby applied himself and advanced to the top of his class. Smaller security companies would've hired him hands down, but he wanted to work for BSI. And so he finally got hired. Since his first BSI paycheck, he hadn't missed a single payment to McBride.

Toby smiled at the memory, waiting for the gas pump to click. He glanced at his watch. He had forty-five minutes before his 1:00 AM shift started. Patchy fog and a near-freezing mist had descended upon the city. Out-of-towners would have a hard time believing San Diego's weather could be like this. A few degrees colder and it would be snowing.

On the opposite side of the intersection, approaching headlights caught his attention. A silver SUV rolled through the green light and pulled into a competing gas station across the road. The vehicle looked familiar—it was the same make, color, and model that BSI used for company vehicles.

Interesting . . . Toby had never bumped into a colleague in this neighborhood. Mildly curious, he tried to glimpse the driver. Another surprise. The driver wasn't merely a colleague of Toby's; he was Chip Hahn, right-hand man and personal bodyguard to BSI Chief of Security Tanner Mason. Toby had often wondered why Mason needed a bodyguard, but he'd never mustered the nerve to ask. Questions like that tended to strangle careers—as would gawking at your boss from the shadows instead of waving hello.

Hahn wore his signature ball cap and sunglasses. In the eighteen months Toby had worked as a private security officer for BSI, he'd never seen Hahn's eyes. Ever. He'd also never seen the man smile.

Toby took an instinctive step back into the concealment of the gas pump and chided himself: *If you're not going to say hello, you'd better not get caught watching the man.* He knew he should mind his own business, but something about Hahn felt . . . off. More than usual.

The rear windows of Hahn's SUV were darkly tinted, screening any occupants. Who besides Mason could Hahn be driving around at this hour? And why? Even more curious, Hahn's SUV had stopped short of the gas pump island. Dressed in black tactical clothing, Hahn got out of the vehicle.

Why didn't he pull up to the pump? Toby wondered.

Rather than reach for his wallet, Hahn pulled a small item from his coat pocket and approached the island. He pointed the object at the top of the pump for a few seconds, then tucked it back into his pocket. Toby quickly looked away and shrank back into the shadow of his gas pump. He was pretty sure he knew what Hahn had just done. The question was why.

Toby leaned to the side to reacquire Hahn. At the same moment, as if sensing he was being watched, Hahn froze. Even though Toby stood more than a hundred yards distant behind a gas pump, he felt the man's eyes penetrate the mist. A shiver raked his body. *Was he blown? Had Hahn seen him?*

In desperation, Toby actually considered stepping out and offering a friendly wave, but Hahn got back into the SUV and pulled forward to the pump.

Toby circled to the driver's side of his white Sentra and got in.

He grabbed a compact pair of field glasses from the glove box and sought out the object that Hahn had reached for earlier. As he'd suspected, a wad of shaving cream was plastered over the orb-shaped security camera overlooking the gas pump area. Given the secretive nature of the corporation Toby worked for, the shaving-cream gambit wasn't totally out of character, but the circumstances didn't seem to warrant such discretion. Something important was going down.

Just drive to work and forget you ever saw this.

But he knew he couldn't. He had to know why Hahn impaired the security camera. Toby bargained with himself: He'd keep the surveillance going as long as it didn't put him at risk of being late to work. He couldn't afford any black marks on his employment record. Getting the BSI job had been a big accomplishment, but these days Toby had his sights set on the San Diego County Sheriff's Department.

Hahn finished pumping the gas and drove the SUV out of the gas station. In world-record time, Toby climbed out and returned the nozzle into its slot. Determined to learn more despite the risk, he turned his headlights off and followed the SUV. Since no one was around, he ran the red light and blew across Clairemont Mesa. Three hundred yards ahead, he saw the SUV make a left.

Not toward BSI.

Toby stomped on the gas, then braked hard at the corner where Hahn had disappeared. Farther ahead, he saw the taillights of the SUV just finishing a right turn. Toby left his headlights off and sped down the street. When he neared the spot where Hahn had turned, he clicked on his headlights. It was a driveway. Cruising past, Toby stole a quick look to the right. The SUV had stopped at the far end of a linear parking lot between two industrial buildings. Its brake lights were on, but as far as Toby could tell, its headlights were dark. Just before he lost sight of it, the driver's door opened and Hahn stepped out. Toby kept going down the block until he found a parking spot at the curb behind a delivery van.

He grabbed his field glasses and night-vision scope—items he used during his nightly BSI beat—and locked his car. If there were any security cameras mounted on the building to his left, he didn't see them, and no lights were on inside. Cautiously, he approached the driveway, then stopped and took a quick look.

The SUV was still there. As was Hahn.

Is that a gun?

He brought his field glasses up and focused on Hahn.

Yes, it was definitely some kind of pistol, and it had a suppressor.

Standing in front of the SUV, Hahn pointed the weapon at the parapet of the roof. Toby followed the man's aim and saw a red laser dot sweep onto a security camera. A second later, the device shuddered and pieces of glass and plastic rained down. There was no sound at all. Not even a faint pop. He estimated the distance at just under one hundred yards. He should've heard something unless Hahn had used a small-caliber subsonic round. Toby knew his way around handguns, and a subsonic round from a suppressed .22 wouldn't be much louder than a dropped apple.

Something big was happening, and Hahn and whoever else was with him didn't want any witnesses. Hahn picked up the expended brass, opened the passenger door, and grabbed a large pair of bolt cutters.

The sudden appearance of an approaching car made Toby's skin tighten. He'd been so focused on the SUV he forgot to watch for other cars.

In a split-second decision, Toby flattened himself on the ground and hoped the low hedge would screen him.

Blinding light blanched the entire area.

Shit, shit!

Panicking could prove costly, and he wasn't just worried about losing his job.

He clenched his teeth as the dual beams bounced. What were the odds? It had to be thousands to one a second vehicle would enter this driveway at this exact moment.

No way was this a coincidence.

He wished he didn't have such a vivid imagination. Here he was, lying on wet grass with a pair of field glasses around his neck, a night-vision scope in his pocket, and absolutely no explanation for any of it.

His stress level eased a bit when the car kept going.

Trembling from the adrenaline rush, he peered over the hedge and saw the intruder was a dark Lexus sedan and its headlights were now off. If he had any brains at all, he'd consider this close call a warning and leave.

The SUV was gone.

He watched the Lexus continue to the end of the aisle and turn right and then stop, but it didn't look like there was anywhere to go out there. There had to be a gate in the fence. That's why Hahn needed the bolt cutters. As if on cue, the bleed light from the Lexus's brakes vanished and the sedan started moving again. Someone had gotten out to close the gate.

Doing his best to stay in the shadows, Toby ran toward the wrecked camera. If he didn't hurry, he'd lose sight of the sedan through the mist. Again, not an altogether bad thing to happen.

He pressed the illumination button on his watch and checked the time. Had only five minutes passed since seeing the SUV? Could that be right? BSI was a ten-minute drive from here, so that left him thirty to forty minutes, depending on how far he ventured on foot.

He slowed to a fast walk when he reached the northwest corner of the building. Like he'd thought, a dark expanse of baseball diamonds and soccer fields bordered this property. From his current position, he couldn't see the Lexus, but he heard the hiss of its tires.

Avoiding the broken pieces of glass and plastic, he angled across the parking lot and found the closed gate. It didn't look like the official entrance to the ball fields—more like a fire-access point. On closer inspection, he saw where a lock had hung.

Beyond the gate, there was only one set of fresh tire tracks on the decomposed granite surface. Check that, two sets, but the Lexus had driven on top of the SUV's impressions. Not accidental, in all likelihood.

Toby used his shirt to wipe the binocular lenses before scanning the area. If there were any sources of light out there, he didn't see them. He switched to NV and immediately found the vehicles. They were creeping along the road toward the interior of the complex. He was about to follow the tire tracks when he realized he shouldn't leave any footprints.

He diverted to the post supporting the gate and used a weed-strewn area to mask his entry. At a safe distance from the gate, he crossed the dirt track, hopped a low center field fence, and sprinted toward home plate. Although he felt exposed out in the open, his footfalls on the grass were silent and the mist provided a good visual screen.

My phone!

He reached into his pocket and changed it to silent mode.

At home plate he found himself trapped by a chain-link fence used for stopping foul balls. He should've anticipated this would be here. Beyond the fence, some kind of tall rectangular structure loomed like a giant tombstone. He diverted to his left, over to the first base side, and found a gate near the dugout.

As far as he could tell, the SUV and Lexus were at least another hundred yards farther north and east of his position. Aside from the background whoosh of the 52 freeway, it was eerily quiet out here.

His soggy clothing produced an involuntary shiver. He should've grabbed his coat and now wished he had. His work uniform—a black security outfit—offered good concealment, but little in the way of thermal protection. He reached up, wiped the dampness from his bald head, and realized he'd forgotten his cover as well. He never wore the BSI hat anywhere other than work, but he kept a Marine Corps hat in the car for everywhere else. *Way to go, Toby. You're two for two.*

The open space to his left was another baseball field, so Toby decided to use it to angle east, back toward the access road where he could use the cover of some trees. Staying close to the road offered a second advantage. The road appeared to be several feet higher than the ball field, which worked in his favor. If headlights swept toward his direction, he could hide in the shadow created by the difference in elevation.

At the tree line, he paralleled the same interior road the vehicles had used and advanced deeper into the complex. The smell of eucalyptus hung in the air like fog. It reminded him of his backyard when he was a kid.

He heard something.

The clunk of a car door—from his three o'clock position.

He focused his NV in that direction and saw the Lexus and SUV sitting in the middle of a soccer field. He hopped the fence and climbed halfway up the bank. Since the trees on the opposite side of the gravel road didn't have low-hanging branches, he stayed where he was.

Standing next to the SUV, Hahn was turning in a circle and appeared to be scanning the area with some sort of device that looked like—

A night-vision scope. Shit!

Toby ducked, praying he'd been quick enough. Hahn had been mere seconds from sweeping past his area. He waited a good ten seconds before risking a look. Hahn was just finishing a 360-degree sweep. The SUV's passenger got out, and to Toby's surprise, it wasn't BSI's chief of security. It was Darla Lyons, a compact brunette in her midthirties. He didn't know much about her, but she worked with Hahn and was obviously part of Mason's inner circle.

Okay, so who's in the Lexus? he wondered. *Maybe Hahn and Lyons have some kind of fling going.* Were they out here for sex? No, that didn't make sense. Why go to all this trouble when a motel would suffice? One thing was certain, if they had something illegal going on behind Mason's back, it was more than reckless. You never crossed Tanner Mason.

For half a minute nothing happened. They just stood there, looking around.

The interior of the Lexus remained dark as its driver exited the vehicle.

In a puzzling move, the sedan chirped and its parking lights flashed. Weird. The driver must've locked the car. Why would he do that?

When the man approached Hahn and Lyons, Toby recognized his boss's commanding presence right away. There was no mistaking Tanner, a.k.a. Skinner, Mason. His long blond hair was always tightly secured in a ponytail. "Skinner" was reputedly a tough-guy nickname or call sign from Mason's BSI Academy days. Toby had only met Mason a couple of times because BSI's structure closely mirrored that of the military. Toby reported to a lieutenant who, in turn, reported up the chain of command.

When Mason reached the SUV, Hahn's body language changed, like that of a corporal in the presence of a general. Like Hahn, Mason and Darla wore gloves and dark clothing, not the standard khaki garb they usually wore at work. They huddled for several seconds before walking over to the Lexus.

Toby took a moment to scan his perimeter with the NV. He didn't think a security guard would be on foot out here, but it was likely a mobile unit cruised the outside every so often as part of a larger patrol loop. He'd once done something similar during his MP days at Camp Pendleton.

He kept alternating his surveillance between the vehicles, wondering what this late-night rendezvous was all about and why they needed such a dark and isolated spot.

Mason raised his hand and the Lexus flashed and chirped again.

Hahn circled to the far side, while Darla stood behind the trunk, her hand tucked inside her coat. Simultaneously, Hahn and Mason opened the rear passenger doors and backed away.

Two men had trouble getting out, and Toby saw why. Their hands were secured behind their backs. He couldn't see a lot of detail, but it looked like they wore formal pants and golf shirts. One of them sported a dark ball cap.

Hahn escorted his man around the vehicle and shoved him into position next to the other guy. Darla closed both of the sedan's doors and stood next to Mason.

With his arms crossed, Mason said something to them. It didn't look like a well-received comment because the man wearing the ball cap jerked his head forward in a spitting type of motion.

Toby inwardly cringed as Mason wiped his face.

It happened fast.

Mason drove his fist into Ball Cap's stomach hard enough to detonate organs. Before the guy could recover, Mason swept his foot and sent the guy sprawling.

The second guy turned to help his buddy, but never got there.

Darla took him down.

Mason produced a suppressed pistol and swung it like a hammer. The blow caught the second man on the side of the head. Mason grabbed the guy's collar, dragged him away from the SUV, and kicked him in the ribs several times.

The man curled into the fetal position and held still.

Some kind of heated exchange took place between Ball Cap and Mason. Toby could only hear bits and pieces, but there was no mistaking the word *chickenshit* being yelled. Still on the ground, Ball Cap made it to his hands and knees, but no farther.

In a casual move, Mason pointed his pistol at Ball Cap's head.

Oh man, no way . . .

There was no sound, but Toby's NV registered the brief flash.

When the other guy tried to get up, Hahn kicked him in the face.

Toby winced as the man's jaw absorbed the full brunt of the energy.

Mason approached the other man and shot him in the head as well. The guy didn't die right away. His body wrenched in violent spasms for several seconds, then went still. Hahn laughed and made some sort of comparison to a headless snake.

Toby couldn't believe what he'd just witnessed. When he tried to swallow, his mouth was dry. He had no business being out here and cursed himself for meddling. How could he have been so stupid?

He wanted to run, but if he did that now, they might see him. The sloped bank he used for concealment didn't extend more than fifty yards along the access road in the direction he needed to go. If he retraced his steps across the baseball field, he'd be out in the open. He should've anticipated Mason would have night vision.

Pinned down, he'd have to wait this out.

Another contraction from the cold raked his body.

He watched Hahn use a penlight to sweep the grass, probably looking for Mason's spent brass. After thirty seconds, Hahn seemed to find what he was looking for. He then arranged the bodies side by side before doing something to their heads, but Toby couldn't see what he did.

He'd never seen anyone get killed—let alone murdered—and it sure as hell wasn't like the movies. There was nothing glamorous or exciting about it. The words "brutal" and "perverse" came to mind. Those were his *colleagues* out there. How could they simply drive to work like none of this had happened? And he wondered the same thing about himself.

Toby zeroed in on Darla. She said something to Mason, but he just shrugged as if to say, *That wasn't so bad.*

A few seconds later, the image in his NV flashed brightly. Four times. Were they taking pictures of the bodies? He then watched Mason open the driver's side door of the SUV, sit down, and remove his shoes. He placed them in a garbage bag and handed it to Hahn. At the sedan, Hahn did the same thing and passed the bag to Darla.

Mason and Hahn got into the sedan, while Darla climbed into the SUV. Both vehicles remained dark as they left the soccer field.

Toby scrambled down the bank and lay flat next to the outfield fence.

In thirty seconds the vehicles would be on top of him.

He'd always believed he was fairly tough, but this sickening feeling of being unarmed and helpless hammered his nerves. He considered bolting again, but knew he'd have no chance against their NV devices. He'd be spotted for sure.

It didn't take a vivid imagination to know what would happen if they stopped. Toby could fight, but he was no match for three of BSI's top military contractors armed with laser-sighted pistols.

The menacing hiss of tires grew louder, and he pressed his forehead into the grass. No more than ten feet away, the two vehicles reached his position. Close to vomiting, Toby clenched his teeth. If the windows of the vehicles were down, they'd hear his retching for sure. Fighting the rising bile, he forced himself to breathe through his nose.

The horrid image of Hahn kicking the downed man in the face invaded his mind. The blow must've destroyed the man's nose—a cruel thing to do before killing him.

Adding to Toby's misery, his wet uniform stuck to his body like frozen plate steel.

Keep going . . . please *keep going.*

Then, as slowly as it had arrived, the sound of crunching tires receded to the south, back toward the fire-access gate.

Toby sucked in a lungful of air and nearly vomited.

His bladder suddenly burned. He hadn't realized how badly he needed to pee.

When the trailing sedan was far enough away, he eased into a kneeling position and took more deep breaths. He was tempted to stick a finger down his throat and just get it over with, but the worst of his fear had passed.

He used the NV to locate the vehicles at the southern edge of the complex. They turned west along the outfield fence where he'd seen the single set of tire tracks on the way out here. In fifteen more seconds, they'd be outside the property and no longer posing a threat.

Toby couldn't wait any longer. He unzipped and relieved himself while kneeling.

Getting up slowly, he looked at the prone forms on the soccer field.

Neither of them moved.

He'd heard of cases where people lived after being shot in the head, but how likely was that? Now wasn't the time for heroics, in any case. For all he knew, someone could be coming to sanitize the scene.

He watched Hahn close the gate behind the two vehicles and hoped they'd turn left out of the driveway. If not, they'd cruise past his parked Sentra.

In a full sprint, he took off toward the tombstone-like structure, and sixty seconds later, he arrived at the fire-access gate. Breathing heavily, he retraced his steps across the weeds and noticed Mason had replaced the cut lock.

He illuminated his watch and saw just under thirty-five minutes remained. Should he call 911? He knew he couldn't use his cell phone to do it. What about a pay phone? No, that wouldn't work—all 911 calls were recorded.

He needed time to think, time to settle his nerves. What about car trouble? A dead battery. With the fog and mist, it would make a believable excuse to be late. But even late, how was he supposed to walk into BSI headquarters like none of this had happened? And he certainly couldn't show up in a wet, disheveled uniform. The spot where he'd lain flat to avoid being seen hadn't been solid grass. There'd been muddy patches. No way. There was no way he could go to work tonight, but it was bad form to call in sick with less than an hour's notice.

Bad form?

He'd just witnessed a double murder, committed by his *employer*!

He stayed close to the building and ran along the landscaped grass strip. When he reached the corner of the street, there were no cars present. He got into his Sentra and drove west, away from the driveway. He didn't want to retrace any of his route over here.

Man, this really sucks, he told himself again. Then he remembered something . . . something from the night that had changed his life.

Feeling a new surge of hope, Toby Haynes reached for his wallet.

CHAPTER 4

Damp with sweat, Nathan awoke from the moth dream again. How many times this week? Four? Wasn't time supposed to be the great healer? *Yeah, right.*

He didn't hate the winged insects, but they'd once tormented him to the brink of insanity.

Two decades ago, the tail end of a CIA mission in Nicaragua had ended badly and he'd fallen into the clutches of a vicious interrogator. At least his spotter Harvey Fontana got away, but Nathan paid a high price ensuring his friend's escape. He'd bought time for Harv with unspeakable humiliation and agony. Their extraction from Nicaragua hadn't been scheduled for two days, and his interrogator was determined to wring the details out of him and set a trap for the other *Americano.* Nathan *held* out and Harvey *got* out, but his vindictive captor had unleashed a lifetime's worth of fury and frustration upon his captive.

Montez de Oca had been exceptionally innovative. Bored with his daily medieval tortures, he'd tied Nathan to a tree one night and put a floodlight in his face. Nathan had thought it was just another wear-the-prisoner-down ploy—the tired, old light-in-the-face trick. The bulb was far enough away not to burn him, but damned bright.

At first nothing happened and he'd thought he might actually get a few hours of sleep. Then a single visitor arrived, drawn to the lure of an artificial sun. The yellow moth landed on his nose and stretched its black-spotted wings. Nathan actually welcomed the moth's company and thought it was a beautiful creature. He remembered cracking a smile—literally, his lips had been scabbed over from countless impacts.

Then a second insect came, bigger than its friend.

It didn't take long for Nathan to understand the true horror of what descended out of the darkness. Within a few minutes there were ten.

Then twenty.

Joy turned to terror as hundreds arrived. They crawled across his face and into his nose, ears, and eyes. The more he shook his head to dislodge them, the more agitated they became. Their wings whirring, they orbited like a menacing swarm of bees before settling onto his face again. The sheer numbers threatened to suffocate him, but that was only part of the terror. Three long, open gashes on his cheeks were especially inviting, and the thirsty moths lined the wounds like antelope drinking at a river. Time stretched and lost all meaning.

When his mind reached the overload point and felt like it was going to snap, the light winked out.

Half an hour later, it started over again. Nathan remembered being so exhausted he thought he might actually die from sleep deprivation, and prayed he would.

But God had other plans for him, because death hadn't come.

Salvation had.

It took twenty-two days, but Harv finally rescued him. Thankfully, Nathan had no memory of being carried through three miles of jungle. His savaged body had been reduced to 130 pounds.

Now fully awake, he focused on the pattern on the ceiling and sighed. At least he was still in bed. Most of the time he woke up on the floor. His record of remaining in bed for five nights in a row might be actually broken tonight.

A glance at the digital clock confirmed he'd only been asleep for two hours. He watched the pale blue number change from 00:45 to 00:46. All things being equal, not a horrible evening. So far . . .

He looked at the woman lying next to him and winced. He must've fallen asleep next to her, a mistake putting her at risk. More often than not, he came out of his dreams violently.

No harm done. This time.

Holly Simpson's shoulder-length dark hair fanned out on the white pillow like a reverse halo. When they'd first met, he thought her hair had been black, but it was actually deep brown. Strands of gray were beginning to take a foothold, but she didn't fight it. Nathan liked that. If men could look distinguished with gray, why not women?

In a different life, Holly could've been a gymnast. She had the body type. Strong facial features reflected her Eastern Bloc lineage. In her midforties, she still silenced a room. Some women just had a commanding presence. It couldn't be bought, borrowed, surgically added, or stolen. It simply existed. Like Nathan, she had no children, but she had several adult nephews by a sister in Boston.

Holly had been the special agent in charge of the FBI's Sacramento field office when a pair of inbred lowlifes nearly ended her life. The massive C4 bomb they'd detonated next to her building had stolen twenty-four lives and wounded dozens more. Holly had been lucky. She'd only been crippled for life. *Only.* Most of the time her limp wasn't too pronounced, except when the weather changed. At least she didn't need that damned cane anymore. It had pained him to see her walk with it. Still, walking with a cane had been infinitely better than the alternative—a rolling chair. Life could be so bad to good people.

They'd often talked about their long-distance relationship, and although Holly said she was okay with it, there were times when Nathan wasn't sure. He felt as though he was preventing her from finding someone else. She'd never voiced it, but he wondered if she wanted a relationship with someone closer to her new home in DC.

One thing was clear: she'd gotten beyond his physical appearance. Nathan didn't consider himself handsome no matter how many times Holly told him otherwise. The last time he'd felt this level of insecurity, he'd been lying next to a different kind of woman, a woman he'd mistakenly believed could give him more than physical pleasure. For two years, denial had hidden the truth. He never told Holly about Mara. What would be the point? What would it accomplish? Besides, he'd never asked Holly about *her* former relationships.

Meeting Holly had changed everything. She'd opened a door that had been closed for so long, he'd forgotten what lay behind it. In one short car ride together on the day they met, Holly had managed to filet him from jaw to groin. Being so exposed had felt . . . what? Unprotected? Was that the right word? Maybe . . . unguarded. Truth be told, he'd found it a cleansing experience. She hadn't pressed the conversation when he'd been initially reluctant to get too personal about his father, even though he ultimately had. She never pried and, more importantly, never judged. Their personalities complemented each other. Trust didn't come easily to Nathan, but he trusted this woman with his life.

"You're staring again," she said.

Her voice startled him. "Huh? Oh, sorry."

"Don't be."

"How long?" he asked.

"Have I been looking at you? Half a minute. Bad dreams again?"

He shrugged. "Hey, I'm still in bed."

Holly rolled onto her side to face him. "Something on your mind?"

"Just thinking about us. It's hard to believe we've only known each other for five years."

"Does it seem longer?"

"If I say yes?"

Holly smiled. "It's a compliment."

"I'm glad you think so."

"I liked the movie we watched tonight. I hadn't seen it since it was in theaters."

"Hannibal Lecter's entrance was pure genius. Letting the camera come to him with him just standing in the cell? It was a powerful scene, set up by Dr. Chilton calling him a monster . . ." Nathan's expression changed.

"You're not."

"There are times . . ." He'd once used the label on himself, and Holly had instantly rebuked it. He changed the subject. "I'm shrinking."

"Shrinking?"

"My annual physical. I'm down to six foot four and a half inches, but my weight hasn't gone down with it."

"Well, grab the pitchforks and light the torches."

"Why do we get along so well?"

"We're self-actualized."

"What does that mean?"

"In theory," she said, "it's the final level of psychological growth achievable when all mental needs are fulfilled, resulting in a complete realization of personal potential."

"What a bunch of psychobabble."

"It definitely is."

"Why'd you switch majors? You would've made a good shrink."

"Hardly."

"I disagree."

"In all seriousness? I wanted to make a tangible stand for something. I suppose law enforcement fit the bill."

Nathan remained silent for a moment. "How's the new job in DC going?"

"Good, so far."

"Good . . . What does Director Lansing have you doing, anyway?" All he knew was that her office was just down the hall.

"It's kinda complicated."

"I'm not trying to pry."

"I know. I guess it's sorta like a management and think tank job all in one. Not exactly high on the action-and-danger spectrum."

Nathan had the distinct impression that by being vague about her new work, Holly was protecting him, but he had no clue from what. Maybe her work really was *that* sensitive. The FBI had its eyes and ears everywhere these days. Well, he didn't need to know right now, or ever, for that matter. Nathan was familiar with secrecy. He'd lived his entire adult life mired in it. And still did. He and Holly often found themselves at a need-to-know dead end. He'd shared his most recent experience in Nicaragua . . . well, most of it. But there remained plenty of things he wasn't comfortable telling her, some of which he'd shared only with a dying man.

Holly traced one of the scars across his torso. "I'm not really tired now; want to watch another movie?"

Nathan smiled. "I kinda had something else in mind."

"And that would be?"

He wanted her. No . . . he needed her. And the thought of ever losing her scared him.

His cell phone rang. Nathan frowned, fell back, and rolled to retrieve the device from the nightstand. A call at this hour needed to be checked—and in this case—answered.

As the caller spoke, he stiffened and sat up straight on the bed. Holly followed suit, her eyes intense, watching for a sign of what the late-night call could mean.

CHAPTER 5

The caller was Gavin, the office manager at First Security, Inc., Nathan and Harv's private security firm. She'd been with the company for thirteen years, and Nathan had never known her to exaggerate an emergency situation.

"I'm sorry to disturb you at this hour, but the answering service operator says she has a man on the phone who insists on speaking to you. He says his life's in danger and it's an emergency."

"It's all right," said Nathan. "Any idea who the caller is?"

"Toby Haynes. He says he knows you."

"Yeah he does, but I don't want his call connected to my cell. I'll call you back on my landline. Can you conference the two calls together?"

"Yes, no problem."

"Tell the answering service to keep Haynes on hold. I'll call you back on the number you're calling from. You're at home, right?"

Across the bed from Nathan, Holly's concerned look had changed to puzzlement.

"Yes."

"Thanks for doing this, Gavin. I want you to log an extra four hours of work today."

"Thank you, but I'm salaried."

"Then expect a healthy gift certificate from Nordstrom's."

"You don't have to do that."

"I'll call you right back. Fifteen seconds." Nathan ended the call and tapped Harv's cell number.

Harv ran the day-to-day operations of the company. He answered on the fourth ring, his deep baritone voice holding a lighthearted tone. "I take it this isn't a social call."

"Toby Haynes is on hold with our answering service. He says it's an emergency, life or death, but I have no idea what it's about. I'm about to call Gavin back, and she's going to conference in Haynes's call."

Harv was all business now. "Let me do that from here. I'll keep you on the line. Did Gavin call from her home number?"

"Yes."

"Hang on."

Nathan listened to a moment of silence before hearing the line ring, presumably at Gavin's house.

Dressed in a T-shirt, Holly came over to his side of the bed and sat next to him.

"Nate, are you there?" Harv asked.

"Yes. Holly's with me. I have you on speaker."

"Hi, Holly."

"Hi, Harvey."

Gavin must've seen Harv's number on her phone console because she spoke Harv's name upon answering. "Mr. Fontana?"

"Hi, Gavin. Nathan's on the line with me. Conference us in with the answering service call and make sure their end disconnects. Sever all the calls if they don't."

"I will." A brief pause followed. "Mr. Haynes, I have Mr. McBride on the line."

"Hello? Mr. McBride?" Toby's voice didn't sound particularly familiar, but it carried the shakiness of a man in shock.

"Call me Nathan. What phone are you using to call me?"

"It's a pay phone, sir. It took forever to find one."

"All right. What's going on?"

"I saw two men get murdered tonight! They both got shot in the head. I—I don't know what to do."

"Murdered? Are you sure?"

"Yes!" Toby nearly shouted. "I saw it happen, and I know the killers. I don't know what to do. I think I made a big mistake. If I call the police and report it, they'll kill me next, I know it."

"Okay, slow down, we believe you. Harv's on the line with us. Are you alone? Can anyone hear you?"

"No. Sorry, sir. I mean yes, I'm alone. I'm just really freaked out."

"Don't say another word about this over the phone. Go home and wait there for us. Do you have a hard line?"

"Yeah."

"Give me the number, your address too."

Toby gave him the info.

"Okay. Sit tight. Don't go anywhere. We'll be there in about twenty-five minutes. Wipe down the pay phone's receiver before you leave."

"I put on my work gloves before I made the call."

"Good going. Try to relax, Toby. I'm assuming you used the First Security business card I gave you to contact us?"

"Yes, sir, it's in my hand right now."

"Burn it over your kitchen sink and wash the ash down the drain."

"I will. I'm sorry, sir. My nerves are shot. I can't stop shaking." He paused for a second. "I'm supposed to be at work in a few minutes."

Nathan asked, "Can you call in sick?"

"Yeah, I think I can get someone to take my shift tonight. He owes me a favor. I took a shift for him last month."

"How does it work? Do you normally get someone to work for you? I mean, do you usually make the arrangements for someone to cover your shift? Will that raise suspicion?"

"I've never called in sick before, but it should be okay."

"Use the hard line at your house to make the call. Your supervisor will probably tell you to stay home. Offer to find someone to take your shift and see what happens."

"Yeah, you're probably right. Man, thanks for helping me. I don't know what I'd do without you guys."

"We'll use a special knock on your door: twice fast, twice slow. You got that?"

"Two fast, two slow."

"See you in twenty-five minutes." Nathan ended the call, knowing Harv would call him right back.

Holly said, "We need to call the police."

"I hear you on that, but Toby said he's afraid for his life if he talks to the police. If he knows the killers, then he really could be in danger." Nathan thought for a moment. "Toby's not a stupid guy. I've known him for a long time. I gave him a loan on just his word he'd pay me back and he never missed a payment. Let's hear why he thinks his life's in danger if the police get involved."

"Well, I'm a sworn law enforcement officer," said Holly. "Not reporting a murder doesn't sit well with me."

"I understand and we'll definitely call them—" His cell chimed. "That's Harv calling . . . Hey, I've got you on speaker again, Holly's right here." Nathan heard Harv's car-door alarm bong three times.

"Sorry, I got dressed during Toby's call. It should switch to the Bluetooth in a few seconds."

"So what do you think?" Nathan asked.

"Let's talk in person," Harv said.

CHAPTER 6

Philippine Sea—fifteen days earlier

Seven hundred miles northeast of Palau, the Republic of Korea container ship *Namkung Khang* slowed to three knots as a small skiff approached its hull. The night watch wasn't worried because the *Khang* wasn't being attacked by pirates—quite the opposite. After all, no sane pirates attacked the *Khang* unless they wanted to meet their creators. This ROK vessel didn't employ water cannons; it employed large-caliber machine guns.

Atop a mountain of precisely stacked containers, Crewman Ryang secured a climbing rope to a hold-down corner and stepped into his rappelling harness. With a second rope slung over his shoulder, he descended past five levels of containers and found the unit he wanted. Unlike its surrounding neighbors, this particular container wasn't secured with lashing rods. Their absence didn't look out of place, as not every container needed them.

Ryang removed his gloves, activated his helmet light, and unlocked the four padlocks securing the container's dual doors. Inside were hundreds of wooden crates containing AK-47s and several dozen boxes of ammunition. Eleven green duffel bags sat atop the ammo boxes. Ryang ignored the rifles and ammo and went to work on the duffels.

Using the second rope, he lowered the bags down to the skiff one at a time.

The operation took just under ten minutes. Per the captain's arrangement, one of the bags didn't make the descent; it ended up tied to the end of his rappelling line, where it dangled in the breeze. While Crewman Ryang attached his ascension pulley system to the rope, the skiff pulled away from the hull, but stayed alongside the container ship, matching its speed. Ryang was a little puzzled, but shrugged it off. Perhaps the skiff remained behind to make sure he made it safely up the vertical wall of containers. He verified his ascension device was installed properly, and he began his climb up the man-made cliff. It was slow going because each pull of the ratchet system only yielded twenty-five centimeters of height.

He focused on the rope, not the foamy black water sliding by the steel hull. A fall into the water from this height would break bones.

Back atop the containers, he left his harness attached for safety and began pulling the rappelling rope up—tough work because the duffel weighed twenty kilograms. Once completed, he took a knee and rested his hands and arms. He sensed a presence and turned around.

"Captain! You startled me."

"I thought you might need help hoisting the bag, but I see you've handled it."

Ryang smiled. "Yes, sir."

The captain nodded toward the bag. "Let's have a look. Here, you'll need this to cut the plastic seal." The captain extended his knife.

To Ryang's astonishment, the knife shot past his outstretched hand and plunged into his abdomen.

Ryang's mind registered the betrayal, but it seemed like a waking dream.

He felt the blade cleave through his flesh, but it didn't hurt at first. A former member of ROK's army, Ryang was no stranger to knife fighting, but he'd never been on the wrong end of one.

Before he could react, the captain stabbed him again. Then again, and again.

Now pain invaded his mind. It started as a mild stinging sensation, but rapidly grew into a horrible burning ache. It was odd what the human mind thought of at times like this. In his limited medical knowledge, Ryang knew his stomach had just been perforated and the burning sensation was caused by gastric acid coming into contact with the surrounding organs and flesh. He also knew it was a mortal wound.

He looked down at the dark stain spreading across his clothes. Why did blood always look so black at night?

Ryang wanted to meet death on his feet, but the captain swept a leg, toppling him to the roof of the container.

It was too shadowy to see the captain's face, but he hoped it held regret. Being killed over money seemed so petty and trivial. Surely there'd been enough for both of them to share.

"My family . . ." Ryang uttered. "Please, give them . . . my share . . ."

"I think not."

He attempted to kick the captain in the groin and missed. He sensed a boot flying toward his face and felt a sickening crack as his front teeth broke free. Semiconscious from the blow, he spat out the pieces as a second man approached. Without saying a word, the man nodded to the captain and hooked himself into the line. A few seconds later, Ryang saw the newcomer disappear over the edge as he rappelled down. It suddenly dawned on Ryang why the skiff hadn't left.

The captain walked past him and looked down the wall of containers. Ryang heard the skiff's motor power up and knew the man had gotten aboard the smaller vessel.

Casually, the captain reached down and unhooked Ryang from the rope. He wanted to fight back, but his mind was shutting down.

He knew weightlessness would come next.

So this is how my life ends? Murdered over money?

The last thing Crewman Ryang thought before his body slammed into the water was, *I hope the fall breaks my neck.*

CHAPTER 7

Nathan and Holly were ready when Harv's one-minute call came. Dressed in black 5.11 Tactical, Nathan would be all but invisible in low light. Holly was a different matter. She'd packed a pair of dark slacks, but she didn't have any dark tops or coats. Improvising, she donned the leather jacket she wore for their Harley rides. He grabbed her gloves too.

He locked the house and used his cell phone to activate the security system.

"I don't think it will be an issue, but Toby might clam up when I tell him you're FBI. It should be his choice to talk to us or not."

"You can say I'm off duty."

"You're never off duty."

"I suppose not." Holly looked at him for a long moment. "Will you reconsider calling the police? Each passing minute degrades the crime scene."

"I get that, but Toby says he knows who did it."

Holly didn't respond.

"I hear Harv's car. He just turned onto our street."

With his headlights off, Harv drove past them and pulled to the curb. Nathan opened the front passenger door for Holly and climbed into the back.

"Holly, nice to see you, even under the circumstances."

"Thanks, Harvey, you too."

"Nate."

"Harv."

No one spoke for a few seconds. Nathan always believed Harv's clean-cut appearance mirrored his father's, but he'd never hold it against him. Half-Hispanic, half-white, he had light-hazel eyes and a dark complexion. Harv looked distinguished—as Holly liked to say. When he spoke, he sounded like James Earl Jones with a Spanish accent. Harv was four inches shorter and thirty pounds lighter than Nathan, but no less deadly when called upon.

Harv already had Toby's address plugged into the nav and the program estimated five minutes.

Harv must've sensed Holly's unease. "This must put you in a difficult situation."

"To put it mildly," she said. "I have to pretend like I don't know about this. Do you guys have a plan you'd like to share?"

Nathan said, "We're kinda figuring that out as we go, but after we talk to Toby, I'd like to go have a look."

"At the dead bodies? You're joking, right?"

"All I want is a look—what could it hurt?"

"You want a list?"

Holly's attitude puzzled Nathan. Before she'd moved to DC, she would've been on board without question. But whatever the reasons for her objections, Nathan wouldn't risk Toby's safety over protocol. A fellow Marine needed his help, and he'd deliver. Simple as that.

The nav took them to a residential area of linear apartments and small homes. Harv slowed when they turned onto Toby's street. Most of the front yards didn't look too bad. A few had accumulated some clutter, but it looked like most people cared about curb appeal.

Harv zoomed the nav to its maximum setting. "I think this is it, the building on the right."

Nathan leaned forward and studied the building and its landscaping as they drove past. It was either a two-story apartment or condo; he couldn't tell which. There were three stairwells along the building, one at each end and one in the middle. It looked like each stairwell served two upstairs units. Toby's apartment building looked like a million others. Rectangular and long, its design reflected cost efficiency, not aesthetics.

On a side street several blocks away, Harv took the first parking place they found. No one spoke as they climbed out and walked toward the apartment building. Toby's unit was on the second level, served from the middle stairwell. The windows on either side of his door were dark. With a hand gesture, Nathan put everyone on hold and listened for several seconds. Detecting no sound, he knocked on the door as they'd agreed.

"The curtain just moved," Harv whispered.

Toby's door flew open. "Nathan McBride!" The big man wrapped him up in a bear hug. Not too many people made Nathan look small.

"Easy, big guy."

"Hi, Harvey. Man, am I glad to see you guys."

Harv looked even smaller in Toby's grasp.

"Toby, this is Holly Simpson. She's a special agent with the FBI from DC."

Toby pulled back, looking from Holly to Nathan. "Am I in trouble?"

"Not at all," Holly said. "I'm off duty. Nathan and I are friends."

"Well, any friend of Nathan's . . ."

Holly's hand disappeared in the handshake.

Nathan noticed a woman sitting on the couch right away, even before the lights came on. Dressed in shorts and a T-shirt, she looked familiar.

When Toby closed the door and flipped on the kitchen lights, Nathan couldn't conceal his shock.

Mara.

She still had the same flawless skin. Her stunning Latina features were nothing short of cover-model material. Twice a week for two years, this woman had been an integral part of his life. Back then, she'd been a call girl. He inwardly flinched at the thought. It felt like a lifetime ago. The last time he'd seen her was the night he'd fought with Toby. Since then, the big man had turned his life around. He wasn't the same person he'd been five years ago. Apparently, neither was Mara.

Oh man, Nathan thought. *Now what?*

He tried to recover, but it was too late. An awkward moment ensued and everyone in the room felt it.

Mara stood.

"This is Mara," Toby said. "My fiancée."

Harv said, "When's the big date?"

"We've decided on December fifteenth."

When Nathan didn't move, Harv took command and stepped forward. He shook her hand. "Congratulations, Mara. That's terrific news." Harv introduced Holly and made an attempt to present Nathan as though they'd never met.

It didn't work.

Mara stepped forward and wrapped Nathan in a sensual hug, pressing her face against his chest. He slowly put his arms around her and looked at Holly.

Her expression told all.

She wouldn't say anything right now, but she'd want an explanation. This wasn't a hug between strangers, quite the contrary. How much should he reveal? Could he tell Holly the truth and not be spurned or judged? He had no reason to assume she'd reject him. In reality, his pre-Holly days were his own. If so, why did he feel so uneasy?

There was no point in pretending. "It's good to see you again, Mara. You look great."

"Thanks, you too."

Nathan was certain Mara and Toby had talked about his previous relationship with her. If not, Toby would've been curious, or even troubled by Mara's intimate embrace.

Everyone settled into the living room.

Mara kept staring at Nathan with pleading eyes. It seemed he wasn't the only one worried about being judged. Nathan offered her a friendly smile, which seemed to have a reassuring effect.

He looked at Toby. "Start at the beginning and tell us where you were and what you saw."

"It happened at the baseball and soccer fields."

"You're talking about Hickman Field?"

"Yeah, I didn't know the name of the place."

"What were you doing?"

"I was on my way to work getting gas and I saw my boss's SUV stop across the street at another gas station. It seemed funny because—"

"Toby, please slow down. You're still at BSI, right? Are you saying your *boss* is involved in a double murder?"

"He's the one who shot them!"

Nathan looked at Harv, then back to Toby. "Who's your boss?"

"Tanner Mason."

"Tanner Mason?" Harv asked. "The chief of security? That Tanner Mason?"

Nathan saw Holly visibly stiffen at hearing Mason's name.

"Yeah, a guy named Charlie Hahn was there too, and Darla Lyons."

"Who are Hahn and Lyons?" Nathan asked.

"They work for Mason. Hahn's his right-hand man. I don't know what Darla does."

"How did you see them?"

"Hahn pulled into the station across the street, but before he pulled up to the pump, he got out and sprayed the security camera with shaving cream. I thought it was weird, and he hadn't seen me yet, so I followed him when he left the gas station. And then . . ." Toby put his head in his hands for a moment, then looked up. "What am I supposed to do?"

"Just tell us what you saw after you followed them."

"They drove into the middle of the soccer fields. They had two cars. Everyone got out, and there were two guys with them and their hands were tied behind their backs. They yelled at Mason and tried to fight, but Mason punched them around. Then he shot them in the head. There wasn't any sound, but his arm shook. One of them didn't die right away."

"How far away were you?" Nathan asked.

"I don't know, maybe about fifty yards. I'm not sure."

"No sound probably means small-caliber subsonic rounds," Harv said. "Did you see any muzzle flashes?"

"No, I mean yes. I had my night-vision scope."

"Did Mason pick up the spent brass?" Harv asked.

"Yeah, he did. He also replaced the lock at the gate. I think they took pictures of the bodies before they left. I saw camera flashes."

"What kind of cell phone do you have?" Nathan hoped it was a fairly new smartphone. He was in luck—Toby's phone was identical to his own. "Now here's what I want you to do. Use your phone's video feature like a dictation device and record everything you can remember about what you saw. Mara can record you. Start at the gas station and be as detailed as you can. Remember what I told you way back when about noticing details?"

"How could I forget?"

"Well, put that to good use. No matter how small or insignificant it may seem, don't leave anything out. If you remember Hahn scratching his head at the gas station, include it in your report. If your phone doesn't have enough memory for the video, just use the dictation feature inside the notes app, but only record a sentence or two at a time."

"I can do the video thing. My phone has lots of memory. I don't keep any music in it."

"After you make the video, stay put. We're going to take a look at the crime scene and then come back."

"What if somebody saw me? I don't think anybody did, but what if they did?"

"You mean someone from BSI?"

"Anyone."

"At the risk of sounding blunt, we wouldn't be talking right now if Mason knew you'd witnessed the murders. They would've intercepted you at the soccer fields."

"What are you gonna do with my phone?"

"I'm going to video your video with my phone and then wipe your phone's memory. Have you backed it up lately?"

"No, but I need to."

Toby sounded a little better now. Giving him a concrete task had had the calming effect Nathan hoped for.

"Back up your phone before you record what you saw. After we capture your video, you can wipe your phone's memory and then use the restore feature of iTunes."

"I've done that before. But what about work? I can't stay sick forever."

"We'll figure that out later."

"What about the dead guys?"

"We'll deal with that. As far as the rest of the world goes, you never saw any of this. You know nothing about it. It never happened."

Toby looked relieved, and so did Mara. Holly didn't react, but Nathan knew she was thinking about courtroom testimony. He was too, but now wasn't the time to mention that.

"Man, this really sucks." Toby looked at Holly. "Sorry about my language, ma'am."

"It's okay," she said.

"Play it cool and you'll get through this. You obviously can't keep working at BSI, so Harv and I will give you a temp job until you find something else. Maybe we'll keep you on. It depends on how you do."

"I'm really grateful you guys are helping me. I don't know what I'd do without you. I'm still really freaked out."

"Your job now is to record what you saw. Be as detailed as you can. If you think of something later—something you forgot—add it to the end of the video. Needless to say, don't mention anything about Harv or me or about calling First Security, and don't use your cell or landline to call us back."

"I won't."

"We'll be back in less than an hour."

CHAPTER 8

Tanner Mason's office reflected a stark, no-nonsense attitude about work. An office was just that. The real work took place outside these sanitized walls.

A few of his cage-fighting trophies sat in a glass cabinet, and some certificates and other memorabilia hung on the walls, but for the most part this room was a painted drywall box with hard, angular furniture. Even though BSI's headquarters occupied one of the most beautiful areas of La Jolla, his office didn't have an ocean view. Neither did old man Beaumont's, for that matter. Thanks to the draconian bureaucrats of the California Coastal Commission, no building west of I-5 could rise higher than thirty feet. Mason's office did, however, overlook a sagebrush canyon and the freeway beyond. He supposed it was better than nothing.

Directly across the street from BSI's headquarters sat the prestigious Scripps Clinic and beyond it, Torrey Pines Golf Course and the cliffs overlooking Black's Beach. Mason wasn't much of a golfer, but he'd gone over there a few times to check out the PGA tournaments. He just couldn't afford the time it took to become a good golfer. Maybe in a different life . . .

He left his office for the break room, where he found Chip sipping coffee and being his usual subdued self. Chip rarely initiated conversation, which suited him just fine. There was nothing worse than a mindless chatterbox who never knew when to shut up. More important, though, was Chip's loyalty. There was only one person in the world Mason trusted with his life: Chip Hahn.

"So what's your gut on Darla?" Mason asked. "If you want to voice any doubts, now's the time."

Darla Lyons was the newest addition to Mason's inner circle. The old man had brought her into BSI's ranks as a favor to a friend, and he'd made it clear she wasn't an ordinary hire. A former Blackwater operative from Desert Storm, she had extensive combat experience as well as computer and countersurveillance training. Her résumé closely mirrored Mason's own, which spoke for itself. About the same height and age as Chip, she had dark eyes and cropped brunette hair. At first glance, most people might use the word "butch" to describe her appearance, but Mason didn't like labels. She was actually quite feminine and possessed a good sense of humor, which allowed her to shrug off the all-too-common macho drollness dominating the PMC world. The bottom line? He liked her.

"I don't think she'll blow the whistle with the old man, if that's what you mean."

"Me either."

"I'll say this about her: she's a team player and doesn't want to let us down."

"Yeah," Mason agreed, "that's my take too. You happy with her training so far?"

"Her long-distance shooting could use some brushing up, but her handgun skills are solid. I'd definitely go into battle with her."

Mason raised his eyebrows. "High praise."

"She'll see her first real action later this morning, but I feel good about her."

"Me too."

Mason left the break room and headed for the restroom down the hall. Since neither Chip nor he was married or had a girlfriend in the traditional sense, they were free to work any hours they wanted. Along with Darla, they'd both been doing graveyard for the last two weeks in anticipation of tonight's two-phased operation. Experience taught him it was always best to acclimatize yourself to a polar shift in time.

Eight years earlier, when he'd first met Chip at BSI's academy in New Mexico, Beaumont Specialists, Inc., had just signed a lucrative contract with the Department of Defense and Mason's job had been to train a special team of security contractors—including Chip Hahn—to spearhead BSI's entry into the theater of Operation Enduring Freedom.

During Mason's early Afghan days, old man Beaumont had made it perfectly clear he didn't want BSI's reputation smeared with sloppy soldiering. There would be no Abu Ghraib–type incidents, or heads would roll. One thing was true back then, which still applied today: you never messed with George Beaumont. Mason had respected the venerable Marine veteran from the start, but he'd also held the personal opinion that what happened in Shindand stayed in Shindand.

Back then, BSI's combat record in OEF had been nothing short of sterling. Thanks to Mason's early successes, BSI's ranks had swelled to more than fifteen hundred. About 40 percent of them had provided security escorts for foreign VIPs and Afghani officials. Another 40 percent were assigned to basic guard duty of installations and infrastructure. The remaining 20 percent were assigned to Mason's special ops units.

Those were the days, Mason thought. *Before having to deal with red tape and spineless bureaucrats here in the States.*

Four years ago, when George Beaumont had come to him and proposed setting up an academy to train undercover agents to infiltrate domestic gangs and cartels, Mason thought he'd been joking. No such endeavor had ever been attempted in the private sector. But the more Mason thought about it, the more it made sense. Private military contractors were already doing every dangerous job known to man, so why not include undercover work on their résumés? It was a perfect fit. And since PMCs weren't considered official military, their use on American soil couldn't be seen as a martial law condition. A loophole, yes, but not a strict violation of the law.

The Mexico division of the November Directive had become an overwhelming success. It couldn't be argued otherwise. Over the last twelve months, five criminal organizations along the Mexican border between California and Arizona had been penetrated. Three of them were dismantled, their leadership imprisoned, and their ranks scattered. According to conservative estimates, the flow of guns crossing into Mexico had been cut in half.

The old man had recently told him there was now a proposal on Attorney General Paul Ames's desk about using PMCs to supplement the US Border Patrol along the international fence. Public outrage over border violence had reached a peak, and Beaumont Specialists, Inc., was perfectly positioned to step up and fill the demand.

The other two divisions of the November Directive, East Asia and Venezuela, were seeing equally positive results. Mason never patted his own back, but he knew the success of the ND sat squarely on his and Chip's shoulders. From the first shovelful of dirt to the insertion of Ramiro into Alfonso Alisio's notorious Mexican narco-trafficking cartel, Mason and Hahn had overseen every aspect of the program. Neither of them had taken a vacation during the first two years. They'd lived and breathed the November Directive, and their hard work was now paying huge dividends.

The men and women who became BSI undercover agents earned their stripes. Only 3 percent of the applicants survived the extensive physical and psychological screening. For security purposes, potential candidates weren't even told what they'd be doing. Every one of them underwent training similar to what SEALs and Recons endured. The lure of $1,200 a day became a huge incentive to finish the three-month boot camp before moving onto the next stage of training, which took fourteen months to complete.

BSI's first undercover graduate, code-named Ramiro, had proven that privately trained undercover agents were not only practical, but also irreplaceable. Ramiro represented the best of the best graduates. The guy could build a toaster out of a hair dryer, shoot a six-inch group at five hundred yards, and speak with a perfect Mexico City or Tijuana dialect. He possessed extensive accounting, computer, surveillance, and countersurveillance skills. In addition to possessing survival training in every environment on the planet, Ramiro could make and disarm most types of bombs, hold his own against black belts, and make HALO jumps from thirty thousand feet. Ramiro felt equally comfortable in an exotic nightclub as he did in an auto mechanic's garage.

Put simply, Ramiro had the mind-set and skills to deal with virtually anything the world could throw at him. If he couldn't solve a problem, he'd work around it. And if he couldn't work around it, he'd make it go away. Ramiro's successful embedment into the highest levels of Alisio's cartel was a testament to all the training and preparation he'd endured.

Like Ramiro, all of BSI's undercover operatives reported directly to Mason, who in turn reported to the old man, who then reported to the various federal agencies involved. That had been a nonnegotiable term of Beaumont's contract with the feds. Since BSI's people were taking the risks, Beaumont wouldn't allow pencil pushers to make the decisions at the street level. Big decisions about policy and other national security issues remained in federal hands, but BSI's operatives couldn't be ordered to do anything without the old man's approval.

Mason washed his hands and headed for his office. He wanted to check for any email messages from his support personnel. The public had no clue how many people it took to maintain a single undercover operative. For every infiltrator, three to four additional people were needed in support roles. Seeing nothing new on his PC, he called Chip to go over their tactical needs for phase two of tonight's operation. They wanted to be stealthy, but it wouldn't hurt to have a few stun grenades and incendiary devices just in case. Like Ramiro, if they couldn't work around a problem, they'd make it go away.

Mason walked over to his window and crossed his arms. Beyond the canyon, the Five displayed its parallel rivers of red and white.

Southern California freeways never sleep . . .

The two men he and his team interrogated and killed earlier tonight had provided some key information. They'd confirmed Ramiro's report last week that something big was happening and it had a South Korean connection. Ramiro had overheard talk about the imminent arrival of ten duffel bags coming in from Seoul. With some careful snooping, Ramiro had determined the bags originated in North Korea and they were being smuggled into the United States through a South Korean crime family.

So far, Ramiro hadn't been able to determine what the duffels held, but he was fairly certain it wasn't the usual money-for-guns deal—it was much bigger.

According to Ramiro, Alisio's lieutenant in San Diego, a guy named Top Hat, was in charge of handling the cartel's gunrunning operations along the border. Top Hat personally transported the black market weapons over to El Centro, where they were warehoused until being smuggled into Mexico by a variety of methods, mostly by truck. Apparently, Top Hat had been given the reins of this new duffel-bag exchange. Mason felt confident Ramiro's intel was accurate because the men they'd killed had confirmed Top Hat's role as the point man. They hadn't given up much, because they hadn't known much, but they'd known enough to convince Mason that Top Hat held an important role in the arrival of the duffel bags.

He turned away from his window at the familiar knock.

"Come in, Chip. What's on your mind?"

"You wanted to be informed when anyone called in sick. Toby Haynes just called."

"He's one of our security guards, as I recall. Isn't he also flagged as a candidate for promotion? I remember seeing his name."

Hahn nodded.

"Has he ever called in sick before?"

"Not once. He's been reliable and prompt, but I should check it out just to be sure."

Mason tried to picture Haynes. Huge. Bald. Kinda tough looking—like a bouncer. He believed Haynes had been with BSI for almost two years, so in Mason's mathematical mind, the odds of a sick call were about one in five hundred. Still, only one sick call in over two years was a damned good track record.

"We're tight on time. Make it quick."

"I'm on it."

After Chip left his office, Mason turned back to the window.

Later tonight, they'd complete phase two, which would likely involve more killing. Mason didn't feel any remorse for slaying those two scumbags on the soccer field. Both of them had grown wealthy from gun trafficking, peddling drugs, prostitution, and worst of all, human trafficking—especially children. What kind of an animal sold children to predators? It was beyond sick. He'd been willing to offer them a more honorable death—to go out in a hand-to-hand fight—but after that jackass spit in his face, Mason's goodwill vanished. He should've known those classless punks had no honor.

The way Mason saw things, he'd just saved the taxpayers more than $4 million in "government housing" expenses, not to mention the free legal fees, free education, free dental and medical care, free sex-change operations, and whatever else those dirtbags would've milked out of the California penal system. Whatever happened to the days of chain gangs, when prisoners actually had to do hard labor? Mason called it the "pussification" of America, and with today's soft-handed, cell phone generation coming through the ranks, it was only going to get worse. All the more reason for warriors like Mason to take command and make the tough decisions.

Along the Mexican border, American citizens were being kidnapped and slaughtered on a near-daily basis. Naturally, the pencil pushers wouldn't get their hands dirty, but that was fine. Mason would do it for them.

Time hadn't diluted the rage he felt toward Alfonso Alisio. If the rumors were true, and Mason had no reason to suspect otherwise, that pudgy Mexican troll had personally tortured Special Agent Hutch to death. Hutch was hardly the first ATF or other federal agent to fall prey to narco-traffickers' sadistic brutality, but what Alisio had done to Hutch was especially monstrous. His men had chosen a streetlight two blocks from the ATF's field office in El Centro and suspended Hutch's body from a meat hook.

Mason shook his head at the memory. He'd been in El Centro at the time and seen his friend's naked form swinging in the wind. It had barely been recognizable as human. Ironically, Hutch's murder had played a key role in the genesis of the November Directive.

He'd first met the ATF agent in Afghanistan inside one of Bagram's dining facilities. Hutch and several of his fellow ATF special agents were seated at a table, and Mason asked if he could join them. Hutch hadn't hesitated in saying yes. It turned out he was an explosives and arson investigator for the ATF. Mason remembered being surprised to hear the ATF was in Afghanistan, but it made perfect sense, given all the ordnance they were finding. Hutch had been genuinely interested in BSI's role in OEF. Although they hadn't been able to talk specifics at the time, they'd both realized they should be working together. Two weeks later, the brass approved Hutch's attachment to Mason's unit. A friendship for life was forged that day, one that survived twenty-two missions.

Tonight's operation, however, would be quite unlike Mason's work in Afghanistan, for he and Hahn planned to profit personally from doing his country's dirty work. Mason supposed the general idea had percolated in his subconscious for years. But it had coalesced into an actual plan when Ramiro passed on the duffel-bag intel. Instinctively, Mason had withheld that information from the old man. And now, tonight, the opportunity was at hand for him and Hahn to reap their reward. And why not? Why shouldn't they enjoy a windfall? Five years ago, he'd played by the rules and finished last. He'd taken one for the team, leaving Afghanistan in disgrace, and for what? A $100K salary? Peanuts. The old man made millions every month.

The box of cash he'd discovered in Mullah Sanjari's compound had opened his eyes to a different future. He didn't have to be a drone for the rest of his life. He and Hahn had dripped blood on Afghan soil and never received Purple Hearts, valor medals, or theater ribbons. The "real" military got all the recognition and accolades—and the benefits to boot. Mason hadn't come home to veterans' benefits, access to the VA, or a college fund. Federal disability or life insurance? Forget about it. A big goose egg. No insurance carrier would touch him, and for good cause. PMCs died with frightening regularity, even post-combat duty. Contractors like Mason and Hahn were five hundred times more likely to commit suicide than the rest of the public, and he almost had.

Okay, his paychecks had been bigger than those of his coalition counterparts. But why shouldn't they have been? After all, he and his men took on the assignments the coalition forces couldn't, or wouldn't, do. All told, Mason's platoon had been the target of seventeen IED and grenade attacks and more than two dozen sniper potshots. That didn't count the two deaths he'd taken eliminating the Taliban mortar teams after raiding the Sanjari compound. His own wound had been far more serious than he'd first thought. Had he not reached Bagram in a timely manner, he would've bled out. Only vascular surgery had saved his life.

Very few people knew of the dangers facing private military contractors until March of 2004 when four Blackwater PMCs were ambushed and murdered. Their mutilated bodies were set on fire and dragged down the streets of Fallujah in a grisly parade of savagery. *That could've been me and Chip.*

Now he was fighting a different kind of war. A war in which criminal cartels were equally as ruthless, just not as visible. In Mason's mind, the only difference was the language they spoke. Terrorist assholes were assholes, in any part of the world.

He took a deep breath and forced himself to focus on the present.

Laptop in hand, Chip reentered his office, but his friend's face didn't display its usual emotionless pallor.

"What?" Mason asked.

"We've got big trouble."

"Show me."

Chip opened his laptop and set it on Mason's desk. "The red line represents Toby Haynes's movements over the past hour. Look at the time stamps where his vehicle was stationary."

Mason's body tensed and his face hardened. *That dumbass.* "Change in plans. Grab our tactical bags and call Darla. We're moving out in thirty seconds."

CHAPTER 9

On the way to Hickman Field, Harv broke the silence. "We're flirting with big trouble here, Nate. You know that, right?"

"Amen," Holly added.

"Toby asked for our help. He's afraid for his life, and Mara's. Turning our backs on them won't sit right with me."

"I'm not saying we shouldn't help," said Holly.

Nathan felt a twinge of irritation. "Then what *are* you saying?"

She didn't respond.

"Look, I'm not planning to wage a war against Mason and his legion of mercenaries . . . excuse me, *private military contractors.* We're looking for a way to put the guy behind bars—ideally without Toby's testimony."

"I have a feeling that's not going to be easy," said Holly.

"Doing the right thing is rarely the easy thing."

"I haven't heard you say that in a long time," Harv said. "I'd forgotten how good it sounds."

He started to respond, but Harv interrupted.

"In fairness to Holly, she's got a point. Maybe we should let the police handle this."

"Thank you, Harvey," she said.

"And we will," Nathan said. "I just want a look first."

"I'm not worried about taking a look," Harv said. "What I'm saying is, we shouldn't underestimate BSI. They aren't just a bunch of yahoos with guns. They're highly skilled and many of them are OEF combat vets who have recon-level training. A company like BSI has a huge budget for ammo, mock-up exercises, survival training, you name it."

Nathan glanced at his friend. "Yeah, I know. I loaned Toby the money he needed to attend the academy."

"Did you know the founder's from New Mexico too?"

"No." Nathan paused. "Then I guess it's likely he knows my father."

"That'd be George Beaumont, and yeah, I'm pretty sure he does. I think they were in the Korean War together."

Nathan wanted to ask how Harv knew that, but it didn't matter right now. He pulled out his smartphone, called up the BSI company web page, and quickly navigated to George Beaumont's bio. "You're right, they were, and in the same unit. Beaumont's a retired major." Next, he skimmed the company-news page. "It says here that late last year, Beaumont signed a lucrative contract with the federal government. Private security for high-risk facilities."

"Makes sense," said Harv. "In many cases, it's actually cheaper for the government to subcontract security work. Does it say what kind of facilities?"

"Oh, nothing too important," Nathan said. "Just all the ATC towers at airports, a couple dozen nuclear power plants, and various federal buildings. What do you think a contract like that's worth?"

"With the way the DOD throws money around and the lack of adequate oversight, it wouldn't be unreasonable to think it could reach nine zeroes."

Nathan rubbed his forehead. "I suppose that could've been us."

"How so?" Holly asked.

"During the First Gulf War, Harv and I considered going that route, like BSI. I guess we're still contractors for security, but only with civilian companies."

"That's true, but some of our clients make toys for the military. It's a little nebulous, but we're not directly supplying personnel to the feds."

"Let's keep it that way. Holly, when Toby mentioned Tanner Mason, you acted like you'd heard of him."

"I'm familiar with BSI. It's become a huge company with several international satellite offices. Actually, the Bureau's considering using BSI to protect our DC headquarters and some of our larger field offices."

Nathan took another look at his smartphone. "I don't see anything about that here. Has the contract been finalized?"

"No, and it's confidential at this point."

"Do you know anything about Tanner Mason?"

"I'm more interested in talking about Mara."

That's twice she'd deflected a question. "What about her?"

"It's pretty clear you two . . . know each other."

"We dated for a while. Before I met you."

"So you *do* have a history?"

"Well, I wasn't exactly . . . celibate. But I wouldn't call it a 'history,' necessarily."

"Don't you think it's interesting that a woman you used to date just happens to be in Toby's apartment? What are the odds of that?"

"I'm . . . not sure what to say."

"You've got good taste. She's incredibly beautiful."

"So what was she doing with me, right?"

Holly looked back over the seat at him. "Relax, Marine, I'm just being a jealous girlfriend."

"No need for that. Seriously. She's ancient history. *Ancient.*" Nathan smiled and raised his eyebrows. "We good?"

Holly nodded. "We're good."

"So," he said, addressing both Holly and Harv, "for the last time, does anyone know anything about this Tanner Mason guy?"

Harv answered first. "Not a whole lot. I've seen him a couple times at conventions. He's kinda hard to miss. Long blond hair, athletic. He had a short career as an MMA fighter, so he carries a bit of celebrity with him. Last year he was at BSI's booth at Shot Show. I actually saw him sign some autographs, but I didn't talk to him."

"What's your take on the guy?"

"He has a condescending demeanor. The few times I've been around him, I got the distinct impression he thought of himself as a superior life-form."

"He sounds like an asshole."

Harv gave a noncommittal shrug. "If he shot two handcuffed men tonight, then I guess that speaks for itself."

Nathan turned to Holly again. "And you? Anything at all about Mason?"

"All I can say is he's on the FBI's radar screen."

"All you can say? Was that before or after tonight?"

"Both, it would seem," she said. "I can tell you that the Bureau's done plenty of due diligence on BSI, including Mason. But if Toby's right and he's responsible for a double murder, then that BSI contract with us is probably toast."

"Right," Harv agreed, "and that's to say nothing of the bigger contract already in place with the government. It sounds like there's tons of money at stake. Toby's concern for his life definitely has merit, but let's avoid being the next casualties in whatever Mason's doing." Harv slowed the car. "We're almost there. What's the plan?"

"The first thing," Nathan said, "is to be sure no one but the victims are out there."

"I concur," said Harv. "We should conduct a thermal scan of the entire area before we go in. The rain and patchy fog will help us get in and out undetected."

Nathan nodded. "Hickman Field seems like an odd choice, doesn't it? There's got to be a reason Mason picked that location."

"Right," said Harv. "If he didn't want anyone to know about the murders, he would've killed them privately and disposed of the bodies."

"So why didn't he?" Holly asked. "If Mason wanted to make a public statement, there are much better places to leave the bodies."

"Maybe it's a territory thing," Nathan said. "As far as I know, Kearny Mesa doesn't have a serious crime problem, so a couple of bodies are bound to stick out in a big way."

"I think what we're saying," Holly said, "is this wasn't a spontaneous act by Mason. And based on them replacing the cut padlock alone, we can conclude premeditation all the way. No one carries a spare padlock around."

Harv made the turn onto the road fronting Hickman Field. "This is it, on the right."

As they passed the main entrance gate, a general lack of activity made it obvious no one had reported the murders. If anyone had, the place would've been swarming with police.

Nathan took a look with the thermal imager. "I'm not seeing any warm signatures out there. Keep going, Harv." Nathan consulted his phone again. "Looking at some satellite photos, I think I know the best place to park and approach the fields. There's an industrial area bordering the north side of the complex. Let's be on the lookout for surveillance cameras. There are bound to be a few around."

As Nathan suspected, most of the low-rise buildings had cameras mounted on their parapets and all of the parking lots between the buildings were brightly lit.

"Keep going, I see a good spot," said Nathan. "Just a little farther."

They approached a smaller industrial building that looked unoccupied. Its doors and windows were covered with painted plywood.

Nathan studied the surrounding area for any movement and detected none. "What do you think about parking in here? The only downside would be a security patrol noticing a newly parked vehicle and recording the license plate. But this place looks inactive."

"I'd say it's low risk," Harv said. "We'll be in and out in fifteen minutes."

They stayed close to the building and walked toward the wrought iron fence surrounding Hickman Field. Nathan brought his night-vision up and scanned the soccer fields again, just to be sure. All clear.

"Ready?"

"And if they aren't dead?" Harv asked.

"We call it in," Holly said.

"I'm already on it." Nathan patted his carry bag. "I'll use the voice-morphing program on my laptop. I can completely change my voice, even into a woman's."

Holly shook her head—in amazement or dismay, it was hard to tell which.

Harv winked at Holly. "He *did* consider working on Broadway."

"Easy, now," said Nathan. "Don't make me hurt you."

"Can we be serious about this?" said Holly.

"Here's the plan. If by some chance one of them is still alive, we'll call 911 and request a bus. I'll use my laptop to create the morphed voice, then we'll play it back into a pay phone, assuming we can find one."

"I guess that'll work," Harv said, "but use the word *ambulance*, not *bus*."

Holly crossed her arms and made an involuntary shiver.

"We'll make this quick. Here, I'll give you a boost."

A few seconds later, they were over the fence, walking toward the site of a double murder.

CHAPTER 10

Philippine Sea—fifteen days earlier

From an aft deck outside the bridge, the captain of *Yoonsuh*, a seventy-meter South Korean–registered luxury yacht with a draft of nearly 1,700 tons, watched the skiff approach the stern of his boat. In the distance, he saw the faint lights of the *Namkung Khang* as it continued its journey south to Palau. His radar indicated there were no other contacts within range. A low-pressure front was moving in from the north, but they'd easily outrun it. Everything looked good.

The skiff's operator maneuvered the small craft up to *Yoonsuh*'s stern diving deck, and a crew member secured its lines.

A state-of-the-art vessel in every respect, *Yoonsuh* had been retrofitted with supplemental diesel tanks, extending its range to forty-five hundred nautical miles at cruising speed. All told, the yacht carried more than forty thousand gallons of fuel.

As he always did, the captain made sure the skiff's special passenger received first-class accommodations. His stateroom suite had a home theater with access to more than two thousand movies and TV series. In addition, there were four women aboard who were highly skilled *masseuses.* And the food? World-class. The two-week journey to the California coast would be lived in extravagance.

The duffel bags were transferred into the closest of six bedroom suites, where they were stacked against the bulkhead. A little later, they'd be moved into a secret double-hull compartment used for smuggling. The modification to the yacht had cost over $1.2 million, but it was a small price to pay in the event *Yoonsuh* were ever boarded. No one but the crew knew the steel deck above the keel had been elevated by two feet, creating a sizable smuggling compartment. The only way to access it involved removing the desalination system, a painstaking operation that required a hydraulic jack to hoist the ship's boiler. His crew practiced removing and replacing the boiler on a regular basis and had the procedure down to a science.

Everyone aboard held proper ID and passports, even the new passenger. The few times *Yoonsuh* had been boarded in US waters, the Coast Guard never found anything out of order and the ship was allowed to continue on its voyages.

The skiff's usefulness expired, its inflatable pontoons were punctured and it was summarily sunk, outboard motor and all. Its plunge to the seabed would be a long one—several miles.

Back inside the bridge, the captain entered a course of 76.65 degrees into the nav computer and dialed their speed to sixteen knots. Their first destination was the Hawaiian Islands for a refueling stop. The voyage would take 237 hours, just under ten days. Until then, they'd just have to endure one of the most prestigious luxury yachts afloat.

CHAPTER 11

Every two minutes, Toby stopped pacing and peered through the curtains. McBride and Fontana couldn't get back here fast enough. Mara had repeatedly asked him to relax, but after what he'd seen, he wouldn't be relaxing anytime soon. For the twentieth time, he wished he'd never followed Hahn.

Despite the circumstances, it felt good to see McBride. They'd kept in touch, even after he'd paid off his academy debt. Toby couldn't consider McBride a close friend, but they shared the brotherhood of the Marines, and that was enough. He wished the auto accident hadn't ended his career as an MP—he'd really liked being a military cop. Looking back on his life, he'd have done a lot of things differently, like taking better care of his finances. When you spend more than you make, the outcome is never good.

At least the video he'd made for McBride was complete. He'd been surprised at the amount of detail he'd remembered.

Mara's reaction at seeing McBride hadn't surprised him. She'd told him they'd seen each other frequently when she'd worked for Karen. Toby had many faults, but hanging onto baggage from the past wasn't one of them. They loved each other and were getting married in a few months. Since Mara had been open and honest about her past, he'd never hold it against her.

He'd finally stopped pacing and settled his nerves when a car alarm went off, and it sounded like his Sentra's. He rushed over to the window and cracked the curtains.

"What's going on?" Mara asked.

"Some dickhead's breaking into my car!"

***

"The curtains just moved," Chip whispered. "He's at the window."

Mason reared back and kicked Haynes's door. It flew open with a loud bang.

Inside, he pivoted toward the window and caught Haynes by surprise.

Movement on his left caught his eye.

A woman stood in the living room, her hand covering her mouth.

Bad move, Mason thought. *You should've screamed.*

Chip was on her before she could remove her hand.

Dressed in a T-shirt and shorts, Haynes reacted quickly. He lowered his head and charged toward Chip.

Mason stepped aside and swung his suppressed handgun. The blow caught the big man squarely on the side of his head. As if short-circuited, Haynes's legs quit working. Mason knelt close and belted him a second time, not as hard. He didn't want Haynes unconscious, only dazed.

He spotted the car keys on the kitchen counter and ended the obnoxious shrieking. The ploy had served its purpose, moving Toby to the window overlooking the street.

Mason propped a chair against the front door to keep it closed.

"Darla, status?"

Her voice came through his ear speaker. *"A few people looked out their windows, but no one's coming out."*

"Keep eyes on the stairwell. We're secure in here."

His radio clicked.

Chip had the woman on the ground, his hand firmly across her mouth. She wasn't struggling, but that could change. Mason stepped forward, took a knee, and pressed his pistol's suppressor against her forehead.

Her eyes widened.

"If you scream, you'll never finish it. Now, my associate here is going to remove his hand. Give me a nod of understanding."

When she didn't respond, Chip maintained his hold.

"Hablas inglés?"

A nod.

"Do you know who I am?"

She shook her head.

Mason squinted and pressed the suppressor against her head hard enough to force it back.

"One more time. Do you know who I am?" Chip removed his hand so she could answer.

"Yes."

"And . . . ?"

"You're from BSI."

"Did Mr. Haynes tell you what he saw tonight?"

Her eyes reflected indecision.

"The truth, please."

She nodded.

"We know Mr. Haynes didn't call the police; we've been monitoring our scanner. Did you or Mr. Haynes tell anyone else?"

"No."

This woman's lack of hesitation with her answer had Mason believing her. In Afghanistan, he'd conducted many interrogations and he usually knew when people were lying. "You're wearing a ring; are you and Mr. Haynes married?"

"Engaged."

"My associate here is going to escort you into the other room to secure your hands and feet and apply a gag. We aren't planning to hurt you; all we want is information. If you don't remain calm, your alternative is unconsciousness. I trust that won't be necessary?"

She shook her head.

After Chip escorted her out of the room, he heard the telltale sound of disposable handcuffs being applied. They sounded like oversized zip ties, and basically were.

Chip reentered the living room. "She's pretty freaked, but I don't think she'll make trouble."

Hahn helped him hoist Haynes into a dining room chair. The big man groaned but offered no resistance.

After they secured his ankles and wrists, Mason said, "Wake his ass up."

Chip activated a smelling salt pack and wafted it under Haynes's nose. The ammonium carbonate did its job, making Haynes stir and shake his head. With anger on his face, he jerked his weight against the binds. Mason was no stranger to this sort of thing and recognized defiance—not a good sign.

"I don't see any reason to waste time," Mason began, "so let's get right to it. We know you saw what happened at Hickman Field. Your fiancée already told us."

Haynes looked around the room.

"And we know you didn't call the police."

"Where's Mara?"

"In the bedroom."

Haynes began a violent struggle against the plastic cuffs. "If you assholes hurt her, I'll—"

"Let me guess," Mason interrupted. "You'll kill us."

Haynes didn't say anything, which Mason thought was appropriate. Any response would sound lame, and the man probably knew it.

"Chip, please fetch the young lady, so Mr. Haynes can see she's unharmed."

A few seconds later, Chip returned with the woman in tow. Her bound ankles forced her to shuffle her feet. A cloth gag occupied her mouth, probably a T-shirt, and her hands were secured behind her back.

"Are you okay?" Toby asked. "Did they hurt you?"

With her eyes full of tears, she shook her head.

Mason motioned with his head, and Chip escorted the woman back to the bedroom.

"It's okay, Mara," Toby called after her. "Everything's gonna be okay."

"That's true for now, Mr. Haynes, but things could change. Chip doesn't have a girlfriend."

"Please don't do that—"

"The truth then. Who else knows about tonight?"

Haynes licked his lips. "No one. I swear."

Mason went into the kitchen and grabbed a plastic garbage bag from under the counter.

In a quick move, he pulled it over the top of Haynes's head and tightened it at the neck. Haynes sucked in a breath, but all he got was plastic. A concave dimple formed at his mouth as he tried to breathe. In a quick move, Mason grabbed Haynes's right hand and cranked his index finger ninety degrees in the wrong direction.

The dimple changed to a protrusion.

A muffled scream followed, but the bag made it more of a mewling sound.

Mason pulled the plastic free.

His eyes watering and his skin red, Haynes sucked in a labored breath.

"It's a horrible feeling . . . being denied air like that. It produces a certain kind of panic that bores into the core of who we are. The fear of suffocation is rooted deep within us."

"Deeply," Toby gasped.

Mason hid his irritation at Toby's correction. Remaining unemotional was key to a proper interrogation. "Since you're so smart, you'll appreciate this irony: the reason we had a tracking bug in your car is because we identified you as a potential candidate for promotion. Funny, huh?"

Still breathing heavily, Toby looked around again.

"Focus on me, Mr. Haynes. Don't think about anything else right now. Now, let's start over. Did you tell anyone about what you saw at the soccer fields?"

Haynes squinted and remained defiant. "I already told you no!"

Mason slapped the side of his head where he'd pistol-whipped him.

"Fuck you," Toby said. "You just broke my fucking finger for nothing!"

"Not so fast, tough guy. I've still got nineteen more fingers to work with."

Toby squinted in thought.

"That's right, I'm including your fiancée in the count."

"Please don't hurt her."

"That's entirely up to you, Mr. Haynes. Now, I'm going to ask you again, did you tell anyone about tonight?"

"No!"

"Where are your cell phones? I'm assuming your fiancée also has one. We didn't see them anywhere."

Haynes said nothing

"You lost both of them."

Again, no response.

Mason brought the plastic bag up.

"Wait! They're hidden."

"And you did that because?"

"I made a video of what I saw."

"A video."

Haynes frowned and closed his eyes for a few seconds.

"I know your finger's throbbing. Stop and think. What video are you talking about?"

"I used the video app on my phone."

"You used it like a dictation device?"

He nodded.

"Why did you do that?"

"I was afraid if you killed me, there wouldn't be any evidence."

"Where are your phones?"

"In the back of the silverware drawer."

He pressed the transmit button. "Darla, status?"

"All quiet, no change."

Mason clicked his radio, strode into the kitchen, and began opening drawers. It didn't take long to find the devices. He assumed the phone with the Hello Kitty cover belonged to the woman—at least he hoped so. The home button on Haynes's phone produced a passcode screen. Irritated, he tried the Hello Kitty phone and saw it wasn't locked with a passcode.

He selected the text message icon and frowned.

"Chip," he called. "Get the woman back in here." He let Haynes see the text message on Mara's phone. "Did you know about this?"

"No! I swear."

"What's your phone's passcode?" Mason asked.

"What about Mara?"

"You're in no position to dictate terms, Mr. Haynes. But I'll give you my word we'll definitely hurt her if you *don't* give me your passcode."

"T-H-X-one-one-three-eight. Uppercase letters."

"Clever. I'm a George Lucas fan myself." Mason tapped the passcode and opened the photos app. He saw the triangle indicating a video and tapped the clip. Haynes's face appeared, looking rather stressed. "How long is the recording?"

"A few minutes. I'm not sure."

"Did you send this to anyone?"

"No."

Mason opened the email and text apps; they didn't show a recent message being sent. Haynes also hadn't made any recent calls. It was possible Haynes had already erased the logs, but Mason had to be sure either way.

"Where's your computer?"

"It's in the spare bedroom. I backed up my phone before I made the recording."

"Why did you do that?"

"In case I decided to wipe its memory."

"And you'd do that because?"

"I didn't call the police—doesn't that mean anything?"

"We'll explore that later. Does your computer have a log-in screen?"

"It's the same code as my phone."

"Sit tight, Mr. Haynes."

***

Nathan now understood why Mason had chosen this particular spot. Despite being in the middle of a huge city, the location was ideal. There weren't any light standards for night play. When the sun went down, this place went to sleep.

So far, they'd avoided walking on any nongrass surfaces that would leave footprints. Once this place became a crime scene, the investigators were going to scour the entire area. As long as they stayed on the thicker areas of grass, they should be okay.

Every twenty seconds or so, Harv scanned for heat signatures. A dead body continued to radiate for a while, but the cold conditions would accelerate the cooling. Still, given the time elapsed, the thermal imager should reveal any objects, human or otherwise, with a warmer signature than the background.

Based on Toby's description, Nathan believed the dead men would be in or near the center of the complex. He angled to the left slightly, believing that would take them in the right direction.

Straight ahead, a line of trees emerged from the mist. As they got closer, they found a gravel access road.

"We need to watch our footprints," Nathan said. "The police will take notice of our missing cleat patterns, and my size thirteen isn't especially common."

"Ya think?" said Holly.

"We'll cross the road up ahead to our right. I see an area where there's more gravel." Nathan noticed the road wasn't just a road: it doubled as a parking aisle and it was at least fifty feet across, probably closer to sixty.

Harv stopped short. "There's no way we'll get across this without leaving some prints. You go first and I'll walk inside your tracks. Holly can follow inside of mine. Can you see well enough to do that?"

"Barely," she said.

"We'll come back across in the same spot. Look for a landmark."

"We'll use that big tree at two o'clock as our anchor point. Walk straight toward it."

Nathan avoided puddles and soft mud, stepping on areas that were mostly gravel. On the opposite side, they paused at the trunk of the tree.

Harv used the thermal imager again. "I've got something. Two signatures at eleven o'clock, maybe fifty yards out. Neither looks bright enough to be alive."

Nathan checked the entire area with his NV and saw the prone forms. "Let's double-time it out there."

They ran at a good clip and slowed as they approached the two motionless forms. It looked as if Toby had seen things pretty accurately. Their hands bound behind their backs with nylon rope, two dead men lay on their sides. The gunshot wounds to the backs of their heads couldn't be missed: both of them were bald. The rest of their exposed skin was covered with expensive tats. Oddly, each man had a 1,000-peso bill tacked to his forehead with a pushpin.

"Check it out," Nathan said. He handed the scope to Harv.

"Weird. It looks like some kind of signature killing."

Harv passed the device to Holly.

"I've seen this before . . ." she said slowly.

"I'll turn on the IR illuminator." Nathan knew the naked eye couldn't see the infrared light. "We'll maintain our perimeter while you check these guys out."

"Toby didn't mention the money pinned to their foreheads," she said.

"He probably couldn't see it," Harv added. "They aren't breathing, but I'm gonna check for a pulse anyway." Harv removed a glove and took a knee. He looked up at Nathan and shook his head. The other man was also dead. Harv put his glove back on and scrubbed the area of their necks he'd just touched to eradicate any possible prints.

"Check for IDs," Nathan said.

"Be careful you don't move the bodies," added Holly.

Harv removed their wallets and used the flashlight app on his phone to illuminate the IDs. "One of them's from Mexico City; the other's from Seoul."

Holly suggested Harv take pictures of the IDs.

Harv nodded. "The mist should mask the flashes. I'll take a couple of overall shots and get some shots of those bills tacked to their foreheads. Their tats as well."

"I'm sure I've seen this before," Holly said.

"The money thing?" Nathan asked.

"Yes. I think it was a few years ago—some kind of ATF operation."

Nathan looked at Holly. "I don't think we should call this in tonight. It's better to let the bodies get discovered in the morning. I know it's important for the police to begin a murder investigation as soon as possible, but we already know who did this."

Holly asked, "Are you thinking Toby's sick call might create a possible link?"

"It's a long shot, but the timing's what worries me. Toby doesn't go to work on the same night his boss commits a double murder. Look, if you insist we call this in, we'll do it. No questions asked."

She didn't answer right away. Nathan knew she was considering all the consequences.

"Since we have an eyewitness to the crime, I'll agree to delay reporting this under protest, but I was never here. I never saw this."

Nathan turned off the IR illuminator. "Let's get back over to Toby's and figure out our next move."

***

Back at Harv's car, Nathan felt strangely deflated. Even if those two dead men were mixed up in a criminal organization, they might've had very different futures ahead of them. Now they'd never have the chance. Nathan had seen his share of death over the years, but it never got any easier.

He again opened the front passenger door for Holly, then climbed into the back.

"Let's find a drive-through and grab some coffee and breakfast sandwiches. We don't know how long we'll be tied up with Toby tonight."

Harv said, "I know a place. It's not far out of our way."

"That okay with you, Holly?"

"Yes."

"Maybe we should start some kind of surveillance on Mason."

"That won't be easy," said Harv. "He's BSI's chief of security, and he's just committed a capital crime. He'll be wary of tails and surveillance, the works. Don't you think?"

"How about his second-in-command? Hahn?"

Harv shrugged. "Same problem, I'd say. Maybe between the three of us we could manage it."

"Holly can't help us with that; she needs to be back in DC tomorrow. It would be useful to get some personal information on Mason, Hahn, and Lyons, though."

"I'll see what we have on them," Holly said.

"If this blows up, that could put you in a difficult spot," Nathan said.

"Define 'blows up.' Never mind. It's better if I don't ask."

"Well," Nathan said, "that brings up the big question: What's our endgame here?"

"Mason and his people need to be held accountable for murdering those men."

"And there are two ways to do it. Through the legal system or . . . privately."

"Nathan, for obvious reasons, I can't sanction any *private* activity."

"Nor should you. I'm only speculating, but I don't like the idea of Toby and Mara living the rest of their lives worrying about Mason coming after them."

"Before you speculate any further," Harv said, "there may be a way to take Mason down within legal boundaries."

"Short of Toby's eyewitness testimony, how would we do that?"

"A confession," Harv said flatly.

Nathan knew what Harv had in mind. "Let's keep that option in reserve for now."

"There's something else we have to think about," Holly said.

"What's that?" Nathan liked how she'd said *we*.

"If Toby ends up testifying in court, he'll need a reason for why he didn't report it right away."

Nathan said, "He could truthfully claim he feared for his life. BSI is not only his employer, it's a powerful company with thousands of employees, and some of them are probably gung ho types who will resent being ratted out. If Toby reports this, he'd be seen as a turncoat, especially by Mason and his inner circle. There's no doubt in my mind if Toby goes to the police, his life will be in danger. Can we all agree on that?"

Harv nodded. "Mason just killed two men execution style, so, yeah, Toby's at risk."

"Holly?"

"Those men were kidnapped before they were murdered. The Lindbergh Law might give us jurisdiction. Either way, the US marshals can keep Toby and Mara safe."

"For how long?"

"As long as it takes," she said.

"We don't have to decide this now. Let's see what Toby has to say first."

They made the fast-food stop as brief as possible, electing to eat in the car. The coffee wasn't strong enough, but it was better than nothing. Nathan glanced at his watch. A little over thirty minutes had passed since leaving Toby's apartment.

"We haven't dealt with the bigger picture here," Harv said. "The people this might affect. George Beaumont is friends with your father, and we certainly don't want to bankrupt Beaumont's company and put thousands of people in the unemployment line."

"More than that," Nathan said, "we don't want to end up in BSI's crosshairs."

Holly asked, "Don't you mean Mason's?"

"I'm not sure what I mean at this point."

"Doesn't this boil down to one simple variable?" she asked.

"What's that?"

"Is George Beaumont complicit? Think about it: if he doesn't know about this, telling him shouldn't pose a risk to us."

"And conversely," Harv added, "if he *is* involved, all of us will be at risk, including you, Holly. There's no telling how far Beaumont will go to cover this up in order to save his company."

"I guess a lot depends on how well your father knows him," she said.

"You mean: Will my dad know if he's lying?"

Holly nodded.

"That's a big if. What's our best-case scenario here? Beaumont doesn't know about this and chooses to deal with Mason privately, leaving the police out."

"I didn't hear that," Holly said.

"Without knowing Beaumont's relationship with Mason," said Harv, "we can't predict what either of them will do."

"Holly, we need to investigate the front end of the crime and find out how those two men ended up on Mason's hit list, or at a minimum, if they have an association with him or BSI."

"You'll need access to the NCIC and other law enforcement databases for that."

Nathan and Harv didn't say anything.

"I'll see what I can do."

"Don't jeopardize your job," Nathan said.

"I'll be okay, but you know, you could just ask your dad for help. He has direct lines of communication to every law enforcement agency in the country—at home and abroad, and he's friends with Attorney General Paul Ames."

"I'll need to make an appointment with my father."

"Come on, Nathan, that's not fair," she said. "Your dad's always been available to you. Twenty-four-seven. If you dialed his cell right now, he'd take your call. I thought you'd patched things up."

Nathan found Holly's defense of his father surprising and was tempted to ask about it, but now wasn't the time. "We had a falling out recently. It's . . . difficult asking him for help. Besides, he's super busy."

"Not too busy for his only son."

Harv asked, "If you tell your father, will he feel obligated to tell Beaumont?"

"I'd certainly ask him not to."

"Would he agree?" Harv asked.

"Probably, but not indefinitely."

Harv didn't sound convinced. "We'll need more than a 'probably.' If your father tells Beaumont about Tanner Mason's little party tonight, then Beaumont'll want to know where your father got the information."

"Which might, and probably will, create a connection to us."

"Not necessarily," Holly said. "Stone's chairman of the Committee on Domestic Terrorism. He could have gotten that kind of info from any number of sources."

"That's true, but so far, the crime's unreported. My father would have to wait until the bodies are discovered before talking to Beaumont. And even so, Beaumont would want to know why Stone is contacting him about an obscure double murder in San Diego. On the surface, it doesn't look like something that warrants the attention of CDT. Since the victims are from Mexico and South Korea, ICE will get involved. Maybe the CIA too, but it still doesn't rise to the level of my father's domestic terrorism committee."

The car fell silent.

"Again, we don't have to decide anything right now," Nathan said. "Let's get back to Toby's and figure out our next move from there. If Toby decides to go to the police, we need to assure him he'll be protected."

"I can definitely arrange that," Holly said.

In the quiet that followed, the clocklike drone of the windshield wipers helped Nathan gather his thoughts. Thinking about his dad had made him edgy. Something else bothered Nathan . . . something about the dead bodies that looked out of place—aside from the pinned money and their citizenships. He tried to bring the thought forward, but it wouldn't come. Shifting gears, he considered Holly's comment. Maybe she was right. Maybe he should call his father. He just hoped doing so wouldn't paint fluorescent targets on all their backs.

Harv turned off the nav when he pulled onto Toby's street. "Do you guys want me to drop you off? It's raining pretty hard now."

"We're okay," Nathan said. "Maybe we'll find the same parking place; it's not that far. Slow down, Harv. Call me paranoid, but I'm gonna take a quick look with the NV."

"You got it."

Everything looked the same. If anyone was out for a stroll in the rain, Nathan couldn't see them. Just before Nathan took the NV scope away from his eye, he saw movement.

"Harv, somebody just ducked out of sight at the top of the stairs."

CHAPTER 12

"Keep going," Nathan told Harv. "Don't slow down."

"Was it Toby?" Holly asked.

"No, it was a woman dressed in dark tactical."

"Are you sure?" Harv asked.

"Positive."

Holly said, "Toby said a woman named Darla Lyons was with Mason and Hahn tonight. What are the odds that a woman dressed in tactical clothing would be hiding at the top of the stairwell leading to Toby's apartment right now?"

"Millions to one," Nathan said. "Which means Mason and Hahn are probably inside."

"Not a nice thought," Harv said.

Nathan tried to sound calm, but he spoke too quickly. "We need to get up there right away."

Harv turned on the same cross street where he had before.

"We're about to get really deep, Nate."

"Tell me about it."

"Toby and Mara know we're coming back, so they could be holding out as best they can. We need a plan. We can't just barge up there with guns blazing."

"I've got an idea. Remember that stunt our old friend pulled on you at the Bahia Hotel?"

"How could I forget? It cost me six months of physical therapy."

"We're going to do the same thing. Once I reach the base of the stairs, all I'll need is a few seconds of distraction. With a little luck, I'll be able to take Lyons down before she's aware I'm there."

"'With a little luck' being the operative words," Holly said.

"I'm open to other suggestions," Nathan said.

"Why not just shoot her?" Holly said flatly.

Nathan didn't respond; he knew she was frustrated at the situation.

"Rules of engagement?" Harv asked.

"Deadly force if needed to save any of our lives, including Toby's and Mara's. Once I've neutralized Lyons, we'll burst into Toby's apartment and catch everyone off guard. We've done this many times."

"Neutralized?" Holly asked.

Harv said, "If we have to shoot our way in there, I won't lose any sleep killing cold-blooded murderers who'd get the needle anyway."

"You guys don't have vests on."

"I doubt they'll be wearing body armor either, but I hear you, Holly. Engaging three military contractors in a gunfight in the middle of a residential neighborhood isn't our first choice. We're not looking for a fight. Our ball ammo will penetrate the walls of these wood-framed buildings."

"I really think we should just call 911."

"Too slow. We'd have to find a pay phone. Unless you want to use your cell."

She didn't say anything.

"Mason's up there torturing them."

"You don't know that," she said. "Toby could be part of some elaborate scheme."

"You saw the way he acted when he saw us. Did you think that was BS?"

Again, she didn't say anything.

"Look, if we call 911, this might turn into a hostage situation, or worse. Mason might kill the first cops to arrive on scene. We've got an opportunity to end this."

"You mean kill them."

"No, that's not what I mean. If we get an opportunity to take them alive, we'll do it."

"That puts us at considerably more risk," Harv said.

"He'll treat this situation like Afghanistan," Holly said under her breath.

"What did you just say about Afghanistan?" he asked.

She didn't respond.

"Holly, if you know something. Let's have it."

"Mason served as a PMC in Afghanistan."

"What? How do you know that?"

"It's in his file. I've seen it."

Harv stopped the car and pivoted toward Holly. No words were needed.

Nathan also waited.

"All I can tell you is that he took on the most dangerous assignments imaginable, jobs our military couldn't or wouldn't do."

"You're talking about black ops and assassinations," Nathan said.

Holly nodded. "He wasn't bound by the same rules as our military. Mason did everything, all of it. IED investigation. Armed security escorts for VIPs and construction personnel. Security for CIA forward operating bases. Surveillance. Infiltration. Interrogation. And, yes, even contract killing. If it weren't for a tragic op at the end of his third tour in Afghanistan, he'd be seen as a hero in every sense of the word."

"You've known this all along? You aren't just remembering it?"

"I've been trying to steer you guys to let the police handle this from the beginning. He's a hardened killer who won't hesitate to shoot both of you."

"And when exactly *were* you planning to tell us all of this?"

"Easy, Nate, we don't share all of our history."

"Damn, Holly . . . I'm sorry. I didn't mean that like it sounded."

"It's okay; don't worry about it."

"It's not okay. I was out of line."

"I know you're stressed about Mason being up there with Toby and Mara."

Nathan nodded. "We don't have time now, but will you tell us what happened with Mason?"

She looked out the window. "It's classified, but, yeah, I'll tell you about it. Now that you know how dangerous Mason is, will you reconsider calling the police?"

"Holly, we've already talked about this. You said you were never here."

"I'm not worried about me. I don't want you guys getting killed out there."

"We won't. With Harv's help, I should be able to approach the stairwell without being seen."

"Unless Toby or Mara have already given you guys up, which is a very real possibility."

"We won't know until we get up there."

Harv found the same parking spot. "Let's wire up."

Between the two of them, they had four radios. Nathan gave Holly one of his. They verified the frequencies and checked them for proper function.

Harv spoke to Holly. "I'm putting the keys on top of the left rear tire. Is there anything in your pockets that will make noise?"

"No."

"Where's your service piece?"

"On my right ankle."

"Do you want a spare nine mil? We have an extra."

She shook her head.

The rain fell even more heavily now, creating cones of orange light under the streetlamps. They huddled on the sidewalk under a tree. "If someone brings a gun up," Nathan said, "we drop 'em and let my father deal with any fallout with Mr. Beaumont. Holly, position yourself on the other side of the street between the parked cars where you can see me approach the stairwell. Report your final position. Harv, you circle around the east side of the building and approach from the south. That will give me the best chance to advance undetected."

"I've got to cover a good two hundred yards. At a brisk walk, count on about two minutes. I'll check in at the south end of the building." Harv put a hand on Nathan's shoulder. "Remember, I like my world with you in it."

"Me too."

"Good hunting, partner."

"Holly, you're with me. Let's go."

***

Darla Lyons saw the approaching vehicle's headlights and ducked behind the stairwell wall with plenty of time to spare.

The sedan rolled past her position and slowed for a right turn at the end of the block. It was probably somebody heading home after a late night of work, or drinking. She didn't think such an expensive vehicle fit this neighborhood, but the possibilities of why it was here were too numerous to consider. Leaning over the rail, Darla watched the Mercedes disappear.

She looked at Haynes's door. There hadn't been much sound in there for the last five minutes. One thing was certain: she never wanted to be the object of Mason's wrath. He was the kind of man who could remove a victim's fingernails with a pair of pliers and maintain a smile while doing it. Although she'd been shaken by the double execution tonight, she was okay with it. Those two scumbags had it coming.

Darla was no stranger to a male-dominated world. She'd been mired in it her entire life. Raised with three brothers, she'd learned how to manipulate males at an early age. Men weren't hard to figure out, but Mason seemed immune to her charm. Although she'd never made a pass at him, or vice versa, he possessed a command presence she found alluring. She imagined a relationship with Mason would be like having a pet rattlesnake. Besides, Mason was consumed by BSI.

She scanned the street again and sighed. Being relegated to sentry duty sucked, but someone had to do it. She'd have preferred to be inside where she could show Mason some of the skills she'd learned in Iraq. Although she might not have seen quite the action Mason and Hahn had, she'd completed three tours in Iraq with Blackwater. Speaking of—

She heard something over the patter of rain.

Somewhere to the south, a man coughed and hacked loud enough to wake the entire neighborhood. Whoever this guy was, he didn't sound good. *Dude, ease off the cigarettes.*

The noise continued to increase until it sounded life threatening. She leaned over the rail and looked toward the source. When the man came into view, he doubled over and clutched his chest. He managed to stagger forward another twenty feet before falling to his hands and knees.

"Skinner, we've got trouble out here. Some guy just collapsed on the sidewalk. If anyone sees him, they'll call 911 for sure."

"What's the story; is he drunk?"

"I don't know, but he's in a bad way. He's coughing loudly. Should I head down there?"

"Ignore him. We're finished in here."

***

Nathan's ear speaker came to life with Holly's voice. *"Nathan, I'm between a light-colored pickup and a dark SUV. I can't tell what color they are. These streetlights are washing out all the color."*

He scanned the line of parked cars. "Are you in front of the house with the two cypress trees?"

"Yes."

"Okay, I've got you." Equidistant between two streetlights, Holly had picked a good spot. Without knowing exactly where she was, Nathan wouldn't have seen her.

"Harv?"

"Ten seconds."

"Holly's in place."

Harv gave him an acknowledgment click. Nathan worked his way along the face of the building, staying in the shadow created by the second-floor walkway. He had to duck below a few glowing windows to avoid creating a silhouette.

Harv checked in from the south end of the building as planned, then began his fake-coughing-spasm diversion when he was halfway down the block.

From Nathan's current location, he couldn't see Lyons, which also meant she couldn't see him. He needed to go another half block before reaching the base of the stairwell, where she'd hidden herself at the top.

Keeping his eyes on the second-floor walkway, he crept forward.

He was about to make his final sprint to the base of the stairwell when Holly's voice came through his ear speaker.

"Mason and Hahn just came out of Toby's apartment."

Nathan heard it then, multiple footsteps coming from above.

Nathan had a big problem. He was out in the open.

The walkway serving the second-floor apartments shielded him from view, but as soon as they started down the stairs, he'd be visible. The low bushes along the building didn't offer enough cover, and there was no way he could move laterally out to the parked cars without being spotted.

He needed to make a split-second decision. He could sprint back to the north corner of the building and *hope* he wasn't seen, or be aggressive and advance south to the stairwell and hide under the stair treads.

He chose the latter option, believing it gave him the best chance.

With Harv too far away to help, Nathan didn't want to engage three hardened mercenaries in a firefight. In his mind, the mission hadn't changed, only its variables. If he could get through the next thirty seconds without discharging his weapon, he'd consider it a victory.

He stayed on the grass to keep his footfalls silent and reached the stairwell with seconds to spare. Thankfully, the wet concrete masked his footprints as he stuffed himself into the hollow under the stairs.

Metallic clanks sounded above his head as Mason, Hahn, and Lyons descended.

Nathan remained motionless as the team of killers made it to the halfway landing. They were now three feet away, directly above his head. He bent lower and felt a spiderweb press into his face.

Shit!

His interrogator in Nicaragua had used spider venom to inflict pain. Clenching his teeth at the image of eight legs crawling down his collar, he took a deep breath, forcing himself to breathe.

The clanking above his head ended. They were down.

I'm not here . . . this is an empty space. I'm just a slab of cracked concrete under here. Cracked concrete . . . cracked concrete. He used the words as a mantra, repeating them silently, over and over.

With his Sig Sauer held tightly against his chest, Nathan froze as three dark figures appeared. In the bleed light coming from the streetlamps, he saw the bulges of weapons under their coats.

If they looked in his direction, he'd likely be blown. It was dark under here, but not pitch black. He might or might not be able to nail all of them before they shot back. To make matters worse, he'd need to score head shots. Their torsos looked bulked up by body armor.

They walked a few steps in Holly's direction and stopped.

What the hell are you doing? Nathan thought. *Get your asses moving!*

"Harv, start coughing again," Holly said. *"Now!"*

Harv complied.

Nathan couldn't see his friend, but he heard the fake coughing spasms. It was difficult to gauge how far away Harv was, but it sounded like a good thirty yards or more.

Harv's coughing did the trick. *Way to go, Holly.*

He watched them turn and focus in that direction. Then, without a word, they angled across the grass and stepped into the street. One thing was instantly clear: Mason, with his blond ponytail dangling, was a big man. Not as big as Nathan, but at least an inch taller than Harv. Hahn and the woman were roughly the same height and build. If she had long hair, it was tucked under her cap. In the low light it was difficult to see much detail, but they were definitely wearing dark tactical clothing.

"Holly, do you have eyes on them?" Nathan whispered.

"They're walking straight toward me."

"Are you secure?"

"Affirm. They'll never see me. I'm using the truck to stay out of sight."

"Harv. Double-time around the rear of the building and form up with Holly."

"Copy."

Down the sidewalk, Harv's coughing went silent.

Nathan quickly wiped his face and neck, dislodging the sticky web. He smashed his clothing at the collar just in case a spider had dropped in there. He suddenly felt itchy, like miniature clawed feet were scrambling across his skin. *There's no spider; it was just an old cobweb.*

He edged out from the cramped space and watched Mason, Hahn, and Lyons cross the street. They moved in a confident, cohesive manner.

Tight, like a military unit.

As soon as they reached the opposite side of the street, all hell broke loose.

CHAPTER 13

Holly moved laterally along the length of the truck to keep it between her and Mason. Two more steps and she'd be behind its tailgate.

Oh no!

She felt the resistance half a second too late and looked down. She'd kicked a plastic cup over, spilling its contents. Crap, she hadn't cleared her path, a gross tactical error. The sound was negligible and she doubted Mason had heard it over the rain. She held perfectly still and slowly raised her head to look through the truck's windows. Mason and his crew hadn't reacted, and she breathed a sigh of relief.

Then things changed.

It started as a low growl, then erupted into an ear-shattering canine tirade. Behind a head-high fence no more than twenty feet away, a large dog barked, snarled, and clawed at the fence. The timing couldn't have been worse. Mason and his team were only a few yards away.

Holly pushed her transmit button. "I'm blown!" she whispered.

"Don't move," Nathan answered. *"The dog might scare them off. Harv, all-out sprint."*

She clicked her radio and crouched lower, willing the animal to stop barking.

It didn't happen.

Her situation got worse when the porch spotlight snapped on. Caught in no-man's land, she was plainly visible from the house. Damning light bleached her like a freeway billboard.

She focused on the window next to the door and saw the shades move.

"Holly, Mason's crew diverted to the middle of the street. They're leaving in a big hurry."

"Someone inside the house just saw me."

"Harv?"

"Twenty seconds."

"Someone's opening the front door!"

"Holly, get ready to bolt south down the sidewalk. I'll cover your exit. Don't pull your piece."

Like something out of a bad dream, she watched a heavy-set man with a baseball bat step onto his porch. Wearing boxer shorts and a T-shirt, he yelled, "What're you doing to my truck?"

The dog's barking got louder and more frantic.

"Five seconds," Harv said, breathing heavily.

Holly pointed to the street, then covered her mouth with her index finger. She hoped the guy would understand her meaning.

He didn't.

And she knew why.

Wafting out the door like fermented fog came the foul stench of alcohol.

He took a step forward and brought the bat up. "Get away from there! I'm callin' the cops!"

Nathan's voice rang through her ear speaker. *"Holly, go!"*

She needed no other prompting. She came out of her crouch and sprinted down the sidewalk.

The drunk yelled, "Hey!"

"Harv?" Nathan asked.

"I have eyes on Mason."

Holly glanced to her left, and saw Mason stop walking.

Then she heard him yell, "Get her!"

***

Not in this Marine's world.

Nathan flew across the lawn, activating the Sig's laser. His sudden appearance had the desired effect. Hahn turned his attention away from Holly and squared off against the new threat.

Nathan slid like a baseball player, took a knee, and leveled his pistol. Hahn reacted quickly and diverted toward the truck where Holly had been. Nathan lost sight of his target.

Now the tables had turned. Nathan was out in the open. He flattened himself on the lawn and pointed the red dot through the truck's windows.

"Harv, two in the air!"

Concussive booms hammered every hard surface in the area and crackled down the street like thunder.

The drunk on the porch cursed and ran back inside, tripping over the jamb.

Nathan saw a black form bolt north from the truck. Hahn was using the line of the parked cars along the curb to retreat. Nathan did his best to keep his laser painted on Hahn as he raced away. He knew Hahn would see the red dot and be strongly motivated to keep going. Mason and Lyons dashed for the line of vehicles as well. Clearly they had no idea where Harv's shots originated, so they did the only logical thing. Retreat or be shot.

Nathan removed his finger from the trigger and looked in Holly's direction. He saw her near the end of the block.

Lights were coming on. Lots of them. The entire neighborhood was alerted.

"Harv, maintain position and make sure our guests leave the area."

"Copy."

Nathan retreated back to the stairwell for cover. "Holly, retrace Harv's route back to the sedan and fire it up. Hold position and be ready to go when we get there."

"On my way."

Nathan heard an engine start in the distance, then another. Headlight intrusion stretched down the street and swept from left to right. Mason and Hahn were turning their vehicles around in a big hurry. There was no way to chase them. They'd be long gone by the time he reached Harv's sedan.

Nathan had more pressing concerns. Every cop within a ten-mile radius would now be speeding to this location.

"How long do you think we have?" Nathan asked.

"Two or three minutes," Harv answered.

"Leave your spent brass. We're going up. Holly, change in plans. Don't start the engine. Put the keys in the ignition, and leave the car unlocked. We need eyes on the street while we check out Toby's apartment. Position yourself where you can see anyone who approaches."

"Copy."

"I'm not worried about people looking out their windows, but let us know if anyone comes outside. There might be a retired or off-duty cop living around here."

"It's my fault the dog barked; I knocked over a plastic cup."

"Put it behind you. Check in when you're in position."

"Copy."

Nathan took a moment to breathe a sigh of relief and offer a silent thank-you. Things could've turned out much worse. He or Holly could've been shot.

With Harv on his way, Nathan held his position. He was tempted to ascend the stairs and check on Toby, but waiting for Harv was the sensible thing to do.

Through the rain Harv materialized, jogging down the sidewalk. Not concerned about the metallic clunks, they hustled up the stairs and hurried toward Toby's door.

Harv pointed. "The jamb is splintered. Mason kicked it in."

Toby's apartment was totally dark.

Nathan tightened his gloves before pulling his Sig. "Watch my six, I'm going in."

"Maybe we should both go."

Nathan reached for the knob. "I want you out here if Mason comes back."

CHAPTER 14

"Toby," he whispered loudly.

No response.

He gave the door a firm rap. "Toby, are you in here?"

Again, nothing.

"Trip wire or booby trap?" Harv asked.

"There'd be no reason for it unless Toby gave us up."

"I'm in place," Holly reported. *"All quiet."*

"Copy," Nathan answered.

Harv put a hand on his shoulder. "We'd better check, then."

"Agreed." Nathan quickly ran his hands along the length of the door, then checked the bottom of the jamb. "Think we're good." He took a step inside, but stopped. "Hang on a sec. I'm doing an NV sweep."

"Nate, we'll need something to prop against the door; it won't stay closed."

"Shit . . ."

"What have you got?"

"Toby's tied to a chair, and he doesn't look good. The place has been tossed; it's completely trashed. We'll use a sofa cushion on the door."

"Kick one over to me."

After verifying the curtains were closed, he focused on the wall next to the door and found a dual light switch. He chose the switch with more handprint grime.

"Harv, eyes." Nathan turned off his NV before flipping the switch.

He grimaced at the sight of Toby leaning back in the chair as if merely passed out from drinking. Seeing the scene in shades of green through the NV scope didn't reflect the true hideousness of the crime. Color added shock value. Especially red.

Directly below Toby's battered head, a perfectly round pool of blood saturated the carpet.

"I don't see Mara. We need to clear the other rooms down the hall."

"Let me do that, Nate."

"We'll both go."

"Nate . . ."

"Both of us."

They found Mara in the first room. Harv turned on the light.

They were greeted by pink. Lots of pink. Like the living room, the room had been crudely searched. The floor was a mess. A crib sat in the corner with a paper butterfly mobile hanging above.

Nathan felt his stomach churn.

Mara's skin wasn't flawless anymore. Her face had taken some hard blows.

She lay on her side, the back of her head caked with fresh blood. Beneath it, a dark pool had soaked into the mattress.

Nathan checked for a pulse.

Nothing.

"Looks like they were expecting a baby girl."

"Nate, man, I'm really sorry . . . But we have to keep moving."

He took a final look and burned the image into his mind, where it would never be removed. Ever. Stealing Mara's life was the filthiest act of theft. It could never be returned to her. He kicked a lamp shade, sending it into the paper mobile.

"We'll get him, Nathan. Count on it."

Looking for Toby's cell phone, they quickly checked every drawer, closet, shower stall, and cabinet. Like the living room and the baby's room, every square inch of the apartment had been tossed, even the bathrooms. The toilet tanks were open, and the lids placed on the countertops. Nothing was broken, just moved aside or on the floor. It was clear Mason and his cohorts didn't make much noise during their search.

"They have his phone," Nathan said.

Harv didn't say anything.

Nathan tried to imagine Toby's and Mara's last minutes. They'd probably held out for as long as possible, thinking they'd be saved by two white knights from First Security, but their rescuers didn't come back. Nathan forced the corrosive thought aside. Now wasn't the time for useless blame or finger-pointing. Toby and Mara were dead because Mason was a cold-blooded asshole. It wasn't more complicated than that.

They returned to the living room, and Nathan put Harv on hold. They held perfectly still, listening for sounds. The muted buzz of a neighbor's television coming through the wall closely matched the volume of the refrigerator's compressor hum.

"Holly, status? Do you hear any sirens?"

"Not yet."

If Toby had a pet, Nathan detected no sign or odor of it. Cats tended to hide, but there definitely wasn't a dog in here. He stepped over to the window, cracked the curtains, and looked down to the street below.

Returning his attention to Toby, he saw the man was dressed only in cargo shorts and a plain white T-shirt. Two holes next to a curved scar on Toby's scalp oozed blood.

"Harv." Nathan nodded toward the kitchen. The contents of Toby's wallet sat on the counter next to his car keys, including eighty dollars in cash. "If he had an electronic access card for work, they took it. At least they don't have our business card."

Harv approached Toby's body. "Nate, this man isn't dead. He's still breathing."

"What! How's that possible?"

"I don't know, but he may not have much longer."

"We're taking him to the ER."

"Wait. You know what that means."

"We're already all-in." He gave Toby a quick examination. "Some of his fingers are broken, and his skin is abraded under the cuffs. They beat his face to a pulp. It's obvious he gave up his cell phone under torture. That's why it isn't here. We need to know what else he told them. We—"

A low-pitched woof rattled the window.

Nathan recognized the sound and rushed to the curtains.

"ID," Harv said, joining him.

Incendiary device.

"Toby's Sentra."

"Are you guys seeing this?" Holly asked.

"Affirm. We're on our way down. Start the sedan and be ready to go." Nathan immediately noticed the rear passenger compartment of Toby's car already glowed. In another minute or so, the entire vehicle would be fully involved. "Why torch Toby's car?"

"A diversion?"

Nathan nodded.

"That car fire actually helps us."

Nathan couldn't hide the tightness in his voice. "Helps us? How the hell does it *help* us?"

"The fire department is already scrambling, and they can usually arrive quicker than the police or an ambulance. They're all first responders and they might have an EMT with them."

Nathan didn't mean to sound incredulous, but it came out that way. "So we just leave him here?"

"At the risk of sounding callous, yes."

"Harv, even if we leave Toby's front door wide open, there's no guarantee the firefighters will see it in time or assume the open door is connected to the car fire. We need to transport him."

"If we take him down to the sidewalk, there's no way they'll miss him. Nate . . . we can't stay. We have to clear the area."

"Shit, Harv. I'm sorry. I didn't mean to snap at you. I'm just *really* pissed off right now."

"Don't worry about it," Harv said.

Nathan pulled his knife and cut the plastic bindings securing Toby's hands and feet, then grasped him under the armpits while Harv picked up Toby's legs. Together they hauled him off the dining room chair.

"This guy weighs a ton," Harv said.

"That might be the only reason he's still alive. They probably used subsonic .22 rounds again."

They moved him through the door onto the walkway.

Just ahead, a door on the opposite side of the stairwell opened and a young woman in a bathrobe stepped out. She approached the rail and stared down at the blazing car. She hadn't seen them yet, but she would soon enough. The entire wall of the apartment building was bathed in orange light.

"Excuse me, ma'am," Nathan said.

She looked at them and covered her mouth. "What happened to Toby?"

"Please call 911 and request an ambulance. I think he may've been injured from the explosion down there."

Without saying another word, she backed into her apartment.

Toby's butt scraped along the stair treads as they hauled him down. At the bottom, they laid him on the sidewalk where he couldn't be missed. Flames now roared from the Sentra's blown-out windows. The rain wasn't going to help much. IDs contained their own fuel and burned hotter than most fires.

Toby's eyes opened for a few seconds, and he turned his head.

"Harv, he's awake." Nathan bent down and spoke softly. "Toby, it's Nathan."

Toby's mouth moved soundlessly, his eyes fluttering closed. "Med hall . . ."

"What's that?" Nathan asked.

"Med . . ."

"I don't understand you, but you're going to be okay. Did you tell Mason about us? Toby? *Toby!* Shit, he's out."

"Nate, we gotta go."

"Did you catch what he said?"

"It sounded like 'med hall.'" Harv nodded toward the other side of the street. "People are watching us."

"Fuck 'em," Nathan said.

"Nate . . ."

"Okay, okay." They walked at a brisk pace along the sidewalk. "I'm ready to burn BSI to the ground."

"A few bad people doesn't make the entire company bad."

"I don't like being in reaction mode. We're going on the offensive."

"We will, but let's get through the next few minutes first."

Nathan issued a dismissive grunt and pictured himself in Mason's shoes. His primary concern would have been finding out if Toby had told anyone what he'd witnessed on the soccer field. He'd obviously beaten Mara as well, and he hoped she'd denied him the satisfaction of breaking her.

By the time they reached the corner of the next street where Harv had parked, the entire neighborhood was awake. Dogs barked, and people stood on the sidewalk with cell phones held to their ears.

They both heard it then: the distant cry of a siren.

Nathan wasn't too worried about the woman they'd seen on the second-floor walkway; it hadn't been brightly lit up there. If questioned, she could give the police a general description of two big men carrying Toby—not terribly useful. Wearing ball caps, they'd also kept their heads down.

When they turned the corner at the end of the block, Nathan felt a certain amount of relief upon seeing Harv's car. They'd be clear of this area in the next twenty seconds.

Getting in the backseat, he asked, "Do you think Toby or Mara caved?"

"It's hard to say. They went at Toby pretty hard, but Mara didn't look as bad. She could've given us up before they got rough, or they might've used her against Toby. There's no way to know until we talk to him."

Holly pulled away from the curb. "Are they alive?"

"Mara's not, and Toby's hanging by a thread. Mason shot both of them in the head multiple times."

"Nathan, I'm so sorry."

"You aren't going to say I told you so?"

"Of course not," she said.

Nathan felt his cell vibrate. He pulled it from his pocket and read the name. *Karen.* A name from another life—from his time with Mara, when he'd first met Toby. Why would she be calling? Especially now?

"Karen?"

"Nathan, I think there's someone in my front yard. The floodlights just came on!"

"How many blinking red lights do you see on the master control unit?"

"I don't know. I think I saw two. I'm looking out the window."

"Stay away from the windows! We're on our way. We'll be there in three minutes. Which zones are blinking red?"

"The front yard."

"Who else is there?"

"No one. I'm alone."

"Karen, don't question me right now: I want you to activate the panic feature on any of the keypads. Do it right now. Keep your phone with you, and put it on silent mode. Get into your emergency hiding place as fast as you can, and clear your recent-call list."

"Nathan—"

"Hide *now*!" Nathan yelled. "And clear that call list!"

CHAPTER 15

Rain pelting off his cap, Mason walked at a good clip down the residential sidewalk. If anyone happened to spot him, he didn't want to look like a burglar. This neighborhood had no apartments or condos, only single-family homes on small lots. *Boring boxes full of boring people*, thought Mason. Aside from an occasional porch light, most of the neighborhood remained dark because the streetlights stood several hundred feet apart.

The address he wanted was the next house on the right. He slowed and looked for motion sensors mounted on the eaves. Detecting none, he angled across the lawn, heading for the front door.

Mason inwardly cursed when four floodlights snapped on. He must've stepped through an IR beam or triggered a hidden motion detector, something he should've anticipated. He left his gun in his waist pack and ran across the brightly lit yard.

***

Karen felt panic tighten her skin. She'd never heard Nathan sound so intense. Dressed only in underwear and a T-shirt, she bolted through the dark house to the kitchen. She jammed the red button on the keypad controller three times in quick succession. The result was instantaneous. The entire house erupted with an ear-piercing electronic shriek—like a hyperactive ambulance siren. And the front and backyard ignited with additional blinding light. To avoid being seen in the bleed light invading the house, Karen crouched below the level of the countertops and crawled over to the kitchen island.

***

"Holly, stop and switch places with me."

Without bothering to pull to the curb, she braked hard in the middle of the street and climbed out. Five seconds later, Nathan floored the accelerator.

Holly asked, "What's going on? Who's Karen?"

"She's Mara's friend; they used to live together."

"You think Mason's at Karen's house?"

Nathan didn't answer.

"They're sterilizing," Harv said.

"Why there?" Holly asked. "Why her?"

Again, Nathan didn't respond; he was too focused on Karen, going over the layout of her house in his head. First Security had upgraded her alarm system a few years ago. There were multiple keypads in the house, so it shouldn't take her more than a few seconds to trigger the panic feature and get into her rabbit hole. He hoped she hadn't used it for storage.

***

Mason knew his way around security systems and believed someone had just triggered the panic button. The increased exterior light and blaring shriek inside the house meant he had very little time to break in, grab the woman, and bug out. Keeping his head down in case there were hidden cameras, he charged the front door and threw his weight against it. No match for his momentum, it flew open and banged against the wall.

***

Karen opened a cabinet door and thanked heaven for finding an empty space. She'd been worried Cindy might've put stuff in here. She scrambled inside and pulled the door closed.

Total blackness engulfed her.

Over the blaring alarm, she heard a loud bang and knew someone had just kicked open her front door. She blindly felt for the small shelf in the upper-right corner and closed her hand over the butt of the .25 automatic pistol. Fighting back tears, she tucked her knees against her chest and waited for Nathan or death to arrive.

***

Nathan's phone vibrated, so did Harv's. If any of their clients ever activated the panic feature, both of their phones received text alerts.

Nathan accelerated to eighty miles an hour along a straight section of road. "Let's hope the noise chases Mason away. He should know the police will treat Karen's alarm like a 911 call."

"Agreed. Our system shows a home invasion's taking place. If she made it into her rabbit hole, she bought some extra time. She's got a gun in there, doesn't she?"

"Yeah, she's supposed to. We'll need to park down the street and proceed on foot."

Holly asked, "Doesn't this seem like overkill? I mean, at some point the crimes you commit to cover things up exceed the original crime."

Harv sighed. "Yeah, they do. It's the same principle as lying. It snowballs."

"Hang on. I'm going through." Nathan approached a red light without slowing.

"Clear on the right," Harv said. "Good driving, partner."

Nathan cranked the windshield wipers to their highest setting.

"So Karen knows Toby and Mara, right?" Holly asked.

"Yes." Nathan ran another red light without incident. "We don't know whether Toby or Mara told Mason about us, but it looks like one of them may have contacted Karen."

"But why?" asked Holly. "Why bring someone else into this? You said not to tell anyone."

"Mara and Karen are close friends," Harv said. "Friends share secret stuff with each other."

Nathan nodded. "Well, let's hope the rabbit hole works. The alarm should force Mason to conduct a quick room-to-room recon, and when he doesn't find anyone, he'll bug out." *Or burn the place down.* Nathan braked hard and made another turn. The wheels drifted on the wet concrete, but he maintained control. "We're almost there. I'll park at the corner and take point on the west side of the street. I'll use whatever landscaping is available to advance. If any of Karen's neighbors see me, that's okay. The more people calling 911, the better. Harv, you take the east side of the street and give me a ten-second lead."

"What about me?" Holly asked.

"You'll take Harv's six, twenty-second delay."

Harv said, "Karen didn't mention seeing any vehicles, did she?"

"No."

"Then we should keep an eye out for their SUV and Lexus. Based on everything that's happened tonight, I know how this is going to sound, but we should avoid a firefight if possible. Again, we don't have vests and we can't risk a stray bullet entering someone's home. Let's agree that our mission objective is to chase them away if they're still around."

"It's tempting to shoot them, but I agree, Harv. We'll get an opportunity later. When we're finished with those BSI . . . *contractors*, they're going to be droolers for the rest of their lives."

"Amen to that."

Nathan made a tight left turn onto Mount Acadia Boulevard and accelerated to twice the speed limit. Every hundred yards or so, he honked his horn. If anyone was out here at 1:43 AM, at least they'd hear the big Mercedes coming.

Harv said, "Be careful, Nate, they could be tearing out of there. If we see some headlights in Karen's neighborhood, there's a good chance it's them."

Nathan braced himself for another high-speed turn.

"There's something else we have to consider," Harv said.

"What's that?"

"If it's Mason, and he finds Karen . . ."

"Yeah, I know. I'm more worried about her being kidnapped. Mason won't hang around to interrogate her; he'll grab her and leave."

"He'll also take her phone."

"I told her to clear her recent calls, but in her current state of mind, who knows. My phone number or name might be front and center in her recent-call list. Let's hope it doesn't say Nathan McBride—First Security."

"Maybe we'll get some footage of them. Karen's security system activated all the cameras—inside and out."

Nathan asked, "It's a live link?"

"Yes, the video is sent directly to our server."

Nathan didn't say anything.

"She's going to be okay, Nate. We'll be there in ninety seconds."

***

Mason rushed through the breached door and crouched at the entrance to the living room. Except for the bleed light from the exterior floods, it was dark in here. If there were any other sounds, they were impossible to hear over the obnoxious shrieking.

Each passing second represented increasing danger. Many Americans owned guns, and he didn't want to be facing the business end of one. He was also worried about dogs, but fortunately, none charged out of the darkness.

He rushed from room to room, pivoting around corners and using furniture for cover when he could. His earpiece came to life with Darla's voice.

"Skinner, we've . . . lights coming on in the house . . . door to the north. Same thing . . . the street . . . think we've got less . . . thirty seconds before . . . coming outside."

"You're unreadable over this alarm. Copy you've got neighbor activity?" Mason reached down and cranked the volume.

"Affirm." Darla's voice was louder.

"It doesn't look like anyone's home, but somebody had to press the panic button."

"It could've been triggered remotely."

"Either way, we're not hanging around to find out. Regroup at the vehicles. I'm on my way. You copy, Chip?"

"Affirm."

Mason looked for framed photos of the people who lived here but saw none. This place was pretty stark. It didn't have the feel of someone's home; it felt more like an office. The infernal noise was getting under his skin. Annoyed at not finding anyone, he kicked a Tiffany table lamp across the room. Its shade shattered on the hardwood floor.

Outside, he kept his head down and sprinted through the blinding light.

"Skinner, we've got more trouble."

"What's going on?"

"I just heard chatter through the scanner. The fire department just requested a code-three bus for an unconscious gunshot victim."

***

Nathan slowed about a hundred yards north of Karen's house and found a parking spot midway between streetlights.

In the distance, multiple sirens pierced the night. The three of them performed a radio check to make sure all their wiring was still good.

With Harv following across the street, Nathan hustled down the sidewalk. He'd cut into people's yards closer to Karen's.

The setting and mood felt eerily familiar and reminded him of the night he'd fought with Toby. Just as they were now, recycle bins had been stationed along the street's curb like sentinels. Contrasting the anger he felt, the soft patter of rain hitting their plastic forms sounded benign, almost calming.

He could now see the glow from Karen's yard and hear the blaring of the security system's alarm—a good sign. If he could hear it at this distance, other neighbors could too. Their system did exactly what it was designed to do. Nathan hoped it would be enough.

He glanced across the street and saw Harv a few paces back, mirroring his forward progress. He couldn't see Holly, but knew she was back there somewhere.

"Holly, status?"

"I've got Harvey in sight."

"Harv, how long ago did we receive the panic-button text?"

"Just over four minutes."

Nathan clicked his radio and kept going, wishing it were darker on this street. When he reached the side yard of Karen's house, he made an all-out sprint for the front door. Its jamb splintered, it lay wide open.

Just inside, he crouched. It was impossible to hear anything over this awful noise. If Mason had discharged his pistol, Nathan ought to be able to smell a trace of it. So far, he didn't.

He took a few seconds to turn off the alarm using a master code. When the noise ended, his nerves settled. That damned racket was beyond hideous. Outside, the spotlights remained on.

From somewhere inside, likely the kitchen, he heard Karen's landline begin ringing. *That's our company calling to see if the button was accidentally pressed.* For now, it would have to wait.

He held still for a moment longer, listening for any activity. If Karen were lying dead in here, a few more seconds wouldn't matter. One thing was certain: Karen's skull wasn't as thick as Toby's. If they'd double-tapped her like Mara, she'd be gone.

"Harv," he whispered. "I'm inside; stand by."

His radio clicked.

Staying low, Nathan advanced to the kitchen's threshold. The octagonal island loomed like a mausoleum. Light from the rear yard's floods reflected off its granite countertop.

He looked to his right, down a dark hall, then back to the kitchen. "Karen, it's Nathan. Are you in here?"

The cabinet door burst open, and Karen flew out with a small semiauto in her hand.

"Karen, your finger's on the trigger!"

Tears streaming down her face, she dropped the gun and wrapped Nathan in a bear hug. He could feel her small frame trembling and understood the terror she'd just experienced. Being in a tight, dark space without knowing what's happening outside could fray even battle-hardened nerves.

"Harv, Karen's okay, but I haven't cleared the house."

"On my way."

"Holly, keep eyes on the street. Let us know if any of those sirens get closer."

He heard his radio click.

Karen's vise-like grasp hadn't loosened.

A few seconds later, Harv ran through the front door and assumed a defensive position, aiming his Sig down the dark hall.

"Karen, wait here; we'll be right back."

"Please don't leave me alone."

"Stay behind us." In a two-man lineup, he and Harv worked their way down the hall, clearing all the open doors. Convinced the intruders were long gone, they returned to the kitchen.

"Did Mara call you tonight?" Nathan asked.

"No, she sent a text. She said Toby saw two men get murdered, and she was really freaked."

"Is the text still in your phone?"

"No way. I erased it. She said not to text her back, so I didn't."

"Can you remember what it said? Did it contain any names?"

"No. It just said what Toby saw."

This confirmed the intruder was Mason, and Karen was lucky to be alive. He'd never know why Mara made such a costly error in judgment by sending that text to Karen, but it no longer mattered. What was done was done.

"Grab an overnight bag; you can't stay here."

"Who broke into my house? Was it the murderers?"

"Yes."

"Were they going to kill me?"

"You're a loose end. Mara told you what Toby witnessed." He looked at Harv, then put a hand on her shoulder. "Karen, I don't know how to tell you this . . . Mara's dead."

"What!" Her face went slack with shock, then changed to anguish.

"I'm really sorry. Whoever killed Mara tried to kill Toby too. He's still alive, but he might not make it."

She covered her face and began crying. "She was pregnant . . . they were getting married."

He didn't know what to say. "We need to get you out of here. The killers might come back any minute."

"What about Cindy?"

"Call her from the road. We're leaving."

"Nathan, I don't—"

"I promise to answer all your questions, but now isn't the time. Pack enough stuff for a couple days."

She didn't move.

"Karen, your life's in danger." He added command tone to his voice. "We're out of here in sixty seconds. Start packing."

That did the trick. Wiping tears, she hurried down the hall.

"I'll check the backyard," Harv said.

Nathan radioed to Holly and asked for an update.

"A few dogs have started barking and more lights are coming on."

"Bring Harv's car up and come in dark." His radio clicked.

Nathan's thoughts returned to Toby and Mara. Her death felt like a punch to the stomach. How could Mason be so cold? Aside from the hideous injustice of it, something else bugged him, something about the incendiary device Mason planted in Toby's car. Why do that? It didn't make sense. If he didn't want any attention drawn to the area, torching Toby's car didn't accomplish that. Clearly, Mason believed Toby and Mara were dead, so maybe he wasn't concerned about how quickly the bodies were discovered. Nathan shook his head. How many people survived two bullets to the head? Subsonic rounds or not, it seemed as though a guardian angel had visited Toby's apartment.

Beyond the sliding glass doors, he saw Harv using the TI to sweep for warm bodies.

"We're clear back here," Harv said. *"I'm gonna check the front yard."*

Nathan clicked his radio.

The nagging question wouldn't go away: Why torch Toby's car?

Her face streaked with tears, Karen returned with a small suitcase.

"Holly's here," Harv reported. *"We need to get outta here. I hear sirens closing."*

"We're coming out." He took Karen's free hand. "None of this is your fault. I'm really sorry you've been pulled into this. I'll have one of our security guards watch your house until we fix your door. The important thing is that you and Cindy are safe, and we're going to protect you. We'll hide you at our cabin on Mount Laguna."

She nodded but didn't say anything.

"Come on, let's go." He escorted her outside to Harv's sedan and opened a rear door for her. From the sound of the sirens, they didn't have more than thirty seconds. "Holly, you're driving. Let's go."

With Karen and Harv in the back, Holly pulled away from the curb and executed a Y-turn.

Karen didn't react when Nathan introduced Holly as a federal agent. Karen was far too distraught to care.

"Where are we going?" Holly asked.

"Back to Toby's apartment. I want to make sure the EMTs have him and find out what hospital they take him to."

"Nate, we need to contact our call center and let them know there's no emergency at Karen's house."

"Yeah, good idea. I heard our dispatcher calling. We also need to assign a security guard to watch the house."

"I'll take care of that right now."

"I want you to think about Mara's message one more time," Nathan told Karen. "Did she text anything else?"

"Only that Toby was in the shower. She didn't want him to know she'd texted me . . . I can't believe she's dead."

He reminded her to call Cindy and warn her about returning to the house.

Nathan saw Holly shift her weight upon hearing a third woman's name. Holly's initial reaction to Karen had been . . . what? Suspicious? No, that wasn't the right word, more like cautious. It was clear Holly sensed something deeper was going on. He didn't want to tell her that Karen, and her . . . *escorts*, had once been under his protective umbrella. He hadn't been a pimp by any definition of the word, but he'd watched out for them, protected them. Seeing Karen had triggered old feelings. Like Mara, she was strikingly beautiful. Long, dark hair flowed across a . . . well-defined chest. Half-Hispanic, half-white, Karen got the best of both. She'd once substituted for Mara, and it had been an amazing evening, one he'd never forgotten.

Holly had to be wondering if he'd ever had a relationship with Karen. Like Mara, there was no way to pretend he and Karen were mere acquaintances. Despite Holly's empathy, he felt tension in the car.

He was about to say something when he suddenly realized what was bothering him. "Toby's car had a tracking bug in it."

"Yeah," Holly said. "That would explain a lot. They torched the Sentra to destroy it. They would've seen his movements and the corresponding time stamps. That's how they knew to come after him."

Harv ended his call and spoke to Karen. "We're all set. We'll have a guard watching your house in twenty minutes. I missed what you guys just said."

Nathan filled him in.

"Of course," said Harv. "Toby calls in sick around the same time as the murders, and he lives within a mile of Hickman Field. They get suspicious, check the data, and he's blown."

Nathan nodded.

"So they torched his car because it's faster and safer than trying to remove the bug in a hurry."

"What are you guys talking about?" Karen asked, ending her call to Cindy.

"We think they put a GPS transmitter in Toby's vehicle."

"Who are *they*?" Karen asked.

"Battle-hardened killers. Just knowing about them puts your life at risk. Do you understand?"

Karen nodded.

"And if you tell Cindy any of this, her life will be in danger too, just like yours."

"I won't tell anyone, I promise."

"How much do you know about Toby's work?"

"Mara said he's a security guard."

"The murderer is Toby's boss, Tanner Mason. He's chief of security at BSI."

"His boss tried to kill me? Because of the text?"

Nathan took a moment to update Karen on what Toby told them. He also told her that BSI was a huge private military contractor with a small army of personnel. He hoped the information would further convince her to keep everything secret.

"What are you going to do?" she asked.

"We're still figuring that out, but our highest priority is to protect you and Toby."

Karen nodded again, her eyes distant.

Holly didn't drive as fast as Nathan had on the way over to Karen's, but she made good time getting back to Toby's neighborhood.

Harv said, "Mason has to know he's just created a link to BSI. It won't take the police long to determine Toby worked there. SDPD is going to be contacting BSI soon, maybe even tonight. At which point Mason will learn that Toby's alive. They'll also want to talk with Toby, assuming he's conscious. I think it's a foregone conclusion Mason will find out he survived. We should post a plainclothes security guard outside his room at whatever hospital he ends up in. Actually, maybe two guards."

"We could do that too," Holly said.

"You'd have to disclose your awareness of everything. Are you sure you want to do that?"

"At this point, I'd prefer it," she said.

"Let's hold off a little longer on your end. In the meantime, we'll get three of our best men assigned to the hospital."

"We've got company," Holly said, turning onto Toby's street. Just behind them, a police cruiser sped around the corner. Its light bar flashing and siren wailing, it raced past them into a multitude of red, blue, and white stroboscopic lights lining the entire length of the street. Every type of first responder was present. Several dozen people stood on the sidewalk with umbrellas, watching the action.

A two-man firefighter team hosed the Sentra, producing a column of steam. Half a block ahead, the street was blocked by a California Highway Patrol cruiser. No doubt the other end was equally impeded.

Holly slowed to a crawl.

Nathan used Harv's field glasses to focus at the base of the stairs, but he didn't see any activity. It probably meant the paramedics had already loaded Toby.

"Turn around, Holly. We don't want to be questioned at that CHP roadblock."

Harv pivoted to look out the rear window. "Nate, one of the ambulances is leaving in a big hurry. That could be Toby's ride."

"If he's conscious, we need to talk to him before they anesthetize him for surgery."

"That won't be easy," Harv said.

"I should have a brief window before the staff calls security on me."

"If you're talking about busting into the ER, you'll be caught on camera for sure," Harv said.

"I'll risk it. Holly, can you follow the ambulance at a safe distance without being too obvious?"

"If I violate a few traffic laws."

"We'll pay our penance later."

"It's going in the right direction for Sharp," Harv said.

Holly handled the sedan like a pro. Burning through red lights was easier with multiple sets of eyes watching for cross traffic. Nathan and Harv kept calling "clear" as Holly approached intersections.

"Good driving," Nathan told her.

"Thanks, but I'd feel better if the roads weren't wet."

"You're doing fine."

"It's definitely heading to Sharp," Harv said.

The streets were deserted except for a distant set of taillights in front of the ambulance. It looked like some kind of minivan.

"That guy should pull over," Holly said.

"Probably a drunk," Nathan muttered. "You know what they say about drivers out at this hour . . . I think he sees the ambulance; he's moving over."

"How much farther is the hospital?" Holly asked.

"About a mile."

"The ambulance crew must know we're following them."

"They do, but they can't do anything about it."

"Nathan, that guy just pulled away from the curb, right in front of the ambulance."

"I see it." As they closed the distance, he realized the minivan wasn't a minivan.

It was a silver SUV.

"Punch it, Holly. That's Mason!"

CHAPTER 16

Mason activated his radio. "We've got the bus in sight." The headlights behind the ambulance were too far away to be a factor. "We'll make our move when it slows for the next turn. Darla, you copy?"

"Affirm."

"Pull in behind, and keep it from backing up."

"I'm paralleling your position one street over. I'll be at the next intersection in ten seconds."

***

"Holly, when was the last time you executed a PIT maneuver?"

"Not since the Crusades were in Jerusalem."

"I'm sure it will come back to you."

"I'm supposed to be on vacation." Holly stomped the accelerator. "What if that's not Mason?"

"We'll offer an apology and exchange insurance information."

"That's not very reassuring."

"You can do this, Holly. You don't have to hit with a lot of force, just a lateral bump. The road is wet, and there's no one else around. You should match Mason's speed or be moving slightly faster when you make contact." Nathan saw her tighten her grip on the steering wheel.

"This is what . . . a $100,000 vehicle?" she asked.

"Harv?"

"More like one twenty."

"Great."

Nathan reached down and pulled his Predator knife.

"What's that for?" she asked.

"Air bags," Harv said flatly. "They might deploy. It depends on the g-force of the impact."

"Maybe this isn't such a good idea," she said.

Nathan sat up as straight as he could and forced his back against the seat. "Stay behind the ambulance for as long as possible, then make your move when I give the word. If the ambulance stops, I'll get out and prevent Mason from approaching it. Switch places with Harv."

The ambulance grew in size as Holly raced toward its rear bumper.

"Here we go, Holly. Be smooth on the wheel. Now!"

She maneuvered the big sedan into the left lane and sped past the shrieking ambulance. Its driver honked, the sound shifting frequency like a passing train.

She braked hard, and yelled, "Everyone hang on!" She swerved to the right and clipped the rear bumper of the SUV. The impact produced a metallic bang, but it didn't jar them too violently.

Karen cried out.

The air bags didn't deploy.

In perfect form, the SUV began a tail slide. The driver tried to recover, but not in time.

"Hot shit, Holly! That was textbook." Nathan looked behind and saw the front end of the ambulance dip. "The bus is slowing down. Get ready to switch places with Harv."

***

Mason saw headlights appear out of nowhere.

"What the hell's that idiot doing?"

He realized too late what was happening.

The impact wasn't violent, but it worked.

He fought to keep the SUV from spinning, but lost the battle. His world turned into a carnival ride. He stomped the brake to slow his forward momentum, but even that was too late.

Mason clenched his teeth as the SUV—moving backward—jumped the curb and plowed through a hedge into a commercial center. Mason thought things might be okay until they slammed into a parked car. Their velocity went from forty miles an hour to zero in less than a second. It felt like he'd been sucker punched as the back of his skull smashed the headrest.

At the same instant, two explosive cracks assaulted all his senses.

For a split second, he was in Afghanistan; then his mind registered the air bags had deployed. A noxious odor like burned plastic filled the compartment.

"Chip, you okay?"

Over the top of the scorching air bag, Mason saw the ambulance swerve to the middle of the street. It slid sideways for a second, then regained its traction.

Chip opened his door and dived out.

All over the parking lot, car alarms blared, adding to the din of the ambulance's siren.

Finishing Toby Haynes would have to wait. "Chip, we're outta here."

It didn't happen.

Mason realized he could barely hear his own voice. Like his own, Chip's eardrums were pounded from the dual air bag detonations.

His friend pulled his handgun and sprinted toward the ambulance.

***

"Stop the car!"

Holly slammed the brakes, pulsing the antilocks.

"Change in plans. Harv, you're with me. Holly, get Karen outta here. Stay within a few blocks. I'll radio you."

Before the sedan had stopped, Nathan and Harv were out. He toggled his laser and lined up on the gunman dashing for the ambulance. He painted the crimson dot on the man's rib cage, then moved it a few inches to the left to lead his target. He had a better chance shooting center mass than risking a missed head shot.

He closed his eyes at the instant he pulled the trigger. Unsuppressed, the report pounded his ears. The gunman shuddered but didn't go down.

***

Mason knew Chip was vulnerable out there. Still semi-dazed from the air bag deployment, he staggered out of the driver's seat and drew his pistol.

He heard an engine roar and looked toward the street. The ambulance crew must've seen Chip running toward them because they were leaving in a big hurry.

A single handgun report rang out.

Mason watched Chip double over.

Thoroughly pissed off, Mason yanked open the rear door of his SUV and grabbed the M4. He leveled it at the man who'd just shot Chip. The guy looked an awful lot like the gunman from Haynes's apartment. He must've followed the ambulance too.

Mason leaned forward and pulled the trigger.

***

Holly screeched the tires on wet pavement as she executed a U-turn and sped away.

"Down!" Harv yelled.

A split second later, a machine-gun burst pierced the night.

Nathan saw a white star of fire spit from the SUV. He dived for the parked cars at the curb and sensed dozens of bullets whizzing past his feet. The staccato roar of the machine gun echoed off every building in the area and crackled down the street.

Behind him, Harv's handgun boomed three times, the muzzle flashes freezing raindrops.

He looked toward the ambulance and was relieved to see it speeding away.

The man Nathan had shot was down on one knee.

Could he have missed? No friggin' way. He'd drilled the guy for sure. The gunman, likely Hahn, given his size, clutched his midsection and limped back toward the SUV in a crouch. Nathan remembered seeing body armor as they'd descended the stairs at Toby's apartment.

A smile touched his lips. "Hey, asshole," he yelled, "you want some barbecue sauce for those ribs?"

He lined up for a head shot at the same instant a second salvo peppered the area around him.

Shit! Nathan covered his face as bullets skipped off the asphalt and whistled away. Mason was spraying the entire area without regard to collateral damage.

"Harv!" Nathan whispered loudly.

"I'm okay."

"We need solid cover! Head for the corner of Boot World. Go!"

He came up and saw no sign of Mason. It didn't matter. He bench-rested his Sig on the hood of the car and sent three quick shots through the SUV's fender into the engine block. A glance in

Harv's direction confirmed he'd made it to safety. At least there weren't any houses around here.

Mason fired again, this time from deeper in the parking lot. More supersonic bullets tore through the car shielding Nathan. Sooner or later, a lucky shot was going to find him. He needed to join Harv behind solid cover.

"Give me suppression fire in three, two, one . . . Now."

Harv's handgun boomed as he sprinted for Harv's position. His friend changed magazines when he arrived.

Nathan peered around the corner. "There were two vehicles at Toby's. Keep eyes on the street. Give me more suppression fire. I've got an idea. A way to advance without being in the open."

"Don't get yourself shot. Like Holly said, we don't have vests and they do."

"You ready?"

Harv nodded.

"Now."

Harv leaned out and fired his pistol toward the SUV, allowing Nathan to pivot around the corner and smack a huge glass window with his Sig. A cascade of tempered shards rained down, and he rushed inside the store. Thankfully, no alarm blared and the inside of the store remained dark. Moving quickly, he worked his way toward the entrance of the store facing the parking lot.

At the same time Nathan's mind registered the cracks, the glass blew inward, followed by the roar of automatic fire. Mason must've seen him breach the window and go inside. Thankfully, the bullets missed to his right. Nathan ducked for cover behind an endcap display as Mason fired another burst.

Like something out of a horror movie, the shoes on the rack came to life as dozens of .223 slugs found them. They jumped into the air and bounced around as if possessed. Nathan heard Harv's gun boom two more times, silencing Mason's machine gun. Without warning, a shrieking security alarm wailed to life and the entire store was invaded with blinding light. Nathan squinted against the visual assault and crawled toward the broken-out door. He rolled onto his back, painted his laser on the closest interior security light, and took it out. Two more shots later and he was in darkness again. He couldn't locate the source of that damned racket; it seemed to be coming from everywhere at once.

"Nate . . . can . . . hear me?"

"I'm okay. Give me three more shots on my mark. I'm going to advance up to a parked RV. Any sign of Hahn?"

"No. The last . . . of him . . . he . . . limping toward . . . SUV."

"Harv, I can't hear you over this damned alarm. Here I go. Stand by . . . Now!"

Nathan waited an extra second to be sure Harv fired before he made his sprint out the door. Harv's gun discharged with slow, deliberate cadence.

Nathan used the interval to advance through the front door's frame. He lowered himself flat behind a short hedge and moved ten feet laterally to his right. If Mason had seen him come out of Boot World, he didn't want to be in the same place for the next salvo.

"When I open fire, follow my path through the store. Keep watching for Darla." Nathan tried to gauge how much time had passed since Holly had sideswiped Mason's SUV. It couldn't have been more than sixty seconds. If Darla were in the area, she'd be showing up fairly quickly. If she did, he wouldn't be able to protect Harv's left flank.

"Change in plan. I'm heading for the landscaped strip along the street. It's—"

Mason's weapon roared again. Bullets tore through the hedge and uprooted grass along Boot World's storefront. When the barrage ended, he popped up and aimed at the spot where he'd seen the flash of the M4, but Mason wasn't there.

"Harv?"

"I'm in the store. I have eyes on you."

"Holly, are you copying all of this?"

"My God, it sounds like a war zone down there."

"Stand by. Harv, on my mark . . . Now."

Harv fired four rounds through the front door.

Nathan had to wait. "I'll be crossing right in front of you; hold your fire."

"Nathan, I didn't copy."

"Hold. Fire."

"Copy, holding fire."

Nathan made an all-out sprint for the landscaping strip next to the street. It wasn't much cover, but it did rise a few feet above the sidewalk and driveway. If he stayed near the curb, Mason's bullets wouldn't be able to find him.

What happened next reminded him of the Robert De Niro movie *Heat*. Two machine guns opened fire. As if sliding headfirst into home plate, Nathan dived into the landscaping and ended up face-to-face with a trio of sago palms. Just in front of him, the ground erupted. Mud, splintered vegetation, and bark trashed him from head to toe. He rolled to his left off the curb, which gave him another six inches of protection.

He heard it then, the roar of an engine. Would Holly come back in the middle of a firefight? She definitely would.

Harv yelled, "Behind you!"

He turned.

And found himself face-to-face with the headlights of a Lexus sedan.

If he didn't move, he'd be run over.

Nathan made a split-second decision to stay there for an instant longer. He didn't think Mason or Hahn would fire at his location once the Lexus arrived.

This is going to be close, he thought. He jumped up and slid over the hood of the Lexus as it turned into the parking lot's driveway. In that moment, he was inches from Darla Lyons's face. They looked at each other, and Nathan saw icy calmness in her eyes. It pissed him off. He'd wanted to smack the glass with his Sig, but there wasn't time.

Nathan landed hard, scraping his left elbow and banging a knee. He rolled back to the safety of the curb as the Lexus angled across the parking lot toward Mason's position.

Darla came to an abrupt halt in front of the SUV, shielding it from further gunfire. *Gutsy move.*

At least Mason and Hahn wouldn't let loose with those damned cannons again; the Lexus was in their way, but it didn't block Harv's line of sight.

Harv popped four more rounds.

Nathan watched the windshields of both vehicles take impacts. *Way to go, Harv. Good shooting.*

With a screeching crunch, the SUV tore free from the parked car. Clearly, Nathan's bullets into the engine block hadn't shut the vehicle down. He should've shot its tires. In reverse gear, Darla mirrored the SUV's movements, maintaining a protective position.

Nathan came up from his crouch, painted the laser on the Lexus's rear window, and sent three bullets through the glass. With a little luck, he'd score a hit, but Darla's sedan continued to speed away.

Boot World's security alarm continued to wail. As if answering a mating call, half a dozen car alarms added to the chaos of the scene.

Harv hustled over to his position. "I thought she was gonna run you over. Please don't ever do that again."

"I'll keep that in mind the next time I'm facing the same situation."

"They could still make a move against the ambulance."

"Holly, you copy?"

"I'm here."

"We're in the street. We need to reacquire the ambulance."

"I'll be there in twenty seconds."

"I'll drive. Slide over when you stop."

They saw headlights appear from an intersection.

"Is that you? Did you just turn onto the street?"

"Affirm."

"If the police get descriptions from anyone who just witnessed any of this, those two vehicles will be hard to miss."

Nathan nodded tightly. "We don't have time to pick up our brass."

"Good thing we have plenty of barrels and firing pins."

To gain a few seconds, they sprinted toward the approaching Mercedes.

Holly cut it pretty close slowing down, but she maintained control. The right front fender was bashed in, but not bad enough to wreck the tire. He watched her scramble over the center console into the passenger seat.

"That was some great driving," Nathan said.

"I second that," Harv added.

"Karen, you okay back there?" he asked.

She didn't respond.

"Harv?"

"She's okay."

"Holly, I need you to reload my Sig. It's in my right thigh pocket; the mags are in my left pocket. I'm going to push things to the limit, so everyone hang on. Call the intersections for me."

At each traffic light—red or green—Harv and Holly cleared him through.

"The proverbial cat's out of the bag," Harv said. "They know Toby's alive and we're protecting him."

"The question is, do they know it's *us*?"

"There's no way to know that without talking to Toby. Put yourself in Mason's shoes," Harv said. "What's his next move?"

"He's definitely worried he's lost containment. Now that he knows Toby's alive, he might flee the area, or go into hiding, or leave the country altogether. Conversely, he might conduct an all-out offensive and try to end the threat tonight, which means he could make a move against Toby while he's in the hospital."

"Based on Mason's actions tonight, we can safely assume he's desperate. We chased him away from Toby's apartment, hid Karen, and just stopped his attempt to kill Toby. We've become wild cards in his little war of cover-up."

"We may not be wild cards if Toby or Mara gave us up."

"Right," Harv agreed. "A lot of maybes, I know."

"Our primary goal is to save Toby's life, and Karen's. We'll worry about his testimony in court later. For now, we do our best to keep Mason away from him."

"We need to think about something. If Toby or Mara gave us up, Mason's next move might be to break into our corporate office to try to get our personal information. We should also post a few guards outside First Security. If nothing happens there tonight, we might be okay."

"For a while," Nathan said. "If Mason has our names and the name of our security company, he'll eventually be able to track us down."

"Not a nice thought. Hang on, I need to call Gavin and get things rolling."

Harv made the call. Security guards would be at the hospital and their headquarters within fifteen minutes or so.

Holly hadn't said much, and it worried him.

"Are you okay?"

"You know where I stand on things. As a federal agent, I'm sworn to uphold the law. I've now participated in a hit-and-run coupled with a firefight in the middle of a mini-mall. And you guys may have just killed one or more of BSI's personnel."

Nathan didn't say anything, ran another red light, and accelerated to seventy miles an hour. He hoped they'd reach Sharp Hospital's ER before Mason.

"Nate, Holly's right. Things have escalated. I'm not sure we should keep this under wraps any longer."

"I'm open to suggestions."

"For one," Holly said, "I should come clean with my boss. The longer I wait, the harder it will be to explain why I waited. Right now, I can claim things have been going at a hundred miles an hour and we're only now getting a break in the action. It's not entirely true, but I can live with it. It should be his decision how to proceed from here."

As much as Nathan wanted to disagree, he couldn't. She was right. Mason was out of control. It was evident he had no compunction about injuring or killing innocent people to keep his crimes secret.

Holly continued. "I also think you should call your father."

"I'm not sure about that," Nathan said.

"Why on earth not? Stone almost surely knows Tanner Mason's boss. He and Beaumont *need* to know what's going on. Furthermore, what Mason's done tonight easily rises to the level of 'domestic terrorism,' don't you think? It's within your father's domain." She paused for a breath. "Did I miss anything?"

"No, that sums it up nicely."

"Look, I'm not trying to beat you up. I know you'd prefer to deal with Mason privately, and that may still happen, but at this point I'm obligated to report what I know. It's the right thing to do. And so is calling your father."

"You're playing Harv's role."

She gave him a puzzled look.

"It's a compliment. Harv has always been the voice of reason and sanity in my world. He's saved my life more times than I can count. We should give you executive override privileges."

"Executive override?"

"Veto power over each other. I'll tell you about it later. We're here."

There was no sign of Mason's SUV or the Lexus; all was quiet. If any of Mason's stray bullets had found anyone, though, this tranquility would soon change. Nathan followed the signs to the

ER and saw the ambulance parked under the sheltered entrance, its rear doors open.

"It looks like they made it," Harv said.

"Let's find a place to park where we can keep an eye on the entrance."

"How about I find a place to watch from the inside?" Holly said. "All ERs have waiting rooms. What's the range of your radios?"

"With an open line of sight, about three miles, but they won't work well inside a big structure."

"Our phones will work."

"It's not ideal, but it's better than nothing. Harv?"

"I think Holly's right. We need someone on the inside, and Holly's a good choice. I doubt Mason got a good look at us during the ambulance shoot-out, but he got an even worse look at Holly back at Toby's apartment."

"What about your report?" Nathan asked. He didn't want to use Director Lansing's name in front of Karen. She'd kept quiet during their discussions, no longer crying but clearly withdrawn.

"Am I okay delaying it a little longer? Yes, but time is running out. We're talking less than thirty minutes. Deal?"

"Deal. Toby will probably be in surgery within the hour, so let's make sure Mason doesn't get to him before that. I seriously doubt he's fanatical enough to burst into a surgical suite and execute Toby on the operating table, but with his cowboy tactics tonight, who knows."

"At this point, I wouldn't put anything past him," Holly said.

"We'll maintain radio contact for as long as possible. Check in with us as you move deeper into the hospital. If the radios stop working, we'll switch to our cells." Nathan turned onto Frost Street and pulled over to the curb next to the main entrance. "Hop out right here. The main entrance is behind us. We'll let you know where we park. Reconnoiter all the ways into the ER, and pick a good spot to keep an eye on things. If anyone questions you, flash that FBI badge of yours."

"Yeah right."

"Stay safe, Special Agent Simpson." An idea came to him, but he shelved it for now. Maybe they'd try it later. He glanced in the rearview mirror as Holly slid out. Karen's expression hadn't changed. Nathan pivoted to face her. "You okay for a few more minutes?"

She nodded.

"Once we're certain Toby's okay, we'll set you up with one of our company cars and directions to our cabin. Call Cindy back and make arrangements to meet her somewhere later this morning. Make it a random place you both know, and whatever you do, don't go back to your house. Even with our security guard stationed there, Mason or his people might make a move."

"She won't have any clothes," Karen said. "Only what she's wearing."

Nathan pulled out his wallet and handed Karen a wad of large bills, mostly hundreds. "This isn't a loan; it's a gift." He usually kept two grand in his wallet for emergencies, and Karen's situation qualified.

"This is way too much money."

"That should tide you and Cindy over. There's plenty of food up at the cabin. The property's ownership is masked by a shell company on the East Coast. There's no way Mason can connect us to it. You'll be safe there. Just lie low and keep your cell phone charged." He read her expression. "You can pick up a charger at Walmart or Best Buy."

"I can't believe she's dead."

Nathan didn't say anything. He felt badly for her, but there were times—like now—when silence was best. Karen needed to mourn her friend's death in her own way.

In the passenger-side mirror, he watched Holly disappear into the hospital.

A few seconds later, her voice sounded off in his ear speaker. *"Radio check."*

"Copy." He turned into the parking structure and pushed the button for a ticket. He noticed the security camera, but believed it wouldn't be a live feed.

"Holly's your girlfriend?" Karen asked.

"Yes."

"Does she know about us, I mean, you know . . . what we used to do?"

He turned into the driveway leading to the ER and the parking garage. "No."

"Are you going to tell her?"

"That wouldn't be my first choice. Look, Karen, I don't regret anything. You're my friend and you always will be, but Holly's helped me in ways I can't even begin to describe."

"Have you ever told her that?" Karen asked.

"Sort of, I mean not in those exact words, but yes."

"You never saw Mara again after you met Holly," said Harv, "so you haven't betrayed her. I'm sure she hasn't told you about every man she's ever been involved with."

"No, she hasn't, and I haven't asked. Hang on . . ." He answered Holly's latest radio check-in.

Harv said, "Your relationship with Holly has been tested on every level imaginable. A couple of years ago, you guys fought side by side in a gunfight. She's proven herself."

"That's not what I'm worried about."

"You don't want her sticking her neck out for us again."

Nathan didn't respond.

"Look, she can handle herself."

"You're right on both counts, but that's still not it."

"You're worried she'll reject you because of me and Mara," Karen said.

"I'm not worried about getting hurt; I'm worried about hurting her. I should've told Holly about you guys a long time ago. If I had, I wouldn't be feeling this way."

"Nate, that's not fair," Harv said. "I haven't told Candace everything from my past before I met her. Especially our . . . questionable evening in Singapore."

"Don't remind me." Nathan pulled into a parking spot on the second level where they had a perfect view of the ER's entrance.

"Karen, Harv and I need to talk. We'll be right outside the car."

They got out and had walked a few paces away when his cell rang.

It was Holly.

"Hey," she said, "you didn't respond to my last radio check, so I'm assuming you didn't hear it."

"No, we didn't. What's going on in there?"

"It's quiet. A few people are in the waiting area, but none of them look like BSI military contractors, whatever they're supposed to look like."

"Okay, good. We're on the second level in the parking structure due east of the ER. We pulled into a spot overlooking the entrance area, so you can't miss us. Stand by. I'll call you back in a few minutes."

Nathan ended the call.

"A lot of our strategy," said Harv, "will depend on whether Toby or Mara gave us up."

"Yeah, I know; if either of them told Mason who we are, we could be fighting a defensive battle, which makes protecting Toby and Karen that much harder. WITSEC might be the only option for them."

"Well, she'll be talking to Lansing soon. We'll see what he wants to do." Nathan looked at a yellow cab heading toward the freeway. "I hope she'll be okay. I mean, she'll have to come clean with Lansing about everything. Holly can say she objected, but she still went along with not reporting it right away."

"We have a personal history with Lansing. Holly does too. He's well aware of our . . . unorthodox methods." Harv half smiled. "He flew all the way out here to visit your hospital bed after that mercenary's bullet skipped off that block of granite you call a head."

Nathan didn't say anything. For some reason, he was seeing the bodies on the soccer field . . . Something about them . . .

"My point is, Lansing isn't going to throw Holly under the bus. In fact, he'll be grateful we've uncovered all of this."

"Don't be too sure about that," Nathan said. "It could be the end of the FBI's contract with Beaumont, and it's likely to cause embarrassment and become a major hassle for Lansing."

"Better he finds out about this before it gets plastered on the nightly news. He'll be grateful he's hearing about it from us first."

"True enough. Do you think my dad's aware of the pending contract?"

"Depending on how close he is with Beaumont, I wouldn't be surprised if he recommended BSI. Why not call and ask him yourself?"

"I will . . . *we* will. You're not off the hook on this one."

"I'm totally okay with that. I like your dad. Now about Toby . . ."

"Got it covered. Here's what I want to do."

CHAPTER 17

Speeding away from the ambush site, Mason cursed his bad luck. He was so close to scoring the perfect heist, but that idiot Haynes had threatened to bring it all crashing down.

Bad luck, he told himself again.

Driving with a spiderwebbed windshield sucked. Every source of light reflected from every crack, making the glass look like fireworks sparklers. Mason was tempted to pull over and kick the glass free, but he didn't want to take the time. He was convinced the second shooter had purposely nailed the driver's side of both their windshields. That guy had also been fast—he'd fired four times in less than three seconds and scored four perfect hits.

Law enforcement or military?

"How you doing, Chip?"

"I'll live. It wasn't a high-powered round. Probably a nine mil."

"Still hurts."

"The asshole taunted me."

Mason said, "I heard him. At least he didn't call you by name. We need to find out who they are and how they know about us."

"It's possible Haynes told someone before we got there, but we worked him over pretty good. His girlfriend too."

"Either they're a whole lot tougher than they acted, or we weren't rough enough."

"What about the text Haynes's girlfriend sent to her friend?" Hahn asked. "Maybe this Karen woman called them in."

"We'll work on the cell phones we took from Haynes's apartment and see what we can glean. Right now, we need to take side streets and clear the area before every cop in San Diego arrives. There's no way we can return to our headquarters or our apartments. Without knowing who's protecting Toby, we can't risk it."

"Do we make one last attempt to kill Haynes?"

Mason thought for a moment. "He's inside the hospital by now, and SDPD is on the way or already there. We stick to the plan. We'll exchange our vehicles at the safe house and proceed with the next phase of the operation."

"That's a long drive. We could get pulled over."

Chip was right. Escondido was a twenty-minute drive—all freeway. Their windshields were still intact, but a CHP officer couldn't miss the wrecked glass. Still, the odds of encountering a state trooper were low. "It's our best option. We need to regroup. Call Darla and let her know the plan."

While Chip made the call, Mason thought about their situation. That dumbass Haynes had caused more trouble than he'd ever know. Mason blamed himself for being so careless at Haynes's apartment. He should've checked for a pulse. How could he be alive? It defied all odds. With a little luck, the guy's brain was scrambled, and he'd be a turnip for the rest of his life. Or at least a victim of serious memory loss. But then again, tonight was no time to trust luck.

He heard Chip end the call. "Darla did well. That was a gutsy move placing herself between us and the gunmen."

Mason nodded. "She's fearless, all right."

"How many are we facing?" Chip asked.

"At least three. I'm pretty sure the woman who ran up the sidewalk outside Haynes's apartment was with the two gunmen. I only saw the guy charging you. He was a big sucker, probably six five or six."

"At Haynes's apartment, he painted me, but he didn't fire. I'm also thinking the other guy purposely fired into the air. Did you get a look at him or see any muzzle flashes?"

"Not him, but I saw the flashes; they came from behind a parked car near the end of the block. Given the accuracy these guys just displayed, I'd agree he purposely missed me at Haynes's apartment."

"That big guy drilled me at the ambulance. Why didn't he shoot me before?"

With Darla's headlights right behind them, Mason sped down the on-ramp onto the freeway. "Because he hadn't been inside Haynes's apartment yet."

"Yeah, that would definitely piss him off," Chip said. "Especially if he knows Haynes. Could he be a Marine?"

Mason thought for a moment. "Yeah, that's a strong possibility and it might give us a starting point to find him. I got the distinct impression he's a formidable player. He felt like Special Forces. The guy charged us with only a handgun."

"The woman with them was dressed differently," Hahn said. "She wasn't wearing tactical clothing like the guy on the grass. She had on a biker jacket."

"Darla didn't report seeing her, but I'm pretty sure she's with them. Someone drove their vehicle away from the ambulance, and it was probably her. I couldn't see any facial details, but I'm pretty sure the big guy who painted you with the laser at Haynes's apartment is the same guy who just shot you."

"If they're former or active SOFs, that's very bad news."

"Tell me about it."

"What about Haynes?"

"He complicates things, but we proceed as planned. We just have to make sure whoever's running interference doesn't reacquire us. The safe house is our best bet. We've got ninety minutes to exchange these wrecked vehicles and execute phase two."

Hahn gave a tight nod.

Mason thought for a moment. "Actually, let's make a quick detour. Get Darla on the phone again."

CHAPTER 18

Kaunakakai Ferry Terminal,
Molokai, Hawaii—five days earlier

Using only thrusters, the captain of *Yoonsuh* maneuvered his ship into position at the end of the dock. The *Molokai Princess* was moored farther down, but there was plenty of room for the ROK private yacht. This part of the island looked quite different from the other side. By all definitions, it was a desert. The mountains made their own rain, but little of it reached the port unless a large storm passed through the area.

As a treat to his passenger and crew, the captain had approached Molokai from the north and navigated around the island's west side. The sea cliffs of Molokai were among the most spectacular on earth. The delay had been minimal, and the captain planned to make up the lost time on the final leg. A sightseeing helicopter had buzzed his ship, but he wasn't concerned; it happened all the time in Hawaiian waters.

Depending on its size, the refueling truck might need to make multiple trips to deliver twenty-five thousand gallons of diesel, and it could take hours to make the transfer. Refueling at Honolulu would've been faster and easier, but also more visible. He supposed a huge purchase like this could raise suspicion, but luxury yachts weren't unheard of in the waters of Molokai. Besides, the fuel company loved the business; it wasn't every day they sold a swimming pool's worth of diesel.

Since no one was getting on or off the ship, he didn't expect to see a customs agent. If an agent happened to show up, the first officer would be happy to give him a tour. More often than not, the inspectors were merely curious, and the captain couldn't blame them. *Yoonsuh*'s elegance and grandeur was a far cry from the rusty old trawlers and cargo ships passing through the area. Charm went a long way in avoiding secondary searches.

The fuel truck rumbled over to the ship. Pleasantries were exchanged, and the refueling hose pulled aboard. Thankfully, it had a bigger diameter than some he'd seen.

Three hours later, the transfer was complete. Not surprisingly, no customs officials or any other federal agents had arrived to inspect his ship. After conducting a head count, the captain maneuvered the ship away from the terminal and set sail for North America.

CHAPTER 19

Nathan entered Sharp Memorial Hospital and found Holly across from the reception counter. Her expression showed puzzlement at his unannounced appearance.

She got up. "Did you try to call me? My cell didn't ring."

"Change in plans. We're going to flash your FBI badge and ask to speak with the ER doctor on duty."

"Okay . . ."

"Since we've agreed to bring Lansing aboard, you can now act in an official FBI manner, can you not?"

"Yes, absolutely."

"You'll take the lead, and I'll be your colleague. Cook up a fake name for me."

"Any preferences?"

"Not really."

They marched down the corridor into the ER and approached the receptionist.

Holly pulled her badge. "I'm FBI Special Agent Holly Simpson, and this is Special Agent Edward Albus. We'd like to speak with the ER physician about a gunshot patient who came in a few minutes ago. It's extremely urgent."

"No problem, ma'am." She focused on Nathan's face. "She, ah . . . might be with the patient. Please wait here. I'll be right back." She left the reception desk and disappeared into the ER.

"Think this is going to work?" Nathan whispered.

"I have no idea. Was this your idea or Harvey's?"

"Mine."

"Should've figured. I think the combination of your blue eyes and scars rattled her. She either wanted to run away from you or have your children. I have no idea which."

"I do."

Dressed in blue scrubs, a tall woman came through the door. Pulled back in a ponytail, her hair was the same color as Holly's—dark brown, bordering on black. She had kind eyes behind rectangular glasses. The receptionist stood off to the side while Holly reintroduced herself and Nathan—Edward—and thanked the doctor for coming out.

"I'm Dr. Lynne Thelan." She locked eyes with Nathan, her expression uncertain. It wasn't hard to read her thoughts.

He smiled and the tension vanished. "I lost a bet," he said.

Holly took the lead. "Your gunshot patient's an important witness in an ongoing FBI investigation. If he's conscious, we really need to speak with him. It's life-and-death urgent."

"He's in X-ray right now. If you make it brief, I'll allow it, but we don't normally do this, even for law enforcement."

"Can you give us his condition? Is he conscious?"

"Yes, but he's been drifting in and out."

"Is he in danger of dying?"

"His life signs are stable, and we're not seeing any signs of brain hemorrhaging, which are both good signs. Look, I don't want to be presumptuous, but it's quite clear he's been interrogated. He has abrasions on both his wrists and ankles. Several of his fingers have been broken or dislocated. He's got a broken nose, lacerations to his ears, cheeks, and lips. He's also sustained a severe concussion. Somebody worked him over pretty hard."

Holly gave a tight nod. "For everyone's safety, we can't comment on that."

"An SDPD detective is also on the way. He wants to talk with Mr. Haynes, but he may not get here in time; we need to get Mr. Haynes prepped for surgery. The detective also wants to talk to the paramedics who brought him in."

Holly feigned a curious look.

"They were caught in the middle of gunfire on the way over here."

"Are they okay?"

"Yes, but a sedan sideswiped an SUV right in front of them, and they were forced to flee the scene. They said they heard a machine gun."

"Sounds like it's going to be a busy night for SDPD."

"When it's busy for them, it's usually busy for us. Like I said, I'm afraid your window to talk with Mr. Haynes will be extremely brief. Follow me, and please keep your voices down; we have an infant in there."

Nathan and Holly trailed Dr. Thelan into the ER.

"There's your man."

An orderly pushed Toby's gurney into a stall.

Toby's eyes were closed and a gauze bandage encircled his head just above his brow line. Nathan hoped Toby was just protecting his eyes against the overhead fluorescents, not unconscious. Nathan knew from firsthand experience that bright light and concussions didn't go well together.

In the stall, she put a hand on Toby's shoulder. "Mr. Haynes, can you hear me? It's Dr. Thelan. You're back in the ER."

Toby's eyes opened.

"I have two FBI agents who want to speak with you. Are you okay with that? May I share your medical information with them?"

He nodded, which caused a wince of pain.

While Dr. Thelan typed her password into the computer, Nathan stepped forward and winked at the patient. "It's *Edward*, Toby. How are you feeling?"

"Where's Mara? Is she okay?"

"I don't know." Nathan hated the lie, but couldn't risk an emotional meltdown right now. He'd tell Toby the truth later, after his surgery.

"She'd be in here if she was alive." Toby looked at the doctor. "Right?"

Dr. Thelan didn't say anything.

Nathan decided to come clean. Fighting back his own emotions, he said, "Mara didn't make it. They shot her . . . just like you."

Toby's face became a mask of pain. His mouth opened, but no words came out.

"I'm sorry," Holly said, putting a hand on Toby's shoulder.

Nathan knew he was seconds from losing it. He instinctively summoned a burst of rage, allowing the red energy to radiate through his body. He used it like a blowtorch to burn away fear and uncertainty. Incinerated, the weaker feelings fell victim to aggression and resolve. Nathan didn't relish killing anyone in cold blood, but exceptions could be—and *would* be—made in this case. An innocent life had been stolen, snuffed out by a phony hard-ass who believed the rules didn't apply to him. *Well, Mason, old pal, you're not the only one who breaks the rules.*

"He killed our baby," Toby cried softly.

"With your help, we'll put him in prison for the rest of his life." Nathan glanced at Holly, who nodded for him to continue. "Toby, to protect Dr. Thelan, we have to be careful what we say, but we need to know something. Did you give the man who shot you our names?"

"No. He kept asking if I told anyone, over and over. Mara didn't talk either. They had her in the baby's room. I couldn't see her." He wiped a tear with his wrapped fingers. "They were hurting her. I heard her say she sent a text to Karen. But I didn't know she did that, I swear. Did they kill Karen too?"

"She's safe," he said. "We got to her first."

Nathan knew his safety had been purchased at a high price. Both Toby and Mara had endured torture to keep his identity secret. Mara had likely given up the text to buy additional time because she knew Nathan was coming back, but her white knight hadn't arrived in time. *Those damned breakfast sandwiches and coffee* . . . Part of him knew he wasn't being fair to himself, but that didn't make it any easier.

Nathan looked at Holly, then to Toby. "You said something to us earlier tonight. It sounded like 'med hall.' What does that mean? Are you taking any medications?"

Toby reached up and grimaced, then let his hand fall. "Metal. I probably said 'metal.'"

"I think I know what Mr. Haynes is talking about," Dr. Thelan said. "Take a look."

Toby's X-rays were on the computer screen. No one said anything; they just stared in stunned disbelief.

The doctor turned toward Toby. "How did you get this?"

"Car wreck at Camp Pendleton. I almost died."

"Based on what I'm seeing here, I'm feeling pretty good about a full recovery." She pointed to some small, irregular white spots on the screen. "The bullets fragmented and didn't penetrate the cranial plate. Titanium?" she asked.

Toby nodded.

"We'll have to remove the pieces, but that's superficial surgery. Hopefully nothing more will be required. How's your pain level?"

"My fingers and nose hurt a little, but I'm okay. I can't believe I'll never see her again."

In Toby's apartment, Nathan had seen several indications that Toby was Christian, but now wasn't the time to say he'd see Mara again.

"When they find out I'm alive, they're going to come after me, aren't they?"

"We'll protect you," Holly said. "Additional agents are on the way."

The doctor turned from the computer and looked at Toby. "I don't want to cut this short, but the neurosurgeon will be here any moment. I still want his opinion on your condition."

Holly shook the doctor's hand. "Thank you, Doctor. We know you didn't have to do this."

"I'm a big fan of law enforcement. My brother's a deputy sheriff in LA County."

Nathan also thanked her and shook hands.

Holly asked, "Will you please keep our visit confidential?"

"As far as I'm concerned, you guys were never here. I'll tell our staff the same thing."

"Do you have hospital security guards?" Holly asked.

"Yes. They'll see that Mr. Haynes is protected as well as possible until your agents arrive, or SDPD."

They thanked the doctor again and said their good-byes. Toby's glazed expression didn't change as they left. Nathan felt bad for the big man. *His world is shattered. Empty. He'll leave the hospital alive, but alone.* Nathan intended to help Toby get back on his feet, starting with a full-time job—and immediate benefits. He wouldn't allow Mason to further destroy Toby's life.

Walking out of the ER, Nathan looked over his shoulder. "SDPD is going to walk in here any minute. Even though Dr. Thelan said she'd keep our visit under wraps, it's probably best if I'm not here when they arrive."

"Lansing?" she asked.

"You're liable to wake him up; it's just after oh five hundred back there."

"He'll take my call."

"You sound certain."

"Let's just say I work closely with him."

"Harv thinks I should call my father at the same time you're talking to Lansing."

"That's a good idea." She took his hand. "Nathan, there's something I've been meaning to tell you. It's about my new job."

"Yeah, I've kinda sensed that."

"It's bigger than I let on."

"Okay . . ."

"I'm the new chief of staff. I report directly to Lansing."

"That's awesome, Holly. But why the hesitation to tell me?"

"There's more. I've replaced Special Agent Leaf Watson."

"Leaf Watson . . . Why is that name familiar?"

"He was the FBI's seat on the CDT."

Nathan couldn't hide his shock. "You're on my father's committee?"

"I've been wanting to tell you."

"Then why didn't you?"

She didn't say anything.

"You don't need my approval, Holly. You know that, right?"

She nodded.

"Is that how you know so much about Mason and BSI?"

"Yes."

He let go of her hand. "Look, I think we should make our respective phone calls." He hadn't intended to put that much ice in his voice, but it happened anyway.

"Yeah, I think you're right. We'll talk about this later, okay?"

"Sure. No problem. I need to update Harv and take care of Karen."

Her expression changed at hearing Karen's name. "Are you okay?"

He wasn't okay. Far from it, but he forced a smile. "I'm fine, Holly. You're still our eyes in here." With that, he left the ER's waiting room. Walking out the front door, he felt a chasm forming. He rounded the corner to get out of Holly's line of sight and stood in the rain, letting the drops hit his face.

It was just like his dad to do something like this. He always had to be the big man on campus. A song from *Annie Get Your Gun* invaded his thoughts. The lyrics mocked him, made him feel snubbed: "Anything you can do, I can do better; I can do anything better than you." *Forget it,* he told himself. *It's nothing.* But it didn't feel like *nothing.* It felt like a betrayal. Maybe that was too strong a word. He didn't feel betrayed, he felt . . . what? Excluded. Deliberately kept in the dark. But for what possible reason? His father wasn't known for transparency—all too typical of career politicians. They never showed all their cards. Senator McBride had a pool of more than thirty thousand FBI personnel, and he chose Holly. Why?

He pushed the radio's transmit button harder than he wanted to. "I'm on my way back. Two minutes."

"Copy, two minutes."

"When will our security guards get here?"

"Ten minutes."

"Meet me outside the car; we need to talk."

"You got it."

Nathan scanned the area as he walked along the sidewalk and tried to put Holly out of his thoughts. She should've told him about her new position with Lansing and her seat on the CDT right away. So why hadn't she? Why hold it back? Being the chief of staff of the FBI had to be an important position, and an even more important stepping stone in her career. He wished he'd handled the news better, but it had caught him by surprise. Thinking about this would have to wait. Right now, he needed to stay focused and get Karen secured with a company car. When he reached the driveway leading to the ER, Harv waved from the parking structure. Nathan returned the wave, then jogged up the ramp to the second level. He huddled with Harv a few car lengths away, where they could still see the ER's entrance.

"How's Karen doing?"

"She's been quiet. I'm giving her space."

"I spoke with Toby. He didn't tell Mason about us. Mara didn't either. We're lucky Mason didn't get his hands on Karen." Nathan gave his friend a quick update on the X-ray he'd seen showing the plate in Toby's head.

"God bless 'em," Harv said. "How did he take the news about Mara?"

"Not well. We need to get closure for him, Harv. Nothing else will do."

"Count on it."

"I wanted to ask him more questions about Mason, but the doctor cut us short."

Harv nodded. "Where was Holly? You said *I*, not *we*."

He squinted and didn't say anything.

"What happened?"

"Holly's new job? She finally told me what it is. She's Lansing's chief of staff."

"That's a big promotion. From a SAC to chief of staff?"

"It gets better. She's replaced Leaf Watson."

"Leaf Watson," Harv said slowly. "Are you saying Holly's the FBI's seat on the CDT?"

"Yep."

"How do you feel about that?"

"It feels like I'm now sharing the most important person in my life with my father."

"Try to see it from Holly's perspective."

"I'm trying, Harv, I really am."

"It's a huge deal for her. She's now got a position on the most prestigious law enforcement panel in the country. She has personal contacts in every federal agency."

"Yeah, I guess. I just wish she'd told me."

"Based on your reaction, I can see why she hesitated."

Nathan didn't respond. He didn't want this distraction right now; he had vermin to kill.

Harv said, “We’re going to need her help to track down Mason. Are you guys okay?”

“I don’t know; it got a little chilly in there.”

“Look, every relationship has friction at one time or another. Everything will be okay. Try not to dwell on it.”

“I’ll be okay, Harv, thanks. We need to get Karen outta here. Do you mind taking her over to First Security and getting her fixed up with one of our company cars and the directions to the cabin? I need to stay here and watch Holly’s back.”

“I’m not jazzed about splitting up, but I’m giving it low odds that Mason will make another move against Toby tonight. He would’ve done it by now. I’ll call you from the office when I’m on my way back. Our security guards will probably pull into this structure to park. Let me do this: I’ll contact them and tell them to use their personal vehicles so there’s no visible link to our company. I’ll also tell them to park right here so you can use one of their vehicles if you need it for any reason.”

“Thanks, Harv.”

“Here, take these.” Harv handed him two extra mags for his Sig. “I know you’re worried about Holly, but things will work out. It’s just a temporary glitch.”

“Before you go, I need to—*we* need to call Senator McBride.”

Harv sighed. “Okay, but don’t call him ‘Senator McBride,’ and try not to be hostile.”

“Me? Hostile?”

CHAPTER 20

An hour after the ambulance shoot-out, Mason, Hahn, and Darla arrived in the Gaslamp Quarter of downtown San Diego and found the streets abandoned. This place wasn't Times Square. The second phase of tonight's operation would be ten times more dangerous than phase one. There was no margin for error. A mistake could mean death for one or all of them.

Mason parked two blocks east of Alisio's nightclub and verified they had everything they needed. Each of them checked their waist packs and confirmed they were good to go. If they crossed paths with a cop while they walked over to the club, they were staying in the Marriott and just taking a late-night stroll around the block. Mason knew how to turn on the charm when needed. Aside from the late hour, they didn't look terribly out of place and they certainly didn't resemble vagrants. If stopped by the police, the contents of their waist packs would be impossible to explain, but Mason wasn't worried about a random search—the cops had no reason to suspect them of anything. With all the action they'd created north of here, they didn't anticipate even seeing a cop.

As planned, Darla hurried ahead of them to find a good spot to watch the street in front of Alisio's nightclub.

The Gaslamp Quarter was composed of older, remodeled low-rise buildings and more modern high-rises. Petco Park, home of the Padres, sat only a few blocks away. Before the redevelopment, this area had been a slum. Now it was a thriving area of retail shops, hotels, and restaurants.

Their target building sat directly ahead, on the opposite corner of the next intersection. Not surprisingly, all the businesses were closed, even the taverns and bars. As far as they could determine, they were the only people in sight. Reflecting the name of the area, the streets were well lit by old-fashioned gas-lamp streetlights, retrofitted with modern bulbs.

Darla's voice came through their ear speakers. *"I've got eyes on you. I'm behind a white pickup with a lumber rack directly across the street from the entrance to the club. No one's around."*

Mason clicked his radio.

Walking past the main entrance to Alisio's nightclub, they heard a deep, rhythmic thump coming from the inside. Their entry point was around the corner, a five-foot-wide pedestrian walkway between the brick buildings. It also doubled as the delivery access for the nightclub. From their interrogation of Alisio's man and his South Korean friend earlier, they knew the narrow alley was protected by an iron gate during evening hours to prevent drunks and derelicts from using it as a public restroom. But the gate would be unlocked tonight, just as it was every Monday and Thursday night between 0330 and 0400.

Alisio's man had told them he'd witnessed the after-hours exchange many times. The drug dealer would push a button next to the door, and within half a minute, an exterior light would snap on and the door would open. After a ritualistic fist-to-fist greeting, a plastic grocery bag went in and an envelope came out. The delivery boy would then tuck the envelope into his coat and leave the alley. A short time later, a short, stocky guy named Fergie came out and locked the gate to the pedestrian alley. The transaction always took less than thirty seconds. Alisio's man had been so willing to talk, he'd even told Mason that the blow was top quality.

Mason looked across the street toward the pickup, offered a compact wave, and received two flashes from Darla's penlight. "Any sign of our delivery boy?"

"Negative, all quiet."

"Check in as soon as you—"

"Shit, he's early! He's crossing the street at the corner."

"How long do we have?"

"Ten seconds."

"No problem. Stand by."

Chip sprang into action and opened the gate.

"I'll take him," Mason said. "Go."

Chip sprinted down the alley and ducked behind a recycle bin.

"Darla, give me a countdown from five."

His radio clicked.

Mason flattened himself against the wall of the building. The drug dealer would appear from his left.

"Five . . . four . . . three . . ."

Mason went through a mental checklist. He'd done this dozens of times. The key was being aggressive and decisive.

"Two . . . one!"

The dealer rounded the corner.

Mason made his move.

In less than two seconds, he had his right hand clamped over the guy's mouth while simultaneously forcing his victim's left wrist up between his shoulder blades.

The plastic bag fell to the ground.

Mason forced his immobilized prey into the alcove and shoved him against the open gate. Dressed in a dark Padres jacket and new jeans, the guy almost looked respectable. His skin matched the color of the sky.

"Listen up," said Mason. "If you cooperate, I won't hurt you. Conversely, if you try anything, you'll be in a sling for three months. Give me a nod of understanding."

When the guy didn't respond, Mason drove his wrist higher and heard a grunt.

"Give me a nod of understanding."

The guy complied.

Darla's voice came through his speaker. *"You're good; all quiet."*

He turned slightly and offered Darla a wink, knowing she had binoculars. After kicking the bag inside the gate, he used his foot to close it. Keeping his face out of head-butting range, he marched the guy down the alley about halfway to the freight door leading into the nightclub. Based on the scrawny build of this clown, he didn't expect a lot of resistance.

"You can relax. I don't want your drugs, or whatever you're peddling." Mason felt the guy loosen up a little. "If you do exactly as I say, you won't be harmed."

When they reached the trash cans, Chip stood up and shoved his pistol under the man's chin. Together, they pinned him against the brick.

"I'm going to remove my hand from your mouth. Screaming or yelling will result in pain. Yours."

The dealer nodded. "Shit, man, do you know who you're jacking?"

"Why don't you tell me."

The guy looked back and forth between Hahn and Mason. "This here's Snowman's territory."

"Well, consider us a heat wave. Now shut the fuck up, act like you always do, and press the button. If you so much as twitch, we'll pop you twice in the skull." Mason looked at Chip. "A demonstration, please."

Chip moved the suppressed pistol in front of the dealer's face, pointed it toward the wall, and pulled the trigger. A small chip flew from the bricks across the alley.

The man flinched, anticipating the report, but no such sound occurred. The spent .22 long-range casing bounced off the man's forehead and clinked on the ground. Chip picked it up.

"Whoa . . . that's some trick."

"That's right: no one will hear you die and the rats will've eaten your lips by the time five-oh finds you."

"Okay, man. Okay."

"We don't want you or your drugs. We want in there." Mason nodded to the metal delivery door down the alley.

"Aw, man," the guy said with resignation. "This is one of my best customers."

"That should be the least of your worries. Now, listen carefully. You will act like you always do. If we suspect you're pulling anything cute, like giving Fergie a secret warning signal, it will be the last thing you ever do. We know everything, even your special fist pump."

"All right, man; I'm just glad you ain't five-oh."

Mason ignored the idiotic comment. "If Fergie doesn't open up, we'll assume you warned him and pain will happen. Are we clear on everything?"

"Yeah, I got it."

"We'll be on either side of you out of camera shot. You've got no place to run." Mason pulled a thick wad of hundred-dollar bills from his coat pocket. "Two grand. It's yours if you play along. If not . . . we keep the money and you get dead."

"You serious about the money?"

"It's yours."

"Shit, man. I ain't gonna make trouble. But you gonna have to knock me around a little before you leave."

Mason exchanged a look with Chip.

"Snowman's gonna think I jacked him otherwise."

"All right, you play along and we'll cover for you."

"Nothin' in the teeth, okay? I just bought this smile."

"Depends on how well you do."

Mason keyed his radio. "Status?"

"No change."

"Come on over."

The muted thump of music they'd heard through the front door was barely audible back here.

Darla arrived a few seconds later. Keeping her face away from the camera, she walked through its cone of vision. If anyone watched the feed, they might come out to investigate who just walked past the door. That would be fine with Mason; they'd make their move then.

"We're going to sit tight for a minute or two," Mason said. "Remain quiet." He removed clear goggles from his waist pack and put them on. Next, he secured a black bandanna over his nose and mouth. Hahn and Darla followed suit. If they were somehow caught on camera, they couldn't be identified. Mason's ponytail was tucked under his ball cap.

Mason listened to the music emanating from inside and didn't hear any change in volume. Ninety seconds later, he let go of the dealer and shoved him toward the door. "Press the button."

Mason and Hahn assumed a back-to-back position with Hahn facing the alley's entrance and Mason facing the dealer. Mason studied the man closely while he pushed the button. Fifteen seconds later, they heard the music grow in volume, then go quiet again. Mason believed someone had just opened and closed the stockroom door to the nightclub beyond.

Time seemed to stretch as the dealer stood there, looking back and forth in a paranoid manner. It looked believable, exactly how a drug dealer might act.

A metallic clank echoed.

Stale cigarette smoke wafted through the door when it opened a few inches.

Mason listened for a chain or hotel-type security latch but heard nothing.

He sprang forward and shouldered the door inward. It smacked the guy's forehead and knocked him off his feet.

Half a second later Mason was inside, pointing his suppressed weapon at the downed man's face. The guy reached out in a futile effort to block the bullets. Mason fired through the man's spread fingers.

The dealer bolted.

Chip kicked his ankle, sending him sprawling.

The man crabbed backward, desperation in his voice. "We had a deal! What the fuck!"

Chip's gun jumped several times, and Mason watched the dealer's legs shudder in a classic death dance, something he'd seen many times. Chip dragged the mortally wounded dealer inside and laid him next to the other man, presumably Fergie, given the giant gold *F* hanging at his chest.

Staying low, Mason pivoted and painted his laser onto the interior camera above the door, dispatching it with a single round. If someone were watching a bank of monitors, they couldn't have missed what had happened. Mason gave Darla a hand signal, so she rushed through the delivery door and flattened herself against the opposite wall of the stockroom.

Within five seconds of breaching the door, they were all inside the building and the exterior camera watching the alley now showed what it always showed.

Mason issued another hand signal. Chip advanced to several columns of stacked chairs and pointed his pistol at the door leading deeper into the nightclub.

He took a few seconds to orient himself. The room was rectangular, maybe twenty feet long and ten feet wide. The only source of light was a single bare bulb on the opposite wall. On the concrete floor, a stained path led to the door where Darla waited.

From their interrogation of Alisio's man earlier, they knew the basic layout of the club, including the location of the three cameras in the main room.

They formed a huddle. "We take out anyone we find in there. I doubt we'll find any children, but they're off-limits. No stun grenades unless absolutely necessary. Pick up spent brass."

Staying off to the side, Mason turned the knob and cracked the door leading into the main room.

The thumping increased by a factor of five, but he wasn't concerned. The techno jam actually helped them. He scanned the pool tables and saw no one. Although it looked like no one was around, he couldn't be sure until he opened the door wider.

On first glance, it seemed Alisio spared no expense. The place had a high-class look. Leather furniture surrounded blue-granite tables. The light fixtures above the pool tables were dimmed, but they still created pyramids of light in the suspended smoke.

Moving ultra slowly, he eased the door open. The other end of the room held an elevated stage. The entire west wall had been converted into a bar with every imaginable brand of liquor on glass shelves. Situated between the stage and pool tables, an empty dance floor waited, complete with chrome poles for exotic dancers. He felt Chip tuck in tight behind him. Since no one sprinted across the room with machine guns, Mason believed their entry had gone undetected. Using fingers, he counted down from three.

When his fist closed, he rushed into the main room and pivoted to the right. Chip was right behind him, protecting his left. Darla took the middle. For several seconds they held that position.

Nothing moved.

The entire ground floor looked deserted.

"Everyone take a camera," he whispered.

They activated their lasers and had no trouble acquiring and destroying them. With the cameras out of commission, they rushed across the dance floor to the hall leading to the restrooms. Off to their right, the main entrance foyer was dark except for the bleed light coming through large transom windows above the carved-wood doors. *This place is incredible.*

He signaled for Chip and Darla to clear the restrooms.

They returned a few seconds later.

The door leading to the stairs was locked. *Shit!* He'd hoped it wouldn't be. This complicated things.

Playing a hunch, he sent Chip back to the man who'd opened the door to look for a set of keys.

Darla remained quiet and focused. With her back to him, she guarded the other end of the hall and the main entrance beyond.

Before reappearing in the hall, Chip issued a soft whistle to Darla, who returned it. With a little luck, one of these keys would unlock the door. Mason pointed to a key that showed the most wear. It didn't work. Chip tried several more with the same result.

Chip was about to try another when they all heard it: the unmistakable thuds of someone descending the stairs.

CHAPTER 21

The expensively dressed man felt restless. They'd had a night of near-record attendance and liquor sales, and he planned to celebrate with several fat lines of the best coke money could buy. "Call Fergie and ask what's going on. He should have our blow by now unless that Padre-loving dipshit is late again."

"He's been on time ever since you slapped him around."

"I feel the need . . . the need for speed!" The well-dressed man high-fived the club's manager and winked at the hookers on the couch. They'd trade off later, but he wanted first dibs on the swanky blonde. Her legs could wrap around the building. At a grand each, they'd do it all. Everything.

The club manager dictated a text: "*Where are you?*"

"Forget texting: just call him."

The manager complied. "He's not answering."

"Check the cameras. He'd better not be shortstopping down there."

From his office, the manager called out, "They aren't working again."

"All of 'em?"

"The back door's working. I'll call the security company in the morning and get this fixed."

"Go find Fergie and tell him to get his dumb ass up here."

***

The descending thuds got louder.

Mason quickly changed weapons, pointed to himself, then to the door.

Darla and Chip nodded and backed up a few steps.

Standing off to the side, Mason waited like a predatory eel.

The door swung outward, in Chip's direction.

When the man stepped into the hall, Mason used the same technique as he had on the delivery boy. He clamped his left hand over the man's mouth, only this time he didn't pin an arm. He drove his knife into the man's torso just under the rib cage and perforated the guy's lung.

Keeping his hand in place, Mason lowered his victim to the floor. He reached out with a foot, nudged Darla, and mouthed: *Three in the head.*

Without hesitating, Darla took careful aim to avoid hitting his hand. Mason turned away as Darla's suppressed pistol flashed. The sound was so faint no one upstairs could have heard it over the music.

Without being prompted, Chip positioned himself just inside the door, where he could watch the staircase leading up to the office.

"I'll take point," he whispered. "Darla, you're down here watching our six."

"You got it."

He liked that about her—she didn't question orders. "Chip, when we make our move up there, I'll take left side of the room, you take the right." Mason wiped the wet knife on the dying man's shirt and sheathed it. With his .22 in hand again, he started up the stairs and sensed Hahn's presence two steps behind. The same music emanated from the office, but not as loud.

Halfway up, he stopped and put Hahn on hold. He looked behind to see what his backdrop was. Good, a dark wall and ceiling.

Moving slowly, he came out of his crouch and looked over the top of the last step.

Flanked by two beautiful young women, a black man in a dark lavender suit, white tie, and some kind of fancy top hat sat on a couch. The guy's hands were occupied between the women's nylon-clad legs. In the mirrored wall behind the couch, Mason saw two doors; both closed. Two other well-dressed men were sitting on a sofa that was positioned at a right angle to Top Hat's couch. In front of them, a glass table awaited their drugs. Complacent, one of the men flanking Top Hat looked bored and the other had his head tilted back with his eyes closed. *Bodyguards, and poor excuses at that.*

He turned to Chip, made a two-finger gesture, and pointed in the direction he'd seen the two men on the couch. He then pointed to his eyes and made an opening-door movement, followed by two fingers. When Mason issued a sweeping motion to the right, Chip offered a nod of understanding.

Mason felt a hand on his back, the signal Chip was ready to go. He reached into his waist pack and grabbed a second gun with his left hand.

With Chip right behind him, Mason bounded up the stairs and sprinted straight toward Top Hat.

The man's shocked expression told all.

Before Top Hat could do more than yank his hands free, Mason fired the Taser and kept his finger on the trigger, giving the guy the full duration of fifty thousand volts.

In the mirror, he saw Chip dispatch the bodyguards with precise forehead shots. The expended .22 casings flipped over the couch and clinked off the wall. In less than three seconds Chip had neutralized both of them.

The women froze but, surprisingly, didn't scream. Perhaps the Taser and Hahn's near-silent pistol reports temporarily confused them.

Their puzzlement ended when Top Hat flopped into the brunette's lap. She flinched as some of the electricity flowed into her body. Top Hat's lips moved, but no sound emerged.

With blank expressions, the bodyguards slumped toward each other, their heads colliding.

Mason pointed the .22 at the blonde's head, made eye contact, and then saw his reflection in the mirror. It made him feel heartless and cruel, and he didn't pull the trigger. These women weren't rabid dogs, and they didn't deserve that kind of end.

He tracked Chip's movements in the mirror as his second-in-command cleared the office and bathroom. Disguising his voice by making it raspy, he told Chip to drag Top Hat away from the couch and secure his hands, feet, and mouth.

The women cringed and covered their chests as Chip stepped forward and yanked Top Hat to the floor.

Mason activated his radio. "We're secure up here, fall back to the gate at the street. Verbal copies from here on." He wasn't sure he'd hear Darla's acknowledgment clicks over the music.

"Copy, on my way out."

He looked at Hahn. "Kill the music."

Hahn walked over to a cabinet behind Top Hat's desk and cranked the receiver's volume down to zero.

Mason locked eyes with the blonde and asked, "What did you just see?"

Despite staring death in the face, her blue eyes radiated intelligence and resolve. "Nothing," she said with a soft voice. "We were in the bathroom."

"Cameras?"

She shook her head. "He hates them."

Mason took a look around, confirming her answer. It made sense; why record illegal activity? Mason didn't discount the possibility of hidden surveillance, but nothing obvious was visible.

He nodded to the dead bodyguards and said, "Mark them."

The women remained motionless as Chip tacked 10,000-peso bills to each of their foreheads.

Mason made eye contact with both women. "I'll be very unhappy if you take those. They've been demonetized since 1996, so they're practically worthless. You can buy them for ten bucks."

The blonde squinted in thought.

Mason reached down and grabbed the blonde's purse. He removed her wallet, pulled her driver's license, and took a picture with his cell phone. He also photographed the brunette's ID.

"Here's the deal: I'm offering a onetime, take-it-or-leave-it proposal. If you two keep what you saw to yourselves and never tell anyone, you'll never see me again and you won't have to worry about looking over your shoulders for the rest of your lives. Trust me: you'll never see me coming anyway. Do we have a deal?"

They both nodded.

"Verbally, please, like this." Mason put his hand up, imitating an oath-of-office pose. "I give you my word I'll never tell anyone about this."

After they repeated what he said, word for word, he pulled the wad of hundreds from his pocket. "A grand each, as a show of sincerity on my part." He tossed the money onto the couch. "The downstairs cameras recorded you earlier, and they're likely time-stamped, so make sure you get your stories straight in the event the police question you. Don't make your stories exactly the same. If you cave under police questioning and tell them you saw us, bad things will happen." Mason paused to let that sink in. "Use the rear door to leave, the gate at the street will be unlocked. Stay right here until we're gone. Give us five minutes before you leave, not a second sooner."

The blonde said, "Thank you."

"Don't make me regret this."

"You won't."

Top Hat was fully conscious now, and his eyes reflected rage, not fear. That would change soon enough.

Mason grabbed him by the collar and dragged him down the stairs. The guy grunted with each step, sounding like slow-motion laughter.

Mason knew Chip would be uneasy about leaving the women alive, but he'd never protest. Chip respected his command decisions, and Mason's actions weren't out of character with their ops in Afghanistan. There'd been many times when Mason could've killed innocents, but let them live.

Downstairs, Mason dragged Top Hat across the dance floor into the stockroom. Hahn returned the set of keys to the dead man's pocket.

He radioed Darla. "Hahn's coming out. He'll watch the alley while you bring the SUV." Mason locked eyes with Top Hat. "If our guest offers any resistance, I'll knock him cold and drag his ass down the alley. Give me a ten-second arrival call."

"Copy."

Before stepping out the door, Chip put a bullet into the exterior camera.

Mason glanced at his watch. From entry to exit, less than five minutes had elapsed. Without a hitch, they'd just kidnapped one of Alisio's most important lieutenants.

When Top Hat made eye contact, Mason winked at him.

CHAPTER 22

Standing with Harv in the parking lot, Nathan glanced toward the sedan to verify the windows were still rolled up. He didn't want Karen to hear any part of this call.

"Well I guess we're about to find out how well my dad knows George Beaumont. You ready?"

"Go easy, Nate."

His father answered on the third ring.

"Hi, Nathan. You're calling awfully early. I always enjoy hearing from you, even at . . . oh, five thirty in the morning."

"I hope I didn't wake you."

"My alarm beat you. I'm prepping for a long day of lobbyists, activists, campaigners, and petitioners. They all want their feel-good programs as long as someone else pays for them."

"Sounds like business as usual."

"It is."

"I have you on speaker. Harv's with me."

"Good morning, Senator."

"Harv, I've been trying to get you to call me Stone for over twenty years."

"Sorry, sir, I'm old-school."

"How're Candace and your boys Dillon and Lucas?"

"Very well, sir, thank you. How's Martha?"

"Nathan's mother has the constitution of a dreadnought."

"I've always wondered where Nathan got his mettle."

"What can I do for my fellow Marines?"

"We've got a situation out here," Nathan said. "How soon can you call us back from a secure landline?"

"A situation. What's the problem?"

"It's best if we don't discuss it over open airwaves. Can you head into your office early today?"

"I was already planning to. Something tells me my hectic day's about to get worse. Can you give me something, at least?"

"Beaumont Specialists, Incorporated."

Silence on the other end.

"I can be in my office in about twenty-five minutes. What number should I call?"

Harv gave Stone his private line at First Security.

"Got it. Let's make it more like thirty in case there's any kind of traffic or road construction."

"We'll talk then." Nathan ended the call.

***

Stone shook his head. Could Nathan's timing be any worse? He was tempted to wake George Beaumont up and find out what the heck was going on but thought better of it. He should hear what Nathan had to say first. Could it be a coincidence that Beaumont was in town and scheduled to speak at today's weekly meeting of the CDT?

Although Nathan hadn't been confrontational, Stone heard the tightness in his son's voice. He wished Nathan wasn't so short-tempered, but after what he went through at the hands of that sadistic madman in Nicaragua, it was completely understandable.

Stone had learned years ago that absorbing his son's anger, rather than reflecting it, worked best.

Martha McBride, Stone's best friend for sixty-four years, entered the kitchen. She was four years younger, but at their current ages, the difference seemed minimal. At eighty-five, Stone had the dubious honor of being the oldest federal legislator currently holding office. He knew the running joke around Capitol Hill was that he got his nickname because his birth certificate was carved on a stone tablet. In reality he'd earned the name during a heroic, perhaps reckless, display of bravery during the Korean War. The men under his command said he'd acted like Stonewall Jackson, the Confederate general who'd rallied his men under heavy Union fire at the First Battle of Manassas. It hadn't been bravery, just blind rage at being shelled by mortars for two straight hours.

Like father, like son.

He liked that Martha didn't dye her hair. At five foot eleven inches, she was taller than 90 percent of the men on the planet. But not Stone. He was six foot four, an inch shorter than Nathan, but no less ornery. Butting heads was a common occurrence in the McBride family. Martha had once referred to them as a couple of bighorn sheep fighting for a crag on a mountaintop.

For his part, he kept his white hair cropped short in the classic Marine cut. Although gravity and the sun had taken a toll on both of them, he'd gladly test his and Martha's stamina against people half their age, because they'd win most of the contests.

"What's wrong, Stone? You've got that look."

"That was Nathan. He wants me to call him back from my office."

"It sounds serious."

Stone's tone was shorter than he intended. "Isn't it always?"

"He'd been calling a lot more, until lately."

Stone didn't respond.

"The phone works in both directions."

Again, Stone said nothing.

"You're going to call him back, aren't you?"

"Just as soon as I get to the office. I'm afraid we'll have to skip our breakfast time together."

"What's your day look like? I can meet you for lunch."

He already knew, but he opened his weekly calendar booklet anyway. Good grief, he was already overbooked and needed to reschedule several appointments. There just weren't enough hours in a workday. If he allowed them, the energy vampires would quite literally drain all of his free time. Not just some of it, *all* of it. He fought a constant battle between the unrelenting weight of political pressure—seemingly from every direction—and maintaining a private life. There were times when his job felt like a gravitational black hole.

"Try to be patient with him," she said.

"He should be more patient with me. He thinks I have a cushy job."

"He doesn't think that. He's never even implied that. Nathan knows how hard you work."

Stone took a final swig of lukewarm coffee and gave her a hug. Despite her height, she disappeared inside his grasp. He smelled her favorite shampoo. He kissed her good-bye, grabbed his briefcase, and headed for the garage.

***

"See? You *can* do it," Harv said.

Nathan attempted a smile. "I didn't even use a single profane word."

"There's hope for you yet. I'd better head over to First Security and get Karen squared away. I'll be back in twenty minutes."

"Don't forget to give her the cabin's gate combination. And remind her not to go back to her house after picking up Cindy. Maybe they should meet up at Lindbergh's long-term parking lot so her car won't be towed. There's no telling how long they'll need to stay at the cabin."

"I'll tell her to do that. See you back here in a few."

From the backseat, Karen made eye contact as Harv got in the car and pulled away, her eyes pleading for some sense of sanity.

Standing there alone in the concrete tomb of the parking structure, his world seemed to compress. A nagging sense of unfairness invaded his thoughts. What was wrong with him? How could he have been so cold to Holly? Okay, she had a seat on his father's committee . . . So what? What's wrong with that? Nothing, he supposed. Then why did it feel so awkward? And why hadn't she told him right away? Why hold it back? Holly knew his relationship with his father had been strained over the last few months—hell, forever—but it seemed like a pretty slim reason not to tell him. Maybe Harv had a point—his reaction to hearing the news spoke for itself.

What if he came clean with Holly and told her about his history with Karen and Mara? But that held inherent risks. Holly might find his previous connection to prostitutes repulsive. *Prostitutes* . . . Such a harsh word. Mara hadn't been a streetwalker turning tricks to support a drug addiction; she'd been an expensive escort. *Escort? Is that what she was?* Deep down, he knew the truth. For two years, his only source of intimacy had come from Mara. Back then, he'd loathed his looks, the scarring that would never go away, and seriously doubted whether he could love or be loved. But Mara had never judged him . . . Of course she hadn't, he'd been a paying customer. A *well-paying* customer.

Ancient history, he reminded himself. He wasn't that person anymore. Holly had shown him a different way of seeing the world, a different way of life. She'd proved he didn't have to be alone.

He was tempted to use the Internet to find out what the FBI director's chief of staff did, but figured it could wait. Now wasn't the time. He needed to keep his head up, not bury it in his cell phone. He'd apologize to Holly in person after Harv returned, and things would return to normal.

The coyote-like wail of a distant siren interrupted his thoughts, a reminder this wasn't over yet—probably first responders headed to or from the ambulance shoot-out scene.

Without knowing Toby's condition, what would Mason do? He imagined himself in Mason's situation. Would the guy make another attempt to kill the witness to his crimes? If so, when? An idea formed. What if it were leaked that Toby never regained consciousness and died on the operating table? Lansing and Holly could work out the details with the hospital's administrator, but if Mason believed Toby never spoke to the police before dying, he might think containment was still possible and not flee. Still, Mason would have to be wondering who he and Harv were. Holly too.

With his father's help, they could crumble Mason's world. If Beaumont cut Mason off and severed his access to BSI's assets he'd likely flee—frustrating to Nathan personally, but not the worst thing that could happen in the short term.

Nathan took a deep breath and dialed Holly. After one ring, he got dumped into her voice mail. He hoped it meant she was talking to Lansing. Either that or she didn't want to talk. He couldn't blame her. He ended the call without leaving a message and dictated a text:

> *I'm still in the parking structure. Harv took Karen to First Security. She'll go from there to the cabin. Three of our security guards are on the way, and I'll send one inside to join you. Maybe ten minutes. After they arrive, Harv and I are heading over to his office to use a landline to call my father. You're welcome to come with us. I'm sorry about what I said, and I offer no excuses. I'm proud of you taking the position on my father's committee.*

He sent the text and stared at his phone, urging it to light up with a return text from Holly. Half a minute later, nothing had changed.

He dictated one more text:

Would it be possible for you to work with the hospital's administrator to leak that Toby never regained consciousness and died on the operating table? Safer for Toby if Mason thinks he's dead.

His phone remained dark for another minute or so. Its sudden vibration felt like a jolt of electricity, and he nearly dropped it. It was Harv, calling to update him on the status of their security guards.

"Okay," he said. "I'll watch for their vehicles. I sent a text to Holly telling her we're heading over to the office once you get back. I also asked her to think about having the hospital leak that Toby died without ever regaining consciousness."

"Good move. You tried calling her first, right?"

"Voice mail."

"She's probably on the phone with Lansing."

Nathan didn't say anything.

"I'll be back in a few minutes. Stay sharp, partner."

"Always."

Standing there, Nathan decided the rain made a lonely sound, like wind through trees.

CHAPTER 23

Sheltered from the mist in the nightclub's pedestrian alley, Mason searched Top Hat and found a cell phone, a wallet, and a set of keys. He kept them, unsure whether Top Hat would need the phone or the keys, but turned the phone to silent mode. Mason knew there was some degree of risk keeping the phone because they could be tracked, but it could prove invaluable if Top Hat needed it to contact someone or vice versa.

After receiving Darla's ten-second call to arrive curbside, he told her they were ready. "Leave your headlights on, but turn them off at the curb." Anything else would look suspicious.

Top Hat's wallet revealed that his name was Javarius Michaels, age thirty-two, of La Mesa, California. Mason considered his approach with Michaels. It was doubtful the guy had ever been interrogated, so breaking him shouldn't present too much of a challenge. The man's attitude had already changed drastically during the past few minutes. He seemed less belligerent and more nervous: a good sign. Once fear replaced resolve and a victim realized his situation was hopeless, interrogation became much easier. In his experience, fear was far more powerful than pain.

He saw a sliver of the brick wall brighten as Darla turned the corner and approached the alley. With a firm grasp on Michaels's arm, he ushered the man toward the gate. Because his ankles were bound loosely, Michaels moved in a chain gang shuffle. Darla pulled the SUV to the curb and killed the headlights.

Stepping out of the shadows, Chip opened the rear passenger door, allowing Mason to shove his captive into the backseat. Mason got in next to Darla.

Looking around, he didn't see anyone. It was possible someone in the low-rise hotel across the street saw the action, but the SUV had only been stationary for a few seconds. Leaving the nightclub, they rode north in silence. Neither Darla nor Chip would say anything. Giving a prisoner the silent treatment was all part of the game.

After Darla got on the southbound Five, Mason pivoted to face his captive.

"By now, you're realizing you're in serious trouble. I have no desire to torture you; that's not my thing. Darla here has a different attitude. If I have to turn you over to her, things will get ugly. Remove his gag."

Chip reached over and pulled the gag free. Top Hat shook his head, but didn't say anything.

Mason locked eyes and waited. After a few seconds, Top Hat looked away.

"Here's what we know," Mason said. "There's an important delivery being made later today. You're going to fill us in on some missing details. We know a South Korean yacht has been used to smuggle weapons into US waters, and for the last eight months you've been the point man, overseeing every aspect of the operation. The delivery isn't guns this time—that much we know. We'd like you to tell us what's being delivered and how it's going to take place."

Top Hat didn't respond.

"Do I have your attention, Mr. Michaels?"

"I have cash. Two hundred grand. It's yours if you let me go."

Mason sucked his teeth and shook his head.

"Okay, five hundred large, but that's all I got, I swear. If you want more, it'll take time."

He nodded to Chip.

As if palming a basketball, Chip wrapped his hand around the side of Michaels's head and shoved. Michaels's skull smacked the glass with a dull thud.

"What the fuck!" he yelled.

Chip dribbled the ball again, harder.

Michaels winced but didn't protest a second time.

"This isn't a negotiation," Mason said patiently. "It's an interrogation."

"If I tell you guys anything, Mr. A's gonna kill me."

"No doubt that's true, but he has to find you first. I have a feeling you've got much more than five hundred grand rat-holed away. Disappearing shouldn't be a problem for you. You'll blend into the Caribbean perfectly. Listen carefully, now: we don't want your money, we want information."

"So I'm supposed to believe you'll just let me walk away?"

"Believe whatever you want, but I'll guarantee you'll be *wheeled away* if you don't tell us what we want to know."

Michaels didn't say anything.

"You're probably thinking, 'If I feed them bullshit, it'll buy some time and I might be able to escape.' Put that out of your head, Mr. Michaels. We've dealt with desert-schooled jihadists who are far tougher than you; trust me on that. See, we aren't going to let you go until after we've verified what you tell. If you give us crap, you'll have to talk with Ms. Lyons."

"The sellers are gonna bolt if they see anyone but me."

"We're aware of that."

"I always pick up and deliver the goods with my two bodyguards, but you killed them. They're going to ask why they aren't there."

"And what will you say?"

"I don't know; it's never happened before. They're always with me."

"You'll say you had a problem with them, and you dealt with it. It's just you this time."

"Yeah, okay, man. Whatever."

"What's being delivered?"

"I don't know yet."

Mason squinted.

"I swear, I don't know. Mr. A's always paranoid."

"Where do you pick up the goods?"

Michaels looked back and forth as if someone were eavesdropping. "Shelter Island Marina."

Mason waited for more.

"Alisio's partner in South Korea owns three commercial fishing boats. One of them goes out to sea to get the goods from the yacht."

"That would be the oceangoing luxury yacht I mentioned, correct?"

Michaels's tone held resentment. "Yeah, man, the *Yoonsuh.* Cost thirty million."

"The best blood-money can buy. So the fishing boat comes back to Shelter Island and the goods are off-loaded?"

"Yeah, that's how it goes down."

"The goods are then transferred into a truck or van?"

"Usually it's a truck, but this time we're using a van."

"Where's the van?"

"It's already in the parking lot at the marina."

"So there are two parts to the deal. The delivery of the goods to the dock, then the exchange of the goods for payment, right?"

Michaels nodded.

"Where does the exchange go down?"

"I don't know yet."

Chip grabbed his head again.

"I swear! I get that info after the stuff arrives. They never use the same place twice. They give me GPS coordinates once the fishing boat arrives."

"Who are *they*?"

"I don't know 'em personally, man. South Korean mafia. That's all I know."

"When do you get the call?"

"Usually within the hour. I park someplace safe and wait."

"If you're lying to me—"

"I'm not lying; that's how it goes down every time. The only thing that's different tonight is what's being delivered."

"And you don't know what it is?"

"No way, man. It's none of my business. I'm just an expensive delivery boy."

Mason didn't believe him.

CHAPTER 24

When Nathan received Harv's call, the only activity on his cell had been from the security guard he'd sent inside the hospital. His man confirmed making contact with Holly. Nathan had asked if she was alone, and the answer was yes. Was Holly on the phone? Again, yes. Apparently, she didn't have time to answer his texts or return his calls. He couldn't worry about it. If Holly didn't think checking in with him was important right now, so be it. There wasn't much he could do. He supposed he could go down there, but he didn't want to force things. If Holly wanted some space, he'd give it to her. Still, the lack of communication bothered him.

They were in a situation where Mason could reappear at any minute. At least she had backup. He personally knew the guard he'd sent inside. He was a capable, intelligent, and well-trained man.

He hustled down the parking structure's ramp and waited near the ticket-dispensing machine. There was no sense having Harv enter the garage again.

When Harv pulled into the ER's driveway, he flashed his high beams.

Nathan dashed through the rain and got in. "How's Karen?"

"Still in shock. I think she can handle the plan, though. She's meeting Cindy at Lindbergh's long-term lot like you suggested. She wanted me to thank you again for the cash."

"Good to hear."

"Holly?"

"She's gone dark on me."

"I don't think it's intentional. She's got her hands full now that the FBI's officially involved and Lansing's calling the shots. It's possible he told her to disengage."

"Yeah, you could be right."

"I'm sure she'll check in as soon as she comes up for air."

Nathan tensed as his phone buzzed. He checked the screen. "You must be prophetic. She just sent me a text. It says, 'All quiet in here. Thanks for the backup. Two SAs on the way. ETA ten minutes. Lansing's very concerned. Buried right now. Do you want your security guard to avoid contact with our SAs?'"

Nathan sent, *Yes, better if he avoids contact with everyone but you.*

She responded: *I'll call you later*, and added a smiley face at the end.

Nathan read their exchange to Harv.

"See? You're overthinking things."

"If you say so."

They arrived at First Security a few minutes later. Harv drove the perimeter, but didn't see anyone other than the two guards they'd assigned to watch the place—both of whom were holding umbrellas. Rather than park in the lot and dash through the rain, Harv used a remote and opened a rolling door on the Batcave. They called it the Batcave because it looked a little like Bruce Wayne's secret lair. Their high-tech garage had all the bells and whistles needed to both install and detect electronic tracking devices and bugs. Three of the six bays were currently occupied by their clients' vehicles. Harv deactivated the security system from a keypad on the wall near the garage door.

Turning on lights, they made their way into the interior of First Security's headquarters. Nathan hadn't been in here since the remodel wrapped up a week ago.

"I've said this before, Harv, but you run a tight ship. The new decor looks great." He added some softness to his voice. "I just *love* what you've done to the place."

"Oh, stop it."

They entered Harv's second-floor office and left the door open. Harv didn't spare any expenses. You could fit two or three pickup trucks in here. Complete with a wet bar, private bathroom, leather couches with matching chairs, several big-screen televisions, and a pink granite desk the size of a small bed, Harv's office was obscenely comfortable. Sealing the deal, he had an awesome view of a natural canyon to the north.

Nathan whistled.

"What?"

"I'll bet this tops Jerry Jones's luxury suite at AT&T Stadium."

"I wouldn't take that bet."

"All right . . . let's get this over with." Nathan pulled out his phone and sent his dad a text.

We're secure in Harv's office.

A few minutes later, Harv's desk phone bleeped to life and Nathan jabbed the speaker button. "Hi, Dad, Harv's with me and I have you on speaker. I hope you'll understand the need for secrecy and why we're doing it this way after you hear what's going on."

"Okay," his dad said. "What's the problem?"

"What can you tell us about Beaumont Specialists?"

"Quite a bit. Why do you ask?"

"BSI's chief of security committed three murders this morning and attempted four others."

Silence on the other end.

"Did you hear me?"

"You must be mistaken. Are you talking about Tanner Mason?"

"Yes. Tanner Mason, chief of security for one of the nation's largest and most prestigious private military companies, is a cold-blooded murderer."

A pause on the other end of the line. "Is this a joke?"

"Do I sound like I'm joking? As we speak, a friend of mine is in emergency surgery after being shot twice in the head."

"Did you witness these so-called murders?"

"No, but I've stood over the *so-called* dead bodies of a Mexican, a South Korean, and a pregnant woman."

"Please, just tell me what you know."

"How about a trade? I give you what we know and in return, you tell me what you know about Beaumont and Mason."

"Are we negotiating here? Is that what we're doing?"

"I'm extremely pissed off, Dad. Someone I once helped, who's also a fellow Marine, has been betrayed, tortured, and left for dead after being shot in the head. Mason murdered his fiancée, along with their unborn baby girl. And he tried to kill Harv, Holly, and me. So *excuse me* if I'm not feeling especially cordial right now."

Stone paused for a moment. "What do you mean he tried to kill you? Tell me what happened."

"Mason tried to intercept an ambulance on its way to the hospital with the intent to kill everyone inside. We drove him off after sideswiping his car and exchanging gunfire."

"Out in the open? On a public street?"

"Yes, Dad, on a public street. We'd like some assurance that Beaumont isn't involved."

"I've known George since before you were born. We fought side by side in Korea. If you're implying he's complicit with Tanner Mason's actions tonight, you're . . . misguided."

"Misguided . . . Then prove me wrong. Tell me about Beaumont's operation. His contracts. His choice of security chief."

"I can't."

"Can't or won't? Harv and I still have the highest security clearances possible."

"It's not that simple."

"Well, I guess we're finished here."

Harv shook his head urgently and raised a hand for Nathan to wait.

"I understand you still have the necessary clearance. That's not the issue."

"Then what is?"

"I'd like to get George's permission before I share sensitive and classified information about himself and his company."

"I see . . ."

"Of all people, you should understand that."

"Well, if George isn't forthcoming with his *permission*, I'm going to firebomb his headquarters and burn the fucking place to the ground. So if your old pal's in there, you might want to suggest he vacate the building."

"You'll do no such thing."

"Watch me."

Another pause. "Actually, George is here in DC. He's speaking before my committee in a few hours on an important domestic-security issue."

"Well, now we're getting somewhere. Is there a connection between these two events? The murder of a South Korean and a Mexican and Beaumont's presence in DC?"

"Why would you think there's any connection?"

"You answered a question with a question. I'll ask again. Is there a connection between these two events? Yes? No? Maybe? I don't know?"

"I refuse to believe that George Beaumont is complicit with Tanner Mason's actions this morning."

"You still haven't answered my question."

Stone put iron in his voice. "I don't report to you, Son."

"Then listen carefully while *I* do the reporting: One way or the other, I'm going to find out what's going on. And right now, I'm looking forward to doing it the *other* way."

"Lawless behavior is answerable, even for you."

"So call the cops."

"Nathan, please—"

"If Beaumont's complicit, Harv, Holly, and I will find ourselves in the crosshairs of BSI's chief of security and his small army of mercenaries, and I can assure you we aren't going to settle our differences by holding hands, drinking Kool-Aid, and singing 'Kumbaya.' Throats will be slit."

"They're called military contractors, not mercenaries."

"Whatever. I'll kill as many as it takes to bring Mason down."

"Good grief, Nathan, listen to yourself."

He didn't respond.

"You're serious, aren't you." It wasn't a question.

"Deadly serious. What part of 'I'm extremely pissed off' don't you understand?"

"George Beaumont is not a party to murder."

"Suppose you're wrong. What do Harv and I do in the meantime? So far we don't think Mason knows who we are. But what if we're wrong? What if he finds out? Do we relocate Harv's family to a safe house as a precaution? How about Angelica and my dogs in La Jolla? What about Jin and Lauren? They could also end up in Mason's gun sights. He won't hesitate to use them as leverage to get to us. And lest you think you're immune, you and Mom could wake up to a home invasion one morning."

"Please do nothing until you hear back from me. Ten minutes, that's all I'm asking. I'm not glossing over any of your concerns, but I'm asking you, as your father, to be patient and stand down. I'll call George's cell as soon as we hang up. I'll ask him to come into my office right away, then call you within ten minutes either way."

"Are you willing to bet our lives on your friendship with Beaumont?"

"Nathan—"

"If you tell Beaumont we're involved and he tells Mason, we're as good as dead. Sooner or later, he'll track us down. We can't hide from BSI's goons for the rest of our lives."

"That's a bit extreme, don't you think?"

"Tell that to families of the murder victims."

"Nathan, you're not listening to—"

"Here's what I can live with. Until we track Mason down, don't tell Beaumont anything. When you see him at your meeting later today, act like everything's normal."

"You're asking me to look the man in the eyes and pretend I don't know anything?"

Nathan wanted to say, *You're a politician, aren't you?* But he restrained himself. "If he ever finds out you knew and didn't tell him, blame it on me. Tell him I insisted you keep all of this confidential. You know, the father-son confidence thing. He should understand that."

His father didn't respond for a few seconds. "How about a compromise? If you agree to temporarily stand down, I'll insist you're included in my conversation with George when he gets to my office."

"What about Harv?"

"Harv too. You'll be hearing everything in real time. You can judge for yourself if you think he's complicit. Agreed?"

"You won't say anything until we're all together on the phone?"

"You have my word."

"And if George refuses?"

"I'll ask him if his property's fire insurance is current."

Nathan glanced at Harv, who nodded approval. "Okay . . . when?"

"Just as soon as he gets here."

"It's still not ideal. We won't be able to look him in the eye."

"I will."

"Let's hope you know him as well as you think you do."

"I'll call you back within ten minutes with an update."

After Nathan hung up, Harv said, "Well, that wasn't horrendously bad."

"For who? Or is it whom?"

"Whom, I think." Harv made a pinching gesture with his fingers. "You were a tad hostile."

"Ya think?"

"I'll give you a passing grade. A C-plus."

"You're being generous. I was an asshole."

"You're not an asshole, you're . . . passionate. Look, your dad's eighty-five."

"I hear you, Harv. I'll go easier on the next call. But his demeanor really frosts me sometimes. He's probably not doing it on purpose, but the man gets under my skin."

"Only if you let him."

"Remember how much money you said the feds were spending with private military companies? Well, money can be a strong lure to corruption. That's why I don't trust Beaumont. I'm not willing to put your family, or mine, at risk solely on my father's faith in the guy. No matter what happens during Beaumont's call, I want to double the number of armed security guards watching our homes and our headquarters."

"Candace won't like the loss of privacy, but she'll deal with it."

"It's not the first time—" Harv's desk phone interrupted him.

Nathan activated the speaker. "That was quick."

"I'm taking this seriously, Nathan. I left a message for Beaumont to call me back. I suspect I'll hear from him quickly."

"I'm sorry about my tone earlier. I'm not mad at you, Dad, I'm just . . . I don't know . . . venting, I guess."

"Forget it. You feel like your lives could be at risk, and you're understandably upset about the situation. I don't blame you; it makes me angry too."

"You're too patient."

"Nonsense. I'm your father. Hang on . . . The other line is ringing. It could be George. This won't take long. I'm going to put you on hold. I'll be back in less than a minute. Stay on the line, okay?"

"Sure, no problem."

There was no sound on the other end, just stifling silence.

Nathan hit the mute button on Harv's desk phone. They'd hear Stone when he came back, but Stone wouldn't hear them. "Is Holly in your contacts list and vice versa?"

"Yes."

"Do you mind calling her and putting it on speaker while the good senator keeps us on hold?"

"No problem."

Harv walked a few steps away and made the call. Nathan noticed Harv got through to her instantly—something Nathan hadn't been able to do. The fact that she hadn't called him back or answered all of his texts spoke for itself. Harv told her she was on speaker, that he and Nathan were in his First Security office, and Nathan was on hold with his dad.

Holly said several special agents from San Diego's field office were with her. Harv asked how her call with Lansing went. She said she'd left an urgent message on his cell's voice mail. If she didn't hear from him in the next five minutes or so, she'd have an emergency page issued.

Right after Harv hung up with Holly, Stone came back on the line. "That was George. He's on his way. I didn't tell him what it was about, only that it's an urgent matter requiring a face-to-face. He's very concerned."

"I have you on speaker again, and Harv is still here."

"One thing, Son, I can't allow our conversation with George to be recorded. I'm not suggesting you'd automatically do that, I'm just saying it needs to be off the record."

"We weren't planning to record anything."

"Good, because I can tell you with one hundred percent certainty he won't talk to us otherwise."

"Dad, may I ask you a question?"

"Sure."

"Is everything discussed in your CDT meetings considered an issue of national security?"

"Most of the time. As you know, our committee is primarily a think tank; we don't make or decide policy, we just propose it."

Think tank, thought Nathan. *Holly had used that term.*

"Why do you ask?"

He wanted to ask his dad how much Holly knew about BSI, but changed his mind at the last second. Maybe it was better if he didn't know. Covering, he said, "I don't know very much about your committee; just curious."

"We do discuss other things. Crime statistics, security for major events like the Super Bowl. High-profile trials. Polling data. You get the picture. All of those things, in combination with other factors, paint a picture of our nation's overall perception of how secure its citizens feel. Right now, the index is fairly low, meaning that the vast majority of Americans don't feel threatened or fear a terrorist attack is pending. The longer we go without a major terrorist incident, the more secure our citizens feel. We have an expectation of feeling safe in public places, and it's the role of CDT to do everything possible to keep things that way without stepping on civil rights."

Nathan rolled his eyes.

Harv smiled and shook his head, his message clear: don't take it personally.

Stone continued. "I've never been a proponent of violating civil rights to combat terrorism. As soon as we go down that road, we're no better than the terrorists. I guess I'm old-school when it comes to the Constitution."

"As well you should be. We've had this debate before, and you know where Harv and I stand on it, so there's no point in rehashing it."

"Let's agree to disagree," Stone said. "I will say this: I admire your determination to go the extra mile when needed. I've always had your best interests at heart, I hope you know that. I'm not speaking as a legislator, I'm speaking as your father when I say it's easier to sweep civil rights aside when it's your own family in jeopardy. I would've broken every law on the books to rescue you from that madman's camp if I could have."

"I know that. I'm sorry for being abrasive." Nathan rubbed his forehead.

"I wonder where you got that from."

"Mom's side, obviously."

"No one's keeping score."

"I'll try to do better. Will you level with me? Do you have any idea what's going on?"

"If it's related to what I think it is, then yes. But I can assure you, no action like this was either planned or sanctioned."

"I know the situation is on a need-to-know basis, but I think we've met that threshold. Speaking of need to know, I'll have to tell you about our last exploit down in Central America sometime."

"Nicaragua."

"You know about that? How—" Nathan stopped himself. "Do I want to know how you found out?"

"It wasn't Holly, if that's what you're thinking. By the way, she's got some news for you . . . it's about her job."

"She told me . . . tonight."

"Tonight? You mean you just found out tonight?"

"Yes."

"I'm a little surprised she didn't say anything sooner."

"You aren't the only one."

"About three weeks ago, I received a call from Director Lansing. He requested that Holly replace Leaf Watson on the CDT. I'd just assumed she'd told you about it right away."

"Holly was Lansing's pick?" Now Nathan felt doubly bad. How could he have been so narrow-minded?

"You sound surprised."

He didn't say anything and looked at Harv, who maintained a neutral expression.

"I'm sure she'd planned to tell you sooner, but she's juggling twenty major projects with twenty more in the wings. It's a prestigious position, but it takes a personal toll. She's hopelessly buried, but I'd have to say she's handling it well. I'm the one who suggested she take a few days off and spend them with you."

"She's been acting kinda edgy lately."

"She's got the right temperament for the job, but it still generates a lot of internal stress. You'll need to be patient with her."

"Like you are with me?"

"Well, maybe not *that* extreme."

"So, what does a chief of staff for the FBI do?"

"Holly spearheads and coordinates new programs and oversees the daily operations of the director's office and its personnel. She personally advises Director Lansing on administrative, criminal, and national-security issues. She also works directly with high-ranking DOJ officials, US attorneys' offices, and the White House. And she oversees programs with federal intelligence agencies, as well as municipal and state law enforcement as needed. Her position as chief of staff made her the perfect candidate for the FBI's seat on the CDT."

"That sounded rehearsed."

"Let's just say I knew we'd have this conversation sooner or later."

Nathan didn't respond.

"Has she contacted Lansing about this?"

"She left him an urgent voice mail."

"Then she's planning to update him on everything?"

"Yes."

"She must be torn about doing that. I'm assuming you'd prefer she didn't?"

"Initially, but things have changed. At this point, we need the FBI's help. We can't protect our injured friend in the long term. He needs witness protection. There's a woman who also needs it. Right after Mason attempted to kill my friends, he broke into her home with the intent to interrogate and kill her, just like Toby and his fiancée. Fortunately, she hid from Mason and we drove him off. We've hidden her in a secure location."

"I'm sorry about this, Son. Very sorry. You and Holly are doing the right thing, though. The FBI should definitely be involved at this point, and it's likely my committee will be too. I'll call Director Lansing later this morning."

"I hope Holly comes out of this okay with Lansing. I may have compromised his trust in her earlier tonight. I asked her to delay reporting all this."

"Holly's relationship with Lansing has already been tested. All debts have been paid in both directions. It's now based purely on trust. I wouldn't worry about it. The delay in informing him isn't ideal, but it sounds like things have been hectic out there."

"I hope you're right. Now, before we talk with Beaumont, what can you tell us about Mason and BSI?"

CHAPTER 25

"What I'm about to share must never be repeated. Only a handful of people know about it."

"No problem, Dad. We know the drill."

"As you know, illegal weapons sales are front and center on the ATF's radar screen."

His dad told them how the borders of California and Arizona, specifically along the San Diego County line, currently sat on the leading edge of the interdiction effort. Over the past four years, Alfonso Alisio's cartel, based out of Mexico City with dozens of criminal gangs in its network, had been smuggling weapons into Mexico from the United States.

Stone continued. "Although there's no way to accurately gauge how many weapons have crossed the border, we believe the number's in the tens of thousands. Around four years ago, a joint task force commanded by the ATF raided a Mexican-owned sweatshop where hundreds of guns were being stockpiled before being moved south. The undercover ATF special agent who'd infiltrated the local gang relayed the location of the guns, and the JTF set up twenty-four-seven surveillance on the sweatshop."

"What kind of sweatshop?" Nathan asked.

"Wide-brimmed straw hats, like you see at the beach."

Nathan exchanged a glance with Harv. Nathan liked wearing those hats when he worked outside in the yard.

"Two days later, a joint terrorism task force consisting of local, state, and federal law enforcement agencies conducted a raid. The ATF spearheaded the operation, and it was successful, but it came at a high price. One ATF agent was killed and several more were wounded in the ensuing firefight. Fifteen Mexican cartel members were killed. No civilians died, but several were wounded when the firefight spilled into the street. Two thousand German-made assault rifles were recovered, along with two hundred and fifty thousand rounds of NATO ammo, most of them armor piercing. I don't need to tell you how devastating AP rounds are against law enforcement. We don't know how it happened, but shortly after the raid, the undercover agent must've been blown because his mutilated body was found hanging from a streetlight a few blocks from the ATF's El Centro satellite office. Needless to say, the man died a horrible, protracted death."

"That's a bad deal," Nathan said.

"It gets worse. Tanner Mason took the fall."

"Mason worked for the ATF?"

"Only as a consultant. Because his gunrunning interdiction ops were so successful in Afghanistan, he made many high-level friends, including ATF Director Martini. When Martini visited Shindand District, he personally asked to meet with Mason. Mason was a private military contractor over there, and . . . Well, we're getting ahead of ourselves here. To be fair to George, I think we should wait to discuss this further until he arrives."

"That's fine."

"Would you object to Director Lansing participating in the discussion?"

Nathan looked at Harv, who offered a "maybe" hand gesture. "I think Harv wants to jump in."

Harv leaned forward a little. "I guess I'm worried about being told to stand down and let the FBI handle everything from here on."

"You said it yourself—the FBI belongs in this. What's wrong with that course of action?"

"Nothing," Harv answered, "as long as Mason doesn't know who we are, but there's no guarantee he won't eventually find us. Nathan shot his right-hand man. They might be looking for some payback, but more than that, we've become huge loose ends. Mason probably believes we know who he is, and he's going to do everything within his power to find out who *we* are."

"You guys told me you exchanged gunfire, but you didn't say anyone was shot. Is he dead?"

Nathan answered, "His vest saved him."

"At this point, maybe you'd better tell me the whole story. Don't leave anything out."

Nathan started with Toby's initial call and ended with the exchange he and Holly had with Dr. Thelan in the ER. Stone asked a few questions, but for the most part didn't interrupt.

Stone said, "The peso bills pinned on the dead men at the soccer field sounds like a signature of some kind."

"We agree."

"As I recall, the dead ATF agent hung from the streetlight had Mexican money tacked to his forehead."

"There's no way that's a coincidence," said Nathan. "Holly told us she thought she recognized the peso thing, but couldn't place it. Maybe that's what she was remembering."

"We'll ask George about it. It's possible Mason knew or worked closely with the dead agent."

"Was your committee involved with the ATF's raid in El Centro?"

"No, not directly. The ATF's seat wasn't at liberty to discuss it. We knew something was in the works, but that's all we knew. The

ATF is a law enforcement agency that reports to the US Attorney General's office."

Harv asked, "Can you try to ID the dead guys on the soccer field? They might have INTERPOL records. Right now, we don't have any leads to help us track Mason down."

"Email me all the photos you took. I'll forward them to Director Lansing."

Nathan's cell phone rang, and he saw it was Holly. "Hang on, Dad, Holly's calling. I'd better take this. I'll be right back, fifteen seconds max."

Nathan hit the mute button on Harv's desk phone. "Holly, we're still on the phone with my father; can I call you right back?"

"Toby's secure; our people have him protected."

"Good to hear. I'll send our security guards home."

"The bodies are gone."

"Gone? You mean from Hickman Field?"

"SDPD went out there and found nothing. They're scouring the area as we speak. We need the photos you took."

We? Nathan thought. "Sure, no problem."

"I'm staying here until San Diego's SAC arrives. I've got to let you go."

And with that, the call ended. No good-byes. No promises to call later. Just a silent phone in his hand.

Shaking his head, Nathan brought his dad back on the line.

"Holly just said the bodies are gone. SDPD went out to the soccer fields and found nothing. She wants the photos we took. We'll let her know you're planning to forward them to Lansing."

"Sounds good. Can you use the notes app in your phone to jot down the sequence of events as best as you remember them and send that to me as well?"

"No problem. I'll do that right away."

"Look, I don't want to cut this short, but I've got to clear some work from my desk. I haven't even looked at yesterday's mail. You have my word I won't discuss anything until George gets here and we're all together on the phone."

"We'll be here. Call this same number. We'll be waiting."

"And Nathan . . . thanks for trusting me."

"No problem. Harv's sending the photos right now."

"I'll look for them."

Harv terminated the call. "Well, that went much better."

He slowly nodded. Something bugged him about the bodies on the soccer field. Something he'd seen. Aside from the cold way they'd been murdered, something was prowling just below the surface of his mind, like a submerged piece of cloth. He could sense its presence, but couldn't grasp it.

"I know that look, Nate. What's on your mind?"

"The dead men from the soccer field; I can't get them out of my head."

"Tell me what's generally bothering you."

"I'm not sure I can."

"Let's walk through it together."

Harv quickly went through everything from the time they left Toby's apartment until they hopped the fence and Harv's TI saw the heat signatures of the two prone forms.

Harv's calm tone had a relaxing, almost hypnotic effect, and Nathan found himself closer to the elusive thought. "It's not the money tacked to their foreheads, it's something else."

"Let's look at the pictures," Harv said. "It might trigger something. Are you thinking it was the position of the bodies?"

"No. It's an image, like a manga cartoon . . . I keep getting a glimpse of something strange . . . Wait, I know what it is! The Asian guy's tattoo. I remember now. I kept thinking it looked expensive. Not like hundreds of dollars, but thousands."

"I remember it too," Harv said. "It was a two-headed dragon with hand-like claws."

Harv pulled his phone and tapped on the photos icon. He thumbed over to the one he wanted and zoomed into the Asian guy's arm. The image was a little fuzzy, but the dragon could clearly be seen. Like a medieval knight, one of its clawed hands held a saber while the other grasped a shield. It had yellow eyes and green scales with some blue mixed in here and there. Nathan had to admit: it was a beautiful piece of artwork. He'd never seen anything like it.

Harv said, "That's an expensive tat, way better than ninety-nine percent of what tattoo artists do in this country. The guy's ID said he was from South Korea. I know Jin's from North Korea, but it couldn't hurt to have her take a look. She might recognize it."

"I guess it's worth waking her up," Nathan said.

"Definitely. We need all the help we can get at this point. If Lansing can't ID the dead men or decides not to share it with us, we'll find ourselves out of the loop and on our own."

"We're hunting Mason down with or without the FBI's help."

Harv didn't respond.

He knew it wasn't disagreement, only concern. Finding Mason would be tremendously easier with Holly working in the background. The question was, would she still help them if Lansing wasn't on board? He didn't know. She'd clearly distanced herself, and Nathan couldn't blame her.

Harv continued to scroll through more photos. "Was there anything about the other guy that stood out in your mind?"

"I'm not sure... Wait, go back. Keep going... That one. Zoom in on the guy's head."

"What did you see?" Harv asked.

"Something looked weird. Can you zoom a little more? There, check out the zeroes on that note."

"Wow. I hadn't noticed that. I didn't look that closely. I'd just assumed they were 1,000. That's a 10,000-peso note. I'm positive they don't print them anymore."

"Are they valuable?"

"Practically worthless," Harv said.

"Then the large denomination might mean something."

"It could be a cartel or gang signature, kinda like the Colombian necktie thing."

"It's a foregone conclusion that ROK has a gang problem similar to Japan's."

"It definitely does," Harv said. "South Korea has organized crime and street gangs, especially a big city like Seoul. I'd bet the yakuza has a presence in ROK."

"The Mexican guy looked a little young to be a made man, don't you think? Then again, I don't know much about Mexico's organized crime. Or ROK's."

"Me either. I'm guessing the Mexican guy's in his twenties, but the ROK guy looks older."

"There's something else . . ."

"What?" Harv asked.

"The location. Why leave the bodies in the middle of a soccer field? Why not dump them on a vacant lot or in a public park, someplace like that? It seems obvious they wanted them to be discovered in the morning."

"Well, it's really isolated and dark, and there aren't any cameras."

"There aren't cameras on vacant lots either."

Harv thought for a moment. "The logical answer is that the location isn't random. Like the peso business, it has some sort of meaning."

"Soccer's a popular sport in Mexico. South Korea too."

"We should find out if there are any games tomorrow and who's playing."

"Could those guys *be* soccer players?" Nathan asked.

"I suppose it's possible, but why would Mason kill them?"

"I remember reading an article during the World Cup about crooked players and refs. There's big money in throwing games. But Hickman Field isn't exactly a large venue."

"The simplest explanation is usually the correct one. Those two dead men were mixed up in some kind of illegal activity that Mason's got going."

"Despite what my father believes, we can't rule out Beaumont's involvement just yet."

"So where does this leave us?"

"Until we hear what he has to say, our options are limited. I don't think Mason's going to let anyone pick up his trail. He definitely knows we were protecting Toby, but I doubt he knows specifically who we are at this point. You've got our security guards watching our homes, right?"

"Yes, they should already be in place. Your La Jolla house is difficult to guard."

"Grant and Sherman are on the job, and no one gets past my dogs without killing them—which would really piss me off."

"You should call Jin while we're waiting."

"Good idea." He glanced at his watch. "I hope she doesn't rip me a new one for calling at oh three thirty. Here goes." Nathan tapped her cell number.

The voice on the other end sounded half-asleep. "This had better be damned important."

"It is. Harv is sending you a text with a photo attached."

"And this couldn't wait a few hours?"

"No."

"It came through. Hang on: I need my glasses . . . What are you sending?"

"It's a tattoo from a dead guy we saw tonight."

"A dead guy," she repeated. "I'm opening it now . . . You saw this tonight, in person."

"Yeah. The man's ID said he was from Seoul."

"Where did you see this? Did anyone see you?" She sounded fully awake now. And seriously concerned.

"No one saw us. Do you recognize the tattoo?"

"Are you one hundred percent sure no one saw you?"

"One hundred percent? No."

"Nathan, your life could be in danger. Mine too."

"Slow down, Jin. What are you talking about?"

"I'm deleting the photo. You should delete it right away too. You need to forget you ever saw this."

"Wait a sec. What's wrong?"

"What's wrong? That dead guy isn't from South Korea; he's a black-ops assassin from North Korea!"

CHAPTER 26

Stone knew Lansing would already be up because Holly had already made contact. He decided to initiate a cell to cell, knowing his caller ID would pop up on Lansing's screen.

"Good morning, Stone. I'm already up, thanks to my new chief of staff."

"How's she working out, by the way?"

"The woman's a human backhoe. I've never met such a hard worker, or a more dedicated public servant. I made the right choice. I can't tell you how many times she's slept on the couch in her office. I'm buying her a convertible sofa so she'll at least have a bed in there."

"The nation's business never sleeps."

"Amen to that."

"Ethan, we need to have a conversation we can't have."

"Where are you?"

"In my office."

"I'll call you right back."

A few seconds later, his desk phone rang.

"Stone?"

"Yeah, it's me. I spoke to Nathan earlier this morning. I imagine my call went a lot like yours with Holly."

"It's troubling news, to say the least," Lansing said.

"At this point, the entire November Directive's at risk."

"For a lot of reasons, we can't let it fail."

"How many undercover operatives does it have?"

"Twelve," Lansing said. "Five of them are in the Mexico division, the other seven are in East Asia and Venezuela. If Mason compromises the November Directive, those operatives could be facing horrible deaths. It doesn't matter how big their paychecks are, they can't spend them if they're dead. Is there any chance Beaumont's behind this?"

"No."

"You sound certain."

"I've known him most of my life. He's a good man. The primary reason people get involved with illegal activity is to make money. George doesn't need it. His net worth is probably close to a billion dollars."

"If you think he's clean, that's good enough for me."

"He's on his way to my office right now. I made a deal with Nathan. I told him if he'd stand down temporarily, I wouldn't discuss anything with George until he arrived so Nathan and Harvey could hear it in real time."

"You're talking about Harvey Fontana, Nathan's business partner?"

"Yes. They agreed to hold off making any moves against Mason until they hear what Beaumont has to say. They didn't have any objections to you joining the call."

"I definitely want in. You said George's on his way to your office right now?"

"Yes. He should be here in a few minutes."

"What about Benson?" Lansing asked.

Stone personally knew the Director of National Intelligence, but it wasn't his job to update him; it was Lansing's. The FBI was one of seventeen agencies under the DNI's umbrella. Lansing had personally kept Benson up to speed on the November Directive's progress. And if DNI Benson knew, the president also knew.

"You'll need to tell him everything," Stone said. "We shouldn't hold anything back at this point. We may lose containment."

"I agree. Hang on a second, Stone. I'll be right back."

The phone line went silent. Stone felt like a hypocrite. He'd always believed Nathan's unorthodox tactics weren't justifiable, but now he and Lansing were about to discuss a black op against an American citizen on American soil. Even if Mason's actions were considered traitorous, he was still entitled to due process. Wasn't he? It was a question Stone didn't want to ask because he didn't like the answer.

"I'm back," Lansing said.

"The way I see it, Ethan, Mason's facing a needle. He's as good as dead already."

"Are we talking about what I think we're talking about?"

"Look, I don't like it any more than you do, but a cascade failure of the November Directive is not an option."

"We've known each other for a lot of years, Stone. This doesn't sound like you. What we're sanctioning isn't within the purest confines of the law. We both took similar oaths."

"I had this conversation with Nathan earlier this morning. He once told me something I've never forgotten. He said, 'Life is never as simple as a book of rules.'"

Lansing said nothing for a moment. "He's right."

"I can tell you this with certainty. Nathan would give his life for any one of us. He's the most loyal man I've ever known. He's a team player through and through, and he's proven it many times."

"Then we turn him loose," Lansing said. "He's already got a head start. We should do everything possible to support him, but I want one of my agents along for the ride."

"I'm not sure that's such a good idea. It complicates things. I don't want him second-guessing himself at the moment of truth because there's a special agent with him."

"Don't worry: I have the perfect person in mind."

Stone thought for a moment. "Then we're on the same page."

"We're here to make the tough decisions and live with the consequences. For the record, I have no desire to tender my resignation just yet."

"We need to be clear on something, Ethan. My son is not taking the fall if things go south. He gets a get-out-of-jail-free card, or no deal. If it takes a presidential pardon, so be it."

"Agreed. Let's just hope it doesn't come to that."

"I can assure you, it won't. Frankly, we're lucky to have him cleaning up our mess."

"It's not our mess, it's George's, but I understand your point. We both know what flows downhill. We talked about this. We never planned to keep the ND secret forever, but it's a whole lot easier to go public when it's got a flawless track record."

"Like I said, we'll know a lot more once we've talked to George."

"Send me a text once he's in your office. I'll set the conference call up from here. I've got Nathan's cell number, but I don't have a landline for him."

Stone gave him Harvey's private number at First Security.

Lansing asked about being off the record.

"Nathan gave me his word we won't be recorded."

CHAPTER 27

A text from his father announced that Beaumont had just entered the parking garage, and they should expect a call within five minutes. Nathan knew it could easily take that long for Beaumont to make his way to Stone's office. He had to go through security twice and walk quite a distance. The Russell Senate Office Building occupied an entire city block.

He sent a return text saying they were waiting.

"This should be an interesting call," Harv said.

Nathan didn't respond. He despised being in a holding pattern. Although he understood the situation, it didn't make it any easier. Intercepting Mason on the way to the hospital had been a lucky break, but Nathan didn't think he'd get another shot at Mason without Lansing's help. If they were going to track the guy down, they needed the resources of the FBI, which dictated Lansing had to be on board. Holly wasn't an option. Nathan didn't plan to ask her for anything. If Lansing didn't sanction their further involvement, they'd have to start from scratch, which consumed time. As Harv believed, sooner or later Mason would discover their involvement, and they didn't want to find themselves in the crosshairs of an OEF combat vet, PMC or not. Nathan had no doubt Mason would make a formidable enemy.

"What's wrong?" Harv asked, breaking Nathan from his thoughts.

"I feel restless; I need to get moving."

"I think Lansing will give us the go-ahead. We have a proven history with him. And we're owed a few favors."

"I don't feel right calling in any IOUs."

"Me either, and I don't think we'll have to."

"So what's Mason's next move? He has to know he's unsupported from here on. He'll bolt and never have to answer for killing Mara."

Harv took a swig of water. "We don't know that. It depends on what he's after—why he killed the guys at the soccer field. Maybe he's doing BSI's business via unconventional means. Maybe it's just a jab in Alisio's eye. More likely, though, I'd guess he's got something to gain. If it's a big enough reward, he might stick around long enough to finish the job. And if he does hang around, how many of his people remain loyal to him? We could be facing a small army."

"I'm giving that low odds. If my father's right, and Beaumont's not complicit, he'll cut Mason off. I seriously doubt anyone outside of Mason's inner circle would be willing to do prison time for the guy."

"I'm only saying we don't know how many people are involved in whatever he's up to."

"At this point, I'm ready to kill anyone who sides with him. Mara's murder really pisses me off. She didn't have a mean bone in her body."

"Did you love her?"

Nathan didn't answer right away. He couldn't recall Harv ever asking him that. "Yeah, I did. At least I thought I did. I'm not sure anymore."

"Maybe you should tell Holly about Mara."

"What would be the point? I'm in no-man's-land. If she wants some space, I should give it to her, and at this point it's looking more and more like that's the case."

"She's on damage control with Lansing. Think about the headache she's facing. The FBI's chief of staff was scouting an unreported murder scene with her boyfriend in the middle of a rainy night, three thousand miles away from her office. Add to that, she participated in a hit-and-run firefight in the middle of a public street. I know she's got Lansing's confidence, but at some point it could be stretched too thin, even for her."

"Maybe you're right. I guess we've still got CIA Director Cantrell. I'm certain she can pull some strings. She'll be able to—"

Harv's desk phone bleeped to life. "Here we go. Maybe we'll get some answers."

"Hi, Dad, I have you on speaker and Harv's with me."

"George Beaumont is here, and Director Ethan Lansing is also on the line with us."

"Hello, Major Beaumont, Director Lansing. Thank you for talking with us."

"Please call me George; I'm long retired from the Marines."

"Let's all use first names," Stone suggested.

"Hello, Nathan," Lansing said. "I hear you've had a busy evening."

"To put it mildly, sir."

Stone jumped in. "George, I told Nathan I didn't want to discuss anything involving BSI unless you were present. You should know that Nathan and Harvey still possess the highest security clearances possible. In theory, they could sit in on presidential briefings. Not even I can do that. Rest assured anything we discuss will be kept in the utmost confidence."

"I'm not worried."

Nathan said, "Thank you. I believe my father and Ethan are up to speed. Why don't I start at the beginning and give you a quick summary of everything that's happened and why we're involved."

It took Nathan about five minutes to tell the story again. Neither Lansing nor Beaumont interrupted, but Stone occasionally added something he thought relevant. When Nathan finished, no one said anything for a few seconds.

"If I may, gentlemen . . ." Lansing said. "Nathan, you aren't aware of this, but a little over three years ago, your father received a handwritten letter from President Obama. In it, the president wanted a two-phased plan for interdicting the gun smuggling taking place along the Mexican border between California and Arizona. Keep in mind what the president wanted wouldn't be easy to do. The fight against ISIS and other radical Islamic factions, both domestic and abroad, had tied up a sizable chunk of our resources. Your father, with the help of everyone on his committee, came up with a totally new concept. We needed a test pilot, and that's where George Beaumont and BSI stepped in. It's called the November Directive."

Nathan listened while Lansing and Beaumont outlined the idea of using privately trained undercover operatives in the fight against criminal gangs and cartels. It had been Tanner Mason's job to manage everything and relay field intelligence to Beaumont, who, in turn, passed it on to ATF Director Martini and Lansing. There were three divisions within the November Directive: Mexico, Venezuela, and East Asia. Beaumont said he now had multiple undercover operatives up and running in each of those areas.

Nathan had to admit, the more he listened, the more he found himself in agreement. Often the best solutions to problems were found through invention and innovation in the private sector.

"The president has a vested interest in the ND," Stone said. "Although he never made it a public campaign promise, he wanted the violence along the border and illegal flow of guns into Mexico stemmed."

Lansing continued. "We knew one of the biggest risks facing the program would be one or more of our operatives being turned or selling out. We just never thought it would be the program's director."

"But hasn't that always been a risk, no matter who the undercover agent is, or what agency he or she works for?" Harv asked.

"Yes, that's right. Many federal agents have been seduced by the lure of the world they're sworn to prosecute. That's why BSI's undercover operatives earn a healthy six-digit salary. While they're inside, they can save a huge amount because they're also on the cartel's bankroll. We believe it helps alleviate the effect of all the money and glamour they're exposed to, knowing they have a huge stash waiting when they come out."

"Seems like a smart idea," Nathan said. "Whatever you're paying those people, it isn't enough."

"On that, we agree," Lansing said. "The program's start-up wasn't without difficulty. It took quite a bit of work just to get the project on Attorney General Paul Ames's desk. Even though it's funded under the Department of Justice, and the ATF is playing the lead role in the interdiction effort, it's a Homeland Security project."

That didn't make sense to Nathan, but he kept quiet. He'd ask his father about it later, privately.

Lansing went on. "At first, Ames didn't buy into the concept of using privately trained undercover operatives on US soil because of the controversial nature of PMCs in general. Truth be told, they played a huge role and were vital to the war effort. Most people don't know this, but at one point during Desert Storm, there were over a hundred thousand private contractors working in Iraq. Not all of them were military personnel, but they were integral to the war effort."

"Your father pushed ND through," Beaumont said. "He paved the way for the program's funding, which is always the most difficult part. Paper is cheap; men and equipment aren't. Because of its early success, the ND has grown into a vital program. Without it, the ATF's gunrunning interdiction would be set back by months, possibly years. A lot's riding on this for everyone involved, especially your father. If the ND succeeds, its address is 1600 Penn, but if it fails, its address changes to the Russell Senate Office Building."

"Politics as usual," Nathan said.

"And it looks like failure is what we're facing," Beaumont said. "Every undercover operative could be exposed and killed, probably horribly."

"They're only at risk if Mason blows their cover," Nathan said. "Are you worried he'll do that?"

"I honestly don't know. I want to believe he's not vindictive, but I used to believe he'd never betray his oath either. Our employees swear an oath, just like the military does. But if he felt up against the wall, the threat of blowing the program would clearly be a source of leverage."

"So, gentlemen, what are we going to do about this?" Stone asked.

"Harvey and I think we have a lead, but we'll need some help pursuing it. Dad, will you show George the photos we took at the soccer fields?"

"Photos?" Beaumont asked. "You took photos of the bodies?"

"It's fortunate they did," Stone said. "Mason went back and removed them. Without Nathan's photos, there'd be no hard evidence the murders took place, even with Mr. Haynes's testimony."

"So Mason did that after he found out about Mr. Haynes?" Beaumont asked.

"Yes," said Stone. "I think we can conclude he initially wanted the bodies to be discovered or he wouldn't have left them there in the first place. I'm showing George the photos."

A brief interval of silence followed.

"If we can ID the dead men," Harvey said, "it might give us some answers. We're also looking into why Mason chose a soccer field for the murder site. We're thinking it wasn't randomly chosen, that it has some underlying meaning."

Nathan added, "Without giving any detail, I showed the double-headed dragon tattoo on the South Korean man to someone I trust. I was told it's a North Korean assassin's tattoo. Harv and I also think the money pinned to their foreheads is a signature of some kind."

"It is," Lansing said.

"We also think our interference in Mason's scheme tonight puts us at risk."

"I believe it does," Lansing said. "That's why I'm going to share some classified information. It's clear you and Harvey are on the right path and you'd eventually discover what I'm about to tell you, so I'll save you the time. The money pinned on the dead men's foreheads is the signature of Alfonso Alisio. He's the crime boss of a huge cartel out of Mexico City with dozens of satellite gangs all over the Western Hemisphere. He uses the gangs to distribute his wares. I'm assuming those are 10,000-peso notes?"

"Yes," Nathan answered.

"They've been demonetized for years."

"So why did Mason do it?" Nathan asked. "And why use a soccer field? Was he hoping to frame Alisio's cartel for the murders?"

"No," Beaumont said.

"You sound certain about that, George," Stone said.

"I am. Our Mexican division of the ND's main mission has been to infiltrate Alisio's cartel. The tattoo on the Mexican guy, the one with the red heart and black dagger piercing it? That's Alisio's trademark. All his people have them, and once they're on, they never come off. Alisio owns a professional soccer team along with several minor-league teams. I can only assume the soccer-field location is somehow related. Maybe one of Alisio's minor-league teams is scheduled to play there tomorrow and Mason left the bodies out there to send a message to Alisio."

"To what end?" Harv asked. "And why would Mason use Alisio's murder signature on the guy's own men?"

"That's what we need to find out," Beaumont said.

"More than that," Nathan added, "we need to know why a North Korean assassin with a South Korean ID was murdered alongside Alisio's man."

"We've long suspected Alisio has a connection with criminal elements inside North Korea, but we've never been able to make a solid connection until a week ago."

"A week ago?" Lansing asked.

Stone's voice was calm, but urgent. "Please tell us what you know, George. Now isn't the time to hold anything back."

"As we all know, counterfeiting is one of North Korea's biggest industries. They counterfeit everything under the sun, from pharmaceuticals to gold bullion. Paper money, tobacco products, liquor, DVDs, firearms, you name it, they're illegally manufacturing it and shipping it all over the world. One of North Korea's biggest markets for counterfeit products is Mexico because it doesn't have nearly the resources to stem the flow."

"May I interrupt?" Nathan asked.

"Of course," Lansing answered for Beaumont.

"Are you saying North Korea's doing business directly with Alisio?"

"Yes. The guns and other contraband from North Korea are being funneled through a South Korean organized-crime connection, probably via container ships. Think of it like a three-link chain, with South Korean smugglers being the middle link between Mexico and DPRK. Once we have our hands on Alisio, we'll know more."

"He'll lawyer up," Nathan said.

"There will be a brief interval of . . . questioning before that happens," Lansing said. "Coupled with Ramiro's testimony, we'll be able to dismantle Alisio's criminal organization and put him behind bars for the rest of his life. We're also coordinating our efforts with South Korea's Ministry of Justice."

Nathan took a sip of water. "Ramiro? He's one of the undercover operatives in the program?"

"Our first November Directive graduate," Beaumont said. "Ramiro's his code name. We've had him inside Alisio's organization for a little over eighteen months."

"I imagine getting him inside Alisio's cartel wasn't easy."

"You're right; it wasn't. We set up a bogus hit on Alisio's Santa Monica nightclub. Fake bullets, fake blood, you get the picture. We knew Alisio's wife was in the club that night, and Ramiro saved her life. We'd spent months training for that sixty-second insert, choreographing the fight; we even built a mock-up of the nightclub at our academy. Needless to say, Alisio was extremely grateful. Adding to the deception, Ramiro refused Alisio's initial offers to join his organization, but Alisio persisted and threw so much cash at Ramiro, he couldn't turn it down."

"And this was all orchestrated by Tanner Mason?" Nathan asked.

"Every step of the way," Beaumont replied.

"So how do we find him?" Lansing asked.

"What I'm about to say," said Beaumont, "is going to take everyone by surprise. There are certain things in an operation like this that must remain on a need-to-know basis, and before now, no one else needed to know."

"What didn't we need to know?" Lansing asked.

Nathan imagined his father's expression mirroring Lansing's: dismay.

"I built a safety catch into the program."

CHAPTER 28

Two hundred miles off the California coast—fifteen hours earlier

The *Yoonsuh*'s captain picked up the radar signature exactly where it should be.

When his ship closed to within three miles, he slowed to five knots and used field glasses to look for the other vessel's nav lights. A quick radio call confirmed the other captain hadn't encountered any problems and no other boats followed him. The *Yoonsuh*'s radar detector had picked up an occasional low-energy sweep, but nothing powerful like a cutter's penetrating EM burst had bounced off them. He knew the Navy and Coast Guard could disguise their sweeps to make them appear more distant, but he wasn't concerned. There weren't any large surface contacts within the twenty-mile range of his own radar. Even at flank speed, a cutter couldn't sneak up on him. He'd have at least thirty minutes to move the ten duffels back into their smuggling compartment and secure the boiler. If a Coast Guard Black Hawk overflew his ship, it wouldn't see anything out of order: the bags were belowdecks. He supposed a submarine could surface next to him, but he gave that pretty low odds. The Navy had bigger concerns.

Being in US waters always created some restlessness. A good captain read his crew's collective mood, and there'd been signs over the last few days that everyone was anxious to dock. They'd been at sea for nearly ten days, and although the *Yoonsuh* offered every available amenity, there was no replacing the feel of being on solid ground. His ship was big, but far from a cruise ship; it pitched and rolled with the swells, often severely. Fortunately, his North Korean gemologist had weathered the voyage well.

Through his field glasses, he watched the fishing boat's skiff racing over the swells toward his boat. As it always did, the transfer of the duffels would take place while moving at a slow speed with a distance of two nautical miles between the two vessels.

The skiff would need to make two trips. One with the cargo, and another with their passenger.

The captain radioed his engine room to verify the duffels had been properly weighted to sink in a hurry. His first officer confirmed the bags were all set. He hated the idea of throwing the bags overboard in the event a cutter intercepted the fishing boat, but it beat spending the next twenty years in a seven-by-ten-foot prison cell.

The gemologist's accommodations aboard the fishing boat would be quite different from what he'd enjoyed on the *Yoonsuh*. There'd be no oil massages, gourmet food, or home theater, proving the old adage that all good things must come to an end. The North Korean would just have to slum it through the last fifteen hours of his voyage.

***

Nestled in the mountains just east of Escondido, Mason's safe house offered complete privacy. The single-story residence wasn't more than a rustic cabin, but it sat low in a valley and no other homes were within eyeshot. The ten-acre property used to be an avocado orchard. The stumps of the trees were all that remained, their timber long ago sold as firewood. And the beauty of this place? It wasn't even his. Its owners, an elderly couple who were friends with the old man, spent half their lives aboard a condominium-style cruise ship. In fact, the old man had no idea that Mason even knew about the place.

The notion of ripping Alisio off had come to him about six months ago after Ramiro reported seeing a huge pile of US cash atop Alisio's desk—a mountain's worth—at least $5 million. The whole idea had crystalized that day for Mason, triggering the long-dormant memories of Mullah Sanjari's compound and that twenty-dollar bill he'd found as a child. The way to hurt Alisio badly, he'd realized, was to hit him where it counted: in the pocketbook.

The question was where and when? And the answer came soon afterward, in the form of critical intel from Ramiro. The news of the upcoming Korean exchange was too good to pass up. Mason had been waiting for the right opportunity to come along, and finally it had.

Recruiting Darla for the eventual heist hadn't been part of the original plan. Hahn and Mason knew that bringing her in would involve risk, but they'd needed a third person. She'd seemed a kindred spirit, and her PMC background mirrored theirs. Sure enough, she'd wanted in on the move against Alisio, especially when Mason offered her an equal share. And the first thing she'd done for them was use her charm on BSI's bookkeeper to locate the safe house they were using today.

He grabbed a bottled water and reentered the living room while Chip and Darla stayed in the kitchen.

Psychologically shattered, Michaels sat with his head hung. It hadn't taken long to break him. Bound to a chair atop painter's plastic, the man was a pitiful sight. Mason gave the guy credit: he'd lasted longer than predicted. But sooner or later, given the right kind of persuasion, the will to resist vanished. Although Mason believed everything Michaels had told them on the drive up here was true, he needed to verify the information with more forceful and—uncomfortable—methods. They hadn't worked on his face and hands, but everything else had been fair game.

Mason didn't enjoy this part of the business, but he knew it should bother him more than it did. Not surprisingly, it had been Darla who'd penetrated Michaels's shell. He'd watched in awe as she'd systematically peeled him down to his core. The finishing touch had come when Darla whispered something in his ear. Michaels had looked at Mason with a shocked, almost disbelieving expression. Mason had shrugged, his message clear: *I have no idea what she said, but I warned you . . .*

Darla had run her hand down Michaels's chest and stomach before brushing his groin. Mason knew from firsthand experience that men don't like being interrogated by women, especially a woman who puts on a convincing act that most men are no better than pigs and deserve to be castrated.

Michaels became very cooperative once he'd been disrobed from the waist down. Darla had asked Mason to spread the man's legs and secure them open for the "procedure." She'd then produced a cigar torch, applied the flame to the business end of her small pocketknife, and hummed "Amazing Grace" during the process. The finishing touch came when she'd put on her goggles.

Whoa! Mason remembered thinking. *Remind me to never cross this woman.*

So they now had what Michaels hadn't spilled on the drive up here. They had a date, time, and location for the arrival of the duffel bags at Shelter Island but no date, time, or location for the exchange of the duffels with Alisio. Michaels received the exchange info after the delivery to the marina was complete. Perhaps most importantly, they knew what the duffel bags contained, and Mason had a hard time wrapping his mind around it.

The bags held 300 million pesos in the form of state-of-the-art counterfeit bills that could fool most bank employees. In American dollars, it was the equivalent of nearly $24 million. Mason didn't yet know how Alisio planned to exchange the bogus money, or how much it would be discounted. But based on what he'd learned from Ramiro over the last six months, he had a pretty good idea. It would be a sweet victory forcibly taking both halves of the exchange from Alisio's grubby little hands.

Mason had re-grilled Michaels about the fishing boat's role because, on the surface, it seemed outrageously risky. Michaels said that the fishing boat always towed a small skiff out to the coordinates, then sent the skiff to pick up the duffels from the yacht while it was still moving. Mason had to hand it to the South Koreans: they were savvy smugglers.

If everything went according to plan, the yacht should've transferred the duffels to the fishing boat about fourteen hours ago. Mason looked at his watch. Michaels said each leg of the fishing boat's journey—out to sea and then back—took fifteen hours, putting the fishing boat's return at 6:00 AM, around ninety minutes from now. An hour before docking, the fishing boat's captain would text Michaels to verify everything was all set.

Mason thought it ironic that Alisio's smuggling activities had become so closely monitored in Mexico that he'd been forced to move his ROK deliveries north of the border. The opposite should've been true. It gave new meaning to the definition of a "porous US border."

Now all Mason and his team had to do was stay away from BSI headquarters, avoid the police, and elude the gunmen who'd protected Toby. None of that should be too difficult.

Everyone needed sleep. They'd been awake for thirty straight hours. One thing Mason had learned during OEF was to get shuteye whenever you could. Depending on the timing of the exchange with Alisio's people later today, they might be able to get some rack time. All things considered, his current fatigue level paled in comparison to what he'd experienced in Afghanistan.

He stepped out the back door and looked up at the smidgen of stars. He missed that about Shindand: the incredibly dark night sky. He felt like knocking down several shots of whiskey, but that self-destructive behavior was no longer an option, especially now, being so close to achieving his lifelong dream. There were times when he wished he'd never seen the box of cash at Mullah Sanjari's compound or the twenty-dollar bill. He still thought it strange that after all the carnage and bloodshed he'd seen—and dished out—the sight of a box full of cash had affected him so deeply. It was the allure of power, he suspected. Power not only to lead soldiers and operatives and succeed in one's endeavors but also to travel the world, buy what you wanted, influence whomever you wished, and ultimately to control your own destiny.

In another ninety minutes, he'd be that much closer.

CHAPTER 29

"When I gave Tanner Mason the reins of the November Directive," George Beaumont explained, "I didn't want his control to be absolute, so I built in a safety catch to verify the information he gave me. Every one of my undercover operatives also reports directly to me or one of my sons, and Mason has no clue they're doing it. Put simply, I've got a direct line of communication to Ramiro."

Stone said, "So may we assume the information Ramiro's been giving you has varied from what Mason's been giving you? And tonight's murders could be related?"

"Yes, I'm afraid so. I can't pinpoint exactly when I began to suspect Mason, but it was several months ago. Just as you said, there were discrepancies in what Mason told me versus what Ramiro told me. At first I thought they were just oversights on Mason's part. I had to remind myself that he's dealing with twelve agents in three countries. The last time I spoke to Mason, a few days ago, there was a bigger . . . inconsistency. He failed to tell me something important that I'd just learned from Ramiro. It involved an unprecedented shipment of duffel bags out of North Korea. There's no way Mason could've overlooked telling me something like that. Mason purposely withheld the intel."

"Is that how it normally works?" Nathan asked. "Do your field agents give you the info before Mason?"

"Not usually. In fact, my updates from the field aren't nearly so frequent as Mason's, or as detailed. They're pretty generalized. When Ramiro reported this latest shipment wasn't being treated like the standard guns-for-money type of deal, I'd expected to hear the same thing from Mason, but he made no mention of it. Since then, Ramiro's gone silent. I understand why Ramiro has to be careful, but when one of my operatives gives me a prolonged period of silence, I get nervous. I have no idea if they're blown or just unable to make contact."

His dad said, "I know exactly how you feel, George. I felt the same way when Nathan and Harvey went on their covert ops. Silence is horrible."

"That's the norm in my world. I have to constantly remind myself they can't just drop what they're doing and call me on their cells."

"So what are we going to do?" Stone asked.

"Based on what I've learned from all of you tonight," Beaumont answered, "I'm going to initiate contact with Ramiro right away. I usually hear back within six to twelve hours if I use an emergency code. Sometimes sooner."

"How do you do that?" Harv asked. "If you don't mind telling us."

"Online gaming," Beaumont said with some pride. "We play a combat video game with other online players. It has the most players of its kind, worldwide. Multiple millions, I'm told. Anyway, we talk to each other in real time using headsets. There's a lot of teasing and trash-talking. It's like a community, and we all have monikers. Ramiro uses his own name so it won't look suspicious. Everyone in Alisio's cartel knows him by Ramiro, anyway. I'm MGK, short for Machine Gun Kelly. Alisio doesn't suspect a thing because Ramiro plays the game right in front of everyone. Some of Alisio's lieutenants play as well. Even Alisio gets online occasionally. He uses the moniker Mr. A. He's pretty good. He's killed me a bunch of times inside the game. Just to be safe, I morph my voice. Lots of players do that, so it doesn't raise any suspicions."

Nathan shook his head and looked at Harv. "So Alisio and his men have no idea they're playing a video game with Ramiro's undercover handler. Remarkable."

"No kidding," Harv said.

"We have one-liners we use as code phrases to communicate. If I say the bolt-code phrase during the game, he knows to get the hell out of there ASAP. I also have a normal 'make contact' phrase and an emergency 'make contact' phrase."

"Can you do that from any computer?" Harv asked.

"Yes, but I like to use my own because I can mask its IP address. Ethan, if I can use one of your computers, I'll be able to contact Ramiro a lot sooner. I won't have to wait until I'm back in San Diego."

"Come by my office after we hang up. I'll get you hooked up."

"Does Ramiro use the same kind of system to contact Mason?" Harv asked. "Online gaming?"

"Yes, but it's a different game run by a completely different gaming company."

"It's brilliant," Nathan said. "Making contact right in front of the boss."

"It's worked well so far," said Beaumont.

Harv asked, "If Mason rips Alisio off, what does that do to your ongoing investigation of Alisio's cartel?"

Lansing cut in. "It could screw everything up. Years of work could be lost. We're an eyelash away from setting up a major sting to nail Alisio and dismantle his cartel. I've been working closely with the ATF and PFM, setting everything up. Which makes the timing of Mason's actions highly suspect. He might be planning to make a move against Alisio before we bring him down."

"Remind me what PFM stands for," Harv said. "Policía Federal . . ."

"Ministerial," Lansing said. "It's very much like our own ATF. It's a federal law enforcement agency under the attorney general of Mexico."

"Is the sting an ATF operation?" Nathan asked.

"No, it's a joint task force under the PFM's command. One of my worries is that Alisio has ears on the inside. It doesn't take much to bribe someone down there. I've had a lot of conversations with the PFM's director, and he's a good man. I think he wants Alisio brought down as badly as we do. Alisio's reign of terror includes the torture and murder of at least five of his federal officers in the last fourteen months. Realistically, the number's more like ten. All of them died horrible deaths and had Alisio's trademark, a 10,000-peso note tacked to their foreheads."

Stone said, "I told Nathan and Harv about the murder of our ATF agent in El Centro with Alisio's signature."

"Yes," Beaumont said. "Mason took Hutch's death badly."

"Was it ever sorted out?" Nathan asked. "Do you know how Hutch's cover was blown?"

"No," Lansing said. "There's no doubt Alisio's behind the murder, we just can't prove it. Personally, I think Mason got a bum deal. It wasn't his fault the agent was killed."

"It definitely wasn't," Beaumont said. "Look, I'm not trying to defend Mason. I picked him for the job because he was the perfect choice. I felt bad we were forced to let him go during OEF's drawdown."

"Holly mentioned that," Nathan said. "She told us he was involved in a botched mission at the end of his tour."

"Holly Simpson?" Beaumont asked. "Your new chief of staff, Ethan?"

"She and Nathan are in a relationship. Holly was with Nathan and Harvey when they saw the bodies on the soccer field."

"How much does she know?" Beaumont asked.

"She knows who Mason is and some of his history, but she doesn't know about the November Directive. She's up to speed on BSI's pending contract with us, though."

Nathan said, "I need to state something for the record, Ethan. The delay in reporting all of this to you is my fault. Holly wanted to tell you from the beginning."

Lansing responded right away. "She's an extremely loyal and dedicated agent. Everything's okay between us, so don't worry about it."

Nathan wondered if Lansing really meant that. He hoped so.

"Getting back to Mason," Beaumont said, "I didn't want to fire him, but keeping him meant the end of BSI. I was told in no uncertain terms to terminate him or lose my contracts with the DOD. At that time, there was considerable heat coming from Capitol Hill to eliminate all PMCs working in Afghanistan, even the noncombat contractors—"

"May I interrupt?" Nathan asked. "What happened? What was Mason's botched mission Holly mentioned?"

"It wasn't botched—"

Nathan said, "To be fair, 'botched' wasn't the word Holly used. I think she said, 'tragic.'"

"It *was* tragic. The objective was accomplished, but two Afghan women got caught in the cross fire and were killed. It caused a local riot that turned bloody. Several Marines were injured. Command pulled everyone out of the area until things settled down. Those women shouldn't have been there, especially so late at night without escorts. The whole thing reeked of a Taliban PR setup and, sadly, it worked. Everyone wanted Mason's head on a platter. I made a big stink and threatened to go public with some classified stuff the coalition had done. I made a deal with the brass. I said I'd accept Mason's resignation if the incident got lost. Fortunately, they took the deal. If they'd called my bluff about blowing the whistle, I wouldn't have done it. I stuck my neck out for Mason because none of his gunrunning interdiction ops ever took a single innocent life. They were textbook raids. Some of Mason's techniques were adopted by the German Army, and they're still in use today."

"But you're only as good as your last op," Nathan said. He hoped his comment didn't sound negative.

"Sadly, that's too often true," Beaumont said.

"I imagine Mason was bitter," Nathan said.

"He was, but there was blood in the water. He faced an inquiry and possible prison time. I shipped him home and made sure he got a healthy severance package, but he was still jobless. He got employment here and there, but nothing lasted. He became depressed and withdrawn."

"That's a common problem," Nathan said. "Combat vets come home from a war zone and can't adjust to mundane civilian life. They need physical and mental challenges. It's difficult for warriors to become nonwarriors."

"Speaking from personal experience?" Beaumont asked.

"Absolutely. Harv and I know it well. Did Mason drink?"

"You have no idea."

"Actually, I do." Nathan saw Harv adjust his weight. Alcohol had nearly destroyed their friendship.

"He'd call me when he was plastered, angry one minute, sobbing the next. I urged Mason to seek counseling for PTSD and managed to get him into an AA program for vets, but he didn't stay with it. He got a part-time job with a national rent-a-cop company that supplied security for shopping malls, but after two months he arm barred and choked out his supervisor and nearly did jail time. I pulled some strings and kept him out of lockup, but he ended up in the unemployment line again and his drinking got worse. I didn't know it at the time, but he'd gambled his savings away. He was close to becoming homeless. He'd pick fights with anyone who'd step up."

Nathan exchanged a glance with Harv.

"When he got arrested for slugging an off-duty cop, guess who he called? I made a deal with him. I told him if he'd permanently lay off the booze, I'd make a call and get him a job, but my offer came with nonnegotiable terms. He'd have to get into therapy with other OEF vets and stick with the AA program for two months before I'd arrange the interview. He came through, and I kept my word. He went to work for a different private military company."

"You got him a job with one of your competitors?" Nathan asked. "You couldn't hire him back?"

"The Afghan incident was still too fresh. He was grateful for the help I gave him, but he still harbored a lot of resentment about what happened. Don't get me wrong: the resentment was one-way. I liked him, and he'd proven he could stay sober."

"What was his new job?" Harv asked.

"His gun-smuggling interdiction experience from OEF made him a perfect candidate to work as a consultant to federal law enforcement agencies, mostly the ATF. Unfortunately, his new assignment evolved into a disaster. This time the arms-interdiction operations were domestic, mostly taking place on the American side of the border with Mexico. The federal agents he instructed resented him and his cowboy tactics. They looked down on him and didn't value the military experience he brought. Instead of working in a Wild West, anything-goes atmosphere, he found himself mired in red tape. He wasn't working with ass kickers, but instead with promotion-hungry ass kissers who feared bad press more than failed ops. And ops *did* fail, but not because of Mason."

Stone said, "I told Nathan and Harvey about the aftermath of the JTF raid in El Centro, about the murdered ATF agent. I didn't know if Mason knew him or not."

"He definitely knew him. Special Agent Hutcheson was assigned to Mason's unit as an explosives and IED expert. Hutch was a good man. I personally approved his embedment. Mason and I spoke about Hutch often. I'd planned to offer him a job if he wasn't happy in the ATF or just wanted a change of scenery."

"How did Mason get tagged for the blame?" Harv asked. "He wasn't responsible for blowing Hutch's cover, was he?"

"No, but before Alisio murdered Hutch, an ATF agent was killed during the raid and several others were seriously wounded. That same midlevel brass concluded the ATF acted too aggressively. Yeah, I know, it sounds ridiculous. They're shooting it out for their lives and they're too aggressive? It's that ass-kisser mentality. I argued that the friendly casualties would've been higher had it not been for Mason's training. The video footage is under lock and key, so I can't confirm what I suspect is true."

"You'll never see it," Nathan added.

"I've concluded the same thing. It was a difficult time for Mason, maybe worse than anything he'd seen overseas. Mason was there when they lowered Hutch from the streetlight. Mason lost control and shoved a TV reporter to the ground. The guy wasn't injured, but the incident went out on the five o'clock news, then went viral on YouTube."

"And Mason lost his job again," Nathan said.

"Yes," Beaumont said. "I guess I'm telling you all of this because I don't want you gentlemen to second-guess why I gave Mason another chance."

"No one here is doing that, George," Stone said. "I'm assuming Mason didn't fall off the wagon and start drinking again after Hutch's death?"

"No, he didn't and that's part of the reason I rehired him. By that time, Afghanistan was old news. Scandals only last as long as cameras are present."

"So what's Mason's endgame?" Nathan asked. "Money?"

"Yes, that's what I'm thinking," said Beaumont.

"If Hutch was his friend and they shared a combat bond from Afghanistan," Harv added, "then there's likely an element of revenge too."

"The perfect double whammy," Nathan said. "He ruins Alisio's deal with the South Koreans and lines his pockets in the process."

"More than that," Lansing said. "He also ruins our entire undercover operation against Alisio and the other ND divisions. We can't let it happen. I'm not just saying that because of the time and money or because the president's behind the project. Lives are at stake."

"He's already taken three lives," said Nathan. "And attempted to murder four others."

"All the more reason to stop Mason before things escalate further." Beaumont sounded genuinely concerned.

"So about this big deal that's in the works," said Harv. "Does Ramiro have any idea what's in the duffel bags?"

"No, but he knows Alisio's been stockpiling Philharmonics and diamonds. He thinks Alisio's going to trade them for whatever's coming in from North Korea. Again, I don't have specific numbers, but Ramiro's under the impression it's a sizable deal."

"Philharmonics . . . you mean the Austrian one-ounce bullion coins?" Harv asked.

"Yes."

"It seems pretty clear Mason's going to make a move and try to raid the exchange," said Stone.

"So how do Harv and I fit in?"

"We want you to get containment," Lansing said.

Nathan knew no one would say more than that. "Understood."

"George needs to initiate emergency contact with Ramiro. Once he does that, we'll have a better idea of exactly how the exchange is working—and what we're up against."

"I assume you'd also like to know whether Mason's compromised the November Directive's undercover agents, and you'd like us to . . . ask him about it?"

Lansing didn't hesitate. "Yes."

Nathan could only imagine what his father was thinking. This was a complete reversal of what they talked about earlier. Nathan wouldn't say anything; his father didn't need the additional stress, and it wasn't in Nathan's nature to say, "I told you so."

He did, however, need to voice a major concern. "What about personal liability for Harv and me?"

"You're covered," Lansing said. "Stone insisted on get-out-of-jail-free cards for both of you. Since you're proven assets, I agreed. But your immunity isn't open-ended."

"Fair enough."

"Once Ramiro checks in with George and relays the info to me, I'll call you and Stone back. I suggest you and Harvey use the downtime to get some sleep; I have a feeling you're going to need it."

"We will."

"George, you look like you want to say something more," Stone said.

"It's a long shot, but I think it's worth a try. All of our company vehicles have antitheft trackers installed. We might be able to track Mason's movements."

"I'm assuming he knows that," Nathan said. "That's why you're calling it a long shot?"

"Yes."

"It's worth a try. When will you know?"

"One of my sons will have to activate the trackers from our headquarters. I'll get that going right after we hang up. What's your cell number? If we get something, I'll text you the GPS coordinates."

Nathan gave him Harv's cell as well.

"One more thing," Lansing said. "Think of it as my own brand of safety catch."

"Okay . . ." Nathan said with some hesitation.

"I'm assigning a special agent to work with you. You might need access to the NCIC database and an FBI badge might come in handy. Chief of Staff Simpson told me she flashed her badge during your ER visit, and it got you access to Mr. Haynes."

"I appreciate the offer, Ethan, but we prefer to work alone."

"I'm aware of that."

Nathan waited for more, but nothing was said. He knew when to be a good soldier and not question orders. "Then the decision's been made."

"It has."

"There's only one person we trust for something like this."

"She's already on her way. Count on about four hours."

Nathan looked at Harv. "I'm assuming this special agent is from your Fresno field office?"

"Indeed she is. I believe you have her cell number."

"Indeed we do."

CHAPTER 30

With sunrise two hours away, Mason drove south on I-15 while Hahn babysat Michaels in the backseat. Darla followed them in a separate vehicle.

Their destination: the Shelter Island Marina in San Diego Harbor. Before leaving the Escondido safe house, Mason had used his tablet to look at satellite images of the surrounding area. He wanted a rough idea of what to expect once they arrived. Mason thought it amusing that Alisio's smuggling operation took place within a few miles of the Coast Guard station.

If all went according to plan, they'd intercept the delivery of the duffels at the marina, learn where Alisio's exchange would take place, and make their move at that location. Mason held no illusions. He knew what they'd be attempting would be difficult and dangerous, but like peeling an onion, they'd tackle each situation one layer at a time.

If things fell through, having the counterfeit pesos was better than nothing, but laundering that much bogus paper wouldn't be easy, and he'd have to warehouse it until he found a wholesale buyer. He couldn't just drive across the international border with 300 million in bogus pesos. Mason knew Alisio wouldn't be paying face value for fake paper. He'd likely be offering around twenty-five cents on the dollar in some form of goods or currency—but that would still be a huge number. Six million or so bucks would go a long way in securing a comfortable lifestyle for the three of them. If his heist succeeded, he might just end up with both the North Koreans' fake pesos and Alisio's loot. Not a bad day's haul.

They arrived at the northeast cove of the marina and followed Michaels's directions onto a street intersecting Harbor Drive. The property to their left held several three-story buildings, separated by a security fence. The place had a military feel, and Mason thought it might be a Navy facility.

He pulled to the side of the road and sent Darla ahead to give the dock area a quick reconnaissance. He told her to scan with both the thermal imager and night vision. The thermal imager wouldn't detect people in cars with the windows up, but the NV might see them.

A few minutes later, she came up on the radio. *"Okay, the marina's office is a small building about the size of a two-car garage. The gate to the dock's ramp is locked with a card-key access and keypad. There are two security cameras. The first one overlooks the gate to the dock, and a second is mounted on the eave of the office, pointing toward the parking lot."*

"Do you see a white Econoline van?"

"It's right where Michaels said it would be, near the north end of the parking lot."

"Can the office camera see it?"

"Unless it's a fish-eye lens, negative. It's tilted down toward the area in front of the door."

"Okay, find a place to park where you can see the driver's side of the van. Let me know if you see anyone walking around or people just sitting in their vehicles. We're coming in."

His radio clicked.

Studying the area, Mason cruised into the marina's parking lot. They passed a nice-looking restaurant called Jimmy's Famous American Tavern. He'd seen its roof on the satellite images, but hadn't known what it was. There were several dozen cars present, most of them close to the dock's entrance.

"Where are Alisio's slips?" Mason asked.

"Right there, the first three slots."

"Why's there only one boat?"

"Sometimes they get chartered. They go on overnight trips to San Clemente Island or wherever."

Mason drove out of the marina's parking lot and radioed Darla. "I've got your location. We're going to sit tight for a few minutes near Harbor Drive."

"There's activity on the dock. Someone's walking toward the gate from a boat near the end."

"Keep eyes on him. Let me know if he enters the parking lot." Mason knew people lived on their boats. The guy could be making a pit stop at the marina's bathroom facilities.

Mason pulled into a small parking lot before reaching Harbor Drive and killed the engine. Michaels reminded Mason he'd promised to let him go once he had the duffel bags. Mason told Michaels that wasn't their agreement. Michaels was going with them to the exchange location, as yet to be determined. Michaels tried to object, but Mason told him to shut up.

Twenty long minutes later, Michaels received his one-hour-ETA text from "Captain Phillips."

Cute, thought Mason.

"Hold the phone so we can see your response and move your fingers slowly. If you scare off Alisio's boat, your usefulness to us is over."

"Yeah, okay man, I get it."

Michaels texted back: *In the van waiting.*

A few seconds later, a return text showed a smiley face.

Even though the text from Phillips came a little late, Mason wasn't worried. Michaels had said the arrival times always varied. In the Escondido safe house, Mason had thoroughly grilled Michaels about the texts, about what was normally exchanged. He didn't want Michaels sending a secret phrase or code alerting the fishing boat to trouble or a stakeout at the dock.

Mason drove back into the marina's parking lot and stopped next to the van. His plan was to put Chip in there with Michaels. It had been a smart move keeping Michaels's keys because the van's key was on the set they'd taken at the nightclub. Mason told Michaels if he made a run for it or attempted to yell for help, Chip would zap him with the Taser. Chip also had a green light to kill Michaels if the guy tried anything funny. As a backup, Darla could nail Michaels if he opened the van's door. Using the same subsonic .22 ammo, her bolt-action rifle wouldn't sound much louder than a soft hand clap. Michaels assured them he wouldn't try anything.

Mason ordered their captive to get behind the wheel and fasten his seat belt. Keeping the keys, Chip got into the back of the van and positioned himself out of Michaels's reach, but where he could still fire the Taser's prongs into the guy's flesh within half a second of any trouble.

With Michaels and Chip squared away in the van, Mason parked several spaces distant, facing away from the dock. He didn't want the SUV to look like it was spying on the action. It also allowed him to screen himself from view and make a quicker escape.

He checked his watch—fifty-five minutes to showtime.

***

Using field glasses, Mason monitored the approaching fishing boat as it crept through the water toward the dock. It looked to be forty or fifty feet long. He knew it was the right boat because it towed a small skiff. It didn't appear to be a commercial tuna boat, more like a day-pass kind of craft. Unlike last night, the weather was dry and no wind blew. The boat cleared the end of the dock and turned straight toward them in the mirror-smooth water. Mason watched the distorted reflection of city lights create an ever-expanding V behind the boat. When the boat neared its slip, an Asian crew member untied the skiff's towline and piloted the inflatable craft over to the dock. The fishing boat's captain then maneuvered his vessel into its slip, and the crew member who'd piloted the skiff secured its lines.

A different crew member, also Asian, hopped off the boat, walked up the ramp to the gate, and retrieved a four-wheeled cart—like the ones used at Costco warehouses. Back on the boat, the skiff's pilot began moving duffel bags to the dock. *Crazy*, Mason thought, *that each bag holds 30 million pesos.* The crew member returned with the cart and began loading the bags. So far, Mason counted ten duffel bags and three men. Two crew members and the captain.

The bags appeared to be heavy; the short man stacking them had to put his weight into the effort.

Then, as if merely moving the day's catch, the guy wheeled the cart toward the ramp. Mason watched him struggle as he pushed the load up the slope, but he made it to the top and took a breather. The cart pusher looked toward the van, then at his watch.

"Here we go," Mason said. "Chip and Darla stand by. Verbal copies."

Both of them acknowledged hearing his transmission.

Mason lost sight of the cart pusher for a brief period when the office building blocked his view.

"I've got the cart pusher," Mason said. "He's entering the parking lot."

"I'm right behind Michaels," Chip said.

"Darla?"

"I've got the van's door in my sights. Standing by."

The man pushed the cart along the wharf, then angled toward the office. When the cart pusher reached the parking lot, he stopped and turned toward the fishing boat.

The other crew member, and someone Mason hadn't yet seen—maybe the captain—hopped onto the dock and began a fast-paced walk toward the gate.

"Two more men are walking toward the gate from the fishing boat. Chip, be ready in there."

"*Copy,*" Chip said.

The newcomers went through the gate and assumed flanking positions next to the cart pusher. Mason cursed under his breath. In the safe house, Michaels had assured them that a single ROK man accompanied the goods, not three. *So who the hell are these guys*? Mason was tempted to order Michaels's summary execution and just settle for the counterfeit pesos. Screw the later exchange. But still . . .

In thirty seconds, the cart would be at the van. He needed to make a decision. Fast.

Believing they had good tactical positions, plenty of firepower, and the element of surprise on their side, Mason decided to play this out. He wasn't willing to write off the operation; he'd come too far to give up now. If this was a trap and Michaels had managed to warn the fishing boat's captain, that dumbass had just signed his own death warrant.

The double escort didn't seem to confuse the cart pusher. Clearly he'd been expecting them. They were dressed in casual attire and had dark coats on. Without a doubt, they were packing.

Mason knew the rear doors of the van were unlocked, and in twenty more seconds, those men were going to swing them open and see Chip holding a Taser on Michaels.

Even though Michaels couldn't hear Chip's ear speaker, Mason kept his voice low and calm. "Chip, they'll be at the van in fifteen seconds. Stand by to shoot your way out of there."

"*What about Michaels?*"

"Nail him with the Taser on my mark. Tell him to lean out the window and wave when they arrive. Darla, you take the shorter guy; I'll take the other. Chip, you're on the cart pusher. Confirm."

Mason listened to the verbal copies.

"Ten seconds. Fire on my mark."

Mason watched the trio approach the rear of the van. The men wearing coats kept looking around, but they didn't seem overly tense. Maybe they weren't expecting trouble after all. Maybe Alisio changed things without telling Michaels, but that was dangerous. Alisio must realize doing something like that could result in a friendly fire incident.

"Tell Michaels to lean out the window and ask about the extras . . . Now."

Mason watched Michaels stick his head out and wave.

"Hey, man, who's the new muscle?"

"Mr. Park wants them here."

"Well he didn't say nothing about this to me."

"Mr. Park doesn't report to you."

"This don't pass the smell test. I've never seen these guys before."

"Shut the fuck up, T-Hat. You don't need to know who they are."

One of the men walked toward the passenger door. Just before Mason lost sight of him, the man reached inside his coat and pulled a suppressed weapon.

"Chip, you're blown! Darla, engage!"

A soft clap pierced the marina.

In a bizarre solo dance, the shorter man spun, looked confused, then crumpled to the ground.

"Zap Michaels!" Mason flew out of the SUV and ran straight toward the van.

A giant bullwhip cracked. The windshield of the car behind him exploded.

Mason knew the sound. Someone had just fired a high-powered suppressed rifle. The supersonic crack of a passing bullet was unmistakable; he'd heard it many times.

Mason changed direction and ducked behind a pickup. "Darla, did you see the muzzle flash?"

"Negative."

"We're pinned until we take out that sniper. Focus on Alisio's boat. I'm going to draw his fire. Stand by . . . Now!" Mason made a sprint toward the van, weaving between the sparsely parked cars.

Another crack echoed across the marina, resulting in more shattered glass. He stopped running and crouched behind a compact.

A third shot broke the passenger window above his head. *Shit!*

"Darla?"

"He's lying prone on the roof of Alisio's boat."

Mason barely heard the muted pop of Darla's rifle.

"He's down," she reported.

"Shoot anyone else you see on the boat."

"Copy."

Darla's rifle discharged again.

"A second man is down. I don't see anyone else."

"Keep eyes on the boat for now."

Mason knew they had to wrap this up quickly. Even though those high-powered rifle reports were suppressed, the bullets weren't. Their supersonic bangs alerted the entire area. The harbor police and the SDPD could be here in minutes, maybe Navy MPs too.

The second gunman who'd joined the cart pusher still posed a threat.

"Darla, fire several shots into the sedan next to the van in . . . three . . . two . . . one. Now."

The windows of the sedan shattered and holes appeared in its fender as Darla fired a shot every second.

Keeping the van between himself and the gunman, Mason sprinted over to the closest car and flattened himself on the asphalt. He toggled the laser and lined up on the man's ankle.

The report of his pistol sounded like a hard-soled footstep. A string of Korean obscenities rang out. Mason gained his feet and rushed to the driver's side of the van. In a crouch, he eased along its front bumper, extended his arm around the fender, and blindly fired along the van's length.

Grunts of pain announced he'd scored more hits.

The passenger door of the van flew open, knocking the gunman sideways.

Way to go, Chip.

Mason used the opportunity to finish the man. He pivoted around the fender, lined up on the guy before he could recover his balance, and fired three quick shots. The shimmering laser jumped with each discharge, but didn't wander from the gunman's forehead.

The man's expression went blank, and his mouth formed an O shape.

Then, as if tired of standing, the man sat down to die.

Mason stepped forward and twisted the Glock out of the gunman's hand, then tossed it into the van.

The man who'd pushed the cart had abandoned his cargo. Making a beeline for the wharf, the guy ran at a full sprint. If he made it to the edge, he might jump in and try to swim under the docks for cover.

"Darla, do you see a gun on the rabbit?"

"Negative."

"Shoot center mass."

Mason leaned against the van to steady his aim and painted the laser on the man's back. He heard Darla's rifle report at the same instant he fired. As before, the subsonic shots were barely audible. The man shuddered but kept going. Mason aimed dead center and sent two more bullets, hoping for a spinal cord hit.

The fleeing man reached back as if trying to wave off a swarm of bees and changed direction. The guy had taken at least five bullets, but they hadn't slowed him down much. Mason knew subsonic .22s didn't deliver a lot of energy, but they had to sting like the devil, and some of them—depending on the thickness of his clothes—might've punctured a lung.

Rather than jump into the water, the guy turned south and paralleled the wharf. He was probably worried he couldn't swim with bullets lodged in his back.

Mason took off in pursuit. He couldn't let that guy report this heist to Alisio.

After he cleared the row of parked cars, Mason angled toward the marina's office building and triggered his radio. "Darla, switch to your handgun and sprint south along the parking lot's perimeter fence. I'll try to drive him to you. I'll be coming in from the north. Let me know if you lose sight of me."

"Copy."

"Chip, make sure Michaels is secure and load the duffels into the van. Do your best to conceal the bodies under the parked cars. Stand by to bug out."

"Michaels is out cold, but I'll cuff him anyway."

Mason saw the cart pusher's head bobbing as he ran. Through a hole in the parked cars, he also saw a handgun in the guy's hand. "Darla, he's got a nonsuppressed pistol."

"Copy. I've still got eyes on you."

The fleeing man looked over his shoulder.

Mason was ready for him to stop and return fire, but the guy kept running. At the wharf, Mason turned south and saw the man run past the access gate to the dock. He disappeared on the far side of the office building inside a group of small boats suspended on blocks.

Mason inserted a full magazine into his pistol. "He's hiding in the dry-docked boats just south of the office. Stay east of them and be ready to move. I'm going to pepper the area. Copy?"

"I'll be ready."

Mason saw the camera above the dock's gate and avoided its cone of vision. He diverted to the west side of the office building, used its wall for cover, and toggled his laser.

"I lost you," Darla said.

"I'm holding position at the office's northwest corner."

"Affirm. I've got you."

"I'm giving you cover fire . . . Now." He painted the hull of the nearest boat, then lowered his aim to the ground and opened fire, walking the rounds along the underside of its keel. Some of the small-caliber bullets whistled as their deformed shapes cartwheeled at 950 feet per second. His goal wasn't to score a direct hit; he just wanted the guy distracted so that he wouldn't see Darla's flanking maneuver.

"Darla?"

"Nothing yet."

Mason changed magazines and sent another barrage.

"I've got a bead," Darla said.

Mason stopped firing and listened for the report of Darla's handgun. A muted clap rang out.

"Affirm: he's down."

"Make sure he's dead and conceal the body as best you can. We're leaving in thirty seconds. Chip?"

"All set."

Back at the van, he found Chip behind the wheel, ready to go. He looked through the driver's side window and saw the duffels piled up next to Michaels. Excitement stirred. He was tempted to open one of them, but it could wait until they cleared the area.

"Darla, cruise out of here without speeding. Get eyes on Harbor Drive, we'll be right behind you."

"Copy."

"Get going, Chip. Normal speed like Darla." As inviting as it was to run, Mason walked over to his SUV. He knew the bodies would be discovered before too long, but he planned to be miles away by then. At best, a witness might be able to offer a general description of some vehicles leaving the marina, but Mason wasn't concerned. The entire gun battle had taken less than two minutes.

Before getting behind the wheel, he scanned the area and didn't see anyone watching him.

"Darla, Chip and I are mobile. Turn right at Harbor, left on Nimitz, then right on Rosecrans. Wait for us to catch up. Chip's driving the van."

"Copy."

In his rearview mirror, Mason saw the prone forms of dead men stuffed under the parked cars and had mixed feelings. He hadn't relished killing them, but if they were associated with Alisio, that made them complicit in murder, human trafficking, smuggling, and everything else illegal.

Three less scumbags walking the planet.

A pleasing thought, but he still felt unsatisfied. For scheming with a scumbag like Alisio, the South Koreans needed a bigger black eye. He made a U-turn, drove down to the wharf, and grabbed his M4 from the backseat.

After a quick look around, he climbed out, leveled the assault rifle at the closest fishing boat, and pulled the trigger.

With a tremendous roar, the M4 answered the call. A curved procession of spent brass flew into the water as he unloaded the entire magazine into a tight group at the waterline of the hull. Fiberglass splintered and cracked. Within a few minutes, that fishing boat would need a submarine for an inspection.

"Mason, you okay? I just heard gunfire."

"Affirm, Chip, just indulging myself. I'm right behind you." He felt relief when he turned onto Harbor and didn't hear any sirens. Darla's vehicle was gone, but he saw the van's taillights just ahead.

Adrenaline stirred as he imagined what 300 million pesos looked like.

He'd know soon enough.

Traffic on Rosecrans was light, and Mason had no trouble spotting the van.

"Chip, I've got eyes on you," Mason said. "Go east on the Eight."

Both Chip and Darla copied they'd heard his transmission.

Now what? Michaels said he got the exchange location via a cell call about an hour after the delivery to the marina. But that assumed there hadn't been a firefight. Mason didn't have a lot of options at this point. He'd keep Michaels alive and hope the call came anyway. He didn't think any of the South Koreans were alive to report the raid, but that didn't mean whoever made the call about the exchange location wouldn't learn of it. *More proof that shit happens*, thought Mason. At least he had 300 million state-of-the-art counterfeit pesos and had ruined Alisio's deal—not the end of the world.

He passed the Econoline and the sedan and radioed for them to follow him onto eastbound I-8. He took the Hotel Circle exit, led them under the freeway over to the Fashion Valley mall, and pulled into the closest parking structure. He scanned the area for security patrols before driving up to the fourth level. At 0615, the parking structure was all but empty. To avoid drawing attention from a security patrol, Mason didn't intend to be in here longer than a few minutes.

The three vehicles parked side by side in the middle of an open expanse of concrete. Mason asked about Top Hat's status, and Chip relayed he was still unconscious.

With Darla at his side, Mason joined Hahn at the van's rear bumper.

"Let's have a look," Mason said. He opened the double doors and pulled his knife. The image from Mullah Sanjari's compound flitted through his mind. A box of cash, ripe for the taking but equally untouchable. Now, things were different. He'd earned this, and he didn't feel any guilt having it.

He cut the plastic tie and pulled the two zippers apart.

What he saw astonished him.

He wasn't looking at bundles of counterfeit pesos but worthless South Korean fashion magazines held together by parcel twine. Red-lipped models with seductive smiles sneered at him.

"What the fuck is this?" Chip asked.

Thinking the money might be underneath, Mason tore the top layer of magazines out and was rewarded with a second layer of equally worthless periodicals. He turned the bag over and dumped its contents on the concrete. Not a single bundle of pesos fell out.

Chip stepped forward and opened a second bag.

More magazines.

Mason opened a third and fourth and found the same thing. "Check the magazines," he said. "Maybe the money's inside."

Darla reached down and grabbed a bundle from the ground. She cut the twine and thumbed through the pages. Nothing fell out but subscription cards. She got the same result with ten other bundles.

"Fuck!" Chip yelled.

Darla smacked the van's side with an open hand.

"Now what?" Chip asked. "We've got shit."

It was worse than that. Not only had they sacrificed their jobs, they were likely on the FBI's most-wanted list. Murder, coupled with kidnapping, was a federal crime. At best, the three of them had around $100,000 stashed at the safe house, but that wasn't going to last long. They could flee the country and scratch out a living for a few years, but that was a far cry from the lifestyle Mason had imagined.

"We can't let Alisio get away with this," Chip said.

"What if it wasn't Alisio?" Darla offered. "Maybe it was the South Koreans, or even Ramiro."

"You mean he set us up?" Hahn asked.

"We'll talk about this later," Mason said. "Right now, we're out of here. Set an IED for ninety seconds. We're torching the van."

Mason thought about Darla's question. It seemed outrageous. Why would Ramiro betray him, and why now? It didn't make sense. Mason held Ramiro's fate in his hands. Mason didn't believe Ramiro would risk an agonizing death by double-crossing him. Ramiro was well aware of how horribly Special Agent Hutch had died. No way. It was far more likely the phony duffels were a sting to test Top Hat's loyalty, and if so, there would be no follow-up call relaying the location of the real exchange. Thinking about it more, it answered lots of questions. The bottom line? It didn't matter because the end result was the same: they had nothing.

"What about Michaels?" Chip asked.

"He's worthless now." Mason climbed in and put three bullets into Michaels's head. *The world won't miss a low-life scumbag like you.*

Anger flared toward the old man, but he knew that wasn't fair. Beaumont had given him another chance when no one else would touch him. For that, he'd always be grateful. He knew Beaumont had cash and other liquid assets, but robbing the old man wasn't an option. There were certain lines he simply wouldn't cross.

One thing was certain, that slimy troll Alisio wasn't off the hook. He pictured the asshole in his lavish lifestyle, complete with expensive cars and homes, wine and women, gold and jewels, suitcases of cash, and the smug certainty he was untouchable. The thought made Mason ill. One way or the other, he'd find a way to kill Alisio, with or without stealing his money. Vengeance was merely delayed, not finished. They'd survive off their reserve cash and use the downtime to plan another move against Alisio.

He looked at Darla and Chip. They needed to hear something positive, something to give them hope.

"Listen up, this is far from over. Alisio's not getting away with this shit. We're going to regroup at the safe house and come up with a new plan. We aren't going to beat ourselves up, and we aren't pulling a *Thelma and Louise*. None of us could've predicted this. I'm going to initiate contact with Ramiro and figure out our next move. Darla, you're with me. Chip, you're in the SUV. Let's get going."

CHAPTER 31

When Special Agent Mary Grangeland stepped out of her car in First Security's parking lot, Nathan and Harv stared despite themselves. Granted, it hadn't been all that long since Nathan had seen her, but Harv hadn't laid eyes on her in several years. Her shoulder-length blond hair was tied in a ponytail. Gleaming in the morning sun, she looked amazing, her light-blue eyes intense. What was her secret? Somehow Grangeland managed to look younger than ever. In any case, it felt good to see their friend again.

"Oh, man . . ." Nathan said under his breath.

"Amen to that."

She rushed forward, wrapped Harv in a bear hug, and took the weight off her feet. Nathan smiled at seeing Grangeland suspended in Harv's grasp. She let go of Harv and gave Nathan a tight hug as well.

They called her Grangeland, not Mary, because she liked it that way. Everyone had been calling her Grangeland since her freshman year in high school, even her teachers. Only her mother used her first name, and only when she was in trouble.

Dressed in khaki 5.11 Tactical pants and a white golf shirt with an embroidered FBI logo, SA Grangeland was the real deal.

There was nothing artificial about her, physically or mentally. He and Harv trusted her with their lives—a litmus test for any friend. The reverse was also true; either of them would lay down his life for hers.

"I must say," Nathan offered, "your clothes . . . They, uh . . . fit you well."

Harv offered a low whistle.

She rolled her eyes. "Hasn't our new chief of staff been here for three days . . . *and* nights?"

Nathan looked at Harv and shrugged as if asking: *And her point is . . . ?*

"Forget it," she said.

"So how've you been?" Nathan asked. "When are they going to promote you to Fresno's ASAC?"

"I hope never; I like working with guns, not pencils."

Nathan exchanged another glance with Harv.

She narrowed her eyes.

Harv nudged him.

"Thank you, Harv."

"Hungry?" Nathan asked.

"Starving. I was going to grab a bite on the way, but figured I'd wait for you guys."

"Glad you did, but we have to pick a place with a pay phone nearby."

"Lansing?"

"Yep. We've been hot racking on Harv's office couch in two-hour shifts."

"Sounds serious. I'm assuming we're going on a bug hunt?"

"Kinda sorta . . . we don't have our marching orders yet."

"Who are the bad guys?"

"Private military contractors from OEF. Two very bad *hombres* and one equally bad *mujer.* We're waiting on a return call from your boss."

"Why is it every time your name gets thrown around, the chain of command goes out the window? I'm supposed to get my assignments from my ASAC, not the big cheese."

"Lansing called you directly again?"

"He said to drop everything and get on the road to your office. He also said he'd handle all the quote, paperwork, unquote. Not only that, I'm to tell no one I'm down here."

"Outstanding," Nathan said. "It's pretty clear he thinks you're the perfect agent for the job. Consider it a compliment."

"Either that or he thinks I'm expendable."

"He doesn't think that."

She didn't respond.

"Trust me: he doesn't."

"So," Grangeland said, taking Nathan's arm as they walked, "how's our new chief of staff doing? It's quite a promotion for her."

Nathan saw no reason to BS with Grangeland; she wouldn't respect it. "I put her in a difficult position. I asked her to delay reporting our activity to Lansing. He told me not to worry about Holly and that his trust in her hasn't been compromised. Still, I probably should've handled things differently."

"Can you tell me what's going on?"

"Yes." Nathan took a moment to give Grangeland a quick summary of everything they knew to date. Grangeland was a good listener; he liked that about her.

"Are you two on the rocks?" she asked, returning to the subject of Holly.

"I don't know."

"You don't know? How can you not know?"

"Nate's more worried than I am," Harv said. "I'm certain Lansing told her to let things cool down a bit."

"Let me guess: he doesn't want his office smeared if things go south."

"Partially, but it's more than that," Nathan said. "Something Lansing and I would never say to Holly."

"Okay . . ."

He looked at Harv, then back to Grangeland. "Physically, Holly's not one hundred percent. She still walks with a slight limp. She's riding a desk now."

"Ouch."

"I didn't mean it like that. What I'm trying to say is, I'd never take her on a combat op against hardened OEF vets."

"But you're comfortable with me?"

"Absolutely, and Lansing is too. You're here to help us get containment."

"Containment . . ."

"His word, not ours."

"So it's a dead-or-alive situation?"

Harv said, "He didn't actually say it, but yeah, that's the gist of it."

"You guys don't need me for that."

"Not true, Grangeland," Nathan said. "We're thankful to have you. But to answer your question, Lansing assigned you to us."

She stopped and faced them. "You guys didn't ask for me?"

"We never got the chance. After Lansing said he insisted one of his people accompany us, we said there was only one agent we'd trust for this kind of thing. That's when he told us you were already on the way."

"He'd already chosen me."

"Yes."

"So I'm an FBI black-ops agent?"

"How do you feel about that?" Harv asked.

"I love it."

Nathan smiled. He and Grangeland were kindred souls. "We're in a holding pattern until we hear from him. All our tactical gear is packed up and ready to go, and our helicopter is sitting on the tarmac at Montgomery Field. We can be in the air within twenty minutes of getting the nod."

“Let’s hope we don’t have a long flight. Spending several hours suspended above the ground inside a giant leaf blower isn’t my idea of fun.”

Harv half laughed. “A giant leaf blower?”

CHAPTER 32

Three hours into George Beaumont's return flight to the West Coast, his first officer patched a phone call through to the cabin. Before leaving Ronald Reagan National, Beaumont had created a new voice mail recording with an emergency number to call if the situation was urgent. Well, Ramiro's situation certainly qualified as urgent, and he wasn't expecting a call from anyone else.

He picked up the phone and spoke two words. "Globular cluster."

"Messier 22."

Beaumont used the speaker feature so that he didn't have to hold the handset. "Ramiro, we've got a real shitstorm up here."

"I'm sorry I couldn't call sooner. I don't have much time. I'm on a pizza run for the gang. What's going on?"

"Mason's gone rogue."

Ramiro didn't respond for a long moment. "What do you mean, 'gone rogue'?"

"He betrayed his oath." Beaumont gave Ramiro a quick summary.

"This is seriously fucked up. I just got off the phone with him."

"How long ago?"

"Shit, five minutes. I told him Alisio doesn't trust his lieutenant in San Diego. There's a new deal going down with new players, and Alisio set up a phony delivery. I just found out about it."

"What's your source? Alisio's second lieutenant again?"

"Yeah, I'm dating the guy's niece, and he totally trusts me. He told me someone tried to raid the fake delivery; everyone's talking about it. Are you saying it was Mason?"

"Yes. Tell me everything you told him."

Ramiro filled him in on the early morning's events at Shelter Island, then paused. "Sorry. I'm just thinking. This news about Mason has me rattled."

"Me too."

"Anyway, the real duffels have already been delivered in the Coronado Cays to Alisio's private residence. There's a dock there big enough to berth the ROK yacht."

"So they're using the *Yoonsuh* again for this newest delivery?"

"Yes."

"Is it guns?"

"No, counterfeit pesos."

"Counterfeit pesos? How much?"

"Three hundred million. The North Korean paper stock is so realistic with all the security features and anticounterfeiting safeguards, it's virtually real money. It even passes the ultraviolet test. Alisio's paying twenty-five cents on the dollar for the funny money, but he's gonna resell it on the streets for twice that. It'll be easy to launder down here because the cash economy's so bad. The South Koreans sent a small sample ahead of time, and we took it to the Banamex branch downtown. The teller tested it with a marker, used a black light, and held it up to see the watermark and then deposited it. It's really good stuff. If this deal goes through successfully, the next shipment will be five times as big."

"How's Alisio paying for it?"

"Like we suspected, it's a combination of bullion, diamonds, and cash. Two million in Philharmonics, two million in round brilliants, and two million in US cash. A DPRK gemologist is going to examine the coins and diamonds for authenticity. It's gonna take several hours because there's four hundred diamonds to check and fifteen hundred gold coins."

"Does Mason know everything you just told me?"

"Yes."

"Where's the exchange taking place?"

"Everyone's tight-lipped, but my friend told me something about an abandoned borrow pit just north of Yuma. Everyone's buzzing about it because Mr. A's gonna be there."

"In person? Are you sure?"

"That's the scuttlebutt. He left yesterday; that's why I'm able to call you like this. The exchange is going down right after sunset tonight. That's all I could get without raising suspicion. I'm pretty sure I heard the word 'reservoir' a few times. Do you want me to press?"

"No, don't risk it. I'll follow up from here. Are you sure you're not compromised? No one's following you or acting strangely?"

"No. Everything's normal."

"I think Mason's planning to ambush the exchange."

"That's crazy. Mr. A took a small army with him."

"How many, best guess?"

"At least ten. His first and second LTs are with him."

"Well, Mason's on his own now. I've cut him off."

"Will he blow my cover?"

Beaumont hesitated. "I don't think he would normally. He respects you a lot. He told me you were his favorite graduate. Having said that, there's still no telling what he'll do. Especially if things go badly at the exchange. I'd feel better if you staged somewhere."

"I can't. I'm in charge until Mr. A gets back."

"He may not be coming back."

"Does that mean what I think it means?"

"Yes."

"What do you want me to do?"

"You're two hours ahead of Pacific time. Tonight at seven, Mexico City time, I want you to make some kind of excuse and get the hell out of there."

"Forever?"

"I don't know yet. It may not be safe at Alisio's compound tonight. The place could be swarming with PFM agents. It's better if you're not there. Do you need anything, any arrangements?"

"No, I'm all set. I've been ready for this for months."

"You've done a terrific job. I'm going to make sure you receive a healthy bonus. I'm giving you the money Mason, Hahn, and Lyons would've gotten this year. It's the least I can do, given what you've risked."

"Thank you, George. I appreciate it. I really miss my mom and dad. I haven't seen them in two years."

"Soon enough."

"Man, I never saw this coming."

"That makes both of us."

"Is there anything I can do to help you between now and tonight?"

"Since Mason already knows about the real delivery, there's nothing you can do. I'll make this brief, but here's what's going to happen." Ramiro didn't interrupt while Beaumont laid out his plan.

"Who are these guys?" Ramiro asked.

"Retired Recons."

"How many?"

"Two."

"Two? You're kidding."

"They'll have an FBI agent with them."

"A SWAT guy?"

"Not exactly."

Ramiro didn't say anything, but Beaumont knew what his man was thinking—*it's a suicide mission.*

"These guys aren't your typical retired grunts."

"For their sakes, let's hope not. I don't need to tell you what Mr. A will do to them if he takes them alive. I'm assuming they know about me?"

"Yes." Beaumont knew Ramiro was worried about being given up under torture. "You've done great work down there. You've saved countless lives on both sides of the border."

"Thank you, sir."

"Stay sharp. Assume nothing. I want you out of there if anyone even looks at you funny."

"No problem. I'm ready."

"I'll see you stateside in a few days. Make contact after you cross the border."

George Beaumont hung up and looked at the passenger sitting across the aisle.

Neither of them spoke. It wasn't needed.

They were both thinking the same thing.

CHAPTER 33

Nathan lifted off from Montgomery Field with Harv and Grangeland twenty minutes after receiving Lansing's call. He'd half expected Beaumont or his father to participate on the call, but Lansing said he'd attempted to reach them and gotten thrown into voice mail.

Lansing had given them GPS coordinates, describing their destination as an abandoned rock quarry, or borrow pit as they were sometimes called. The quarry sat approximately fifteen miles north of Yuma, Arizona. Lansing had thoroughly checked the satellite photos, and only one location fit Ramiro's description.

Harv's preliminary flight planning indicated it was approximately 150 miles to their destination. If they pushed the Bell 407's engine a little, they could make it in seventy-five minutes, plus or minus. Given the timing of Ramiro's earlier conversation with Mason, Nathan believed they'd arrive at least an hour before Mason, Hahn, and Lyons could possibly get there.

Having a helicopter and the ability to pilot it was a huge speed advantage, but Nathan knew it still didn't offer much of a margin. They had to land at a safe distance, conceal the ship, hump over to the pit on foot, and then find tactical locations to set up their shooting positions.

The weather remained a positive aspect. Conditions were perfect. The previous night's rain had cleared the air, and bright sunshine dominated the entire southwest quadrant of the country. Nathan hadn't flown in several weeks, and lifting off reminded him how much he enjoyed flying and the feeling of freedom it offered.

Though Harv had only been licensed for a few years, he'd become a skilled pilot. In some ways, he was better than Nathan. Harv had an instinctive feel for performing autorotations, a crucial procedure pilots had to master in the event of an engine failure or other mechanical problems. Fortunately, it rarely happened, but Nathan supposed all pilots, both fixed wing and rotary wing, felt the same underlying fear. Flying wasn't like driving; you couldn't just pull over to the curb when the engine stopped.

Despite her hesitation to travel in helicopters, Grangeland was a good passenger. If she felt any unease, she hid it well, and after an uneventful flight following the I-8 corridor, they reached an expanse of sand dunes on the outskirts of Yuma. Harv told Nathan to fly a course of zero-five-nine.

Harv studied the chart for a few seconds, then pointed. "Head for the second line of peaks. The borrow pit should be just north of them."

Fifteen minutes later, Harv gave a course correction to the east.

Nathan slowed to fifty knots as he approached their target area. "I see the quarry. Eleven o'clock at two miles."

"Got it," Harv said. "We'll need to turn south before we reach the river to avoid entering Yuma Proving Ground's airspace. After you make the turn, stay west of the river. We'll maintain that heading for a minute or two before turning around and retracing our path. I don't think we should risk orbiting the area. Someone could be down there."

Nathan flew directly over the center of the quarry.

"I'm getting some good video footage. We'll take a look after we land."

A few miles southeast of the quarry, Harv told him to turn around and head back. Nathan executed a steep 180-degree turn, increasing the g-force.

Grangeland groaned, but she didn't sound as bad as the first time they'd flown together.

"You okay back there?" Nathan asked.

"Yeah, I think so. Can you keep the maneuvering to a minimum?"

"Sorry. No more steep turns, I promise."

"Thanks. I didn't take any Dramamine. It makes me a little drowsy, and I want to be fully alert."

"Here we go, Nate. Twenty seconds to the turn . . ."

"I'm on it."

"Right about . . . here."

Nathan gently pushed the cyclic to the left, added some left pedal, and watched the compass spin.

Sitting on Nathan's left, Harv filmed the quarry's southern hemisphere as they overflew it in the opposite direction.

Nathan burned the landscape into his head, making mental notes of the prominent geographical features. Accessed by a dirt road that wound its way up a canyon, there was no mistaking the borrow pit's distinctive form—a giant, craterlike wound on the south side of a mountain. A lake, about the size of a soccer field, dominated the center of the pit.

The pit had roughly the same size and shape as a football stadium. At the open end of its south hemisphere—where the water nearly flowed out—several small buildings stood in various stages of decay. A rusty conveyor for moving and piling excavated earth had collapsed. Some wrecked hulks of cars dotted the area. The pit's access road terminated at a large expanse of level ground where the buildings, the cars, and the collapsed conveyor sat.

It was hard to judge, but Nathan believed the overall depth of the quarry was somewhere around 150 feet measured from the highest point on its north rim. Thirty-foot-high terraces ringed the pit, each terrace measuring some thirty to forty feet wide. A fall from one of those ledges would break bones and likely be fatal. The man-made cliffs were nearly vertical.

Nathan saw a separate road following the rim of the quarry, but it didn't connect to the tiers below. About a quarter mile west of the pit, they overflew another road running north and south, but it didn't appear to be associated with the quarry.

The more Nathan thought about it, the more this place made sense. It was an ideal location to conduct business away from prying eyes, but only if sentries were posted along the rim. Otherwise, it could become a shooting gallery. It was defensible and isolated. Conversely, there was only one way in, or out, of the place.

"What do you guys think?" Nathan asked.

"It looks like a prime spot," Harv offered, voicing his exact thoughts on the high sniping positions.

"Grangeland?"

"I agree with Harvey. I'd definitely want shooters overlooking the pit. From the west rim, they'd have a clear line of sight along the access road all the way to the Colorado River."

"Harv, how far's the river?"

"I'd say . . . two miles."

"Did anyone see any vehicles in the immediate area surrounding the quarry?"

"Besides the junked cars . . . no," said Grangeland. "But I saw a few cars and RVs parked at the river. It looked like a campground. There were some tents. I'm pretty sure I saw boat ramps at both of the lakes."

"Those would be Squaw Lake and Senator Wash Reservoir," Harv said. "I've camped here before, a long time ago. Squaw is the smaller lake below the dam."

"Did you film those?" Nathan asked Harv.

"Yeah, I figured it couldn't hurt."

"We'll land a mile west of the quarry, take a look at your footage, and hump in from there."

"Let's hope your ballistic vests are . . . improved models," Grangeland said.

"Indeed they are," Harv said. "We upgraded them right after your incident."

"Great timing," she said dryly.

Nathan didn't have the heart to tell Grangeland that Mason and crew were probably using armor-piercing rounds; she didn't need the added distraction.

"Start descending," Harv said. "I spotted a good place to land on our first pass."

"Power lines?" Nathan asked.

"Negative, no poles or transmission towers are present. Turn to two-three-zero, keep descending."

Nathan slowed and bled off more altitude. "I see it—that dry wash?"

"Yep."

"Looks good. We're going to kick up a sizable dust cloud. Grangeland, do you see any cars or people?"

Her voice sounded tight. "No."

Nathan slowed and continued to descend. The spot they wanted sat in the middle of a sandy wash shielded by sloping twenty-foot-high banks on either side. The borrow pit sat about a mile to the east across a relatively flat expanse of desert. The wash flowed north to south, so Nathan pivoted the Bell, allowing it to touch down with the front of the skids first. He estimated he had thirty feet of clearance on either side of the main rotor.

No one traversing the road they'd overflown would be able to see the helicopter. It could be seen from the air, but night was coming soon. Still, to be safe, Nathan intended to cover its fuselage with desert camouflage netting.

Dust and loose weeds flew in every direction as Nathan brought the two-and-a-half-ton machine into a hover. Grangeland's description of a giant leaf blower seemed accurate.

"Looking good," Harv said. "We're clear on the left."

The helicopter jolted slightly as its left skid landed on a small rock and slid off.

"Talk about a pucker factor," Grangeland said. "Is landing this thing as difficult as it looks?"

"Not really," Nathan answered. "You try not to think about it. You do it by feel, using a visual reference to the ground. I focus on a spot about fifty to sixty feet away and then slowly lower the collective until the ship can't fly anymore. I know that sounds overly simple, but the weight of the ship just settles to the ground."

"If you say so."

"If Holly had been here, she could've made this landing."

"Holly knows how to fly this thing?"

"Yep, I've been teaching her. She doesn't have a license yet, but she can fly it. Tell you what, on the way back I'll give you some time on the controls . . ." He grinned. "If you think you can handle it."

"We'll see."

Nathan started the shutdown procedure. After the main rotor stopped, they climbed out into an arid landscape. Nathan glanced at his watch: 1602. Sunset was around seventy-five minutes away.

All three of them were dressed in desert MARPAT. Grangeland's combat uniform fit her well because she was roughly the same size and build as Holly. Several years ago, Nathan had bought Holly two sets of both woodland and desert MARPATs as Christmas presents. Holly had been thrilled and immediately put them on—with nothing underneath. He smiled at the memory, but it vanished. Whatever the outcome between them, he just wanted her to be happy.

Not now, he told himself. He needed to remain focused on the task at hand: taking out the trash.

"Let's get the ship covered," Nathan said. He opened the luggage compartment and froze. A chill raked his skin. "Helicopter!"

"Shit!" Harv said.

Nathan yanked a camo-netting bag from the compartment. "Harv, get the other."

"What can I do to help?" Grangeland asked.

"Get on the other side. I'm going to toss the net. We don't have time to cover the main rotor." Nathan threw the camo netting as if casting it from a fishing boat.

Coming from the east, the helicopter's whooping grew in volume.

Harv tossed his netting over the rear of the ship. It draped the tail rotor and vertical stabilizer perfectly.

"Good toss," Nathan said. "Mine's caught on the cable cutter."

Harv raced to the opposite side and opened the door. He lifted the net as best he could, but it kept getting caught on the fin-shaped device.

"Good enough. Everybody under the net!"

They huddled under the belly of the ship. "It's going to pass north of us," Harv said. "It's deep, sounds like a big one."

"Could be a Navy or Marine Super Stallion from Yuma MCAS."

"Did we fly through their airspace?" Grangeland asked.

"No. The air station is well south of here and Yuma Proving Ground is east of us. They saw us on radar, but pilots fly these corridors all the time to stay out of military airspace."

The thumping grew louder, then reached a peak. "Harv, can you see it?"

"It's a Stallion, but it's half a mile away and not changing course. Might be heading out to El Centro or Miramar. No way to know."

The whooping of its big main rotor faded, and silence fell across the desert once more.

"You feelin' it, Grangeland?" Nathan asked with a smile.

"If you're talking about this tingling all over my body, yes."

He offered her a high five. She grinned and smacked his hand.

"Let's get these nets squared away."

They used large rocks to secure the corners. When they were finished, the netting resembled a sheer tent over the aircraft.

"That looks amazing," Grangeland said. "No way anyone'll see it from the air."

Nathan took a moment to gauge the temperature and wind. Around seventy degrees and ten miles an hour out of the northeast, respectively.

"Let's get underneath for a minute."

They ducked under the mesh and formed a huddle next to the ship.

"Here's the video I shot." Harv wirelessly linked his video recorder to his laptop, opened the Bell's door, and placed the computer on the rear seat. "We can slow it down, freeze the stream, and take screenshots."

Nathan leaned in for a better look. "I have a pretty good idea where to position everyone, but we should scout the area before we make the final decision. Ramiro told Beaumont the exchange is going down about an hour after sunset, so we'll need to choose locations near large rocks or boulders. That way, if Mason or Alisio's men have thermal imagers, the rocks will help mask our signatures."

"Our ghillie suits will help too," Harv said.

Nathan and Harv's handmade ghillie suits were vital pieces of gear. Consisting of pants and a poncho-like coat, once donned, they broke up the sharp edges of a human form by employing thousands of tattered pieces of fabric. A motionless wearer looked much like a shaggy bush or small tree.

"I think one of us should be positioned inside the pit somewhere, maybe near or in one of those abandoned vehicles." Nathan thought for a moment. "Scratch that. Those might be the first places they'd search."

He asked Harv to zoom in on certain features like the abandoned cars and the buildings. As Nathan suspected, all the structures' windows had been destroyed long ago. Same with the vehicles.

"Maybe there's a good place to hide inside this collapsed conveyor belt," Harv offered.

"We'll give it a look from the rim."

"So what are the rules of engagement here?" Harv asked.

"We'll have to see how things shake out," Nathan said. "We know Alisio's arriving with the cash, Philharmonics, and diamonds, and the South Koreans are bringing the counterfeit pesos in duffel bags. Mason might want all of it, but if he had to settle for one or the other, he'd pick Alisio's half of the equation. It's much more portable than the bulky duffel bags."

Grangeland nodded. "The cash, diamonds, and gold would be my priority too."

"Right. So you might expect him to wait for the exchange to occur, then raid Alisio's payment from the Koreans on their way out. The wild card, though, is Alisio's presence at the exchange."

"The revenge motive," Harv said.

"Exactly. If Mason got word that Alisio's going to be here, then he may see it as an unplanned bonus."

"Why's Alisio coming?" Grangeland asked.

"There's no way to know. Beaumont told us this counterfeit-money thing is a new venture for Alisio; he probably wants to be there for the first exchange."

"And Alisio's presence would be seen as a show of good faith," Harv said. "That he's willing to stand behind his money, so to speak. But speaking of Alisio, let's say Mason does hit the Koreans after the exchange. Alisio's not going to stand idly by while someone rips off his business partners, right? For one thing, he's gonna feel threatened. For another, if his people don't fight back, the South Koreans will assume he's behind the heist. They might end up shooting at each other."

"Which could be Mason's plan," Grangeland said.

"It's entirely possible. They thin each other out, and he mops up the rest." Nathan thought for a moment. "Pulling this off is a tall order for Mason's team of three. Like us, they haven't had a lot of time to plan."

"Are you thinking they'll bring some extra bodies? BSI personnel?" she asked.

"That's another variable we can't predict," Nathan said. "We'll deal with what we're facing as best we can." He wished he had a squad of Recons to supplement their effort, but this had been an under-the-table operation from the start. Lansing had made that abundantly clear.

"Back to what's gonna happen down there," he said. "If what Ramiro heard is accurate, the South Koreans will have a North Korean gemologist with them, and he'll need time to examine the diamonds and Philharmonics. He may not check every one, but I doubt the South Koreans will leave without checking a large random sampling. That means a long wait while both parties are in the quarry. Given that, do you still think Mason waits to make his move until after the exchange?"

Grangeland spoke first. "Yeah, I do. We can safely assume there will be multiple vehicles arriving, and Mason will need to know which one to hit on the way out. He won't know that until the end when everyone is leaving."

"So he'll hide and observe until they're ready to leave, then make his move."

"Yes," Grangeland said. "That makes the most sense to me."

Nathan nodded in agreement. "Me too. Like Mason, we'll have to sit tight and observe what initially happens. We don't know who's who either. But keep in mind that our targets are Mason, Hahn, and Lyons. We'll try not to kill anyone else, but if the situation warrants it, we shoot first and ask questions later." Harv knew the gig, but Nathan needed to be clear Grangeland fully understood their situation. He looked at her, waiting for an acknowledgment, but she seemed to be evaluating what she'd just heard. "Special Agent Grangeland, we are in a shoot-to-kill situation. Period. All you have to do is imagine what they'd do to you if they take you prisoner. I'll guarantee you'll wish you'd killed them."

"I'm shooting to kill," she said with conviction.

"Have you ever—"

"No," she interrupted, "but it won't be a problem."

Nathan nodded approval and grabbed the rifle cases from the seats behind the cockpit. "Mason's crew will likely have vests on. We brought armor-piercing ammo for all of our weapons. I'm assuming your service piece is a Glock 22 like Holly's?"

"Yes. But I didn't bring it. I've got my old Sig 226 in forty."

"You're in luck. We brought our 226s in forty as well. We'll give you a couple of spare mags. We'll also swap out your ammo with our AP rounds. Harv and I have a couple of suppressed 226s in nine mil. Those subsonic rounds won't penetrate their vests, but they'll bruise ribs. Our forties may or may not penetrate their vests, so let's make sure we follow up with head shots. Our rifles will definitely punch through. Harv and I will have Remington 700s in 308. Are you okay with a Springfield M1A? It's match conditioned with a night-vision scope and thermal capability."

"No problem. I know that weapon well."

Nathan handed the M1A to Grangeland.

"This is a beautiful rifle." She pulled the bolt back and looked in the chamber. "Just checking."

"As you should."

"What's its zero?"

"Three hundred yards."

"How accurate?"

"Very. It'll hold a six-inch group at six hundred yards."

"That's way better than I am."

"Don't worry, that will be Harv's job."

"Harv's a shooter?"

"Absolutely. We used to alternate on ops. It kept both of us sharp. Harv's better at wind calls, and I'm better beyond six hundred, but basically we're interchangeable. Remember to keep the rubber boot tight to your face while the NV's turned on, or you'll light yourself up like a Christmas tree. Keep the rifle firmly shouldered; the soft rubber boot will absorb the kick."

"I volunteer to be down in the pit," she said.

"I appreciate the offer, but that's my job."

Harv didn't say anything, but Nathan knew his friend was concerned about splitting up.

Nathan continued. "We've got a huge area to cover." He pointed to the borrow pit on the screen. "Let's partition it like a football stadium. The north side is the highest point. We'll call that section one. Moving in a clockwise direction, each ten-degree span will be a section, kinda like a real stadium. The south end where the lake nearly flows out is section eighteen, representing one hundred eighty degrees. So if I say I saw someone at section nine, upper deck, everyone looks to the eastern rim. If I say section twenty-seven loge, everyone focuses at the west side about halfway up the pit. Everyone follow?"

"Got it," Harv said.

"Grangeland?"

"Got it," she said. "My dad took me to a few 49ers games. I think the stadium references will work great. Field level will be the lowest tier, pond, and buildings."

"Exactly. The loge is the middle two tiers, and upper deck is the top two tiers and rim. We'll use standard clock references for our respective positions, so it's important we all understand each other's orientations. We'll verify that by radio after we're in position. When we reach the rim of the pit, we'll use the range finder to get some exact distances. Let's get ready to move out."

While Harv closed his laptop and put it on the floor of the rear compartment, Nathan scanned up and down the wash with field glasses again. His friend then grabbed their backpacks, waist packs, and ghillie suits from the storage compartment. They only had two ghillies, and only he and Harv had experience working in them. Grangeland would have to rely on her desert MARPATs for concealment. Nathan watched his friend conduct a quick check of the handguns, making sure they were ready to shoot with rounds in the chambers.

"Everyone check their phones for a connection. I've got three bars."

"Me too," Harv said.

Grangeland had the same.

"Make sure they're on silent and pocket them with the screens facing in. Night vision can see their glow through clothing. Even facing inward, they're still visible, just not as brightly. We may have to turn them off completely to prevent an untimely illumination from an incoming signal or text."

"Before we go," Harv said, "I'm going to show Grangeland how to activate the helicopter's emergency-locator transmitter. You never know."

"Good idea. If all else fails, she can hustle out here and flip the switch. Why don't you set the radio to 'Guard,' so she can transmit a distress message? One more thing, this mission is off the books. We can't call 911 unless one of us is quite literally bleeding to death."

"I don't like the sound of that," she said.

"We have to pretend 911 isn't an option. We'll have to solve our own problems out here."

Grangeland slowly nodded.

After Harv set the Bell's radio to 121.5 and showed Grangeland the master switch and ELT, he locked the helicopter. "I'm hiding the key under this rock over here." Harv took a few seconds to create some random footprints around the area to mask the trail over to the rock and back.

"Let's get moving," Nathan said. "Ten-yard separation. Once we're out of this wash, we'll double-time it over to the rock quarry. I'm on point. Harv will take six."

With the helicopter secure, they diverted to an area where the bank of the sandy ravine wasn't as steep and scrambled up the slope. Nathan took a final look at the helicopter, then began a medium-paced jog due east.

The terrain was dotted with low, scrubby bushes, creosote, yucca, and saguaro cactus. The cactus reminded Nathan of the old *Quick Draw McGraw* cartoons he used to watch as a kid, but he couldn't remember the name of Quick Draw's little sidekick. Funny, the things a person thought about when facing a life-or-death situation. Maybe it was a protection mechanism insulating him from the harsh truth of having to kill again. Either way, he didn't question it. He'd stayed sane so far . . .

Every two minutes, Nathan put everyone on hold and conducted a sweep of the area with his field glasses. Grangeland and Harv did the same. Of all the environments on earth—and Nathan had worked in all types—he liked deserts best. He also knew the Mojave well. The last time he'd been in the Mojave, Lauren had been with him. He still couldn't believe how well she'd handled herself. An amazing kid. He hoped things had settled down with her mom.

They crossed the dirt track they'd seen from the air, but Nathan wasn't worried about leaving footprints this far from the rim. After traversing another dry wash of rock-strewn sand, they still couldn't see the borrow pit. Nathan thought it was another quarter mile or so.

A few minutes later, they stopped at a barbed wire fence. It appeared to follow an unmaintained road that was little more than two tire ruts. Nathan issued a hand signal to form a huddle.

"If anyone's down in the pit, we'll know soon enough. No quick movements from here on." Harv already knew the drill—Nathan said it to remind Grangeland. They carefully stepped over the old fence and approached the west side of the rim in a crouch.

"Try to minimize footprints," Nathan said. "Alisio might send people up here, probably will."

There was no warning: the ground suddenly ended, and they were looking over a sheer drop-off. The rusty barbed wire probably saved lives. At night, you could easily walk over this precipice.

"Holy shit," Grangeland whispered. "This makes my knees weak." A gust of wind moved her ponytail, and she grabbed the bill of her hat.

Nathan and Harv scanned the pit carefully with their field glasses. Still no one in sight. Nathan eased forward and peered over the edge.

"You're making me really nervous," she said.

"I just want a quick look."

Grangeland was right: this was one massive hole. The upper tier's wall wasn't as steep as the lower levels, but from this perspective, it looked straight down. The thirty-foot fall to the next tier would yield a very unhappy result. On the north side of the pit, he saw where bulldozers had moved up and down the tiers. A zigzagging series of switchbacks worked its way up the walls of the pit. Other than the perimeter, where the excavated hole merged with the mountain's natural slope, it was the only place to move up and down the pit without using rock climbing gear.

Harv pointed to the east at the Senator Wash Reservoir visible from their vantage point. "I was wondering why this borrow pit was here. There's our answer."

"The fill material for the dams," Grangeland said.

"Yep," Harv said.

Looking at the collapsed conveyor belt at the south end of the pit, Nathan saw it would make a good place to conceal himself. The contraption looked to be 150 feet long and five feet wide. In most places, it lay heavily on the ground, but a few spots buckled upward from its collapse. In a crouch, he should be able to traverse back and forth along its length without being seen. If he had to make a quick retreat, he could bolt over to the pond and use its drop in elevation for cover. He didn't like retreating to lower ground, but it beat being trapped inside the twisted steel of the conveyor.

Next, he studied the bottleneck. The access road serving the pit was carved into the north side of a canyon sandwiched between two mountain peaks. At the bottleneck, one side of the road sloped up the rocky terrain; the other dropped away into a dry creek. For about a hundred yards, there was no place to leave the road. If Nathan were to attack, he'd choose that location. All Mason would have to do is disable a vehicle and the road would be blocked.

"Harv, do you still like the saddle on the north side of the canyon above the access road as a shooting position?"

"It looks good from here. It's got a clear line of sight to the conveyor and buildings. I'm not seeing much for cover though. It looks like an open area."

Grangeland asked, "What about that big rock outcropping above the saddle?"

"I like it better," Harv said. "It's more defensible."

"Harv, how long will it take you to relocate down to the rock outcropping from the peak?"

"Depends on how stealthy you want me to be. It's at least five hundred yards."

"Here's what I'm thinking: you start at the top where you can keep an eye on the river and the reservoirs, then drop down when you see vehicles approaching."

"If I don't have to worry about being seen, I can probably make it in three or four minutes. It's not super steep."

"Grangeland, we'll put you on the opposite side of the access road, about two hundred yards up the canyon's slope. I'm seeing a few places that look good. Pick a spot where you can see the bottleneck and flat area of the pit. You're my artillery. You can lay down a lot of fire if needed. You've got four hundred rounds in twenty magazines in your pack; that's why it's so heavy. Harv and I have fifty rounds each, but our bolt-action rifles are slower to fire and reload. Like I said before, your weapon sight can switch between thermal or NV, or use a combo of each."

"You'll need to show me how it works."

"No problem."

"I'm going to get some distances." Harv took out the range finder and rattled off some numbers to the buildings, the conveyor, and other landmarks in the hole. Harv reported the east rim was just over 750 yards away and the center of the pit was half that distance.

Nathan asked, "If I have to shoot up here from the conveyor, what's the hold if I don't click it in?"

"Best guess? About twenty inches above your three hundred zero."

Nathan nodded toward the saddle they'd located on the video. "Shoot the rock outcropping above the saddle."

Harv brought the device to his eye. "Eleven hundred yards. Given my current skill level, that's beyond my effective range. From down there, I'll be able to put some suppression fire on the rim up here, but don't ask me to score a hit."

"Suppression's good enough. The reverse is also true. No one's going to shoot you guys from up here."

"That's a comforting thought," Grangeland said.

"You okay?"

"I don't like heights."

"How far is the saddle from the center of the pit?" Nathan waited while Harv shot the pit and did the subtraction.

"About seven hundred twenty-five yards."

"Grangeland, you okay at that distance?" Nathan asked.

"For center-mass shots, yes. I'll need wind and elevation corrections, though."

"We'll give you those once you're in place. Now that we've seen the layout close-up, any new thoughts?" Nathan asked.

Harv pointed to the bottleneck in the access road. "If Mason's looking to ambush them before or after the exchange, he might make his move there. The vehicles can't leave the road."

"True," said Grangeland, "but ambushing at the bottleneck separates them from their rides. They'd have to park at a distance and hike in on foot. I suppose they could do a combination. They could have Lyons staged somewhere with a vehicle while Mason and Hahn attack on foot. After they make the hit, Lyons races in and picks them up. The Philharmonics and diamonds won't be bulky. But two million in gold bullion has got to weigh close to a hundred pounds."

"I doubt they'll try to take off on foot with that much weight," Harv said. "They'll need a vehicle for sure."

"Agreed." Nathan sighed. "Look, clearly it's impossible to predict everything that's gonna happen. We'll do what we can *as* it happens and stay in close communication with each other." Nathan looked at Grangeland. "This is where we part company with Harv. He's going north to that peak. We're going south along the rim down to the pit. Let's do a radio check."

Their radios worked perfectly, and just like that, Harv walked away.

Grangeland looked confused. Nathan knew what she was thinking, that they should've said some sort of good-byes to each other. It wasn't their preferred way of parting company under the circumstances. Saying good-bye was like mentioning a no-hitter in the bottom of the ninth inning. Each of them had to believe they'd see each other again. Confidence played a large role in any op. As far as Nathan and Harv were concerned, Mason, Lyons, and Hahn were going to get exactly what they deserved: a one-way ticket to the underworld. Nathan didn't care if Mason was a war hero or not. He'd murdered a pregnant woman while she was handcuffed.

Nathan met her gaze. "Ten-meter separation: let's go."

She nodded tightly, and Nathan knew she was beginning to feel the gravity of what they faced. Recognizing Grangeland didn't have Harv's experience in this kind of operation, he stopped and waved her over.

"It's gonna be okay, all right? You're a proven asset."

"I'd be lying if I said I wasn't nervous," she said. "It feels like there's a brick in my stomach."

"I'm always nervous before ops."

"So it's not just me?"

"Hell no. Truthfully, I'd be worried if you weren't nervous. You'd either be a sociopath or overly confident. Either one would spell disaster."

She didn't say anything.

Nathan put a hand on her shoulder. "Don't worry, we're going to kick their asses. Those clowns don't stand a chance against us."

Following the barbed wire, Nathan resumed their hike along the rim, losing elevation as they moved south. The borrow pit's walls became lower and lower until the rim terminated in the flat area in the pit.

Once on level ground, Nathan showed her how to work the M1A's scope. He reminded her again to keep her face against the soft rubber boot while it was powered on. It was an older model that didn't employ a pressure switch to turn off and on when moved against or away from her face.

"No good-byes," he said. "Check in when you're in position and also give me a flash with your penlight. I want to know exactly where you are."

"Will do."

"Harv, status."

"I'm about halfway up. I'll have a clear view all the way past the Senator Wash Reservoir to the Imperial Reservoir. Ditto the area surrounding the access road and that dirt track we crossed on the way to the rim."

"I'm heading for the conveyor. You won't be able to see me, but Grangeland will from the south side of the access canyon."

"I'll check in from the peak."

Nathan walked the perimeter of the pit, which took him around the lake. He made mental notes of the abandoned buildings in relationship to the wrecked cars. The central building was about the size of a two-car garage and probably served as the office. The smallest building looked like a prefab structure and could've been used for an on-site residence; he wasn't sure. A metal frame was all that was left of the biggest building. It had probably been a service garage to repair the excavating equipment, loaders, and dump trucks. Building an earthen dam was a huge project, and the machines would've needed on-site maintenance.

Fortunately, the ground wouldn't leave much in the way of footprints. It was largely composed of medium to small gravel, with a few patches of dirt scattered here and there. Thousands of spent .22 casings littered the entire area. Trash shooters had left the remains of their slovenly target practice. Broken glass, five-gallon cans, wooden pallets, and various other makeshift objectives plagued the area. All of the vehicles had dozens of bullet holes, and the walls of the buildings were pockmarked.

He diverted to the closest building, looked through the broken-out windows, and found what he'd expected—broken glass, trash, hanging wires, and a few fist-sized rocks. There was no need to explore the four derelict cars, but he created a designation for each of them.

"Grangeland, hold position and get eyes on me."

"Copy."

"I'm giving these rusted cars names for reference purposes. See the one I'm pointing at?"

"Yes."

"We're calling it D1 for Derelict One. Moving in a clockwise direction, we'll call the others D2, D3, and D4, respectively."

"Got it."

"Harv, you can't see it, but D1 is closest to field level, section three. Did you copy the references?"

"Affirm. D2, D3, and D4 are in a clockwise direction from D1."

"Grangeland, after you set up your shooting position, I want you to practice sighting in on each designation. Randomly move from one target to the next. I want you to create an instinctive feel for each movement of your M1A. Do the same for the buildings. Imagine shooting three shots at D1, then adjusting aim for D3, etc. The building I'm standing next to looks like an abandoned office. We'll call it the office. The one I'm pointing at looks like a prefab of some kind; we'll call that one prefab. The metal-framed building without walls was probably a repair garage, so we'll call it garage. Everyone follow? Office, prefab, and garage. You copy all that, Harv?"

"Affirm."

"Practice adjusting aim from building to building as well."

"No problem," she said. *"I'll start doing that once I'm in position."*

"Your muzzle flashes will reveal your SP, so be ready to relocate. Have a backup location identified before you set up your SP. Everyone double-check their radio batteries. All of us should have ninety to ninety-five percent remaining."

Harv and Grangeland confirmed that was true. "To save battery power, we'll use acknowledgment clicks unless verbal copies are requested."

His radio clicked, and he smiled. A second later, he heard a second click from Harv.

He looked up to the rim and assured himself that this wasn't a coliseum, that there weren't any lions being released. He knew preop jitters were normal and didn't second-guess them. Holding a certain amount of apprehension kept him sharp.

He hustled over to the collapsed conveyor and circled its form. As he'd thought, it was about 150 feet long and lying in a north-south orientation with one end terminating about thirty feet from the man-made lake. Weeds and tall grass had grown inside the truss-like structure. Tactically, he liked it. In a crouch, he could run back and forth along its length and remain out of sight. And the combination of the deepening twilight coupled with his ghillie suit would give him excellent concealment. On the other hand, it didn't offer bullet-resistant cover. He'd have to rely solely on stealth until the shooting started, then switch to mobility.

He chose a location near the end terminating at the lake and hollowed out a small area inside its lattice frame. He made it big enough to sit in a cross-legged position. As always, he checked for ants, a mistake he'd once made, at great cost.

"Grangeland, do you have my position?"

"Affirm, you're inside the north end of the conveyor."

It wasn't dark enough for night-vision devices yet, but thermal imagers would work. The metal struts surrounding him would be brightly delineated. As long as he stayed behind the conveyor's rubber belt, he should be okay.

He looked toward section nine of the borrow pit's rim. The massive cliff face was highlighted against a watercolor sky of orange and blue. He liked evening twilight, but liked morning twilight better. A gradually lightening sky appealed to him—maybe it signified a new beginning, or something even more intangible, but Nathan never took a single day for granted.

His radio crackled to life with Harv's voice. *"I've got a caravan of three SUVs moving north, paralleling the river. Here we go."*

CHAPTER 34

"Do you see any other vehicles?" Nathan asked.

"Negative, just those three."

"Grangeland? You all set?"

"Affirm. I'm between two large boulders directly across the canyon from the saddle. I've got a good shooting lane down to the bottleneck and the flat area of the borrow pit."

"I can't see you. Give me a signal with your penlight." A few seconds later, he saw the camera-like flash. "Affirm. I've got you. I want you to add thirty-six clicks on the elevation knob. Confirm?"

"Copy, adding thirty-six."

"Let me know when you got that dialed in." He waited for her to come back on the radio.

"Okay, I added the clicks."

"That will zero you pretty close to the center of the pit. Now add six clicks to the right for the wind."

"Got it."

He was tempted to ask Grangeland which way she turned the windage knob, but he didn't want to rattle her confidence by asking. She knew her way around rifles. "Harv, you concur?"

"Yeah, that's close enough for center-mass stuff. I'd have her add two more clicks for wind. Her bullets won't be sheltered by the pit until their last 150 yards or so and that canyon amplifies the wind."

"Grangeland, add two more right clicks."

"Will do."

"Nate, do you want me to drop down to the saddle opposite Grangeland?"

"Not yet. I need you looking for more vehicles. Let me know if any of the SUVs stop."

"They're about two minutes from turning onto the access road up the canyon to the pit."

Nathan didn't know if the SUVs belonged to Alisio or the South Koreans, but if the caravan drove straight up here without stopping, he felt confident it wouldn't be Mason and his crew. Based on the time it took to drive out here from San Diego, though, they could be arriving any minute.

Nathan waited through a silent interval. *Patience*, he told himself.

Harv said, *"The caravan just turned onto the access road. They'll be passing Grangeland's position in . . . ninety seconds. They're moving slowly."*

"Headlights still on?" Nathan asked.

"Affirm."

Definitely not Mason, then. "Grangeland, do you have eyes on the caravan?"

"Not yet."

"Let me know when they pass your position and again when they're ten seconds from the pit. Harv, come up on the radio if something changes or if you see additional vehicles enter the area."

"I see them," Grangeland said. *"Their headlights are bouncing like crazy. It looks like a pretty rough ride. Wait . . . They're stopping."*

"What are they doing? Is anyone getting out?"

"Yes, one of them is opening a gate."

"What gate?"

"It's almost invisible. It's just three strands of barbed wire attached to a post."

"Is there a fence on either side of the road?"

"Yes, but it stops following the road farther up. It angles away on both sides. Okay . . . the guy got back in, and they're moving again. They left the gate open."

"Harv, any other vehicles?"

"No, just those three, but I lost sight of them in the canyon."

Half a minute later, Nathan received his ten-second warning from Grangeland.

His body tightened with adrenaline. If he had any doubts about being in the lions' den, it was just confirmed. He took some deep breaths and loosened his grip on the Remington.

The crunch of tires interrupted the silence, and headlight intrusion swept the north tiers of the pit.

Nathan followed the arriving vehicles with his field glasses as they made sweeping turns and parked facing the exit.

Each SUV disgorged four Hispanic-looking men. Ten of them carried compact automatic weapons, one had a sniper rifle, and one sported a white fedora and a huge gold-plated sidearm.

Alisio.

Confirming Nathan's suspicion, six of the gunmen formed a loose circle around the man with the fedora.

The cartel boss was a short, heavyset man with a thin mustache and goatee. His diamond stud earrings had to be four carats each. Below a double chin, huge gold chains hung like Broadway stage curtains. His fingers were lousy with gold—every one of them. Even his hat sported a band of gold. This guy wore enough jewelry to feed an orphanage for twenty years. *What a friggin' douche bag,* Nathan thought. *Look how rich I am.* The words "slimy" and "pimp" came to mind. No other description fit.

Nathan could imagine the guy giving the order to kill Special Agent Hutch as easily as ordering a club sandwich.

Alisio's men carried Heckler & Koch MP5s, bad news for anyone on the business end of those things. Nathan might be able to take down four or five of them before the others returned fire, but even with a vest on, and even if he avoided a head shot, he'd be bleeding from multiple holes. Not a nice thought.

Several of Alisio's gunmen strolled over to the derelict cars, then diverted to the abandoned structures before returning to the SUVs.

A single gunman walked toward the conveyor. Halfway there, he turned right and headed for its south end, away from Nathan's location. Expecting the gunman to circle the conveyor, Nathan bent low until his head nearly touched the ground. He pulled his suppressed Sig from his waist pack and held still.

A smile touched his lips.

If forced to, he was ready to send the first of Alisio's men to the underworld.

***

Harv wished he could be closer to the action, but he understood the need to maintain a lookout position. Despite the circumstances, it was a beautiful view from up here. The Colorado River weaved through the desert landscape like a never-ending snake.

Like Nathan's, his ghillie suit offered him ideal cover. Its beige colors blended perfectly with the parched desert environment. Clearly the area hadn't received its first winter downpour yet. The tall grass pockets and low vegetation were still brown, and the reservoirs were low: the result of a three-year drought crippling the Southwest. In the deepening twilight, the ghillie suit's colors wouldn't be as critical.

Grangeland's voice cut into his thoughts. *"Nathan, do you see that guy approaching the south end of the conveyor?"*

"Yep, I've got him," he replied in a whisper. *"Don't fire unless I'm blown. If I have to drop him, be ready to open up on Alisio's group with as much firepower as you can lay down. You won't hear my shot, but you'll see the guy go down."*

Harv saw a linear dust cloud about two miles distant to the southwest and focused on the leading edge. "I've got something west of here. A vehicle is speeding north on that first road we crossed. It's raising a huge dust cloud."

"Is it an SUV?" Nathan asked.

"No, it's a compact."

"Nathan, that gunman's at the end of the conveyor; he's about to get behind you."

"Stand by, Grangeland. Harv, what's that compact doing?"

"It's still speeding along the road."

Grangeland said, *"One of the gunmen is walking past the office and around the lake toward the zigzags. I think he's going up to the top. He's carrying a scoped rifle."*

"I've got eyes on him," Nathan said. *"Where's the guy who approached the conveyor? Is he walking north behind it?"*

"No, he stopped at the end and looked along its length. He's walking back toward the others. Stay low, he's still looking in your direction."

"The compact stopped," Harv said. "It's turning around. Whoever's driving nearly got stuck in the sand. The driver's getting out."

"Is it Mason?" Nathan asked.

"I can't tell at this distance, but he's wearing desert camo with a rifle slung across his chest. I see a sidearm too. He's making a sprint across the desert directly toward the rim."

"Harv, change in plans. Start down toward section nine of the rim, but don't lose eyes on that runner coming in from the west. We need to know where he sets up his SP. If we lose sight of him, we're all in trouble."

Harv nodded to himself. "I might lose him while I'm relocating."

"Go slow and keep him in sight: that's your priority."

"No problem. I'm on it."

"Grangeland, we've got two hostile forces converging on the rim. Alisio's man will arrive at the top of section one where the switchbacks end. We'll designate him as Lookout. Harv's man is Runner. Unless Runner diverts to another location, he'll arrive around section twenty-seven. Harv's heading for section nine. Let us know when Lookout is thirty seconds from reaching the top, then give us a five-second warning."

"Copy. He just started up the switchbacks."

"Do you have eyes on Harv?"

"Negative. He dropped out of my line of sight when he moved down toward the rim."

"Harv, best guess on Runner's ETA to the rim?"

"Two minutes."

"Grangeland?"

"Lookout's going to arrive at the rim about the same time."

"Harv, unless Lookout makes it to the top first, Runner will see him from section twenty-seven. Concur?"

"Affirm. The switchbacks are plainly visible from there, but it looks like Runner's going to arrive closer to section twenty-four."

"Let me know if he checks the ground at the fence where we arrived."

"Our footprints?"

"Yep."

Harv watched the guy continue across the desert, weaving his way through the bushes and cactus. Whoever it was, he wasn't concerned about being seen.

Harv kept descending the rocky slope as fast as possible. Still, it felt painstakingly slow because he couldn't go too fast without creating movement Runner would detect. He'd done this many times, and it never got easier. "I've lost eyes on the reservoir and the road paralleling the river."

"Thirty seconds," Grangeland said.

Harv cut in. "Runner's almost to the rim, and it's . . . definitely . . . a woman."

"Darla Lyons," Nathan said. *"We're changing her designation to Lyons."*

"Lyons just went over the barbed wire. She's approaching the rim in a crouch . . . She's got two rifles, not one. One of them's suppressed . . . Oh man, she's packing some serious firepower. I'm seeing an M4 carbine with an M203 attached."

"Grenade launcher," Nathan said for Grangeland.

"Shit! She's sweeping toward me with field glasses." Staying right where he was, Harv slowly took a knee. If he made a sudden movement, Lyons would see him for sure.

"Did she see you?" Nathan asked.

"Stand by . . ."

"Harv, talk to me. Her carbine can punch a silver dollar at three hundred yards. Are you blown?"

"No. She's focusing on Lookout."

"Does Lyons have a radio?"

"Not that I can see. All I see are her rifles and a sidearm. I don't see anything else clipped to her belt besides some mag holsters. She's got a small backpack and waist pack. If she's got an earpiece wire, it's tucked tight behind her ear."

"Keep her in sight at all costs, even if you have to blow your cover and drop her."

"Understood. She's on the move again, heading north toward section one." Harv studied her movements, evaluating her tactics and looking for any kind of discernable pattern or repetition. So far, she seemed to be a capable adversary. Her only mistake was assuming no one else was up here, and Harv intended to make her pay for it. "She's working her way along the barbed wire and not making any attempt to be stealthy. If she'd seen me, she wouldn't be doing that. She just blew through the area where we crossed the fence. She didn't see our prints."

"Lookout is five seconds from the rim," Grangeland said.

"Lyons stopped running. She's looking for an SP. I think she's gonna nail Lookout when he reaches the top."

"If Alisio's men have radios, they'll know Lookout's gone silent, even if they don't hear Lyons's rifle. Grangeland, I need you on that peak above you to the south. Head up the mountainside and get eyes on the Imperial Reservoir and the road following the river. We need to know if Mason's got other vehicles in the area. Go slowly. Lyons is eleven hundred yards away, but she could still detect quick movement at that distance."

"It will take me several minutes to get up there," she said.

"Understood; get going."

"If I circle the mountain to the east and maintain the same elevation, I'll be able to see the reservoir and road paralleling the river from there. That will be faster and make me less visible from Lyons's position."

"Stand by. Harv, after you drop down to section nine, will you be able to see if anyone else uses that north-south track we crossed?"

"No. The low angle will screen it from view, but I'll be able to see a dust cloud."

"When will you reach the rim?"

"At least three minutes. There's no way I can advance quickly. I'm in Lyons's peripheral vision. I have eyes on Lookout now; he's at the top."

"Grangeland, proceed due east and maintain current elevation. I'm okay down here until Harv arrives at the rim. Harv, what's Lyons doing?"

"She's sitting in a cross-legged position, lined up on Lookout."

"Harv, you're cleared to take her down if I hear her rifle report down here. Alisio's men will hear it too, and all hell will break loose."

"Copy that, cleared to shoot . . . Lookout's bent over. He's gassed from the hike up there. Lyons is still lined up on him, but she hasn't fired. He just pulled a radio. He's talking on it and looking down into the pit. Okay, he just put it away. He's scanning the rim with field glasses."

"Will he see Lyons?"

"No way."

"If you have to drop Lyons, things will escalate quickly, so make a beeline to the closest part of the rim after you shoot. Grangeland, hold position for the next thirty seconds and be ready to double-time back to your SP. I might need your firepower with that M1A. Copy?"

"Copy. Holding position."

"Once the shooting starts, Alisio and his men could bolt," Harv said. "They might be racing out of that pit in a big hurry. If they leave, Mason will likely follow them, and we could lose him. Should I disable their vehicles?"

"Take down live targets first, then go for their vehicles if it looks like they're making a run for it. Once the shooting starts, they'll probably take cover in the buildings. I doubt those SUVs are armored."

"That pins them down. They—"

Grangeland cut in. *"Two more cars are coming up the access road."*

"Will they see you?"

"I don't know, but I'm out in the open."

"Are their headlights on?"

"Yes."

"What's in your immediate area?"

"Just some rocks, but they aren't big enough to hide behind."

"I want you to drop right where you are and curl into a ball. Don't make any sudden movements at all and don't look at the headlights."

"Shit!"

Harv knew what was coming next; he'd heard it many times—Nathan's cool and composed tone in the face of a potential disaster.

"Listen up, Grangeland. Drop down and slowly form a ball. Please do it right now. Their headlights actually help you. Drivers and passengers tend to look at the cone of light in front of them. You're at least six hundred feet away from the road, well beyond their visual range. That road is also bumpy and rutted. Their heads are jarring around. They can't focus well. Those vehicles are going to pass harmlessly beneath you."

She didn't respond, and Harv knew she was probably holding her breath.

"Breathe, Grangeland," Nathan said. *"You're invisible up there."*

"I'm okay, thanks. I'm just not used to this kind of thing. Okay, I'm curled into a ball. I guess I just became a big rock."

"That's exactly what you are. I wish you could see Alisio. He looks like a caricature from a comic book. He's as clichéd as they get. Mustache, goatee, gold everywhere, white fedora—the works. I hope he gives me an excuse to kill him. A fashion asshole of this magnitude shouldn't be allowed to reproduce himself."

"Hey, I've got dibs on him," she said.

"Now that's *the Grangeland I know and love."*

Harv smiled at their exchange. Lyons must've heard the crunch of gravel from the arriving vehicles. She kept glancing toward the pit, but never took her eyes off Lookout for more than a few seconds.

"They're passing below me, just like you said they would."

"Copy that," Nathan said. *"Good work."*

So far, Lyons hadn't fired. If Grangeland's new arrivals were the South Koreans, then Lookout would be expected to make contact with the others to warn them. A lack of a warning radio call would likely raise suspicion. Suppressed rifle or not, Harv thought Lyons wouldn't shoot Lookout until after the new vehicles arrived in the pit.

"Grangeland, we still need to get your eyes on the road paralleling the river. The next vehicles to arrive are likely to be Mason and Hahn, and their headlights will probably be dark."

"I'll be watching for them," she said.

"Use your thermal imager. It'll work well in this growing twilight. Any vehicle on that road will be a bright object. Harv and I will handle the action in the pit, but be ready to beat feet back to your SP on my mark. Harv, what's Lyons doing? Is she still lined up on Lookout?"

"Affirm, but I think she's waiting to nail him until the other vehicles arrive."

"Agreed. Can Lookout see the arriving vehicles from section one of the rim?"

"No, not until they get closer to the pit, but he should be able to hear their tires and see the glow from their headlights."

"Grangeland, what are those new vehicles doing? Did either of them stop?"

"Negative, they just went through the barbed wire gate. Shit, I hear more vehicles coming!"

CHAPTER 35

Special Agent Mary Grangeland didn't feel so special. What she felt was an upwelling of anxiety, bordering on panic.

She quickly looked around her but saw nothing taller than a shoe box.

Not again . . .

Nathan's voice prompted her to get moving. *"Grangeland, that's probably Mason and Hahn. Find solid cover immediately! Do it now!"*

Her best bet was a trio of large boulders a hundred feet uphill. If she could reach them before the vehicles turned onto the access road, she might be okay.

"There's a spot above me."

"Balls-out sprint. Get your ass moving! If that's our bad guys, they'll have night-vision or thermal-weapon sights."

Abandoning all stealth, she slung the Springfield over her shoulder and scrambled up the steep mountainside toward the boulders. At least she couldn't be seen from Lyons's position. From the urgency in Nathan's voice, he believed the newcomers were Mason and Hahn. And if they got eyes on her, she'd have a firefight on her hands while her backup was several minutes away. A lot could happen in several minutes. Like death . . .

She focused on the ground directly in front of her and drove her legs. If ever she needed a burst of energy, this was it. She couldn't tune out the radio chatter, but she couldn't let it distract her either.

"Harv, you're on Lyons. If she shoots Alisio's man with the suppressed rifle and it doesn't alert everyone, don't fire, and stay with her no matter what. She may relocate."

Despite her desperate situation and her lack of a ghillie suit, Grangeland found the experience strangely exhilarating. Part fear, part excitement, she imagined blue mixing with red to form a beautiful purple—her favorite color. She used the visual to stay focused and calm and to avoid tripping in the minefield of rocks, cacti, and spiked plants. Falling now would be a disaster. A face-plant into one of the many cactus patches would definitely ruin her evening.

Halfway to her cover, the slope got steeper, and finding solid footholds became a problem.

She shut out the unnerving sound of vehicles speeding along the road and kept driving her legs, reminding herself she was in peak shape. She could run several miles without breaking a sweat. This was—

Nathan's voice interrupted her thoughts. *"Grangeland, status?"*

"I'm halfway there, but it's kind of steep. My feet keep slipping."

"Can you see the vehicles?"

"Not yet, but it's going to be close."

"Will you have eyes on the pit from the boulders?"

"I don't know. Probably not. I'm too far around the mountain to the east."

"ETA to your cover?"

She wanted to say, "Sooner if you'd let me concentrate," but instead said, "Fifteen seconds."

"Harv?"

"Lyons is still lined up on Lookout."

"Let me know if the guy uses his radio. The South Korean vehicles are almost in visual range."

"Copy. You called it, Nate. He's on the radio. I can hear the crunch of tires and see headlight intrusion. Lyons is hearing and seeing the same thing I am. We have to assume she's in radio contact with Mason and Hahn."

"Grangeland?"

"Ten more feet . . ." She nearly fell, but regained her balance. Huffing a little, she said, "Shit, I made it." She brought her field glasses up, took a deep breath, and tried to hold still. "Their headlights are dark, and they're slowing for the access road."

"Definitely Mason and Hahn," Nathan said. *"What are they driving?"*

"A dark SUV and a sedan. The SUV's in front. I lost sight of the South Korean SUVs. They should be arriving at your location any second."

"Grangeland, your job is to keep eyes on Mason and Hahn. We have to know where they are at all times. If one or both of them get out, let us know right away."

"I will."

"If they spot you, lay down a barrage of fire and keep shooting until you score a hit. The NV scope will automatically dim to your muzzle flashes. Shoot every second or so, then reload quickly. Each magazine gives you about twenty to thirty seconds of suppression-fire time."

"Copy."

"Be relentless and pour it on them. No mercy. Harv will drop Lyons and hustle down to the rim to support us."

"Got it . . . wait, something's happening. The SUV turned onto the access road, but the sedan kept going. Okay, it stopped. Now the sedan's in reverse behind the SUV. It looks like it's going to back up the road."

"They're setting up a getaway car. They might park the vehicles at the bottleneck to block the road. The driver of the sedan will either transfer into the SUV or take off on foot to high ground. Harv, you copy that?"

"Affirm."

Grangeland listened while Nathan and Harv continued.

"Harv, if someone gets out, I don't see them going up on Grangeland's side of the canyon. Mason or Hahn will go northwest up the mountain, then turn left toward the rim. That will have him arriving at section seven or eight up there. Are you visually secure from that direction?"

"Yes, I'll be ready."

"Grangeland, confirm you can't see the eastern side of the rim from your current position or your original SP."

"Confirmed."

"Harv, if things get heavy, drop Lyons first. You don't want her using that grenade launcher on you. The first of us with eyes on Mason and Hahn outside their vehicles, check in right away. We need to know if they're armed like Lyons."

Grangeland copied Nathan.

"Harv, are you still on the move toward the rim?"

"Yeah, but it's slow going. I'm still a good fifty yards out."

"We may have to initiate the shooting. I don't want you bracketed up there. Grangeland, where are Mason's vehicles?"

"They're halfway to the gate."

"Stand by to open fire. Have five or six mags in your belly pack ready to go."

"I'm all set."

Then Nathan said, *"The South Koreans just arrived in the pit. They're getting out."*

***

From his vantage point inside the conveyor, Nathan watched eight Asian men climb out of two SUVs. All four from the lead vehicle assumed a defensive perimeter around the second SUV. Including Alisio, there were now twenty heavily armed men in the quarry. Darla Lyons occupied the west rim with an M4 carbine and a grenade launcher at her disposal.

Nathan was quick with a pistol, but he didn't possess Harv's skills. At this distance of a football field to where the men were standing outside their vehicles, Nathan could use his bolt-action rifle against them, but because of their numbers, it was far from ideal. The semiauto M1A would've been better. All factors considered, Grangeland needed that weapon. She wouldn't be nearly as fast as Harv or him cycling a bolt-action weapon. She also didn't have the one-shot-one-kill expertise, but he had no doubt she could take down multiple targets once the shooting started.

As tempting as it was to give the order, Harv couldn't drop Lyons yet. It would alert everyone to Harv's presence because his rifle wasn't suppressed. The report would echo through the pit like a thunderclap, and everyone would immediately scramble for cover. Patience was the hardest part of an op like this. Being the first to shoot wasn't always to a sniper's advantage.

Two of the South Koreans walked over and shook hands with Alisio. Nathan heard them speaking English, but couldn't make out more than a few words. Alisio made more introductions, followed by more handshakes.

"Everyone listen up. Including Alisio's lookout on the rim, we're facing twenty gunmen. Twelve are Alisio's; eight are ROK. Grangeland, status?"

"Mason and Hahn are still coming, but they're going slowly. They haven't reached the barbed wire gate yet."

"Maintain eyes on them with your field glasses. Be ready to switch to the M1A on my mark. Are you working your way back to your original SP above the bottleneck in the access road?"

"Yes."

Harv said, *"Alisio's lookout on the rim just used his radio and put it away. He's not acting very watchful. He's . . . taking a leak. Oh, man."*

"What?" Nathan asked.

"Lyons just killed him. She shot the guy in the head while he was relieving himself."

"I didn't hear the shot down here."

"I didn't either. She just fired twice more; I guess to make sure the guy's dead. She may be switching to the M4 with the grenade launcher. Its weapon sight is bigger than a normal optical. She'll have NV for sure, maybe thermal too."

"Hold off dropping her, Harv. It's a brutal reality, but every gunman she eliminates is one less we have to deal with."

"I'm ready; just give the word."

"Mason can't drive up here like he's part of the exchange. The players have already arrived. And he can't sneak up here with his headlights dark or they'll hear his tires crunching on the gravel. He'll need a distraction."

"I'm confirming Lyons just switched to the M4," Harv said.

"Harv, once an unsuppressed shot rings out or she uses the launcher, take her down quickly. Grangeland, what are Mason's vehicles doing? Are they still coming up the road?"

"Yes."

Harv cut in. *"Lyons just loaded the grenade launcher. The rounds are in her belly pack."*

"I doubt she'll target Alisio's vehicles yet. She doesn't know which one has the money. Are you at the rim?"

"Sixty seconds. It's slow going. I'm still in Lyons's cone of vision. If she swings her rifle scope toward me, it might be the last thing I'll ever see."

Grangeland cut in. *"Sorry to interrupt, but Mason and Hahn just went through the gate. Both vehicles."*

"Copy. One of the South Koreans opened the back of an SUV. I can't see it from my angle, but I suspect the duffel bags are in there. Alisio's checking it out. Stand by . . . we might have trouble. One of his men is looking at the rim through field glasses and talking on a radio. Harv, hold position and get a bead on Lyons. If I have to start shooting down here, drop her right away. I don't want to end up on the business end of that M203."

"Copy."

"The sedan stopped," Grangeland said. *"Someone's getting out. He's not big enough to be Mason. Gotta be Hahn. He's getting in the SUV. He left the sedan blocking the road."*

"Can a vehicle get past it?"

"No."

"Weapons?"

"Hahn's carrying an M4 with a big sight, but it doesn't have a launcher. He's wearing desert camo with a backpack and belly pack."

"Keep eyes on Mason's SUV. If they keep going at their present pace, when will they reach the pit?"

"Thirty seconds, maybe a little more."

"Will you make your SP before they reach the pit?"

"I think so. It'll be close."

"Don't shoot until you have solid cover. Get into a prone position. If you have to, stack some rocks in front of you. Check for ants before you lie down. Copy?"

"Copy."

Harv cut in. *"Nate, can you hear Mason's SUV?"*

"Not yet. The South Koreans are unloading the duffel bags. They're also setting up a small folding table and a chair. It's partially blocked from my line of sight."

"To examine the diamonds and coins," Harv said.

"Alisio's walking over to his SUV. He grabbed a briefcase; it probably holds the two million in cash. He's looking at his man, the one who tried to contact his lookout. Everyone give me a short interval of radio silence. I want to hear what he's saying."

Nathan spoke fluent Spanish and couldn't miss what Alisio yelled up to the rim.

"Julio! Where the fuck are you?" The crime boss cursed again and ordered one of his men to hustle up there and find "Julio's dumb ass."

The South Koreans suddenly looked edgy, eyeing the rim, then their vehicles. Alisio assured them everything was okay. He told them his lookout was probably scouting the area up there and couldn't hear him.

They exchanged a few more words, and one of the South Korean gunmen joined Alisio's man. Together, they began a jog around the perimeter of the lake toward the switchbacks.

There were now seventeen gunmen left in the pit.

"Harv, two gunmen are heading for the switchbacks. One of them has an MP5; the other's got an AK. How close is Lyons to the rim? Will she be able to see them once they start up?"

"Yes, she's several feet from the edge behind a large creosote bush, but she can see the pit and the switchbacks for sure."

"If she relocates for any reason, use the opportunity to advance. I need you on the rim."

"Will do. Those guys are going to find Alisio's dead lookout. They can't miss him."

"Mason's SUV just stopped," Grangeland said. *"Hahn got out . . . he's running up the mountain to the north."*

"Grangeland, your responsibility is now Hahn. Keep track of him at all costs. We absolutely need to know where he sets up his SP. Expect him to make a left turn and head for section eight or nine on the rim. If Mason's SUV stops again, let me know."

"Okay, I'm back at my original SP. Shit, my phone just vibrated," she said.

"Ignore it and stay on Hahn."

"Mine too," Harv said.

"Leave them in your pockets. Harv, stay on Lyons. Will Hahn be in your line of sight once he makes his move toward the rim?"

"Affirm. He'll be on fairly open ground."

"Mason slowed to a crawl. I don't hear the crunch of his tires," Grangeland said.

"Harv?"

"I don't hear it either."

"The two men are at the bottom of the switchbacks. They're starting up in a jog. Alisio put his briefcase on the table. Grangeland, be ready to drop Hahn simultaneously with Harv dropping Lyons. Will you be able to track Hahn's progress all the way to the rim?"

"Yes."

Nathan eased forward a little to give himself a better field of view. He couldn't see the mouth of the road, but everything else was visible. He had to be careful. One of the truss braces of the conveyor went diagonally through his shooting lane.

"Grangeland, keep your field glasses handy and switch to the M1A's optical. For reference purposes, there are five SUVs in the pit. Alisio's three are parked near the office, and the two ROK vehicles are closer to the prefab."

Grangeland and Harv copied.

"Mason stopped, but he's not getting out," Grangeland said.

"How far from the mouth of the pit? Is his SUV blocking the road at that spot?"

"One hundred yards, and yes."

"Harv, can you see that?"

"No, I'm not close enough to the rim to see over the edge, and I've got no cover directly ahead. Lyons saw the two guys run over to the switchback, so she's sighting in on section one at the switchback's upper terminus."

"Grangeland, do you have frontal cover?"

"If I move some big rocks."

"Make it quick and watch for scorpions. Their sting isn't fatal, but you'll wish it was."

"I'll be careful."

"Harv, those two guys are halfway up the switchbacks. Does Lyons still have the M4 shouldered?"

"Yes, and I can see Hahn now. He made his turn west, toward section nine."

"Copy." He needed to say something to Grangeland and couldn't worry if she'd be insulted or not. "Listen up, Grangeland. You already know this, but I'm saying it anyway. Take a few deep breaths and settle your nerves. I want you smooth on that trigger. We're saving lives by taking lives, that's how you get through it."

"You guys used to do this for a living?"

"Shoot center mass; don't attempt head shots. Your wind and elevation are dialed in. In about fifteen seconds, those two guys hustling up the switchbacks are going to discover the body, at which point Lyons will likely drop them. What's Mason doing?"

"Nothing, his SUV's just sitting—"

Harv cut into Grangeland's transmission. *"Lyons just aimed her M4 into the pit!"*

CHAPTER 36

Nathan heard the unmistakable thunk of Lyons's grenade launcher. He took a deep breath and lowered his head. If she'd fired an antipersonnel round, he didn't want to take a piece of it. He was about to order Harv to drop her, but no loud explosion rocked the pit; it was more like a muted pop.

A second thunk reverberated through the pit, followed by another pop.

Nathan saw yellow smoke belching. Lyons had fired two smoke rounds into the pit near the parked SUVs. Everyone in the pit froze for several seconds.

Grangeland said, *"Mason's SUV is on the move! He's racing toward the pit."*

"Stand by, Grangeland. You're still on Hahn. Switch to thermal mode."

"Copy, switching to thermal."

"Lyons has a bead on the two men," Harv said. *"They stopped running. They're staring at the smoke. She's going to nail them."*

"Let her," Nathan said. "Take her down after she shoots them."

Two quick rifle reports crackled around the rock walls. Still using field glasses, Nathan looked toward the top of the switchbacks and saw the men go down.

All of the gunmen in the pit were now scrambling for cover in every direction. Alisio barked orders, but it was every man for himself. Some of the gunmen ran toward their vehicles; others bolted for the buildings.

Another pop rang out, and Nathan couldn't place the source. He swept the rim and saw white smoke at section thirty. Had Lyons's grenade launcher malfunctioned?

Harv said, *"Lyons just popped smoke up here. I lost eyes on her!"*

Shit! He should've anticipated that. Identical to his own, Harv's scope didn't have thermal capacity—only Grangeland had TI mode. "Harv, use the opportunity to advance to the rim and find cover. Everyone is scrambling down here. Get eyes on Lyons when she fires again and drop her."

"Copy that," Harv said. *"Grangeland, give section thirty a quick look with your thermal."*

Nathan watched Alisio pull his handgun and bolt for the closest building. "Alisio and five of his men just ducked into the office. Some of the South Koreans are beelining for their SUVs. Grangeland, can you see Lyons?"

"No."

"Where's Mason's SUV?"

"It's still racing up the road."

From the windows of the buildings, bursts of automatic fire crackled. Nathan saw the stroboscopic effect of the discharges illuminate the ground. Alisio's men were firing at the cloud of white smoke on the rim. Dozens of bullet impacts peppered the wall, some of them creating sparks.

"Grangeland, on my mark, stand by to open fire on Mason's vehicle when it reaches the flat area at the pit. Your AP rounds will penetrate the sheet metal. Shoot out its tires. Keep pouring it on until I give you new orders."

"Copy that. What about Hahn?"

"Harv's got him for now."

Nathan watched five South Koreans rush toward their vehicles. Their leader yelled something in Korean, seemingly a reprimand because none of them had grabbed the briefcase.

One of them made a mad dash back to the folding table, and it saved his life.

Nathan didn't hear the thunk of Lyons's grenade launcher, but the South Korean SUV, where the other men had huddled, exploded. Smoking parts arced through the air. Two men screamed and rolled away from the ruined vehicle, clearly wounded. Two seconds later, the second ROK vehicle exploded. Nathan saw the glow of fire begin inside its destroyed interior. Clutching his leg, a third South Korean fell to the ground. Three of the eight South Koreans were now out of the fight.

The ROK gunman who'd run back toward the folding table to retrieve the loot changed his mind and scrambled toward the prefab.

Alisio was yelling, but Nathan couldn't tell what he said.

"I've got Lyons!" said Harv.

"Drop her."

Nathan waited for Harv's shot, but it didn't come.

"Shit. She popped more smoke just before she fired. I lost her again."

Nathan saw a second cloud forming up on the rim. "Grangeland, where's Mason?"

"He's seconds out. The smoke is still pretty thick in the pit, but I can see bodies on the ground. Most of Alisio's men are in the office. The South Koreans are running toward the prefab. Several others are crouching behind an intact SUV. Wait, they just bolted for the prefab."

Alisio's gunmen continued firing from the office. The roars of their automatics sounded like crackling thunderclaps. Just before they disappeared behind the smoke screen, the wounded ROK gunmen cried out in anger as some of Alisio's men walked their machine-gun bursts over their prone forms. Alisio's men either suspected the ROK gunmen were part of the raid, or they were confused and didn't know who was who.

"Harv, can Hahn see the conveyor from his position? He's on the rim directly behind me, concur?"

"Yes, he can definitely see the conveyor."

"Grangeland, change in plan. On my mark, open fire on Hahn's position. Keep laying it on until I tell you to stop. Don't fire too quickly, just a bullet every two seconds or so. Stay in thermal mode. Copy?"

"Copy, but I don't have a clear shot at him; he's between two large boulders."

"Do your best to keep him pinned. Try for a cornering shot off the rock face behind him."

"Standing by," she said.

"Harv, be ready to nail Lyons. I'm dropping Mason as soon as I get eyes on him."

Chaos reigned in the pit, made worse by the dust and smoke obscuring everyone's vision. The echo of gunfire kept rattling around the rock ledges in random intervals. Both vehicles Lyons had destroyed were now burning, creating twin columns of black smoke that twisted into one.

"Still no sign of Lyons," Harv reported.

Nathan steeled himself. If he took a bullet within the next few minutes, he hoped it would find his vest. He didn't like how he'd left things with Holly and didn't want to die without reconciling with her. He forced the thought aside; hopefully he could ponder the virtues of regret later.

"Grangeland, open fire on Hahn's position!"

***

Mason consciously loosened his left-hand grip on the steering wheel. The other hand held his M4, currently aimed out the passenger window. From the sound of things, Darla had done a great job disabling the vehicles up ahead. Alisio should be pissing his pants by now. He pressed the gas harder and endured the teeth-chipping ruts and bumps.

Mason heard a steady pounding of individual rifle reports at the same time his earpiece crackled to life.

"*I'm taking fire!*" Hahn yelled.

"Darla, can you see the shooter?"

"*Affirm, it's coming from the south side of the canyon above the access road. I'm seeing muzzle flashes, but the shooter's out of my range.*"

"Chip, do you have cover?"

"*Yeah, barely. Shit!*"

"Stay down. I'll try to take out the shooter. Darla, am I in that shooter's line of sight?"

"*Yes.*"

"Empty a magazine into the cinder block building where Alisio's holed up, and take out those remaining vehicles. Any sign of more shooters?"

"*No.*"

Mason began swerving back and forth along the narrow road as best he could, but if he wasn't careful, he'd end up stuck in the ditch.

"Relocate after your shot, be ready to—"

Darla interrupted him. "*Someone just came out from under the collapsed conveyor. He's running toward its south end where you're coming in.*"

So there were two new players now, and maybe more than that. One was firing at Hahn from above and behind him, and the other was in the pit. He had no idea if they were with Alisio, the South Koreans, or independent. It didn't matter. They had to be neutralized. Unfortunately, shooting a man in full sprint was tough. Given Darla's skill level and the distance, she had little chance of nailing the guy. "Pin that runner down with the 203, then try to nail him when he stops. What's he carrying?"

"A sniper rifle and a sidearm."

"Send an HE round, now!"

Mason kept weaving his car from side to side as he approached the mouth of the pit. If Darla didn't kill that sniper running along the conveyor, this raid might be over. He already had to contend with Alisio's machine guns and couldn't risk the added worry of facing a shooter. From his tours in Afghanistan, he knew how deadly they could be.

Another explosion came from the pit—Darla's grenade launcher.

He listened for the follow-up report of her rifle, but there were too many other gunshots and machine-gun bursts to hear it.

A bullet penetrated the top of his SUV and tore through the passenger seat. "I'm taking fire! How about you, Chip?"

"The shooting stopped for the moment. I'd better relocate."

"Do it. And take out the shooter who tried to nail you."

***

Nathan slung his Remington across his chest, scrambled backward from his hiding place, and *shit* . . . banged his head on a brace. Fortunately the metallic bong couldn't be heard over the sounds of war. Irritated at himself, he crawled out from the hollow space and hoped Hahn wasn't crazy enough to attempt a shot while taking constant fire from Grangeland.

Lyons was a different matter. "Harv, stand by to reacquire Lyons. I doubt she's finished with that grenade launcher. Watch for the flash. Grangeland, keep firing on Hahn's position."

Like a distant metronome, Grangeland's rifle boomed every two seconds. Some of the South Koreans were shooting toward Grangeland's position, but their subcompacts were useless at that range.

By her fifth shot, Nathan had his Sig in his hand and sprinted in a crouch toward the south end of the conveyor. He needed to get eyes on Mason before the reverse happened. He also needed to alternate his forward speed. If Lyons had a bead on him, he didn't want to be a predictable target.

He stopped running and took a knee.

Good thing. Thirty feet in front of him, the conveyor exploded.

The concussive blast and white flash of the detonation overloaded his senses. Disoriented and stunned, he fell forward to his hands and nearly vomited. He didn't feel any wounds, but knew it could take a few seconds for shock to wear off. Instinctively, he reversed direction, crawling quickly to avoid remaining a stationary target.

The ground in front of him erupted with the supersonic crack of an arriving bullet.

His chin and lip took fragments, but the wounds didn't feel too bad. Were it not for his protective goggles, he'd have two eyes full of dirt, pulverized rock, and shredded copper. Blood began to ooze over his lips and the familiar taste of his own blood was back—again.

He scrambled over to the conveyor. Just ahead, Lyons's grenade had twisted and mangled the metal braces and ignited the grass inside the conveyor. Gray smoke began to stalk him. Time to get moving.

"Harv!"

"I've got her."

Over the clatter of automatic gunfire, he heard the boom of Harv's Remington, a sound he knew well.

"Center mass," Harv said calmly. *"She's down."*

"Good shooting, partner."

Lyons never had a clue Harv was up there. She'd used the smoke screens effectively, but patience had paid off. Harv's steel-core bullet had cleaved through Lyons's body armor. She'd be in a bad way for sure. Nathan didn't wish her a slow death, but it wouldn't break his heart either. She'd played a role in the murder of Mara and her unborn baby.

Encouraged by Harv's success, Nathan cleared the dirt out of the Sig's barrel and gained his feet. He'd just resumed his sprint along the conveyor when Grangeland's frantic voice sounded in his earpiece.

"There's another vehicle coming in!"

CHAPTER 37

Nathan had to hand it to Mason; he'd played this well. The incoming vehicle was obviously reinforcements, a getaway car, or both. As soon as it arrived, the momentum of the battle would shift back to Mason. Nathan had a very short window to neutralize Mason before more PMCs joined the fight.

He needed to keep Grangeland focused. "Hahn is Harv's responsibility now. Switch your fire to Mason's SUV. Ignore the incoming vehicle; light Mason up." He heard Grangeland's Springfield start pounding away again.

"Hahn's in a full sprint," Harv reported. *"I can't get a good bead on him."*

"Stay with him no matter what, Harv."

Nathan reached the end of the conveyor just as Mason's SUV shot from the mouth of the canyon. Weaving back and forth and kicking up a huge dust cloud, it raced toward the burning vehicles inside the thinning cloud of yellow smoke.

Nathan shook the earth from his hat and painted the Sig's laser on Mason's windshield. A burst of automatic fire from the prefab building forced him to duck and relocate. Apparently the

South Koreans were alerted to his presence now. He wanted to return fire at the Koreans, but kept his attention on Mason.

Grangeland kept firing, but few of her rounds found Mason's SUV, and those that punched holes in it didn't find Mason.

Fifty yards from the trio of burning SUVs, Mason swerved to the left and slid to a stop.

Nathan saw why.

The business end of an M4 hung out the passenger window, and it had the menacing outline of a grenade launcher.

Not knowing Mason's target, Nathan hit the deck. The broken-out windows of the office and prefab buildings came to life with starlike muzzle flashes as the Mexicans and South Koreans opened fire at Mason's SUV.

The grenade launcher spit fire.

A second later, thick white smoke blasted in all directions, engulfing Alisio's burning vehicles and the folding table containing the loot.

Bursting smoke grenade.

Mason then sprayed the entire area with the .223. Dozens of rounds peppered the office building, forcing Alisio's men to stop firing. Mason gunned the engine and circled back toward the access road. He hadn't been stationary for more than two or three seconds. The combination of cover smoke and failing light made him a difficult target to acquire.

In grudging admiration, Nathan watched Mason swing around for another pass. Grangeland continued to shoot, and miss. Nathan saw her rounds cratering the rocky soil.

From somewhere above, he heard the boom of Harv's Remington. Obviously, his friend had his hands full, and requesting an update would only distract him. He needed to believe that Harv was keeping Hahn from getting a bead on him. Either that, or his life might come to a quick end. So far, no one had taken another potshot at him from the rim.

The break in Grangeland's barrage meant she was changing magazines.

"Grangeland, where's that new vehicle?"

"It just came through the gate. It looks like a Humvee."

"A Humvee? Are you sure?"

"Yes."

"I'll deal with it. Keep shooting at Mason."

Nathan painted his Sig's laser on the SUV's windshield and popped off three quick shots. Only one of his bullets found its mark, creating a spiderwebbed break on the passenger's side. Then he lost sight of the SUV behind the mass of white smoke. The reduced wind in the pit gave Mason a tactical advantage, and he used it well.

A few seconds later, Mason's vehicle reemerged from the smoke, his M4 no longer hanging out the window. Nathan lined up for another shot but had to duck for cover when several of the South Koreans in the prefab opened fire on his position again. He heard bullets thump and clang off the metal braces to his left. Staying low, he advanced to the tip of the conveyor. Beyond it, he'd have no cover. The closest object was a pockmarked washing machine or dryer; he couldn't tell which.

Nathan watched Mason's SUV straighten out and head straight for the folding table. Nathan came up for another shot, but was immediately pinned by more automatic fire from the South Koreans.

He needed Harv's help and risked a call. "Harv?"

"I'm CM with Hahn. He's wounded but still in the fight."

"Keep after him." CM was code for cat and mouse. At least Hahn was fighting for his life up there and wouldn't be shooting into the pit. With the added firepower the newly arrived Humvee introduced, Nathan would soon find himself seriously outgunned. As it was, he couldn't even shoot at Mason—the South Koreans were keeping him pinned down. It was beginning to look like Mason might actually get his hands on the money and escape.

He couldn't let that happen, but short of making a suicidal charge into a maelstrom of bullets, his options were limited.

Grangeland's voice was intermittent. *"The Humvee just . . . pushed . . . the . . . road."*

Shit, he didn't catch all of Grangeland's last transmission. Her rifle reports were drowning out her voice.

Something flew from the driver's window of Mason's vehicle. It arced through the air and landed next to the last intact SUV.

The resulting explosion ruined Nathan's vision. Temporarily flash blinded, he cursed himself for being so careless. He should have anticipated it. Now a purple blotch dominated the center of his field of view, even as he again lost sight of Mason's SUV.

"Grangeland, cease fire! Cease fire." The pounding of her reports stopped. "Does the Humvee have a turret gun?"

"Yes."

Shit. That was very bad news. This fight might be over. "Mason's heading for the folding table. Try to nail the briefcase before he gets there. Copy?"

"Copy."

Nathan heard the roar of a diesel engine and had to make a decision. That rusty washing machine would offer little protection against the Humvee's turret gun; neither would the sparsely spaced braces of this conveyor.

He had an idea. If he could score a driver's-side-window or windshield shot into the Humvee with an armor-piercing .308 round, it might penetrate its bulletproof glass and take out the driver.

He holstered the Sig and shouldered his Remington. As he did, Grangeland's Springfield began another barrage, slower this time. He imagined her walking the bullets onto the folding table. Hopefully she could nail the briefcase—anything to delay Mason.

Harv's rifle boomed again, but Nathan didn't dare distract his friend by asking for an update.

"I got it!" Grangeland said. *"Alisio's bundles of cash are scattered all over the place!"*

"Good shooting. I'll take the Humvee. You switch back to Mason's SUV. Can you still see it through the smoke?"

"Affirm: it's a bright object."

"Pour it on."

At that moment, like a vision out of Operation Desert Storm, a tan Humvee roared into the pit.

Nathan couldn't believe what he saw and heard next.

"Nathan!"

Oh, no way. No possible way! This couldn't be happening.

His father was in the Humvee's gun turret, manning its fifty-caliber machine gun.

The voice rang out again. "Nathan, are you in here?"

"Over here! Mason's got a grenade launcher. Get that thing moving!"

Nathan heard his dad yell, "George, punch it over to the south end of the conveyor!"

George? George Beaumont was driving? Incredible. What the hell were those old Marines doing? Trying to get themselves killed? He couldn't believe they were here. What on earth had possessed them? Part of him thought it was reckless; the other part admired the pure moxie of it. Either way, he welcomed the firepower.

"Grangeland, what direction does that Humvee have to fire to nail Mason?"

"What?"

"Cease fire again! Give me a clock vector for the Humvee to shoot at Mason's SUV."

She didn't answer, and he realized the reason for her confusion.

"The Humvee's a friendly! My father's in it! What direction should he shoot?"

"Eight o'clock!"

Nathan yelled, "Dad, fire the M2 at your eight!"

"Roger that!"

A grin took Nathan's face. Once a Marine, always a Marine. His eighty-five-year-old father looked like a World War II destroyerman shooting at an incoming kamikaze. A ten-foot javelin of mushrooming flame spat from the Browning's muzzle.

Nathan couldn't help himself, and yelled, "Get some, Dad! Get some!"

A line of bright tracers pulsed into the fog-like smoke and disappeared. The roar of the discharge was beyond deafening.

Grangeland said, *"Tell him to adjust to the left slightly."*

Nathan knew it was useless to repeat her correction; his dad would never hear it.

The Humvee roared toward his position. Pouring it on, his father continued to hammer away at the center of the pit. *Keep it up*, thought Nathan. If just one of those bullets found Mason, it was lights-out for the former PMC.

The Humvee turned, paralleling the conveyor.

Nathan made his move.

He dashed from his position and felt his face vibrate from the Browning's concussive reports. His earpiece came to life with Grangeland's voice, but the roar of the fifty caliber drowned it. He was about to open the door and jump in when he glimpsed an unbelievable sight.

Like a demon emerging from hell, Mason walked out of the smoke with his M4 leveled at the hip.

Before his dad could walk the fifty-caliber barrage onto Mason's body, the grenade launcher flashed.

CHAPTER 38

The opposite side of the Humvee detonated in a blinding explosion.

Nathan's stomach twisted as a plume of gray smoke gushed from the turret's opening.

"Dad!"

He rushed to the Humvee, shouldered his Remington, and aimed at the center of Mason's chest.

From no more than thirty yards distant, Mason aligned the M4 on Nathan's body.

Nathan stood firm.

This could be it.

An image of his father, standing like a stone wall during the Korean War, formed in his mind, and the visual hardened his resolve. As Stone McBride had done more than sixty years ago, Nathan looked death in the eyes and felt no fear. Like an ever-heightening whistle from a teakettle, all of his senses expanded to the bursting point, then instantaneously compressed.

Mason's flash suppressor ignited with an alluring white star. The sight of it was strangely beautiful, like an airport beacon to a lost pilot.

Nathan felt warmth engulf his body as three separate yet interlinked images formed in his mind.

Holly's smile.

Harv's deep laughter.

His father's warm hand in his own.

And in that instant, Nathan knew it was okay to die. He didn't question it. Didn't fight it. And didn't regret it.

I am ready to walk with God . . .

When his senses returned to normal, he heard the staccato growl of Mason's M4 echoing around the pit. Dozens of bullets thumped on the ground in front of him and clanked off the Humvee. The sleeve of his ghillie jumped, but he didn't feel anything penetrate his flesh.

Before Mason's salvo ended, Nathan pulled the trigger.

His Remington answered the request.

When he came back on target, Tanner Mason stood there, looking down at his chest with an expression of disbelief. The man dropped the M4, issued a nod of understanding, and collapsed.

"Grangeland, open fire on the office and prefab buildings where the gunmen are holed up. Alternate between them like you practiced. I need as much cover fire as you can lay down."

"Copy."

Grangeland's crackling reports resumed. Nathan used the lapse in enemy fire to climb onto the smoking Humvee. He found his father bent at the waist, slumped against the turret's armor. Smoke still belched from the opening, but it wasn't dangerously thick or hot.

"Nathan—" His dad coughed and tried to straighten up.

"I've got you."

"Help George . . ."

Nathan pulled his father from the turret and laid him on the sloped rear hatch. He jumped to the ground, muscled his dad over his shoulder, and ran him over to the protected side of the conveyor. Thankfully, Stone didn't look severely burned, but there was blood on his left calf—lots of it. The grass fire under the conveyor wouldn't reach his dad's position for several minutes.

"I'm okay . . . get George."

Nathan handed him a bandanna. "Tie that off."

Nathan opened the driver's door and found George drooped over the center console. Nathan saw the damage right away. A chunk of George's head was gone. It looked like something had cleaved through his skull like a broadsword. He grabbed the retired Marine under his arms and pulled him out of the smoldering compartment, and carried him over to his father's position.

Mason must've fired a standard high-explosive round. If it had been a dual-purpose, the armored Humvee would've sustained more damage. From what Nathan saw, the grenade had detonated just below the window, but some of the explosive force had blown through the bulletproof glass, instantly killing George. If Mason's aim had been six inches higher, the grenade would've struck the glass directly, killing his dad as well.

Nathan ran back to the Humvee and found what he was looking for: cans of fifty-caliber ammo secured by a strap. The M2's high-energy slugs were capable of punching through the cinder block walls of the office. And that's what Nathan intended to do. Working quickly, he released the strap.

As much as Nathan wanted to mourn George's passing, this fight wasn't over.

"Grangeland, cease fire. Cease fire. Get down here fast!"

"On my way."

The smoke near the middle of the pit was thinning. He didn't have much time before the Humvee would be visible to the remaining gunmen hiding in the two buildings.

He wondered about Harv. Their radios were set for auto transmission, so Harv would've been hearing everything that happened. Should he risk checking in? He decided to wait. The last message from his friend had mentioned he was chasing Hahn.

There was no reason to believe that had changed. Distracting Harv with a radio call at the wrong instant could cost Harv his life.

He ran back to his dad, who was in the process of securing the bandanna around his calf wound. "George didn't make it. I'm sorry."

Stone nodded. "Look, I'm okay. I'm not worried about the fire yet. Get up there and man that Browning."

"I'll be right back; sit tight."

"Nathan—"

With Grangeland providing cover fire, he dashed over to Mason's prone form. The man was still breathing, but it sounded wet and labored. Nathan felt Mason's waist pack and knew there were at least half a dozen grenades left inside. He zipped it closed, pulled his Predator knife, and cut the waist pack's belt. Thinking it held the M4's magazines, he yanked Mason's backpack free.

He was about to run back to the conveyor when Mason grabbed his ankle.

"How did I . . . miss you . . . from here?"

Nathan didn't say anything or try to jerk free. Less than ten seconds remained before he'd be visible through the thinning smoke.

All the anger he felt toward this man melted, didn't seem important anymore.

"Don't let Alisio . . . get away." Mason coughed blood and grimaced in pain.

This could've been me.

"We need to know something," Nathan told Mason. "Did you compromise the November Directive's operatives?"

Mason's eyes were losing their brightness as he stared past Nathan. "Never . . . Never do that. Tell the old man I'm . . . sorry. He helped me when . . . I was—"

He didn't tell Mason the grenade attack had killed George Beaumont. There was no point in tormenting a dying man.

"I'll tell him."

Mason managed a half smile and tried to finish his sentence, but only blood came out. The man's eyes went blank, then closed for good. As he did in the presence of any death, Nathan grieved a loss, but Mason had made his own choices. He could've walked a different path.

He grabbed Mason's M4 and hustled back to his dad's position at the conveyor. He reloaded the carbine's magazine and cycled the bolt. Next he opened the M203, put a dual-purpose grenade into its breech, and snapped it closed.

"This is loaded with a HEDP grenade. You good to go?"

"Yes, now get up there and kick some ass. The turret should still work."

Bursts of automatic fire from the remaining gunmen in the buildings began echoing around the pit. A few of the bullets clanked off the Humvee.

Nathan opened the other door on the protected side of the vehicle to free the acrid smoke, then went inside and stood on the plate under the roof's hatch. He glanced at the ammo can feeding the M2 and saw about half of the one hundred rounds remained. He needed to fire in short, controlled bursts to avoid blowing through the rest of the can too quickly. Reloading this weapon wasn't like changing an M4's magazine; it could take five to fifteen seconds, especially since he hadn't done it in over twenty years.

In truth, there was no reason that he, Harv, and Grangeland couldn't leave at this point. Technically, their mission was accomplished, but bugging out without emptying the remaining trash wouldn't sit right with him, and Nathan was determined to be a good janitor.

Anger flared at Alisio, for all of this. None of this would be happening without the man's bloodthirsty love of money. He relaxed his jaw and steeled himself for the living hell he was going to unleash. Nathan hadn't known Special Agent Hutch, but from everything he'd learned, Hutch had been a good man and loyal public servant and certainly hadn't deserved to be tortured to death and hung from a streetlamp. As payback for that heinous act, Nathan planned to kill everyone associated with Alisio, which meant killing everyone in this forsaken pit.

So be it.

Nathan looked beyond the burning SUVs and saw the office building had partially materialized through the white smoke. Occasional bursts of machine-gun fire emanated from its windows. He pivoted the turret and lined up on the prefab building, the closer of the two.

Nathan tapped the trigger to be sure the weapon answered the call.

It did.

The short burst tore into the structure.

All his senses were instantly assaulted, worst of all his eardrums. *Damn, this thing's loud!*

In response, the South Koreans fired back. Some of their nine-millimeter bullets clanked off the turret's faceted armor and whistled away.

Okay, suit yourselves.

He pushed the thumb trigger, and this time kept it depressed.

Even though the weapon was firmly anchored to the turret, Nathan's body shuddered. A smile touched his lips at the visual of his father up here, hammering away at Alisio's men. He emptied the remainder of the can, walking the barrage back and forth across the length of the wall. He battered the wood-framed building like there was no tomorrow, which was true for most of the men cowering inside. Being on the wrong end of John Browning's invention was a wholly unpleasant experience. If anyone were hit and remained alive in there, he wouldn't be for long.

When the gun stopped firing, he went to work reloading it. He tossed the empty can to the ground, reached into the interior of the Humvee, and grabbed another. He unlatched the lid, secured the can to the left side of the weapon, and fed the belt into the breech.

Three cranks later, the Browning was good to go.

He rotated the turret to the cinder block office building, but held his fire.

In a move that surprised himself, he yelled, "Everyone come out with your hands in the air!"

Nothing happened. The only sound was the crackling of the burning SUVs.

"This is your last chance, Alisio. You and your men come out."

A few seconds later, someone yelled, *"No hablamos inglés."*

He pushed the trigger.

The supersonic slugs delivered their kinetic energy with frightening efficiency. Lining the weapon up at knee level, he watched chunks of concrete explode off the wall as baseball-sized holes materialized. It looked as though the building were imploding from dozens of invisible sledgehammer blows.

He ceased fire and yelled, "*Cómo sobre ahora*?" (*How about now?)*

"Sí, hablamos inglés!"

"Then drop all your weapons and get your dumb asses out of there."

Looking like tattered war refugees, Alisio and two other men came out of the office building. Taking up the rear, Alisio had a pronounced limp. Even though the man looked out of the fight, Nathan watched him closely. He wouldn't put it past the crime boss to make a move once he got closer.

The orange glow from the burning SUVs illuminated the men's faces and added to the battleground feel of the place.

"Grangeland?"

"I'll be there in ninety seconds."

Keeping his eyes on the three men walking toward him, he yelled, "Dad, are you okay?"

"You tell me . . ."

Startled, Nathan turned and saw his father standing next to the Humvee with Mason's M4. The bandanna on his calf wound was soaked.

"Are you trying to bleed out? Sit down. A fall at your age could be fatal."

His dad didn't budge. "I'm still in this fight, Son."

Nathan refocused on Alisio's group. "Keep coming and keep your hands where I can see them."

Alisio looked over both shoulders, probably wondering if anyone else was still alive.

Nathan heard a rifle report somewhere above the rim.

Harv's Remington.

Alisio stopped and cringed.

"Keep moving," said Nathan.

"Hahn's toast," Harv said.

"Good work, old friend. We could use some help down here, but head over to Lyons's last known position and make sure she's dead."

"And if she's not?"

"No comment."

"Understood. It sounds like your dad needs a ride to the nearest hospital. After I check Lyons, I'll beat feet over to the Bell and fly her into the pit."

"Be careful approaching her, Harv. Assume nothing."

Grangeland said, *"I'm just reaching the flat area of the pit. I can see you in the Humvee."*

"Stay sharp and keep the Humvee between yourself and Alisio's men."

"I'll be careful. Remember my cell phone buzzing earlier? I just checked. It was a text from your father saying he and George Beaumont were on their way in a Humvee and not to shoot at them."

"Expect the unexpected," he said.

"I need to make a call."

"Lansing?"

"Yes."

"That's far enough," Nathan yelled. "Everyone turn around." When no one complied, he aimed the Browning to their left and fired a short burst. The staccato roar echoed around the pit for several seconds. *"Cada uno da vuelta alrededor. Ahora!"*

The men turned around, and as Nathan suspected, Alisio had a small handgun tucked into the small of his back.

"Alisio, keep your back to me, reach back, and lose the gun."

In slow motion, the crime boss complied. Nathan felt hatred radiate from the man like heat from a stove. Part of him hoped the murderer would try something. If Alisio ended up in a Mexican prison, he'd probably manage to bribe his way out eventually. If that ever happened, he would certainly come after Nathan.

"Keep walking toward me," Nathan yelled.

M1A in hand, Grangeland arrived and stood next to Nathan's father.

"Special Agent Grangeland, I presume?" Stone asked.

"It's nice to meet you, Senator." She glanced at the damaged Humvee. "I'm very sorry about Mr. Beaumont."

"George was a good man. He died fighting for something he believed in, not a terrible way to go."

"Grangeland, I'm covering the office and Alisio's men. Hustle over to the prefab building and make sure no one's hiding out in there, then check the office. Stay sharp. Let me know what you find." He glanced down at his father. "Dad, you need to get off your feet."

"I will as soon as Special Agent Grangeland returns. I—Grangeland, get down!"

She hit the deck at the same time one of the South Koreans fired from a window of the prefab.

"Fire the launcher!" Nathan yelled.

The M203 made a loud thunk. The wall of the prefab ignited in a blinding flash. Grangeland used the detonation time to sprint the remaining distance. *She's got brass*, Nathan thought. Handgun blazing, she dashed into the smoking building and disappeared.

Alisio's two cohorts used the opportunity to bolt in opposite directions. One ran toward the conveyor, and the other toward the derelict vehicles. It seemed pointless; there was no place to go.

Nathan was about to fire the Browning when a single report echoed across the pit. The man running toward the derelict cars did a face-plant and slid to a stop.

"Hold your fire, Dad. Just watch . . ."

Two seconds later, another loud crack shook the pit. The other man stopped running and fell to his knees.

"Finish him, Harv."

"Copy."

A third report rang out. The kneeling man's head jerked before he slumped sideways and lay still.

"How about you, Alisio? Want to give it a try?" When he didn't move, Nathan yelled, "Then keep walking."

His dad was looking at the smoking end of the grenade launcher. "I've always wanted to do that. I guess I can cross it off my bucket list."

"Prefab's clear," Grangeland said. *"It's a bloody mess. Two are still alive, but they won't be for long. I'm heading over to the office."*

Nathan wiped blood from his chin and mouth from Lyons's earlier rifle shot that had exploded in front of his face—a close call.

In defiance, Alisio stopped short. "I don't know who you are, but you obviously have no idea who you're fucking with. You and that old-timer just committed multiple murders. I own the Mexican government and the courts. I'll be free in a few days."

"This old-timer is none other than Stone McBride, the senior senator from New Mexico. He's chairman of the Committee on Domestic Terrorism and a member of the Committee on Finance and Homeland Security and Governmental Affairs. Oh, and he's also my father."

"And I'm supposed to be impressed?"

Nathan held up a hand, silencing Alisio.

Grangeland reported no one alive in the office.

"Good work; hustle back here."

"What?" Alisio said.

"I wasn't talking to you." Nathan climbed out of the turret and walked up to Alisio. He towered over the crime boss by at least a foot.

"Am I supposed to be intimidated?" Alisio laughed. "Maybe you should read me my rights now."

Nathan turned toward Stone. "Do you remember how that goes? Isn't it something about remaining silent and something being used against someone?"

"Some cop you are," Alisio said.

"I'm not a cop."

Alisio's expression changed from smug to uncertain. "Then who the fuck are you?"

"Please watch your language. We have a lady present."

Alisio turned toward Grangeland as she jogged back over and stood next to Stone.

Nathan stared at Alisio without saying anything.

"Ooh, I'm scared . . . What? You think I can't get to you? You think you'll all be safe in your pathetic little houses? I'm going to enjoy watching you *and* your families die slow deaths. You'll be screaming for mercy, biting your tongues off. I've seen it hundreds of times. You'll be no different." He pointed at Grangeland. "We'll keep that blond bitch alive for months."

Nathan felt his face flush. An image of Special Agent Hutch being slowly tortured to death by this vile being invaded his mind. He hoped Hutch hadn't sobbed in agony, pleading for his life.

Grangeland stepped over and put a hand on Nathan's shoulder. "It's too bad Mr. Alisio was killed in the firefight."

Nathan's expression brightened. "Yeah, that *is* too bad." He painted the Sig's laser on Alisio's forehead.

"A horrible shame," Stone said. "May I quote our president?"

"By all means," Nathan said.

Stone cleared his throat. "'It should be noted that while on American soil, Mexican nationals engaged in the wanton murder of US citizens do not fall under the umbrella of our Constitution and therefore do not enjoy the protections thereof.'"

Nathan nodded in agreement. "Elegantly stated. No need for reading his rights anyway, then." He kept the gun trained on Alisio's head.

"Wait! I have cash and diamonds. It's right over there. Gold too. Lots of gold!"

"He has lots of gold," Nathan said. "Do you see any gold, Special Agent Grangeland? How about you, Dad? Do you see any gold?"

"Not a nugget."

Nathan pursed his lips, shook his head.

Alisio pointed toward the burning cars. "Wait! It's right over—"

Nathan pulled the trigger.

A blank expression took Alisio's face, as if his scrambled brain were unable to comprehend the damage it had just sustained.

Nathan raised a brow and looked at Grangeland.

She shrugged as if to say, *That wasn't so bad.*

"I had no idea you knew all that about me," Stone said.

"Well, don't let it go to your head."

His dad looked at Alisio's lifeless form. "I wasn't sure you'd do it."

"Honestly, neither was I. Then I thought about Mara and all the other deaths and misery surrounding this man and said: *Screw him.* God can be his judge; I'll just be the conduit for the introduction."

"That's a rather unorthodox approach to being a Christian, isn't it?" Grangeland asked.

"Yeah, I suppose it is."

She gave him a long, tight hug. "In a different life," she whispered.

"Dad, you okay with what just happened?"

"That hug? I think I should've gotten it."

Grangeland stepped over and wrapped him up.

"Easy, Grangeland, you're gonna give that old jarhead a heart attack."

"It's not every day I get to hug the chairman of the CDT." She kissed his cheek.

"Don't you have a call to make?"

"Special Agent Grangeland is doing just fine."

"Dad, need I remind you that you're leaking? Grangeland, would you mind grabbing the first aid kit from the Hummer and putting a few more wraps around that wound? I'll be right back. I'm gonna do a quick head count. Everyone stay sharp; there could be a straggler." He turned to go, but stopped. "I'm really sorry about George. I shouldn't have doubted him."

His dad nodded.

Nathan took off toward the burning SUVs and the buildings beyond. It took a couple of minutes to do the survey. Including Alisio, he counted seventeen in the pit. The three men Lyons killed at the top completed the tally at twenty.

Harv checked in and said Lyons had managed to crawl fifty feet before expiring. Nathan affirmed, unwilling to mourn her passing any more than that of the other criminals here. They'd made their choices.

When he returned to the Humvee, Grangeland told him his dad was on the phone to Lansing, doing his best to explain how he and George had managed to get their hands on a Marine Corps Humvee and why they thought it necessary to insert themselves into the fight. All in all, it sounded like the call was going fairly well.

He heard his father say something along the lines of "the results speak for themselves." Lansing wanted to speak to him, as evidenced by his father extending Grangeland's phone.

"Director Lansing, it's Nathan."

"I want to personally thank you. And like I said before, please call me Ethan."

"We couldn't have pulled this off without Special Agent Grangeland."

"She's got a solid future with us."

"Good to hear. Don't be too angry with my dad. He showed up at a critical time and helped turn the tide of the fight."

"I'm very sorry we lost George. No one knows what I'm about to tell you because he wanted it kept confidential, but he had metastasized pancreatic cancer. He might've lived another year, but it would've been a slow, drawn-out ending. He died serving his country. He'll get a full Honor Guard service at Arlington, and I hope you and Harv will be there."

"Count on it."

"I've got an FBI bird on the way. It's been standing by at Imperial County Airport. It would be best if you guys weren't around when it arrives."

"No problem; we've got our own ride. My dad's got a pretty serious calf wound. It's not life threatening, but he needs an ER visit."

"Let me make a call. I may want you to take him to the flight surgeon at NAF El Centro. Can you receive cell calls in your helicopter?"

"Yes."

"Okay, get in the air and head west."

"What about local law enforcement? They're on their way by now."

"Attorney General Ames and I have that covered. It's best if you don't know the specific details. The BSI personnel won't be found. They were never there, and neither were you."

"Good enough. Mason's two accomplices are up on the rim and three more bodies are near the top of the switchbacks." Nathan used the stadium references and gave Lansing their exact locations. He also reminded Lansing about the cash, diamonds, and gold coins.

"Got it," Lansing said. "I want to thank you and Harvey again. It seems the IOUs keep adding up."

"We aren't keeping them."

"You're a lot like your father."

"Thanks, Ethan. I consider that very high praise. Will you do me a favor?"

"Sure, name it."

"Please tell Holly we're okay."

"Consider it done."

EPILOGUE

One week later

Under a flawless La Jolla sky, Chief of Staff Holly Simpson parked her rental car and climbed out. The two men she'd met at Harry's Coffee Shop pulled in behind her and joined her on the sidewalk. Across the street, the pop of tennis balls mixed with a mockingbird's song. She liked this neighborhood—it triggered a childhood memory of walking to school. Draper Avenue held a nice mix of small residences, apartments, and retail shops.

Before leaving Harry's, she'd gone over some dos and don'ts and let them know that Nathan McBride tended to be an extremely private person who didn't want attention or public recognition.

Just ahead, she saw the sign. Given the size of La Jolla Presbyterian Church, the modest sign seemed too small, and yet it somehow fit. She asked the men to wait at a planter in front of the chapel.

At the double doors, the music of a pipe organ filtered from within. She smiled when she recognized it.

"Adagio for Strings" by Samuel Barber.

***

Nathan marveled at how something so mathematical could sound so beautiful. He didn't think the organ rendition lost any of the emotional aura of the piece.

He came here when his soul was troubled, like now . . .

The short calls and texts he'd exchanged with Holly seemed synthetic. Their relationship felt damaged, and he didn't know if it could be repaired. Maybe it shouldn't be. Maybe his destiny was solitude, and he'd been naïve to believe otherwise. Nathan blamed himself. He hadn't intended to chase Holly away, but he couldn't help thinking she'd be better off without him, without his baggage.

He was about to leave when he caught a familiar scent.

Light Blue by Dolce & Gabbana.

Holly.

He stood when she entered the pew.

Tight jeans. A white buttoned shirt. Turquoise and silver belt. *She's so incredibly beautiful . . .*

Without a word, they embraced each other. Tightly. Neither wanted to let go, and didn't.

He rested his chin on top of her head. "Are you here to give me bad news?"

She shook her head.

"I need you in my life. I used to think Harv's friendship was enough, but it's not."

She wiped a tear.

"Can you ever forgive me?" he asked. "I shouldn't have doubted you."

"I was about to ask you the same thing. I wanted to tell you about my seat on your father's committee, but I didn't."

"We'll forgive each other and move on. That's what friends do. You're much more than that, but you're my friend before anything else."

"There's so much I want to tell you; I don't know where to begin."

"Me too."

They sat down and listened to the music reach its peak.

"In Yuma, I executed Alisio. I shot him right in front of my father and Grangeland."

"Lansing told me."

"I wanted to believe I'd moved on, that I didn't do that sort of thing anymore."

"It won't make you feel any better, but Grangeland said you beat her to it. Alisio was as good as dead."

"The guy made some depraved threats, and I believed he would've carried them out. I couldn't let that happen."

She nodded. "Do you regret killing him?"

"No. But that's not what's bothering me. I should've disliked it more than I did. So what does that make me?"

"Nathan," she said quietly, "if you weren't asking yourself that question, I wouldn't be here. Don't second-guess the gift you've been given."

"Gift . . ."

"I believe there are a chosen few who step up when called upon, and you're one of them. You're a good man with a deep conscience. I trust my instincts."

"I guess I needed to hear that."

"I wish you heard it more often."

He looked at the cross beyond the chancel. "I felt something . . . at the quarry. It's hard to describe. There was no burning bush or booming voice from the heavens, but when Tanner Mason fired his M4 at me, I felt protected. The white star from its flash suppressor was beautiful, not frightening." He stopped. "Listen to me: I probably sound like I'm crazy."

"Not at all. You faced death and survived. It's happened before. You're processing the experience and finding meaning as best you can. It's a good thing, Nathan."

"I wish knowing that made it easier." For another long moment, he said nothing. "There's something else bothering me, something I should've shared with you years ago." Nathan felt his face tighten. "You sensed it . . . at Toby's apartment."

"You're talking about Mara . . . Karen and Cindy too."

He looked down.

"They were call girls, weren't they." It wasn't a question.

"How could you possibly know that?"

"I just knew."

"For two years I thought Mara could give me more than I paid for. I guess I knew the truth deep down, but I couldn't face it."

"Nathan, I can't . . . won't judge you. Confession time? In my sophomore year in college, I once traded my body for a couple grams of coke. The guy wasn't a stranger, but I sold myself just the same."

"We aren't those people anymore."

"No, we aren't."

"I was worried you came here to give me my walking papers."

"You can't get rid of me that easily. I've become partial to Marines."

"Heaven help you."

They enjoyed a comfortable silence. "This is a beautiful sanctuary," she said. "The stained glass is amazing."

"Each one represents a ministry of Christ." He looked back to her. "Did Harv tell you where to find me?"

"Actually, it was your mother's suggestion. Your dad relayed it to me."

"I'm not surprised."

"How long have you been in here?"

"A few hours."

Holly suddenly seemed a little uneasy.

"What?" he asked.

"Remember when we first met, and we were really good listeners?"

"Uh-oh."

"There are two men outside who want to meet you."

He started to object, but she stopped him by putting a hand on his chest.

"It wasn't my doing; it was Lansing's and your father's. You haven't been set up. I made it abundantly clear the decision's yours. You don't have to meet them."

Nathan wasn't sure what to say. He didn't like the idea. Hated it, really.

"It's important to them. They want to thank you in person. I think I know you pretty well, and you'll be okay with it."

"They're outside right now? Who are they?"

"Vincent Beaumont and Ramiro."

"Holly, I don't—"

"You need to trust me."

That got through. He smiled and said, "Done."

Nathan waved a thank-you to the organist and followed Holly down the center aisle. Outside the vestibule, he saw the men right away. He recognized Vincent Beaumont from the memorial service. Both of them stood when he approached.

"I'm Vince Beaumont."

"Nathan McBride." He shook hands. "I'm very sorry about your father."

"Thank you."

Nathan reached toward the other man. "Ramiro."

The tall Hispanic man pumped his hand and offered a genuine smile, nothing plastic about it. "My real name's Tomas Bustamante, but everyone calls me Tommy. It's going to be a little weird adjusting to it again."

"I can imagine." Nathan liked that neither of them had reacted to seeing his scars. Maybe Holly had prepped them.

"It's an honor to meet you," Tommy said. "Thank you for protecting my identity. You and Mr. Fontana and SA Grangeland risked your lives for me, and I won't ever forget it."

"You have my gratitude as well," Vince said. "I wish I could do more than just say thank you."

"It's more than enough," said Nathan.

Vince smiled. "That's what Director Lansing told me you'd say."

"In case it matters," Nathan told them, "Mason said something to me just before he died. He claimed he would never have blown the cover of his operatives. It seemed genuine to me. He had nothing to gain by lying."

"Even if he was telling the truth," Ramiro said, "it doesn't diminish the thanks we owe you. There was no guarantee he wouldn't have eventually sold us out for money. I once believed he'd never betray his oath."

"Well," Vince said, "the important thing is that the November Directive's secure and the other operatives are safe."

"The president will be happy about that," Holly said to Vince.

"He already is. He's going to invite Nathan and Harv to the White House. Apparently your names have crossed his desk before. It's happening sometime next month, but you didn't hear that from me."

"We'll go, but only if Holly and SA Grangeland can come with us."

"I can't guarantee that, but I don't think it will be a problem. As you know, the plan for implementing the ND came from your father's committee as a result of a presidential edict, and the president's been following its progress closely. For a lot of reasons, he's extremely pleased the ND was saved."

"Harv and I will go no matter what, but don't tell anyone that. Even though we're not aligned politically, I have no desire to see the president look bad. When he looks bad, the entire nation looks bad. Refusing an invitation would be very bad form, and it would also reflect poorly on my father. Besides, I've heard he can be quite charming. I'm curious to see for myself."

"Guard your pocketbook," Vince said with some humor, but Nathan saw pain on the man's face. Although the ND was secure, his father was dead—the last casualty in Mason's private war.

"I'll leave my checkbook in the car." He looked at Tommy. "Was being undercover as bad as I imagine? It has to be the worst kind of stress imaginable."

"You get used to it."

Nathan waited.

"Okay, not really. It's pretty bad."

No one said anything, and Nathan suspected Holly may have told them not to fill in the silent intervals. Either way, he appreciated the break to gather his thoughts.

Vince said, "I wish I could've been there to see our fathers fighting side by side. That must've been quite a sight."

"It was. I have this incredible visual of my dad firing the Browning while George drove. Your father died a true warrior's death, and it was far from meaningless. We might not have made it without him."

Vince shook his head. "I still can't believe he did it. He called me that afternoon and said he didn't feel right about you and Harvey cleaning up his mess. But I never expected him to go to Yuma, much less with your father."

Nathan thought about his last moments with Mason. "Why do you think he did it? Tanner Mason, I mean."

"I've been asking myself the same thing," said Vince. "We paid him an exorbitant salary, nearly twice the industry standard."

"He hated Alisio," Tommy said. "Maybe defeating the man wasn't enough. He had to destroy him. Mason told me many times he didn't want Alisio getting away with murdering Special Agent Hutcheson."

"So in the process of destroying him," said Nathan, "he became him."

"My father and I talked about various risks," Vince said, "but we never suspected it would be Mason. If anyone was going to go rogue, we always believed it would be one of our ND operatives."

Tommy cleared his throat.

"Present company excluded," Vince said.

"Despite Mason, have some of the November Directive's goals been reached?" asked Nathan. "Alisio's cartel is in disarray, at least, right?"

"Better than that," Vince said. "It's been dismantled. Two dozen arrests were made in four Mexican cities."

"Has there been any fallout from Mr. Alisio's unfortunate . . . demise?"

"Nothing we can't handle. It seems you have some friends on Capitol Hill."

Nathan glanced at Holly, who nodded.

"How's Harvey doing?" Vince asked.

"He's okay; Hahn's bullet only nicked him. He just needed a few stitches."

Harv hadn't mentioned getting winged on the rim, and Nathan had chewed him a new one for bleeding on his helicopter. The flight surgeon at NAF El Centro did the needlework on his thigh. His dad's calf wound turned out to be more serious than they first thought, but the venerable Stonewall McBride was expected to make a full recovery.

"Is BSI otherwise unscathed?" Nathan asked.

"So far, so good. We had to act quickly, and I think we made the right call."

"You're talking Mason, Hahn, and Lyons?" George Beaumont's death had been publicly explained as being due to natural causes. But he hadn't heard how BSI explained the sudden disappearance of three of its key personnel.

Vince nodded. "This may not sit well with you, but officially they were killed in the line of duty, doing BSI work. That's what we told their families."

Nathan looked at Holly, then back at Vince.

"Given the circumstances," Vince continued, "it seemed the right way to go. For the record, Mason and the others were KIA during a covert mission related to the takedown of Alisio's cartel. Because of the classified nature of their work, that's the only information BSI or the government can confirm. When Mason and the others signed contracts with us, they formally acknowledged that this kind of thing could happen, so their family members have accepted the situation about as well as anyone could."

"So they're unsung heroes," Nathan said. "Like fallen CIA officers."

Vince looked a little uneasy. "Yes, that's a fair analogy. Their families will receive full death benefits, the works. I hope this doesn't . . . you know, sit badly with you, given what really happened."

Nathan wasn't concerned. "I'm okay with it. It seems like a good solution to me. I can't imagine how else you could've done it without compromising the program. And the families certainly don't deserve to be punished."

Vince nodded, as did Tommy. "That's how we see it."

"I have one personal favor to ask," Nathan said. "I looked at your bio and noticed you'd climbed pretty high in the San Diego Sheriff's Department before you became a co-owner in BSI with your brother and dad. Do you still have any connections over there?"

"Yes, I know lots of people."

"Toby Haynes really wants to be a deputy sheriff. Since he literally took one for the team, could you put in a good word for him?"

"I absolutely can. And will. And if he'd rather stay with us, he's got a bright future."

"He told me he doesn't think he can do that."

"Yeah, I kind of figured, but the offer's good if he changes his mind. BSI's covering all of his out-of-pocket medical expenses and offering a healthy parting gift. It's enough to make a down payment on a house, so he won't have to be a renter for the rest of his life. All we're asking is that he keeps everything confidential."

"Toby's not a gold digger; he's a hard worker and an honest man. We offered him a job as well, but I'm pretty sure he's set on being a deputy sheriff."

"Please let me know if I can help, I mean, more than I already have."

"Will do. You would've made a respectable Marine."

"Thank you, that's what my dad kept telling me."

"So what's next for you, Tommy? Sun, wine, and women? Sorry, Holly."

"No offense taken."

"I think I'll chill for a while, then start a nursery business. I've always liked gardening."

"Outstanding."

"Well, we just wanted to say thank you in person," Vince said. "If my father were alive, he'd be here."

"He'll be remembered." Nathan shook hands with them.

They turned to go, but Tommy stopped. Nathan knew what was coming, and let it happen. Tommy gave him a handshake, then a brief hug.

After they left, Nathan said, "Thank you, Holly. I wasn't big on meeting them, but I'm glad I did. Can we go for a walk?"

"Sure." She turned to go, but Nathan didn't move.

"What is it?" Holly asked.

"A question's been bugging me ever since the fight in the borrow pit. When we were jogging across the desert, the saguaro cacti triggered a memory of a cartoon I used to watch."

"Which one?"

"Quick Draw McGraw."

"Are you serious?"

Nathan nodded.

She smiled. "I loved that cartoon. I laughed when Quick Draw played El Kabong and hit the bad guys on the head with his guitar."

"Oh, man, I'd forgotten about that. He wore a mask and black cape and yelled '*Kabong!*'"

"Yep. So why are you thinking about it now?"

"Because I can't remember the name of his little sidekick."

"And *that's* what's bugging you?"

"Yeah, it's making me crazy. I guess I could use the Internet, but that seems lazy. What on earth did people ever do before smartphones? I guess they went to the library or actually talked to each other."

"His name was Baba Looey."

"Yes! That's it. Thanks, now I don't have to cheat to get the answer. Harv didn't know, and I told him not to look it up."

"I'm speechless, Nathan. I had no idea."

"What?"

"You just constantly surprise me."

Holly took his hand, and they wandered north along the sidewalk. Nathan had played some pickup basketball games in the rec center across the street, but he hadn't done it in years.

"I saw you at George's memorial service," Holly said.

"You were on the other end of the bleachers."

"You knew I was there?"

He nodded.

"I wasn't ready to talk."

"That made two of us."

"I've never seen such a beautiful service. It made me cry."

"The Marine Corps Honor Guard units are volunteers. It's hard for me to hold it together when I attend those services. I wish more young people appreciated veterans."

"You looked really sharp in your Dress Blues. I know I'm biased, but you Marines have the best uniforms."

"Hey, at least it still fits."

"In hindsight, talking to you at the service would've been easy."

Nathan didn't say anything.

"Ethan says I've been really grouchy lately."

"That's hard to picture."

"Trust me, I can be really mean."

"Everyone can. Want to head down to the breakwater?"

"The breakwater?"

"It's an old La Jolla icon. It created the Children's Pool, a small sheltered cove of beach, but the seals have reclaimed it. I think it's a preserve now, not sure."

Neither of them spoke while they walked. Life was so amazing and rich, and yet so equally full of disappointment and heartache. Such was the human condition—a continuous struggle to overcome obstacles. Nathan hoped it never got easier.

As if reading his mind, she said, "We're going to take things one day at a time."

He squeezed her hand tighter.

And felt safe.

ACKNOWLEDGMENTS

Thanks are owed to the following people:

Dr. Douglas Reavie, FACS, for his input on and insights about the Sharp Memorial Hospital scene.

Tom Davin, CEO of 5.11 Tactical, for allowing me to use his products and clothing lines in the books. Tom also served as a Recon with the 1st Battalion, 1st Marines—"First of the First."

John Torres, former ATF deputy assistant director. I first met John at the ATF Citizens' Academy in 2010 when he was the SAC of the Los Angeles field office, and he's been a good friend ever since. Anything stated correctly about the ATF is to John's credit; anything missed is on me.

Corporal Tim Haley, a retired US Marine. Tim served with the 1st Battalion, 9th Marines—"The Walking Dead." Tim saw action at Khe Sanh; what more needs to be said?

Pastor Charlie Little of Templeton Presbyterian Church for his permission to use him as a real character in the book. Charlie's guidance and leadership in my life are essential for my spiritual health.

Mike Holmes of Molokai Fishing, for his help with the Kaunakakai Ferry Terminal scene.

Erick and Mary Ann Reinstedt: their friendship is treasured.

Jake Elwell, my agent. Jake stuck with me during the early years!

Alan Turkus, Jacque Ben-Zekry, Jeff Belle, and the entire Thomas & Mercer team. My journey with Amazon Publishing has been extraordinary in every sense of the word. Writing novels is hard work, but the T&M team makes the publication experience enjoyable.

Perhaps most important, my freelance editor Ed Stackler. From original story concept to finished product, Ed plays a vital role in the Nathan McBride adventures. I couldn't write these books without his help.

AUTHOR'S NOTE

The Nathan McBride books employ a combination of real and imagined locations and people. In *First to Kill*, I created a completely fictional FBI field office in Sacramento. In *Option to Kill*, I used the actual Fashion Valley mall and its surrounding area.

I stepped out of my comfort zone to write *Contract to Kill*. I think authors need to do that every so often to challenge themselves. I don't like painting the military or law enforcement with a dark brush. I believe our service members, law enforcement personnel, and first responders are heroes in every sense of the word. Are there bad apples in those professions? Yes, of course, but we shouldn't allow the actions of an extremely small minority to be representative of everyone else.

The world of private military contractors (PMCs) is nebulous. Lots of money exchanges hands at many different levels, and, with that, there's always the possibility of corruption. I believe most PMCs are honest, hardworking, and dedicated individuals. Sadly, for some people, money becomes an addictive drug, and its obsessive pursuit can change a good person into a wicked person.

Having said that, I believe people are people, no matter what their socioeconomic background is. Proof can be found in the following example: take a Wall Street millionaire and a small-town barber, and put them in a sealed room together with no food or water. In a few days, they're the same. They're both hungry and thirsty and miserable. My point is this: basic human needs are universal, and at the core—male or female—we're all the same.

Nathan McBride is far from perfect. His character is larger than life, but he's not superhuman, and he makes mistakes. Nathan has many flaws, but he'll never compromise his core beliefs.

ABOUT THE AUTHOR

Photo © 2011 Mike Theiler

Andrew Peterson is the international bestselling author of the Nathan McBride series. A native of San Diego, he holds an architectural degree from the University of Oklahoma. Andrew is an avid marksman who has won numerous high-power rifle competitions. He enjoys flying helicopters, camping and hiking, scuba diving, and an occasional round of golf.

Andrew has donated more than two thousand books to American troops serving overseas and wounded soldiers recovering in military hospitals. He lives in Monterey County, California, with his wife, Carla, and their two dogs.

Visit Andrew's website at www.andrewpeterson.com, and follow him on Twitter at @APetersonNovels, and on Facebook at www.facebook.com/Andrew.Peterson.Author.